TO A FAR WESTERN LAND

CARSON MCCLOUD

1

J im Heston scowled at a white, knobby rock laying in his field.

This wasn't the first rock he'd found lying in such a way, not the hundredth, not the thousandth, but some number far greater than both. After every rain or plowing, the chalky bleached rocks popped up like fresh mushrooms. He picked this one up in his fist. Warm from the springtime sun, it was the size of a large potato. He hefted it once, felt the weight of it, brought his arm back, and then let it fly. Spinning in a high arc, the offending rock cleared the field by a few feet, striking the ground hard, tumbled twice end-over-end, and smacked into one of its brethren at the base of a long pile.

"Another one for you Pa," Jim said aloud.

Wiping the fine dust from his hands onto his pants, he took up his hoe and returned to cultivating the row of corn. Already six inches tall, the rich green spouts were coming along nicely. *All I have to do now is protect them from the deer and hope no hailstorm comes through in the next month or two and pray that no locust swarm flies in to chew them off into the dirt.* Those were not the only dangers of course, only the most immediate. It was still too early to worry about a windstorms, drought, an early freeze, or the neighbor's cattle tearing down the fence to kill his crop.

Plenty of time for those troubles later.

At the end of the row another rock waited. Jim tossed it under-handed at the top of the pile. It landed with a solid thunk and rolled away down the far side.

"One more Pa. That's only two today. Best day yet, but it is early."

The Heston farm had never grown much, barely enough to survive on when it was the four of them, but what it lacked in food it made up for in chalk rocks and hard luck.

Jim's hoe work resumed. The sharp blade whisked through the dirt, severing goatheads and other stray weeds that threatened to choke his corn. The work was important but mindless and Jim's thoughts strayed.

Food really wasn't a problem these days. The War Between the States had taken a vicious toll on the Hestons. Travis Heston, Jim's father, had gone off to fight early-on, and then Jim's older brother, John, followed their Pa first to the war and then into the grave at some far-off place called Gettysburg.

"That man was too soft for this place. Left us to it alone," Ma said when news came of Pa's fate. After he went to war she never called him Pa anymore just 'that man'.

When John died she'd already taken to bed with the fever sick-ness, and a week later, after digging a hole his own two hands, Jim carefully wrapped his mother up in bedsheets and buried her in the local cemetery. Alma Heston—good woman that she was—deserved better but coffins were expensive and so the bedsheet had to do. Prac-tical as she'd been in life, he thought she would have approved. He could almost hear her. "No need to put a perfectly good piece of wood in the ground on my account."

Jim wiped sweat from his face and started chopping along the next row when hoofbeats sounded from up the lane. He closed his eyes, smiling faintly, listening to the stepping horse. The horse was a good one, taking confident, easy steps and had a lively gait. *Someday I'll have a fine horse like that and then we'll ride away from here forever.* Horse and rider soon cleared the mesquite and live oak that squeezed in around the Heston homestead like a giant's fist. Jim looked at the horse first, a tall chestnut stallion with powerful legs and four white stockings. His smile widened. Stepper was an old friend.

"Hey Jim," the rider stood in the stirrups and waved his hat from the field's edge.

Will Trimble, like Stepper, was a friend, one of only two men Jim could claim that about. They'd gone to school together down on Clear Creek until Will's folks moved their family to town.

"Will, how are you?" Jim said and crossed the field.

"Awww, you know me. No complaints."

Jim moved to the horse's head and Stepper nuzzled him.

"How's Stepper treating you?"

Will flashed a toothy smile. "Like a dream. I still don't know how you did it though. He bucked off every man I hired to break him. Real cowboys all of them."

"He just needed some time." Jim patted the stallion's great head and blew into his open nostril.

He didn't believe in 'breaking' horses. Making friends with them, that was the best way if you wanted a real horse. The old way of 'breaking' ruined a lot of good animals. Sure, they'd be ridable enough afterwards, but they'd never trust you, never give you their absolute best.

Time, patience, trust, that was how you taught a horse to want to be ridden. Not with some damned cowboy digging his spurs, tying himself on, and praying.

"I'm sure you didn't ride out all this way to talk about Stepper," Jim said.

"Afraid not," Will's face soured. "I'm here for the loan."

Jim nodded. Nothing he hadn't expected. Will had been patient with him—patient as only a true friend might be—but the day was finally come. "I've got it in the house. Light and set?"

"Of course," Will said and stepped out of the saddle.

Will put both hands behind his back, stretched, and then started to walk awkwardly. "Too much time behind a desk," he said.

Jim only grunted. He'd known nothing but hard work since he was six and couldn't imagine anything else. Sitting at a desk all day, dealing with people, it sounded utterly miserable.

"Say, I think you've gotten bigger since the last time I saw you," Will eyed him over. "You got to be well over six foot now and arms like an ox."

"Farm work," Jim said.

"You know, you was always good in a fight Jim. If you've a notion to make some money I could see about setting something up. Those boys south of the river like a good scrap. They'd pay too. My father always said you could be a top-notch fighter. Quick with your hands, bull strong, and cagey like a fox. He saw you whip Ned Schooner that time behind the..."

Jim gave him a sideways look and Will's voice trailed off.

"Alright. Alright." Will held up his hands, palms out. "No more talk about fighting."

He followed Jim up to the house. Two handsome rocking chairs sat on the porch. Jim's mother had inherited them from her father, a craftsman of some renown, and she'd dearly loved resting in hers after a long day of work. Will started to sit in the one on the right. Jim coughed, and Will jerked upright as if he'd been stung by a hornet. "Sorry," he mumbled before taking the leftmost chair.

"Coffee?" Jim said.

"Please."

Jim brought out a tin cup of dark liquid then went back inside. Beneath his parent's bed, behind an old wooden crate, was a small jar of money. He retrieved it and slowly counted out the loan payment. Ten dollars. A year's worth of earnings and more money than he'd ever seen. Still his mother hadn't raised him to be in debt nor to shirk one. He sighed and then folded the money in half. Nothing remained in the jar but a few loose coins. Jim rattled the jar. Enough for a meal in town, maybe two. He needed that crop of corn to come in.

Will put the coffee down when he returned to the porch.

Jim counted out the money, cringing inwardly with every dollar.

Relieved as he was to have the loan repaid, he didn't know when he'd ever see a sum like that again.

"Real sorry about this Jim. Only things are slow at the store and I'm flat busted myself." Will tucked the money into his pocket.

"A loan's a loan," Jim said.

"All that confederate cash we had ended up being worthless. I lost a thousand dollars. Damned Yankees."

Jim looked out at his field. The breeze rippled the little shoots making them whisper. This crop had to survive. One good crop, just one, and he'd have cash enough to hold on for another year. Surely his luck would turn by then.

The old house wasn't much, never had been, a dirt floor, some thin lumber for walls, most of that warped by rain and the blistering Texas sun, all topped off by a sod roof. Only the fireplace was nice. Jim and his brother had made that themselves, after hauling up rounded stones from the river and mortaring them together. The chalky field rocks weren't even good for that.

Useless things.

"It's hard all over," Jim said. "How's life in the big city?"

"Same old San Antone. You know how it-" Will took a sip of coffee and his face convulsed before spitting it out. "That's awful," he said.

Jim laughed. "Ran out of real coffee two weeks ago. Been using mesquite beans."

Will's face screwed up tight, "Tastes like gunpowder."

"You get used to it."

"I'd rather not."

Jim pulled up a stool he'd fashioned for himself and sat beside the second rocking chair. Ma's chair wasn't to be sat in, not by him or anyone else.

"There's carpetbaggers in town," Will said. "A whole mess of them. They been talking about taxes and fees and regulations and such."

Jim gave him a lopsided look. "Not much out here to tax. We're all broke."

"They don't seem to see it that way," Will cleared his throat. "I've got a bit put by, but I've got to find a way to hide it."

"Cash money?"

Will licked his lips. "Gold."

"I thought you said you needed money?"

"I do. I need cash. If I get caught flashing gold around there'll be questions."

"So change it at the bank," Jim said. Having gold money sounded like a good problem to have. "Sutherland will treat you right."

"Sutherland doesn't run the bank anymore."

"What?"

"The Yankees ran him out. That's what I'm trying to tell you. That's why I need a place to hide the gold."

Will looked Jim in the eye for a time.

"No. I don't want it here," Jim raised his hands.

"C'mon Jim, why not? This place is perfect, no one will think to look for it in a..." Will's words trailed off. He gestured with his hands at the cabin.

"In a what? A two-bit outfit like mine?" Jim said.

"Well...yes," Will stammered. "It's perfect."

"No."

"Look, I'll pay you of course. A tenth of what I've got. That's twenty dollars to you. All you have to do is keep it safe and hidden."

"No." Even as he said it Jim's mind echoed with the number. *Twenty dollars. I won't see that much in three years.* Enough for a horse, a plow, maybe some left over to fix the place up a bit.

"Jim, please," Will said. "I can't lose everything. Look if it makes it easier, I can buy you out."

"What?"

"I can buy you out. I'll give you a hundred dollars gold for this place. Then I can hide the rest here. You can buy yourself another place. They say there's land in California where you can set up with a real farm."

"Then why don't you go?"

"I can't. I've thought about it believe me," Will's jaw bulged. "But Millie won't leave her folks."

"Got you by the tail does she?"

"You know how she is Jim."

Jim did know and only too well. Millie Van Court, now Millie Trimble, wasn't about to let any man tell her what to do, much less her husband. She set her cap for Will years ago and the fool went and married her.

Jim stood and moved to the steps looking out over the little farm. Without a neighbor closer than two miles, the place was quiet and peaceful. It was also backbreaking work. Unending work. The soil wasn't much good it took everything he had to scratch out a living. Twenty dollars to watch over Will's gold or a hundred to sell out and start over. A tempting offer either way.

"I'll need to think it over," he said.

"That's all I ask," Will said and moved beside him. "Whatever you decide let me know."

Neither spoke for a long time.

"So quiet out here it hurts my ears," Will said. "I'll never understand why you stay. You did well enough in school and I know how hard a worker you are. In San Antone you could do anything you set your mind to."

"You know how I am Will."

"I do," Will dipped his head.

"Did that cottonseed I ordered arrive yet?" Jim asked.

"Not yet. I saw the salesman the other day though. Said as long as it's in the ground before the next moon you should be fine. He thinks it will do well here."

The next moon. No more than two weeks off. Jim looked at the weed-covered field he'd reserved for his new crop. There was still time to plow it clear if he could swing a deal with Brett Yost, his nearest neighbor.

Will smiled with a twinkle bright in his eye. "He also said the market was up by double over last year. Not much being planted in the old south. No one to do the work these days."

"I imagine not," Jim said.

Will stood and dumped out his coffee over the porch edge. "Say hello to Jose when you see him."

"Sure."

With that, Will mounted Stepper and set off for town.

Jim listened to the beautiful horse's hooves fade into the lane.

California, land of grapes and honey. Even the name held a kind of far-off magic. The whole country was talking about it. Seemed like everyone wanted to sell out and start over again out west.

Jim rapped his knuckles once on his stool and stood.

California. Let them go and good luck to them. Texas was too deep in his blood. His thoughts came back to his current situation and Will's offer. *I'll never see a hundred dollars all at once. Not if I farm this place until I'm fifty.* Despite what Will might think the Yankees very well might try to take this place though. Pa never paid a tax in his life. He smiled at the thought of Travis Heston dealing with a tax man.

The old man might not have been much of a farmer, but he could sure fight. As a boy, Jim saw him shoot a Comanche in the chest, and club another to death just outside the front door. Then the old man jumped a third brave with no more than a knife.

There had been more of course, with Indians there always were, but one look at Pa covered in their friend's gore and blood and they lit out. No Comanche ever returned to the Heston farm after that.

In any kind of fight Pa had been a real terror. John had taken after him in a lot of ways. Jim flexed his big left fist. Though only nineteen he'd fought a few battles as well, always with his fists, school bullies and the like—the country ran short on Comanches these days—but he liked to think he was a little more like his mother, calm and peaceful.

Jim looked at the rows of precious corn. Those weeds wouldn't chop themselves. Always more work to be done on a farm. He picked up the hoe and trudged back toward the field.

. . .

"Every day when I wake up, I lay in bed staring up at the ceiling for a time, and I think to myself, I am so glad that Jim Heston will be here to work with me today," said a thin Mexican with a neat mustache.

"And why is that Jose?" Jim said.

"Two things," Jose held up a finger. "One, he does twice the work so I can get by with only half."

Jim set his pack of tools on the ground and took up the axe Jose had just sharpened. He inspected the edge—good enough for today—then put a log atop a thick stump. His first swing split the log neatly in two pieces and sent each flying.

Jose set another log upright for splitting.

"You said two things."

Jose grinned. He held up a second finger. "Two, when big strong Jim is here Miss Nancy makes those heavenly sweet potato pies."

Jim growled at his friend and brought the axe down again.

Jose replaced the log and moved back. "I notice amigo, you don't deny it."

"I'm sure she feeds you well enough when I'm not here."

"Well enough, Si. But not sweet potato pie," Jose smiled. His teeth gleamed in the morning light. "Those are special. Those are only on Jim Heston days."

The axe sung and struck a third log, this time grazing one side, before sticking in the heavy stump. Jim pried it loose with the handle and set for another swing. He eyed Jose.

"Everyone misses sometime," Jose said with a shrug and a grin.

"How would you know? You never do the splitting," Jim said.

Jose only laughed.

Jim was setting up for another try when a woman's voice rang out. Anna Yost was a tall woman, almost tall as Jim's six-two, and strong as a country mule. With eight children, she had to be. She was coming back from the shed with a bucket of creamy milk in one hand and cradling, Caleb, her youngest, with the other.

"Oh, Jim you're here good," Mrs. Yost said. "I'm teaching Nancy to make Pecan pie today. You can taste it for us."

"Sounds good, ma'am," Jim said and gave her a wave.

He turned back to work and sent the next log flying. "Not a word," he breathed.

"Me? I would never," Jose said with mock innocence.

They split wood for another hour, until the sun was well up on the horizon, then set about working on the new fence with the farm's owner, Brett Yost. Mr. Yost was a good man, hard though, a little less than his wife's height, but what he lacked in height he made up for in brute strength. Jim once saw him lift a barrel of flour out of a wagon by himself. His chin was like a slab of carved granite and his chest was thick as an old oak.

At noon Mrs. Yost and Nancy emerged from the house with plates and covered dishes. Nancy wore a new blue dress, though it hung a little loose around the middle. Following her mother, she was a near mirror-image, a little shorter maybe, and leaner, but the broad strokes were all there. They all sat down in the shade of a tall oak tree. Nancy smiled at Jim as she served him, and then sat by while he ate. The food was good as always, a thick hunk of broiled beef, yellow cornbread, potatoes, and cool milk to wash it all down. When it was done Nancy took the empty plates and piled them off to one side.

"I made this just for you," she said with eyes only for Jim. "I hope you like it."

She lifted the lid on a pan and carved out a big slice of pecan pie. Jim's mouth watered at just the sight of it and the smell was beyond anything he'd ever imagined.

The first few bites were gone in a flash, and then he had to force himself to slow down and savor every mouthful. Nothing he'd ever tasted was so good. Too soon the slice was gone.

"More?" Nancy offered.

"I'd better not," Jim raised a hand. His eyes were drawn to the pan though. Another slice couldn't hurt.

"He'll sleep all afternoon," Brett laughed knowingly, and the others chuckled along.

Mrs. Yost gave Jim a broad smile, and patted Nancy on the back. "It was great honey," she said. "Don't you all think so?"

"Just fine," her husband said.

"Muy Bueno," Jose said. "Don't you agree Jim?"

Jim started to say something to Jose about minding his own business, but they all looked at him expectantly. "Very good, Nancy," he said. "Thank you."

"I'm so glad you liked it," Nancy said shyly. She smoothed out the front of her dress.

Then she and her mother rose, gathered up all the plates, and returned to the house. Halfway there, Mrs. Yost leaned over and whispered something to her daughter. Both giggled.

"A man could do worse than a woman who can cook. Least that's what I always say," Mr. Yost said.

"Si," Jose answered.

Jim felt his face warm. He got to his feet and wiped his mouth with a hand. "Those rails won't hang themselves."

They spent the rest of the afternoon sweating beneath the hot South Texas sun, hanging fence rails. The fence lengthened quickly until by late afternoon it enclosed the new pasture for the Yost's pair of Holstein milk cows.

"A fine job," Brett said when they were done. "Not used to this kind of heat though. Tennessee wasn't near so warm."

"I'll come get Sam and Jack tomorrow. Should have my seeds any day now."

"You're welcome to them," Brett said. "You really think the cotton will do well here."

"Everyone seems to say so. Just needs heat and sun."

"We've plenty of that," Brett said and mopped sweat from his forehead.

"If it's alright with you Señor Brett, I'll make my way home," Jose said.

"Alright by me, Jose. You put in more than a full day. I'll see you Monday. Need to get new shingles on the chickenhouse roof."

"Of course," Jose said.

"Think I'll take off as well," Jim said. He picked up his tool pack and slung it over a shoulder.

"You sure you won't stay for supper Jim?" Brett said. "Unless the boys found it, there's bound to be some of that pie left."

"I've got several rows of corn to finish," Jim said. "You know how it is."

"Weeds popping up thick as hair," Brett laughed. "Nancy will miss you, but I won't keep you from it. Farmin' is hard work."

"I'll be over for Sam and Jack," Jim said with a wave.

"Come round breakfast time. We'll have something on," Brett answered.

Jose waited until they were down the road and well out of earshot before sprawling on the ground, rolling around like a loon, and laughing. Jim watched him impassively. He knew Jose well. Protesting would not make things better.

"The look on your face when he wanted you to stay for supper," Jose barked. "Then when he mentioned that pie." He sat up and rested on his arms. "I thought you were going to stay. You looked like a hungry dog choosing between a pair of big meaty bones."

Jim nudged him over with his boot toe. "Enough already."

Jose smiled up at the sky. "Ahh amigo. Sometimes I am not sure which of us is the lucky one. You for having Miss Nancy's affections or me getting the crumbs for free."

Jim offered his friend a hand up. "Will said to give you his best, by the way."

"Bueno. Did you tell him the same from me?"

"Next time I see him."

Jose took Jim's hand and the bigger man lifted him up to his feet.

"Not so rough, you oaf. You must learn to be more gentle with Miss Nancy."

Jim started off ahead of Jose. Like Will, he and Jose had been friends since school on Clear Creek, but once Jose got his teeth into something he never let go. Nancy Yost and her plan to capture a husband was his latest obsession. It had gone on for a month now.

Jim shook his head. *Surely he'll tire of it eventually.*

"My friend, you know I'm only trying to help you out. It is no good living alone as you do on that place."

"I'm living just fine. You know how I am."

"Yes, I do. Lonely, withdrawn, locked away from the world."

"I'm just waiting until I get the old place fixed up some. Then I'll settle down and find someone."

"If you say so," Jose shrugged. "But if you keep waiting for perfection you'll miss out on everything good in life. Sounds lonesome to me."

"With friends like you and Will how can I ever be lonely?" Jim said.

"Friends like me and Will are all you have," Jose ran to catch up and walk beside him. "You need to get out and meet people. There's a whole wide world out there."

"And you?"

"And me what?"

"Why don't you go see this wide world of yours."

Jose's face fell. "You know why."

"You still haven't talked your way out of it?"

"No, Uncle Tomas comes by every week." Jose scowled. "He says I should honor my mother's wishes, obey my father, but you know me. I can never join the priesthood. I would give up much."

"Father Jose Santos. It does have a ring to it," Jim said, happy to be past the Nancy business. "I bet you'd be a good priest."

"But of course," Jose shrugged. "How could I not? But the cost. Think of the cost."

"No more of Nancy Yost's pie," Jim grinned. No one could stay mad at Jose for long.

Jose laughed. "No more of Nancy Yost's pie nor anyone else's."

"You could have gone off with the others."

"Driving cattle to Kansas. Months in the saddle with dust and rain and no pretty senioritas just a bunch of skinny cows, and at the end... not much money to show for it. No thanks. If anyone should have gone it was you. Do you some good out in the world."

"You know they didn't want me to go."

"The cowboys didn't. But the drivers, the men who mattered, they did. No one else can take care of horses like you."

"There would have been trouble."

"Only until you whipped a few of them. Reminded them how you handled their business back in school."

"Half those fights were defending you if I remember right."

"I think that was Will," Jose's teeth shined.

"No, it was you and your chasing after all their girls."

"I cannot help it if women love me," Jose said. "It is my one great flaw."

"Anyway, I couldn't go with Ma sick like she was." Jim's voice was low and rough.

Jose faltered a stop and they walked in silence for a time. The turnoff toward Jose's home was just ahead. His father had a nice spread down on a wide bend in the Blanco.

"Besides," Jose finally said. "Who would keep watch over you?"

"I'm sure Will would."

"Will," Jose snorted. He shook his head. "I love him like a brother, and you as well, but Will can't even keep watch over that terror of a wife of his."

"That's true enough," Jim grunted. "He was talking about California yesterday."

"Ahh California, a land of gold and pretty women," Jose smiled. "Now that sounds like the place for me."

They were at the turnoff now and Jose offered his hand. Jim shook it.

"Via con dios," Jose said. Then, whistling to himself, he was off toward his father's place.

"Via con dios," Jim repeated, and Jose raised an arm without looking.

Afternoon was turning into evening by the time Jim caught sight of home. There wasn't much for dinner, a couple leftover biscuits and a thin slice of cured ham. *I bet the Yost's had a nice dinner this evening.* Nancy had surely saved another slice of pecan pie for him.

She was certainly a pretty enough girl, but it just wasn't for him. Nancy Yost meant settling down. It meant joining his place to theirs forever. It meant no matter how hard he worked on his farm he'd be expected to help them as well. He couldn't even keep one farm running, much less two.

And is that life what I truly want?

No, this thing with Nancy wasn't right, not for him anyways. Someday the right girl would come along. Once he had his farm running well. Once he'd made himself into something.

2

Jim rose early, well short of dawn, and started out for the Yost homestead.

He smiled at the shin high weeds growing in his future cotton field. *By tomorrow they'll be done and soon I'll be sowing my future in a beautiful new field.*

Another of the white rocks lay where his cornfield bordered the unplowed ground. He laughed and kicked it toward the edge. Soon enough he was well along the trail to the Yost's place and whistling a tune Pa had taught him years ago.

He still hadn't settled on what to do about Will's problem. He could hide the gold easy enough. Lots of places on a farm to hide things. But gold did funny things to a man, or at least that's what he'd always heard. Made them crazy. 'Gold Fever' they called it.

He passed the cutoff to Jose's place and glanced down along it.

California, Jim grinned.

Even Jose seemed seduced by it. As if any of them would ever leave Texas. No, they were Texas born and bred. Their families had been here before there even was a Texas. Jose's grandfather loaded supplies into the Alamo before the siege, and Will's uncle rode with Houston at San Jacinto. *Pa carried messages for the great General.* Twice

Santa Anna's patrols chased after him, but few men could outride Travis Heston and those that did sure couldn't outfight him.

The Yost's house lay dark and sleeping when he arrived. Dawn was yet an hour off. He'd planned to get an early start with Sam and Jack, and as it was he wouldn't be back at his place for another hour.

Two days to plow the field, another to run into town and see if Will had the seed yet, one more to plant. He still had time.

Jim kept a good distance from the house and headed for the barn. There was a light on in the kitchen. Mrs. Yost must be up cooking already. Sam and Jack, two of the biggest mules he'd ever seen, stood patiently in their stalls. Quiet as he could manage, he hooked the mules up in tandem, Jack on the left, Sam on the right, just as they preferred.

He started past the house when a voice stopped him cold.

"Sneaking off like a thieving Comanche are you?"

"Nancy," he let out a breath. "Just trying to get an early start."

She came down off the back step, dressed in an old robe. "I don't think Papa knew you'd be over quite this early. Mama and me are putting bacon and biscuits on. We've butter and some honey too. If you want to stay…"

Jim's stomach rumbled. All of it sounded heavenly.

"I don't know. I've got a lot to do."

"Big plans," Nancy nodded. "I understand."

She moved up beside him, close enough he could smell the bacon grease and flour. "Jim," her voice lowered, "if you ask my Papa he'd be happy to give us his blessing."

Jim coughed. "Nancy, well I uh…I don't know that I uh…"

"It must be awful lonely over on your place. That kind of living is hard on a man. I could help you Jim. I could be good to you."

"Nancy, look I'm not ready for all that yet," Jim said.

Nancy giggled. "Mama and Papa were two years younger than us and they done fine. We could have Parson John over tomorrow and do it all right and proper if that's what you want."

"I don't want to rush things," Jim said. His chest grew tight, breath coming hard and rough, his heart pounded like thunder. Surely Nancy could hear it too.

"Who's rushing," she purred. She moved closer yet, leaned up on her toes, and kissed him.

Her breath on his skin burned like fire and Jim felt a jolt through to his bootheels. "No, I can't I just can't," he said and tore himself away. The sudden movement caused Nancy to fall back with a hard plop. She stared up at Jim, face reddening and nostrils flaring.

Mules in tow, he fled down the road at a trot.

Behind him, still on her backside, Nancy laughed. "Why big Jim Heston? So strong and so brave. Whipped all the school bullies, but he's afraid of a little old girl."

"This isn't what I want," Jim said. "I don't want anything to do with you. I just want to be left alone."

"Run all you want Jim Heston," Nancy said. "You'll be alone forever. No one will ever want a coward like you."

He heard her laugh over and over again even when he'd put a mile behind him. Why had she said those things? Why had she kissed him? He didn't want to be married, not yet especially. He had too much to do. He couldn't have someone living with him. There wasn't time enough for anyone else.

When he got back to his place he went straight to work. The old plow waited eagerly at the edge of the new field, ready to go, and soon he had Jack and Sam hitched to it.

He moved up beside the pair and tugged on their harness straps to make sure all was secure. Satisfied, he circled around behind the plow.

"Let's go boys," he said and lightly popped the reins on their backs. He didn't like the whip, most men would use one, but he'd never owned nor needed one. The mules strained. The plow moved two feet, started sinking down, and stopped dead.

"Come on now," Jim urged. He lent his own strength to the plow and it started forward. He had it moving then; he cut another eight feet, the plow clanged against something hard, lurched a little, and then slid up and over whatever it was. Immediately, it clanged again and stopped completely. Jim popped the mules with the reins. He put his back into the plow while Sam and Jack strained. Finally, it moved. A little more and then the first row was done.

Breathing like he'd plowed for a half-day, Jim clung to the plow to hold himself upright. He glanced at the sun. An hour had passed. *An hour for each row? I'll never finish. No, I have to. If the cotton comes through it will all be worth it.* Every row couldn't be as hard as the first. He looked back over his handiwork.

Dozens of white rocks lay spilled in the new field. Many were small—just pebbles really—some though were the size of an apple or larger. Dumbstruck, Jim stared at them. *How am I ever going to get them all?*

He picked himself up off the plow and brought the team around. Every row couldn't be so full of rocks. The lower ground had to be better. Maybe these had gathered at the edge of the cornfield when the plow pushed them over into it. That had to be it.

Sam and Jack pulled for three steps before the plow stopped again. Jim gritted his teeth and shoved and the plow moved ahead another three feet before clanging to a halt.

He leaned into the plow's handle again and the wood strained until it cracked and split apart. Jim held the broken handle. There wasn't time enough for this. How would he finish with a broken plow?

He coaxed Sam and Jack to pull harder. The pair strained. Sweat rolled off their flanks until there was a loud pop and Jack stumbled ahead.

"No...No...No," Jim said. "Please be alright."

He abandoned the plow and circled around to the big mule. The leather harness had snapped through the middle. He inspected Jack's legs, feeling the muscles for any sign of strain. The big mule snorted and tossed his head.

"Please, don't be hurt," Jim pleaded. Leaving Sam hitched as he was, he led Jack around the field by his bridle. The mule moved fine, a little stiff on his left foreleg, but he was putting weight on it. In a few days he'd be fine.

Days Jim did not have. There had to be another way to finish. He just needed to think of it.

Jim took him to the water trough and tied the injured mule to a post. Then he did the same for Sam.

With the animals cared for he looked at his handiwork. Three hours and he only had a row and a half done. Worse, the second row already had twice as many rocks as the first.

Jim fell to his knees beside the newest row. Two inches beyond his right knee, a rock taunted him. He scowled and picked it up, squeezing tight until it dug into his palm.

"More for you Pa," Jim roared. He looked out at the row of rocks. "A whole mess more."

With all his strength he hurled it into the brush well beyond the field. He had a broken plow, a busted harness, and two tired mules, one of whom was injured. Rocks and hard luck year after year. *Damn this evil place.* There would be nowhere to plant the cotton.

What will I do now?

JIM WALKED Sam and Jack back to the Yost farm. With his plow and harness busted he had no need for the mules.

Brett Yost met him at the front gate. "Must have been easy plowing. You finished early."

"I did," Jim agreed and returned the pair to the barn. No need to talk about his broken dream.

On the way out he stopped by Brett. "Sir, I'd like to apologize to Nancy if I offended her."

"Offended her?"

"We had words."

"Oh," Brett gave him a questioning look. "She hasn't left her room all morning. Been feeling sickly."

Jim paused. She didn't seem sickly when he saw her. And why didn't her father realize she'd been out?

"Please pass along my apologies anyway."

"I will," Brett said. "Sometimes these things happen. It's normal. Me and Anna fought often enough those first few years together."

"That's just it sir, Nancy and I aren't together. She's a fine girl and all, but I just don't..."

Brett gave him a hard look. "Jim, what has happened?"

Jim took a deep breath. He looked into the distance. "I'm done. I'm selling the farm and moving on."

"You what?" Brett's eyes flashed.

"I'm selling the place to Will Martin and I'm going out West. Maybe California."

"But what about Nancy?"

"That's why I wanted to apologize. I'm not coming back this way again."

Anna Yost came out to stand by her husband. She smiled gently at Jim.

"Done plowing already?"

"Yes, ma'am I decided—" Jim started.

"He sold out," Brett interrupted.

"What? You're giving up? But what about Nancy?" Anna's hands fell to her sides.

"We had words this morning and I wanted to apologize."

"This morning?" Brett said. He was standing now, fists clinched.

"She was outside when I came by to get the mules."

"She was?" Brett turned to his wife. "Did you know about this?"

"I did," Anna nodded.

"I thought she was in bed sickly. Just what's been going on around here?" Brett said.

"I'll be on my way," Jim said.

Mrs. Yost opened her mouth to speak again when her husband interrupted.

"Anna? What aren't you telling me?"

Deciding it was time to leave, Jim started down the road. He didn't stop at his own place—no point wasting time there—and walked straight for San Antonio.

Eight miles lay between Jim's farm and San Antonio. He made it in half a day's walk. The town had grown since the last time he'd been there, more shops and stores, a few new rows of houses.

Will Martin's general store stood in the heart of town, and from the look of the place was doing good business.

Will's office was on the second floor, but Jim met him as soon as he entered.

"Jim," the storekeeper said. "Didn't expect you for a few days yet."

"Will, I'm selling out."

The words rang out like a leaden bell and Jim felt a pressure release in his chest like just he'd shrugged off some deep burden. Was this the right thing?

Will looked at him in confusion.

"I'm done," Jim said. "If you want the farm I'll sell it to you right now today."

"Well...uh...alright," Will said. "I didn't actually think you would."

Jim sat down at the desk across from his old friend. "You offered a hundred dollars in gold for the farm. I'll take a hundred and ten today plus some supplies for a trip."

"I did," Will nodded. "But you know Jim I'm not sure..."

"A hundred and ten dollars gold money today," Jim knocked on the desktop and held out a hand.

Will eyed the offered hand for minute then took it. "Why not. Let me draw up some papers real quick." He opened a desk drawer and scratched out a Bill-of-Sale on a sheet of clean paper.

Jim read it over twice; he signed his name at the bottom while Will counted out a hundred dollars in gold eagles.

"What changed your mind?" Will said. "I can't believe you'd ever sell."

Jim started to answer but Will went on.

"Ohh, your cottonseed came in this morning by the way. I even had a man came in wanting to buy it. Offered me five dollars, but I told him it was all yours."

Jim sighed. Where to begin? He started to explain about the rocks, the broken harness, the injured mule, Nancy, all of it, when a man's voice boomed downstairs.

"Will Martin," the man said. "I'm looking for Will Martin."

Jim knew the voice, they both did. Will gave him a strange look. What was Brett Yost doing in town?

Will and Jim descended the stairs. Anna and Brett Yost were both inside the store, everyone else had cleared out. Face clouded over like a thunderhead, Brett had his feet spread and his big hands clenched tight. His wife stood slightly behind him.

"Just who I was looking for," Brett said.

"Deal's done," Jim said. "Will Martin owns my place now."

"No, it isn't. You can give him his money back," Anna Yost said.

"I'm through," Jim said.

"No, you're not. You're going to pay this man back, then you're coming with me to Parson Smith's place where you and Nancy can get married."

"I'm not marrying anyone," Jim said. He eyed Brett warily. He'd never seen Brett mad before.

Will held up his hands. "Now, Mr. Yost I'm sure we can all reach some kind of..."

"Shut it," Brett growled and pointed. "I'll deal with you later."

"I am not marrying Nancy," Jim repeated.

"Then you shouldn't have gotten her pregnant," Brett said.

"What?"

"You got my daughter pregnant and now you're going to make it right."

"I didn't."

"You lying son of a—" Brett was suddenly across the room then and swinging one of his big fists.

Jim slipped back from the punch and hopped out of range. "What are you—" Then Brett's other fist caught him across the jaw and sent him reeling.

Colliding with a rack of blankets, Jim righted himself. He dabbed blood off his lips. His heart quickened and pounded like a racing horse.

Brett Yost stood just off to the side. "Had enough or do I need to persuade you some more?"

Jim came off the ground with a lunge at the bigger man's knees. Yost tried to jump back but proved too slow and went down in a heap. Then Jim was on top punching away with both fists like a man possessed.

The older man strained and threw him aside and they both came up at the same time.

Yost threw a vicious haymaker that Jim ducked beneath. He whipped two quick rights into the older man's ribs then a left. Even big as Yost was, Jim's fists were rock hard, and the bigger man fell back a step. He jabbed at Jim's face.

The punch connected and Jim's vision blurred. He turned to take the following punch to the shoulder and swung back with a hook. The big man's granite chin absorbed the blow.

Swinging away, they went toe-to-toe. Jim scored with an uppercut and the other man's legs wobbled. Yost steadied himself, charged, and grabbed for Jim.

Jim popped him on the way in and Yost's head snapped back hard, but one arm swept him up. Desperate to get away, Jim spun free as Yost staggered past.

Throwing lefts and rights, Jim went to work on the big man's side. He felt something crack with his last punch and Yost howled.

In desperation, he reached out and flung Jim away.

Jim bounced off another set of shelves and sent them flying. The he was on Yost before he could recover, slugging away at him with everything he had. The bigger man took every blow, refusing to go down.

Yost finally fell to one knee. Jim lined up a final blow and brought his right fist across the kneeling man's blocky head.

Yost went down in a heap.

"Brett," Mrs. Yost screamed.

Weaving on his feet, Jim moved to the stairs and plopped down. He looked around the store. The place was wrecked. Every shelf in the place had been busted and broken. Oddly enough he didn't remember smashing more than one or two.

"Will, this place is kind of a mess."

Will Martin, speechless for once, leaned on the counter rubbing at his jaw.

"What happened to you?" Jim asked.

"Stray shot."

"Ohh, he got you with one did he?"

"Not him." Will glared. "If you wanted to fight you could have just said so. Those boys across the river would have paid good money to see this."

"I guess you'd better go ahead and sell that cottonseed to pay for all this," Jim grinned.

3

Despite the pain in his ribs, Jim rode tall on his new roan horse. The roan wouldn't win any races or beauty contests, his racing days were a little behind him and his whole head looked a size too small for his body, but he was powerful and he carried himself in a prideful way that had drawn Jim's eyes and warmed his heart.

Two days had passed since the big brawl. Along with the sore ribs, Jim wore a purple shiner and his nose was swollen to half again its normal size. Doctor Benton said it would never be straight again. *Guess I won't be winning any beauty contests either.* Will Martin said it made him look like a real boxer. By the fight's end Marshall Wilkes arrived with a scattergun to sort things out. Jim made sure to keep the Marshall between himself and Brett Yost when the big man finally woke and picked himself up off the floor.

Nancy Yost admitted, eventually, that she'd lied about her baby's father. One of the cowboys from town had gotten her pregnant before he rode off for the railhead in Kansas. The Yosts didn't seem to care. They still wanted Jim to buy back the farm and marry Nancy.

Calmly, Jim had explained to them that there wouldn't be a farm. Never would be, not on that stretch of ground. Those fields grew nothing but rocks and heartache. The best thing anyone could do was let it grass over.

The trail he rode was decent if dusty. Most trade in San Antonio went to and from the coast, but more than a few traveled up this way to Austin. Trees, Mesquite mainly, but a few scattered Pecan or Live Oak, covered the land in a blanket of green. Here and there clumps of prickly-pear cactus, nearly as tall as his horse, rose up in a little clearing.

With only the vaguest notions of his destination, Jim rode north most of the afternoon. California lay west of course, but between Comanches, Apaches, and almost a thousand miles of desert, the safest way was to join up with a wagon train. Of course the wagon trains left from Independence or somewhere else along the river, a detour north of several hundred miles.

The gold Will paid him for the farm weighed heavy in his saddle-bags. Unconsciously, his hand rested on it. A hundred and ten dollars. Ten more than Will originally promised, but he'd been desperate and would have gone higher if Jim had pushed him. Jim didn't feel too bad about it. Will would sell the cottonseed and make the extra back quick enough. The rest would cover the damages to Will's store, though Yost was supposed to cover most of that. A hundred and ten dollars. Even with the cost of the roan the sum was substantial.

Enough to buy a decent farm though? Who knew the price of land in California?

The irony of the last few days—that he should be the one going West while both his friends longed for California and he'd wanted only to stay in Texas—was not lost on him. He still worried about the money though. How much did good land in California cost?

There might be work in Independence and I can add to my savings.

He was young and strong, good with his hands, good with horses. He could find work easy enough and then be on his way.

By noon he dismounted and led his horse across the Blanco river. On the far bank he paused and looked back toward the southern shore. He and Will and Jose had often ridden here as children to hunt after squirrels or deer and fish for perch or the big channel cats that prowled the river's moss-green depths. On rare occasions, they'd go home empty-handed but more often they brought a stringer full of fish and a brace of squirrels. They might get scolded for sneaking off, but their parents, even Will's, never turned down an extra meal.

"The farthest I've ever been from home," Jim confided to the horse. So far he hadn't named the roan. He had a few names in mind, but none seemed to fit just yet.

He gave the far bank a final look. *Not home for me. Not anymore and likely never again.*

Jim remounted then and set out. To the north the sky was clouding over with high white thunderheads. Like all farmers, he knew a lot about clouds, he'd studied them often enough, and these promised a pounding rain, hail, lightning, and driving wind. That meant a long cold night for a man out-of-doors.

In an hour, maybe two, he and the roan would need to be in shelter.

There was supposed to be a few old homesteads scattered up this way, mostly abandoned. A lot of good folks found out the hard way that being out in the wilderness alone wasn't the life they'd been hoping for.

Jim coaxed the roan into a trot and scanned both sides of the trail for a dry place to spend the night. A half-hour later and with nothing in sight the wind shifted from a warm southern breeze to a hard chilly norther. The roan's nostril's flared and his ears rose when he smelled the storm's cool breath.

"C'mon boy, we gotta find us a place to ride this one out," Jim said.

They circled a bend and dipped into a gap between two hills and Jim reined the roan in. There was a faint trail to the east, old, unused for a long time, and just the sort than might lead to an abandoned farm.

On faith, Jim swung off the trail and rode the roan onward. They passed through a copse of thick mesquite and emerged into a little open area and an abandoned field. The sky was dark now. Lightning flashed in the distance. At the far end of the field stood a little house.

When they reached it, Jim dismounted and tried the door. Instead of opening it fell off the rotted leather hinges.

The place wasn't big, two rooms with just enough space for himself and the roan. He checked inside for rattlers or skunks then led the horse on in.

There was a small hearth in the corner and trash and debris scattered all around. Jim nudged a little girl's abandoned doll with his boot.

Whoever left here had been in a hurry.

He tied the roan in one corner, removed his saddle and blankets, then set about finding some wood for the fire. There was a little stack of firewood laying against the back of the house and he scooped up an armload. Just as he returned inside the thunder crashed and the sky opened up in a great torrent of driving rain. Wind howled through the old house and in moments, the rain turned to hail, falling hard and loud as gunfire on the thin roof.

"Lucky to find this place weren't we," Jim said. He eyed the horse for a long time. "Nah you don't look much like a Lucky."

Jim watched the storm through the open door. The hail lasted a few minutes, enough to coat the ground in slippery white marbles, and then the storm tapered down into rain. Drops fell through several holes in the roof. The wind fell away completely as the fury of the storm passed south and east.

Will's corn would appreciate the rain if not the hail. The stalks were young though and tender the hail wouldn't damage them much.

There was an old, overturned stool at the edge of the room. Jim righted it and sat down beside the hearth. How many evenings had he spent sitting on the stool at home beside his mother's chair. Will had promised to look after it, but more than giving up the farm, leaving it behind felt like a betrayal.

"I just couldn't make that place work Ma," he said aloud.

Jim fed firewood into the hearth and watched the long yellow flames rise. He hadn't made it far, but he had a good horse, gold in his pocket, and he was warm and dry. Besides he was already more north than he ever had gone before. California might be a thousand miles off, but he was well on his way.

"If I keep at it, I'll make it one way or the other," he told the night.

Jim's second day proved better than the first. He reached Austin, stopping to top off his supplies and grab a quick meal from a tiny adobe cafe. On a whim, he strolled to the Capitol building and found a place to sit and eat.

Still under construction, the building would be a big one. An army of masons, bricklayers, and carpenters attacked the project with a chorus of banging hammers, ringing chisels, and buzzing saws. To Jim they looked like ants struggling with a fat grasshopper, only instead of taking him apart, they were putting him back together.

How could a place be rich enough to support so many men?

Proud as he was of his home state and its Capitol, he couldn't help but think of all the honest folks being taxed into poverty down in San Antonio by the Yankees. So many people suffering to pay for buildings like this to be built up.

The Yanks would take their own cut first of course. Men like that always did.

One of the workmen yelled out when his carthorses got away from him. Frightened by the noise, the team tore off down one of the muddy streets, spilling barrels and tools all the way.

Finishing his meal, Jim put his hat back on and started north again. He'd asked for directions back at the adobe and now had a good idea of where he was headed.

Waco would be next good-sized town, then east toward Louisiana, and on up into Arkansas and Missouri. Again, he was struck by how strange it was, traveling east and north to reach California in the far west. But trying to cross Comanche and Apache territory alone he wouldn't have much of a chance. For similar reasons the Indian territory, due north, was out of the question. Even in San Antonio they heard stories about the bandits and renegades living there.

No, he had his gold, and it was better to arrive slow and safe than rush in and wind up with his scalp hanging on some Comanche's lodge-pole.

Two days out of Austin he was crossing between some low hills when he saw smoke rising ahead. Jim stopped the roan long enough to study the smoke.

He'd seen traffic on the road, mostly heading in the other direction, toward Austin. Generally, the travelers had been pleasant enough, doffing a hat or exchanging a bit about the trail ahead. But there had been a few hard-eyed types who hinted around after lawmen who might be laying for them. With that type, Jim kept his answers short and to the point. Yes, there was a Sheriff in the last town. No, he wasn't stopping travelers.

Jim kept his pistol handy and loose while he talked. His father had taught him how to use a belt gun and Jim proved a good student. The war had made people desperate and desperate people were apt to do all sorts of things to survive, especially to an unknown traveler with gold on him.

Twice, he'd seen a group of Yankee soldiers, and once a pair of men wearing the gray.

Just south of Dallas, Jim came to a grove of pines and then a little meadow with a creek rolling through it. There were a half-dozen young men in it, eating breakfast. Most were little more than boys, only one or two looked as old as Jim.

They watched him approach.

"Howdy," one of the older boys saluted.

"Howdy yourself," Jim said.

"Set down if you like and have some coffee. We'll have some biscuits in a few minutes. Unless Tobe burns them again." The oldest of them said. He gave a half smile to one of the younger ones.

"Only a little brown on that last batch," Tobe said.

"Coulda made them into horseshoes," another boy answered.

"It's been some time since I had burned biscuits. I've grown to dearly miss them," Jim grinned.

"You won't miss them once you try one," the first boy said. "I'm Roper and this is Jace, Bill, Andy, Ned, and you've already met Tobe."

"Jim, nice to meet ya." Jim swung down off his horse and walked to their fire.

The rest of them were eyeing him pretty close, their eyes lingering on the rifle in its scabbard, his horse, his pistol.

"Traveled far?" Roper asked. He was tall and lithe, but wide across the shoulders, and he had an easy smile.

"San Antone. Thought I might see some new country." Jim eased his hat up with one hand and kept the other down near the butt of his pistol. "You all?"

"From all over. Waco or Austin mostly. We had us a spot of trouble and decided we might as well ride west and see what all the fuss is about."

Several of the boys chuckled.

"Headed that way myself. Independence and then over the trail. I'd like to see the Pacific."

"Well Jim, we're of like mind." Roper said with a grin. "After a little breakfast we're setting out. You're welcome to join us."

"Sounds good." Jim crinkled his nose. "Though it smells like those biscuits might be burnt already."

Tobe swore and scrambled toward the fire.

"Dammit Tobe," Roper smiled as he said it though. "Once again you've ruint breakfast. Now our new friend's gonna decide to ride off without us."

Jim ate breakfast with them, Tobe's biscuits weren't burned nearly so bad as they'd smelled. Then they mounted up and headed out.

The boy's horses were good—too good—for a group of traveling cowboys. All wore a K-Bar branded on their hips.

"K-Bar," Jim said when he saw it.

"Used to work for them," Roper said. "You know them."

"Nope."

"Big outfit, over east of Austin," Roper volunteered. "They owed us some back wages and couldn't pay what with money being scarce an all, so they paid us in horses."

"Back wages," Andy snickered.

They were a rough lot with dirty clothes, worn boots, and

patched saddles, but most people were poor these days. Tobe didn't even have a proper saddle just a wood and rawhide affair like an Indian might use. Tobe and Roper did the talking, the others kept mainly to themselves. Now and then Jim caught them staring at his guns and saddlebags. He fought to keep himself from placing a protective hand over his gold. He'd only draw more of their attention.

By midday he realized he'd made a mistake riding with Roper and his gang. Traveling alone was dangerous, there were thieves and renegades all through the country, but he was fairly certain Roper was deciding whether or not to try and rob him.

The young man himself was pleasant enough. He had an easy way of speaking that caused a man to let down his guard if he wasn't careful. He asked about San Antonio and if Jim had people back there and what Jim planned on doing out in California.

Jim kept his answers vague, and if they frustrated Roper he gave no sign of it.

Three days they journeyed along. Roper did most of the talking, but gradually the others joined in. Though he got the know them all, Jim's unease didn't subside. They studied him close anytime he opened his saddlebags to contribute supplies for their meals.

For his own part Jim never left any of his gear more than an arm's length away.

He needed to get free of them. But how?

At night they always kept a careful watch. Fighting his way free was out of the question. Jim could fight certainly, he was good with his pistol and rifle, but one against so many. He hadn't a chance.

A distraction, I need something to distract them long enough for me to escape.

It was almost noon on the fourth day when they saw the Indian. The county here was wide and opened up onto the flat prairie. Shimmering heat made him look watery and distorted. At first, the Indian was no more than a brown dot on a carpet of green grass, but details emerged as he rode closer.

"By Gawd," Roper said. "It's a Comanche."

"What?" Ned said. They were alert now, all of them, rifles drawn as they leaned forward and squinted for a better look.

The approaching Indian neither turned nor stopped but kept on coming.

Jim could see him clear now. He was a tall man, clad in faded blue cavalry pants, shirtless, brown-skinned, and with several white feathers dangling from his long black hair.

"Get him," Roper said and spurred his horse into a run. The others fell in quickly behind him and, caught up along with them, Jim followed suit. This wasn't the distraction he'd hoped for. If anything it was a reminder that he had to keep in a group for safety.

The Indian stopped and straightened. He waited for three long breaths, let out a long war cry, turned his horse, and raced in the opposite direction.

"We got him on the run," Roper said. He let out a long whoop and raised his pistol for a shot.

Roper's gun roared and sent smoke bellowing. The shot missed, and the Indian lowered his body closer to the horse, making a more difficult target. Ned and Bill drew their own pistols and began firing away quick as they could bring the hammers back.

Then the flat land ended and broke up into ridges and deep cuts. Suddenly on either side, more Indians began popping up from the ground like prairie dogs.

They were all around now. At least a dozen of them, armed with bows or old rifles. Roper stopped his horse with a cloud of dust. Jim almost crashed into him. No sense of the danger, Ned and Bill kept riding after the first Indian. They fell in the first volley.

"Back like we came," Jim said. "Hurry before they close in."

He spun the roan around, but it was too late. Four armed Indians had closed the gap behind.

Then Jim's pistol was in his hand, coughing smoke and flame. A bullet zipped past his ear and an arrow struck into the leather of his saddle.

Everyone was fighting then. Roper emptied his pistol into an Indian with a long war club. He started to reload then his face took on a look of horror. The first Comanche they'd seen, the only one mounted, rode into Roper and split his skull with a stone axe.

Jim snapped off a shot at the mounted brave, saw the bullet strike him on the shoulder.

Then the roan bucked and Jim fell off onto the ground. The air rushed out of him and he fought for breath. Gunfire sounded all around him. He got to his feet and looked around.

Knife raised, one of the Comanches had Tobe down beneath him. They were close enough to touch and Jim beat the Comanche over the head with the barrel of his pistol.

Off to his left, Andy screamed. Jim whipped around. There was an arrow in the young man's leg. A second struck him in the chest and his screams died off.

An older Comanche was running toward Jim and he put two bullets in the man's stomach. Then his pistol clicked on an empty chamber.

His rifle was still in its scabbard, but where was the roan?

He saw it then. One of the Comanches was holding the reins as the frightened horse bucked and fought. Jim took off at a run. An arrow hit the ground ahead of him and he ignored it. He had to get that rifle.

The Indian holding his horse saw him at the last moment. He dropped the reins and raised his tomahawk, but too late. Jim's beltknife took him in the ribs and drove deep. With his other hand, Jim punched the smaller man and sent him flying.

Then the rifle was in his grasp and Jim opened up. He didn't fire quickly; this wasn't the time for wasted shots. He killed one, then two Comanches who were fighting with Jace. Then the first one they'd seen, still mounted despite the bleeding shoulder, charged him. Jim's first shot missed, but the second sent the man flying off his pony.

Somewhere a bugle bellowed, and more guns joined the battle.

Men in blue coats raced by. One hacked down at a brave with a long, gleaming saber.

The Indians took to running, and half of the Cavalry soldiers tore out after them.

"Comanches," Jace said between breaths. He was bleeding from the scalp and a bullet hole in his right arm.

One of the soldiers approached.

"Are you men alright?" he said. He was a tall, lanky man with gray eyes and a long brown mustache.

"We're alive," Jim nodded.

"Corporal McLane, see to these men."

"Yes, Lieutenant," a young soldier said.

He dismounted and took a white medical bag from his horse.

"Sergeant Smith have your men recover the bodies," the Lieutenant said.

"Savages too?"

"Savages too," the Lieutenant nodded. Then, while the Sergeant set about his work, he dismounted and removed his hat.

"I am Lieutenant Travis Bell. Can one of you tell me what happened here?"

"We were making our way north to Independence to join up with a wagon train east. We came across a lone Comanche. Roper," Jim pointed with his chin, "set out after him along with the rest of us."

"It was a trap, of course," Travis said.

"It was. We rode right into them and before we knew what was happening they had Ned and Bill dead and the rest of us surrounded."

"You were lucky we were close." Travis put his hat back on. "We've been trailing them for three days after they left the reservation."

"Lieutenant," the Sergeant said. He was standing over Roper. "You might want to look at this."

"Excuse me," Travis said and joined his Sergeant.

"You'll have a nasty scar," the doctor told Jace.

"Just patch me up best you can," Jace answered.

"You'll have to have stitches on the arm."

"Jim," Tobe said. The boy seemed to have escaped harm completely. His eyes were wet with tears. "Jim, you saved my life back there. That Injun was surely going to..."

"Yeah, I'm sure you would have done the same," Jim answered.

"Jim, we was planning to ro—"

"What did you call this man?" the Lieutenant interrupted.

"Roper," Jim answered. "He told me his name was Roper."

The Sergeant held open a piece of unfolded paper. Both soldiers were looking from it to the body.

"Sure looks like him," the Lieutenant said.

Both men then turned back toward Jim and the others. Any sympathy they had given after the Comanche attack was gone now.

"You boys have some explaining to do," the Lieutenant said.

4

Jim Heston mopped sweat from his forehead with the back of his hand. All around him hammers rung as his fellow prisoners pounded white limestone boulders down into gravel for the railroad. The sun bore down on him, hot and pitiless. Armed with rifles, blue-coat soldiers stood scattered around the quarry, mostly in shadowed ledges or sheltered inside towers where the brutal sun couldn't reach them.

How did I ever end up in a place like this?

Jim hoisted his hammer and brought it down.

There wasn't a trial. Not a real one anyway. Jim, Jace, and Tobe were dragged in before Lieutenant Bell's commanding officer, General Killian, a stern man of about forty with an ugly scar over his left cheek and a bald head.

The Lieutenant unrolled the paper and then he and the General had gone out to view Roper's body.

"What are they going on about?" Jim asked Tobe.

"Quiet you," one of the guards said and curled his hands up into fists. "Or I'll make you quiet."

Jim eyed the Sergeant. He wasn't so big as Brett Yost, but by the scars on his knuckles he had a lot of experience beating men into submission. This was not a man to take lightly.

General Killian and his Lieutenant returned then.

"Do you three know who that man is?" Killian asked.

"He told me his name was Roper," Jim said. "I only fell in with them a few days ago, south of Dallas."

"Hmm, another Texan," Killian said. "And you others? Lost your tongues?"

Tobe and Jace gave each other a long look and Tobe spoke. "We don't know who he was either, it's like Jim said we fell in with him a couple days earlier."

"And yet each of you rode K-Bar horses. Stolen K-Bar horses."

"I didn't," Jim protested.

"No?" Killian said. "And which horse was yours?"

"The big roan."

"Ahh, the big roan," Killian gave him a dangerous smile. "The one with over a hundred dollars in gold money in his saddlebags." The Lieutenant dumped gold coins out on the General's desk.

Jim heard Jace and Tobe's breath catch.

"Too much money for a poor dirt farmer from Texas," Killian said. "Luke Davensport and his gang robbed the outfit of a man named Kincaid just outside of Waco two weeks ago."

"Who is Luke Davensport?" Jim said.

Lieutenant Bell held up the paper. The script read: Luke Davensport, horse-thief and murderer, wanted for $350. The picture below the words showed a smiling Roper.

"I had no idea," Jim said.

"Of course you didn't," Killian grinned. "Mr. Kincaid said your friend Roper stole a number of horses off him along with a cashbox of gold coins."

Killian picked up one of the coins where it caught the sun. "Coins like these."

"I had nothi—"

"Lieutenant, escort these men to Reedsville quarry for hard labor."

"What about a trial?" Jim protested.

"You were caught with stolen property in Indian Territory, you just had your trial and I found you guilty."

"I sold my farm to Will Trimble in San Antonio. He can vouch for me," Jim protested.

"Get this rebel trash out of my sight," Killian said.

The Sergeant and two other men dragged all three out, brought them to the quarry, turned them over, and that had been the end of it. The end of Jim's California dreams. The end of his freedom. The end of his life. He'd be busting rocks for the rest of his days.

White, chalk rocks just like the ones that ended his farm.

Jim frowned at the irony.

"Heston," one of the guards called.

"Here, boss," Jim said and lowered his hammer.

"Stanton wants you up top."

Relief washed over Jim. Hot and full of air that choked, working down in the pit was hell itself. The only relief was in the evening when the prisoners were all chained together and marched up top for a greasy dinner then locked in their bunkhouse on the quarry's rim. The following morning, after a bowl of cold gruel, the hammering began all over again. Young or old, everyone hammered.

There was a single exception to the back-breaking work. Stable duty.

Under the watchful eyes of the guards, Jim made his way up the winding path to the rim. At the top he stopped at the guard post and waited.

"Wanted in the stables?" a guard said.

"Yes, boss," Jim nodded. Jim hadn't learned the guard's names. No prisoner did. They rotated out often and they were all boss. It was easier to remember to call them that if you didn't know their names.

Two more guards came out and placed a pair of shackles around Jim's ankles.

"All right, go on with you," the guard said.

The stables, along with the cells and barracks, stood just a hundred yards or so from the quarry, but Jim gave no thought to escape. Some had. Jace tried it on their third day here. He made it fifty yards before the guards shot him dead. The newcomers, Jim and Tobe included, buried him in an unmarked grave that very evening.

Jim kept straightaway for the stables. His ankle chains were purposefully short, enough so that a man couldn't make a full running stride.

The stables were shaded and offered a respite from the sun's heat. Jim took a deep breath of that coolness as soon as he entered. In the far corner an old man stood beside a workbench repairing a bridle.

"Jim?" the old man said and looked up from his work.

"Yes, boss," Jim said.

"None of that boss nonsense in here," Stanton scowled. "I'm no guard."

"Yes," Jim smiled.

"Go fill the water troughs and then start mucking out the stalls," Stanton said.

Two buckets hung from pegs on one wall. Jim took both down and headed for the pump. He filled each then helped himself to a long drink. He rubbed water over his head and face. The water here was brackish but cool.

It took five trips to fill all the water troughs and then Jim found the shovel and wheelbarrow before starting to muck the stables clean.

Jim didn't mind the smell of the stables, nor the backbreaking work. Shoveling was harder than merely swinging a hammer—quite a bit harder—but it kept him up top where there was open sky and wind and fresh air to breathe.

Old man Stanton finished his work and came over to watch him.

"Take a rest," he said.

"Yes boss," Jim answered and stopped.

Stanton sighed and held out a cup of water.

Jim took it gratefully.

"Come along. I've got something I want you to look at," the old man started for one of the far stalls. Jim followed.

At the very back stalls were the horses belonging to the officers.

Jim had never been allowed back here, not while the horses were present anyways. Whenever these needed mucked Stanton would move the horses out into one of the pens outside.

In the farthest stall stood a magnificent bay horse. A full eighteen hands tall, the bay had long, powerful legs and a deep chest. His head came up and he stared at Jim.

Stanton raised his hands to the bay. "Easy now. This is my friend, Jim."

The horse snorted.

"Yes, I know he smells very bad," Stanton said. He turned to Jim. "What do you think?"

"He's beautiful." Jim said. His hands reached up to pat the big horse's side.

"He belongs to the Warden."

Jim's hands jerked back like he'd been burned.

"I want you to watch him walk," Stanton said. He slipped the repaired bridle over the bay's ears and fastened the clasp.

"Why?"

"You'll see." The old man took the bay by the reins and swung the door open. Then he walked the big horse out into one of the larger pens and around into a circle.

Immediately Jim knew something wasn't right. Jim watched the big horse move in around the pen. There was a limp, slight, barely noticeable, and it came and went.

"What happened?"

"He fell when the Warden was riding back from Dallas," Stanton said.

"How long ago?" Jim said.

"A month."

A month. The bay shouldn't be limping from an injury so old.

When Stanton came closer and stopped Jim moved up beside the bay. He ran his hands down over each of the horse's legs. The right, front one trembled when he touched near the knee joint. "Sprain of some kind."

"How would you treat it?" Stanton said.

"Cloth wrap, tight but not enough to cut off circulation. Daily walks without a rider to keep it loose," Jim said. He stood and patted the bay's flank. The horse nuzzled at him.

"Good," Stanton said. "I'll see you back here tomorrow then and you can begin treatment."

"Me?" Jim said. "I'm just a prisoner. I'm not allowed to."

"Nonsense," Stanton said. "You know horses and I'm too old to babysit a horse like this. You're the man for the job."

"Look I know a few things, but I'm hardly..."

"I'll make sure the guards know your schedule. They won't shoot you," the old man gave him a long look. "Get the Warden's horse back to health and I'll have them keep you up here permanently."

"Up here?"

"I'm getting old for this sort of work. Eyes are too blurry and my hands aren't steady enough."

"There's a lot I don't know," Jim said. "My Pa taught me a few things is all."

"You've the knack for it. A way with animals. I'll teach you the rest."

One of the guards entered the pen then. "Everything alright here?"

"It is," Stanton said. "I want this man up here tomorrow and every day after for a month. He'll be taking care of the Warden's horse from now on."

The guard's eyes narrowed as he looked at Jim. "You're sure?"

"I am. He won't go anywhere."

That was the beginning of Jim's time in the stables and his escape from the hellish quarry. At night he'd be mixed in with the other prisoners, same food, same living arrangements, but in the morning Stanton sent for him and he took up work in the stables.

If the other prisoners grew jealous none said anything. Jim had been in several fights when he'd first arrived. Men tried taking his boots or clothing. After he beat down the first three, word got out that Jim Heston was not a man to be fought.

The guards grew to treat him better than the other men. They wanted their horses well cared for. Stanton taught him how to repair old tack, an easy way to shoe, even how to take care of a full team, the prison had a cart sometimes used to collect prisoners from the distant forts.

His skills grew and each day the quarry seemed a little farther away. He could still smell it. Despite being up on the rim, chalky limestone dust drifted out and settled onto everything. But it wasn't the choking cloud the men in the quarry took in. Other than his confinement and the lousy food he could almost have enjoyed himself.

FIVE MONTHS after Jim started helping Stanton the guards came to the stables for him.

"Jim Heston," the one in charge said.

"Yes boss," Jim answered. He didn't recognize this one, a big burly man with a heavy black beard. *Not a new recruit, not at his age, someone being punished then.* None of the guards liked prison duty. They complained about it often enough. Jim looked at the other two guards, but neither were familiar.

"You are to come with us immediately," the guard said.

"Yes boss." Jim looked to Stanton but the old man only shrugged.

The burly guard turned then and led Jim to the main prison compound. Two more guards, armed with rifles, fell in behind them.

Jim's neck began sweating as he felt the eyes of the two men behind him.

They led them past the prisoner barracks, the cookhouse, and the soldier's housing to a modest little house at the end.

The Warden's quarters, Jim swallowed. What was this? Had he done something wrong? In the months since he'd come to this place he'd never once even seen the Warden.

The door was open when they arrived, and the bearded man brought Jim directly inside. Warden Simmons sat behind a big oak desk holding a thick cigar in one hand and a paper in the other.

"Have a seat," he gestured with the cigar. "Please."

Reluctantly, Jim eased down into the chair and sat quietly.

"You are Jim Heston," the Warden kept studying the paper.

"Yes boss."

"You are the one who looked after my horse."

"Yes boss."

The Warden lowered the paper then and regarded Jim. Jim felt his breath catch. The man was older than Jim's father would have been, but he had the same look about him, the same sandy-gray hair, the same narrow face, the same strong jaw, even the eyes were the same shade of bright green.

"Are you alright?" the Warden asked.

With the question Jim took a second look. He studied the man's blue coat. This was not his father.

"Sorry, you looked like," Jim coughed. "That is to say yes boss."

"You've been a model prisoner, Heston. A few fights early on. Most of the men have those until they find their place in the pecking order. Such is the way of prisoners."

Jim sat silent.

"Arch says you've done good work with the horses. He said you did a fine job with my bay. Best horse I ever owned."

Jim bit his lips. The Warden knew. He knew Jim had been taking care of the horses and now he was being sent back down into the pit. It was over.

"Anyway, I want you to consider my next offer closely."

"Offer?"

"Yes, it seems a friend of yours, one Will Trimble from San Antonio, he's written a letter on your behalf. He claims you sold a farm to him and he paid you with gold. He also claims there's no way you were involved with the K-Bar incident or Luke Davensport. Says you grew up together."

"It's true. I had nothing to do with K-Bar. Just a run of bad luck," Jim's voice cracked.

The Warden drew on his cigar. "Mr. Trimble had this document drawn up before a local judge and it's signed by a half-dozen men. It says you were in San Antonio the day the K-Bar was robbed."

"Will is a good friend."

"A very good friend. It seems based on this that you're a free man Mr. Heston. Furthermore," the Warden took a small sack from his desk and set it on the table. It rattled when it struck. "It seems this gold is rightfully yours."

"A free man," Jim felt tears burn his eyes.

"Free," the Warden smiled and nodded. "I have to say that you are the first man I've freed since I've been here. Before you go though, I want you to consider an offer."

"An offer?"

"Arch Stanton and I have been friends for a long time. That old man is an excellent judge of horseflesh and people. I respect him and his opinions and he thinks very highly of you. If you're as good with horses as he claims you would do well serving the army."

"Serving the army?" Jim choked out. The Yankee army. The men who'd killed his Pa and brother.

"Yes, we could use another man in the stables. The position would be paid of course and you'd bunk with the soldiers."

Jim's thoughts flew. This couldn't be happening. Will had come through for him and now the blue-bellies were offering him a job. He thought of that stinking pit. The endless ringing of hammers. The choking dust. Men's spirits being ground down to nothing.

"I don't think—" Jim started.

"If it's the guards I assure you they've all been told about your situation. They'll be nothing but accommodating."

At that, the bearded guard cleared his throat.

"I had a plan to go to California," Jim said. "Up to Independence first and then on to buy a farm beside the ocean."

"I expected as much," he smiled. "I don't really blame you. That sounds more appealing to me as well."

The Warden stood and held out a hand then.

Jim shook his hand and when they were done the Warden

dropped the bag of coins into it. Then he gave Jim a rolled-up piece of paper. "Your gold, plus some for the work you've done here, and your release papers, signed by myself. Good luck, Mr. Heston. On behalf of the US Army, I can offer nothing but an apology. I hope you find everything you wish for in sunny California."

5

Ellen Wilson ate a silent dinner with the man who called himself her husband. But for the two of them, the great house was empty. Clive preferred his family estate that way, silent, dark, cold. Ellen shuddered. He was a handsome man, by all accounts the most eligible bachelor in Illinois, and she had been the girl lucky enough to land him. Captain Clive Wilson was a tall man, proud, strong, dashing —a war hero who'd risen through the ranks with valor. Dozens of women envied her. They envied her status, her wealth, her respect.

Ellen in turn envied them.

"Is our meal to your liking?" she asked. He'd attacked his dinner without ceremony and hadn't spoken since.

"It is," he said without so much as looking up.

"How was your business today?"

"Profitable," he looked at her then and she caught the warning glare of those deep brown eyes.

Ellen knew that look. Knew it enough to know she was on dangerous ground. Her husband had many moods. None were predictable, even by her, even after four years of marriage. All were dangerous. But this...this was his most dangerous mood.

"Where is Walter?" he said.

"He stayed over at my parents," Ellen said. She tried to keep the tremble from her voice.

"He spends too much time over there in that shack of theirs," Clive said.

"He loves them. He only wants—," Ellen started then caught herself. *Do not anger him.* "I will keep him at home more."

"Good."

Ellen let out a sigh. She'd come close to provoking him. That he hadn't exploded into rage at her insolence was a sign of just how profitable his day must have been.

Clive pushed back his plate and belched. He ran a hand through his dark mane of hair and looked at her.

Ellen felt his eyes on her, weighing and measuring. Her breath caught. She kept her head down and took another spoonful. *Not tonight, please not tonight. If he touches me tonight I will scream.*

Their marriage started out happy enough, had stayed happy enough, until Walt had been born. Clive had been the perfect husband just as he'd been the perfect gentlemen during their courtship. There had been some fraying around the edges of course. A sharp comment here, a hard word there, nothing all couples didn't go through. Her mother said it would pass once they settled into each other's ways.

Then Walt was born, and Clive changed.

Even before they married there been rumors of course. Ellen ignored them. She'd chalked them up to business rivals jealous of his success or his looks or his family status.

Clive's chair rumbled as he lay back in it. Ellen risked a glance up. He watched her now with his eyes almost shut. Ellen studied her hands, folding them tight. Her mother always said she had beautiful hands. The last two fingers of her right hand were crooked, the knuckles thicker than the others.

Three years ago, Clive had broken them in a fit of rage after she'd overcooked a roast.

Ellen shifted her misshapen fingers out of sight. She fought to keep her expression plain and neutral.

He must not guess my plan.

Those premarriage rumors didn't cover half of it. Clive became a monster. No, that wasn't right he'd always been a monster, after Walt was born he'd merely removed the mask. When his work went poorly he beat her. When he lost at cards he beat her. When the baby cried he beat her. When he found things he didn't like he beat her. Whenever he was frustrated in any way his response was to beat her.

At first, she thought the beatings were her fault. She had done something wrong failed him in some way—and had to be punished. Gradually, she'd learned the truth.

Dashing Clive Wilson simply enjoyed beating his wife.

Not just his wife of course. She heard those rumors too. He beat the girls in town when they displeased him. He visited those places often, and he beat them mercilessly, but he had money enough to smooth everything over. When money didn't work he used his family's power and influence.

The Wilson family ran this part of Illinois. Anyone who thought to accuse Clive Wilson of wrongdoing was quickly shown the error of their ways.

"I'm going into Shawneetown tonight," he said. He rose and stretched like a lion who'd just eaten a fresh gazelle.

Ellen tried not to imagine herself as that gazelle.

"Should I have breakfast ready in the morning?" Ellen ventured. The question was a risk, with Clive every question was. But she had her plans. Plans that depended on his answer. Freedom from this terrible prison awaited. Everything depended though on her husband's absence.

"No. I've a job to do and I'll be gone for at least a week Little Mouse," Clive said.

Little Mouse—his nickname for her. She'd been content with it while they courted, thought it was sweet that he wanted to protect her from harm. Now she knew the truth. Now she knew heard clear the scorn in it.

How had everything all gone so wrong?

Clive came over beside her chair. He leaned down, rested his hands on her shoulders, kissed the top of her head. She smelled the whiskey he'd spilled on his shirt mingled with the pure stench of him.

Ellen fought down a scream.

"I will see you after that Little Mouse," he said. "And we will catch up."

"I will have Walter here when you do," she answered.

"See that you do." Clive laughed. And with that he took up his coat and left.

After the front door slammed shut Ellen let out a breath. She began to sob into her hands.

This nightmare has to end.

She allowed herself a few minutes to cry, then stood, and went upstairs. She left their dirty dishes on the table. Clive would be furious about that. *Everything had to be in its place. Everything had to be perfect. Always.*

At the door to their bedroom, she paused.

How many nights had she spent crying on that bed? She'd lost count two years ago. Even today, a month since the last time he'd laid hands on her, her body was covered in fading bruises. Bruises were far from the worst of it. He'd broken her arm twice, her ribs once, along with her fingers.

She'd lied to the Doctors of course. She was a clumsy little mouse. Fell down the stairs again. Stuck her fingers where she shouldn't.

Ellen wiped away a stray tear. *Enough crying for yourself. There's work to be done.*

She took the bags from her closet and began packing.

"Take only trail-worthy clothes," her father had said. As if she didn't know better. This had been her idea after all. She knew what was required better than any of them.

Sleep would come hard tonight, but tomorrow—if all went as planned—she would finally begin her escape from this gilded cage.

"I'll never come back," she said. "He'll have to kill me first."

. . .

JIM LEFT Reedsville prison that very evening.

He could have stayed another night and set off in the morning. Instead he'd thanked Stanton for saving him from the pit, gathered what little amounted to his things, and set out east for the trail to Independence.

The Warden had given him a set of clothes and once he put Reedsville out of sight he changed into them, abandoning the blue prisoner uniform. Then he walked until his feet hurt and walked some more. He couldn't get far enough away from the foul place. Finally, sometime after midnight, he collapsed at the base of a tall maple. Resting his head against the trunk he closed his eyes, and for the first time in almost a year he breathed fresh clean air, without even a hint of limestone, and slept beneath the outstretched branches and cold, distant stars.

The morning proved bitterly cold. Jim woke covered in dew and shivering. His teeth clattered like stones rattling in an empty can. With no way to light a fire, he rose and started out again.

A good walk will get me warm enough.

The sun was well up when he saw the covered wagon.

A man and his wife, along with a pair of children, one older boy and a very little girl, huddled around a campfire. Jim heard the sizzle of bacon and caught the sweet scent of it. His mouth watered.

"Hello," he said.

The man stood quickly; his hand fell to the butt of a pistol. Jim was unarmed, the Warden didn't have his guns or anything more than the gold he'd been carrying.

"Don't come any closer," the man said.

"I am unarmed," Jim offered. "Only hungry. Had a run-in with Comanches."

"Comanches," the woman hissed and her eyes went wild.

"Where are they?" the man said.

"Quite a ways back," Jim said. "Haven't seen them in some time now."

It wasn't strictly a lie. He needed these people's help very badly. He had no water, no food, no means of travel. Even if they just told him where the nearest town was he would be grateful.

"You lost your outfit?" the man said.

"Lost everything."

"Come on in and we'll feed you," the wife said. "I'm Sarah Sides and this is Mack and our children, Matthew and Lily."

"Nice to meet you all. I'm Jim Heston from San Antone."

"You're a long way from home then," Mack said.

"Don't I know it."

Jim took a seat by the fire and fought back the urge to grab the sizzling bacon straight from the pan. The smell was intoxicating. "Was going up to Independence then on out west to California."

"Ahh," Mack said. "You following the gold fields?"

"Gold?" Jim said. "No, just a farmer. My land played out down south. Nothing but rocks and stones. Soil couldn't even grow a proper weed."

"I've seen it," Mack nodded. His hand eased away from the pistol. "We tried farming up in the Ozarks. Same problem. Planted corn, potatoes, rye, but nothing grew but rocks. Then we moved on to Louisiana, but I don't care for that country. You ever seen a swamp?"

"No," Jim shook his head. Mrs. Sides fished out a strip of bacon with a fork and passed it over.

"Guests first," she said.

The bacon threatened to burn his hands so Jim blew on it a little before wolfing it down. The flavor hit him like a hammer and he chewed slow, squeezing out as much as he could. When it was gone, he licked each finger in turn.

He caught the little girl staring at him.

"I'm Jim," he said.

"I'm Lily," she answered shyly. "Pleased to meet you."

Mrs. Sides doled out more bacon for her husband and children followed by warm buttermilk biscuits and a cup of hot coffee. Jim rolled the coffee around in his mouth. He hadn't had coffee in so long.

"What's a swamp?" Jim asked.

"It's a black place," Mack said. "Just oozing mud or brown water as far as you can see. Full of snakes and alligators. No place fit for farming nor even living. How those Cajuns stand it I will never know."

Mrs. Sides leaned over to her husband and whispered in his ear. Jim tried not to eavesdrop. The breakfast sat in his stomach warm and perfect. He felt like a real person again. All he needed now was a bit of directions and he could be on his way.

"Ahem," Mack coughed. "The Missus and I are heading up North ourselves. We'd appreciate some company."

"You're sure?" Jim said. "I've got nothing but the clothes I'm wearing and a little spending money."

"Well there are renegades and the like, Injuns like you said. One more man to help with the stock and keep watch would be a real blessing."

"I don't even have a gun," Jim said. "But if you're serious I'd thank you."

"We are," Mrs. Sides nodded.

Jim stood then and shook their hands in turn. "I'll do everything I can to help out."

He hitched up the team, a pair of sturdy old plowhorses, and helped Mack pack the wagon back up. An hour later they were rolling north.

"Is there a town ahead?" Jim said.

"Nearest is Fort Smith. We should be there this afternoon. At least that's what a traveling man told me two days ago," Mack answered.

"What are you folks going to do in California?"

"Same as you, settle in on a little farm," Mack's eyes darkened a little. "I'm afraid we set out too late though. The trains leave in the spring."

"Why's that?"

"Gotta cross the Sierras before winter hits."

"The Sierras?"

"Big chain of mountains. High enough to touch the clouds, not so tall as the Rockies, but rough and rugged as all get out," Mack said. "They wall California off from the desert."

Jim had never seen a mountain. *High enough to touch the clouds.* He couldn't imagine it.

"If it's too late leave Independence what will you do in the meantime?" Jim asked.

"We'll see," Mack shrugged.

Fort Smith wasn't so big as San Antonio, nor Austin. But there was a general store and Jim was able to outfit himself with a set of new clothes, a rifle, a pistol, and ammunition. He bought a couple pounds of bacon, a bit of flour, and some sugar. He considered buying a horse, but his gold was dwindling and the prices were too high. He could walk at the wagon's pace easy enough.

There was a barber shop and Jim got a proper shave, haircut, and paid two bits for a scalding hot bath.

Mack was waiting for him at the wagon when he returned.

"Cleans up nice don't he, Sarah?"

"I bought some supplies," Jim loaded the bacon, flour, and sugar into the wagon.

"You didn't need to do that," Sarah said.

"I've been eating your food, only right I should chip in some."

"What happened to your face?" Lily asked.

"Why, I don't know," Jim rubbed at his clean cheeks. "Say where did my whiskers go? I must have lost them in town."

"Did you shave?" she said. "Sometimes my Pa shaves, but he doesn't like it."

"Must have. Or maybe some sneaking Indian shaved me while I was asleep."

"I thought Indians took the hair from your head, not your face," Matthew said.

"Maybe their knives weren't sharp enough to whittle down my scalp," Jim said. "Good thing too. I'd look scary with no hair."

"Sure would," Lily giggled.

"You've done it now," Mack chuckled from the wagon seat.

"Done what?"

"You've got her talking," Sarah said. "Now she'll never leave you alone."

"Got a thousand questions," Mack added. "She'll have your whole life story by the time we get to Independence."

They set out at a walk and, true to her parent's predictions, Lily began peppering Jim with questions.

Where was he from? What did he do for a living? Did he have a brother like she did? Why wasn't his brother with him?

She went on endlessly, asking whatever came to mind, considering the answers, then firing back another round. In hopes of a respite, Jim tried asking her a few, but she rarely gave more than a word or two.

"Five years old isn't enough time to have long answers," she said.

Mealtime offered no relief. Jim wasn't sure how she managed to eat and keeping talking, but she did. Her parents gave him sympathetic looks and her older brother grew disgusted.

"Girls," Matthew mumbled, "have to know everything."

Mercifully, she fell asleep soon after their dinner. Jim sat for a long time, listening to the crackling fire, the breeze in the treetops, and the incredible silence. He'd missed it. Reedsville had never been silent and talking to Lily was like wrestling a tornado.

"How long to Independence?" he finally asked Mack.

"Days and days yet," Mack chuckled. "By then she'll have you plumb wore down."

6

For the tenth time that afternoon, Ellen Barton opened her front
door, shaded her blue eyes, and searched the western horizon.
Nothing. Where are they?

Her mother and father should have been here hours ago. They
knew how important it was for her to be as far from her home as
possible.

She shut the door again. She ran her hand over the smooth, oak
railing that led upstairs. *I will miss this house.* Perched on a hill like
some medieval castle and with clear views of the river, the long
rolling fields, the forest, there was a lot to love here. By rights, this
should have been the perfect home, warm and inviting. No one could
argue it wasn't the grandest house in all of southern Illinois. When
they were first married she'd imagined hosting parties for their
friends and neighbors. She would fill the great mansion with light
and warmth.

Only Clive did not want that. Instead, her husband filled their
home with cruelty and suffering. Not his own suffering of course,
never his own. Clive Wilson would not suffer.

A wagon wheel creaked on the road outside; Ellen opened the
door enough to peek out. She could see nothing.

Please, please let it me them.

Anyone else would be a risk. Everyone knew her husband. His family was among the earliest settlers in Illinois. His father, a proud vain man, had been a riverboat Captain, sailing up and down the Ohio and the Mississippi beyond, carrying furs, grain, and timber all the way to New Orleans. The old Captain built this place and settled the whole clan out here.

Now they practically ran Shawneetown and all of Southern Illinois. Every political office in the county was held by either a family member or someone with their blessing. Clive though hadn't gone into politico. He certainly could have. He had all the tools—intelligence, cunning, charm enough for two men—and an utter ruthlessness.

The wagon creaked closer and Ellen slammed the door. Eyes closed, she leaned back against it. Her bags stood next to the door waiting.

What if it's Clive? What if he's back early?

The wagon came to a stop. Through the door she heard the horses stomp their feet. *Please don't let it be him.*

"Ellen," her father called from outside.

"Papa." She threw the door open and ran to her father, enveloping him in a fierce hug.

He hugged her back then stepped away.

"Are you well?"

"Fine. Better now than in ages," Ellen dabbed at her damp eyes. "We've got to hurry."

"Two bags, like we discussed?"

"Just inside," Ellen nodded.

"Good girl. Go on up with your mother," he said.

Ellen climbed into the wagon to her waiting mother.

"Oh, dear heart, it will be alright," Abigail said.

"Where's Walt?"

"In the back with Colton and Martha, he fell asleep as soon as we left the house."

"I don't know how I'll explain all of this to him," Ellen said.

Her father returned with the two bags and took them behind the wagon. "Colton, take these," he said.

In moments, he returned and climbed into the wagon seat beside Ellen. He took her hand, squeezing it once. Then he took the reins in hand and stared up at the great house.

"Evil place. Always gave me the creeps," he muttered. Then he turned to Ellen. "No second thoughts?"

"Not one."

He popped the reins, and the wagon began to roll south.

"What kept you?" Ellen asked.

Her parents looked at each other for a moment then at her.

"Sheriff Thomas stopped by this morning," her mother said.

Ellen felt a dagger of fear lodge just under her breastbone. Thomas Wilson, Clive's first cousin and the county Sheriff. What if he knew? What if Clive asked him to check up on her?

"He didn't suspect anything?" Ellen asked. She despised the note of fear in her voice, but there was no hiding it.

"No," her father said.

"We had the wagon ready and hidden away in the barn. He came in for breakfast, but I don't think he suspected a thing," her mother said. She draped an arm over Ellen and pulled her closer. "Anyway, he can't force you to stay. No one can."

Ellen forced a smile. *How naive her parents were.*

David and Abigail Barton were loving parents who cared deeply for their children, but they always had their blind spots. They understood, now at least, how evil her husband was, but they underestimated his family. The Wilson clan was the law out here. Nothing was beyond their power and influence. If Clive wanted to keep Ellen here he certainly would. That's why the secrecy was so important. Secrecy and speed. They must get far, far away.

"We're on our way now dear," her father smiled. "And no one suspects a thing. It will take them days to realize we're gone, and by then we'll be miles down the trail."

Ellen didn't believe that for a minute. Clive was the most

dangerous man she'd ever met. If he decided to stretch out his hand no distance would prove too great.

What a fool I was to marry him.

He'd been so charming when they met, fresh back from the war, and handsome in his navy-blue cavalry uniform. He was so much more mature than boys her own age. Six years made a difference. After the war he'd started a freight business. It soon made more profit than his competitors, and he'd quickly become the richest man in southern Illinois. Later—two years into their marriage—Ellen finally learned the truth.

The business was a lie; one that lost money. Clive's real profit came from riverboat piracy and outright murder. Heaven only know how many barges he'd captured and sank after killing everyone aboard.

Ellen shivered. She couldn't guess at how many men he'd killed.

"I won't feel safe until we reach California," she said.

And perhaps not even then.

If Jim thought the questions would taper off, Lily proved him mistaken. Night and day she peppered him with questions. He answered until his voice turned raw and then she wanted to know all about why he sounded like a strangled toad as well.

Three weeks out of Ft. Smith they finally reached Independence. An exhausted Lily lay on the seat, sleeping, head resting in her mother's lap. Though he couldn't stop the questions entirely, Jim came up with a way to at least limit them. If he walked out front of the wagon Lily was forced to walk beside him to be heard. She was young. She would walk for hours, but around noontime she'd wear down and have to ride in the wagon. Three weeks of travel with the Sides and Jim felt like an old paper-thin rag who'd been rung out day-after-day. He imagined a person could look right through him to see daylight on the other side.

At first glance Independence didn't seem any more or less impressive than any of the other towns he'd passed through. Certainly it didn't have the bustle of Austin.

Mack brought them up to the outskirts of town and, though the day was young, they began setting up camp. By now Jim had been accepted as part of the family and he set about his usual tasks. Getting down the cooking supplies, the tent, a shovel for digging a fire pit.

When he was done, Mack leaned against the wagon, watching him over a hand-rolled cigarette.

"What will you do now?"

"See about a wagon train I guess," Jim shrugged.

"I'll come along with you," Mack offered.

"If you come across some fresh apples I'll bake a pie tomorrow," Sarah said. "You're welcome at out our fire anytime Jim." She gave a meaningful look at the sleeping Lily, then followed up with a sympathetic smile for Jim. "Though we understand if you need a break."

Jim weighed the pie against Lily in his mind. Mrs. Sides proved an excellent cook, and he had no doubt she would work magic on that pie.

"I'll be there," Jim said. By now he'd built up his stamina. An hour or two of Lily's questions would surely be worth it for a slice of pie.

Once they were in town, Jim revised his opinion on Independence. There were people everywhere, workmen carrying picks and hammers and saws, teamsters wrestling with their wagons, cowboys, soldiers, storekeepers calling out prices to call in more trade.

"I've never seen the like," Mack confided.

"Neither have I," Jim said.

Ahead a man stood on a barrel trying to sell soap of all things. He didn't seem to be doing well. Filth covered him head to toe.

Mack approached him.

"Sell you some soap sir," the man said. "Only five cents."

"Not today," Mack shook his head. "Can you tell me where I might join up with one of the caravans heading west?"

"You don't want to buy this soap?" the man said.

"No. Just looking for travel west." Mack said.

The man on the barrel gave him a scowl, dismissed them both, and began bellaring again. "SOAP. Soap for five cents!"

"I'll give you five cents to use that soap and take a bath," someone laughed.

"Let's try somewhere else," Mack said and led the way through the crowd.

The thoroughfare grew more and more packed as they walked deeper into town, until everyone was pressed almost shoulder-to-shoulder.

They came to a cleared area where a man in a long black cloak stood on a barrel talking to a spellbound crowd.

Deep in sermon, the Reverend called out, "The Lord shall deliver us from Evil and punish the wicked. Whiskey sellers, liars, cheats, murderers, all will come to ruin but through the blood of the lamb."

Jim and Mack listened for a bit as were many others. One of the Reverend's assistants had a washtub in the back and men were lined up for a dunking.

Jim didn't think the Reverend or his assistants would stop preaching long enough to help them so he took Mack by the arm and moved them along. They turned off the main road and up a side street and paused to catch his breath.

"Needed a break from all that," he said.

"A good choice," Mack agreed. "I can't imagine how we'll find a train west in all of that mess."

"Is it a wagon train you're after?" The voice came from the shadowed alley behind the nearest building.

Hesitating, Jim leaned around for a better look.

A disheveled man sat on the ground in the alley, legs outstretched, where Jim could see the holes in his boot soles. An old gray cavalry hat covered his face, and the rest of his clothing matched the boots.

Mack gave Jim a questioning look and shrugged.

"We're looking for a wagon train west," Jim said.

"That's Texican I hear in your voice," the man said. "What part I wonder? Not Dallas. Not Nacogdoches either, not enough Cajun slur for that. Austin?"

"San Antone," Jim said.

"I might have know'd it." The man pushed back his hat. He had an ugly scar running up from left cheek, through the eye, the brow, and all the way to his scalp. "I served with a few Texicans. Fighters they were. Had to keep them pointed in the right direction though or they'd set the whole company to fighting itself."

The man took a long pull from a bottle, wiped his mouth with a dirty sleeve and regarded them.

Jim started to go. This man could do nothing to help them.

Mack caught his sleeve. "Did you say you knew about the wagon trains?"

"I surely do," the man said. "I been out there once or twice. Nothing but desert and Indians and bandits." He lifted the bottle again, scowling when it proved empty. "Don't suppose either of you has a drink on you."

"We only just arrived," Mack said. "No drink. But we are looking to travel west."

"You're too late," the drunk said. "Too late by half a year."

"Let's go," Jim said. "We can find our own way we don't need help from a-"

"From a what?" the man said. "From a drunk? Well you can take my help or no, either way boy I don't give a damn."

"Look," Mack said. "My friend is just wanting to find a way to travel west. We've been on the road for a month now."

"A month," the drunk barked out a laugh. "A child could do that. You'll be six months crossing to California. Six months of disease, starvation, and bad water. There's ten thousand graves between here and California. Ten thousand men, women, children who fell. No markers for them, no wood out there to build one out of."

Jim gave the man a look of disgust. *This is going nowhere.* The drunk was just wasting their time.

"Let's go," Jim repeated.

"Now just a minute," the drunk said. He got to his feet unsteadily, weaving for a moment, then he fell against the wall and reached out for support.

Mack grabbed for him. He took hold of the man's arm.

The drunk steadied and looked at him gratefully. Then he stepped away from the wall, adjusting first his coat then his hat.

"Captain Neill Patrick of Virginia at your service," he swept off his battered cavalry had to give them a bow.

"Mack Sides out of Arkansas," Mack said with an awkward bow of his own.

They both turned to look at Jim expectantly.

"Jim Heston," he said. He did not bow.

"If you gentlemen will follow me then," the Captain said. "I know a man who might be able to help you."

7

"Too late, you're far too late."

Donovan was a big man, built like an ox from the waist up, and if he had another name he did not give it. He wore his shaggy brown hair loose and it draped down to his shoulders. By contrast his beard was neatly trimmed.

"There's no other way though?" Mack asked.

Donovan shook his head. "Not unless you want to cut down toward Santa Fe and brave the desert. The Sonora. Hot, dry, filled with Apaches and worse. A few men have tried that route—some made it through—it's far more dangerous though. Comanches and Apaches are trouble enough, but they say there's a tribe down in the Sonora that eats the dead."

"Cannibals?" Mack whispered.

Donovan nodded.

"What are the dangers in leaving now? Going over the usual route?" Jim said. It seemed to him that the coming winter might drive the plains Indians into their lodges and give them an easier way through.

"Snow," Donovan said. "Worst possible enemy. Can't outthink it, can't outfight it, can't outrun it. In the Rockies it piles up in the passes maybe ten or fifteen feet deep. In the Sierras it's worse."

"So your advice is?" Mack said.

"Wait for spring." Donovan took a drink of coffee. "I'll be leading a group through then and you both seem steady enough to travel with me."

Jim gave Captain Neill a hard look. So much for the man's help. The drunk had been useless. *We'll have to find another wagon train led by someone willing to brave the winter.*

Donovan gave him a half-smile and long look. "Right now you're thinking you can find another train. You're thinking there's someone out there willing to try and take you on through."

The big man took another swallow of coffee.

"You're partly right. There are men in this town who'll offer what you want. They'll promise you safe passage. They'll have either a paper treaty with the Indians or know some secret pass through the mountains, one that doesn't snow over."

Donovan smiled. "And they're lying. They'll take you out a ways, a good fifty miles or so—far enough there won't be any help—and then they'll turn on you. Murder the men, take the women and supplies. Then they'll—"

"There are men like that in town?" Mack interrupted.

Donovan held up a hand. "I won't tell you or anyone else their names, or whatever they call themselves anyway, wouldn't be good for my health, but I will warn you against what sounds too good to be true."

"So the best we can do, the only thing we can do, is to sit around and wait?" Jim said. He couldn't afford to do that of course and neither could the Sides. They'd be flat broke by spring.

"I didn't say you had to sit around and do nothing," Donovan said. "This town has needs. In the spring a hundred wagon trains will leave and they'll want supplies for the trip. Supplies which are being made or gathered here even as we speak."

"I told you he'd be able to help," Neill said.

"My help will depend on them," Donovan said. "What sort of skills do each of you have?"

"I haven't done much more than farm," Mack shrugged. "My wife can sew very well though."

"Good," Donovan nodded. "Farming slows down a good bit this time of year. Do you know anything about hogs though?"

"I do. Had a dozen of them down in Louisiana."

"There's a farm east of town raising hogs. They feed them all winter then slaughter and cure them before springtime. They're looking for a few hired men. Your wife will have no trouble finding work. Everybody needs canvas sewn. Wagon tops are big business."

Donovan turned to the Captain. "Neill take Mr. Sides to Job Tennyson's place. First though, talk to Lamont at the Emporium. He's handling my order for canvas and will need all the help he can get."

"I'll be grateful," Mack said.

"You'll curse me plenty before spring," Donovan smiled. "The work is hard and brutal, but if you're frugal by spring you'll have more money than you arrived with and be in good shape for the journey."

Captain Neill stood and turned to go.

"And Neill? Don't stop for a drink until you get Mr. Sides where he's going."

Neill's face slipped a little. "I won't."

The Captain and Mack left then, and Donovan and Jim watched them go. When they were gone Donovan turned to Jim again.

"And what will you do until springtime?"

"I'm pretty handy around a place, good with horses or stock," Jim said.

"Not much stock in town at the moment, but that will change the closer to spring we get. Place fills up with oxen, mules, and horses all. You ever work with wood?"

"Fixing up the home place. Replacing shingles, patching holes, fencing, and the like."

"Come with me," Donovan paid their bill and rose.

Jim followed the man out into the nearly empty street.

"Where is everyone? When we got into town the streets were full to bursting."

"Weather's turning," Donovan said. "Big storm tonight, first blast of Old Man Winter has everybody hunkering down tight."

Jim eyed the northern horizon. There was a bank of low, dark clouds. "That it?"

"Yep, we got a couple hours yet, but it looks like a bad one."

They went through the empty streets heading south and west. At the edge of town a huge wooden building stood alone. Jim heard the buzzing of a saws inside along with a chorus of falling hammers.

"What is this place?" Jim asked.

Donovan opened the door and led them inside. "This is the most important building in Independence. This is where we make the wagons."

"Donovan, you great bear, it's been too long since you darkened my door." an older man wearing an apron greeted them.

"Charles Hightower this is Jim Heston," Donovan said. "Jim is new in town and looking for work."

"Work is one thing we have in abundance," Charles laughed and regarded Jim. "What are your skills Mr. Heston?"

"I had a homestead down in Texas. Kept the place up by myself. Good with animals. Show me what you want done and I can do it."

"You're certainly built strong enough," Charles said appraising him. "But working with wood requires a sense of touch. Too much strength and it will fail you. You have to listen to the wood."

Jim nodded. Right away he liked the smaller man. He had an earnestness that Jim respected. It reminded him of old man Stanton. "Same as horses."

"How so?"

"If you want the best out of a horse you have to earn his trust. Listen to him, not fight him down into the ground."

"Hmm," the small man said.

"What type of woodworking have you done?"

"Built fences, shingled a roof or two, repairs around the home place."

"Ever worked with steel or leather?"

"None with steel, except for shoeing horses. I repaired harnesses and saddles quite a bit," Jim said.

"How did you replace the shingles?"

"We cut them ourselves after finding a big enough cedar and then—"

Donovan cleared his throat. "I'll leave you fellas to it then." Then he headed back for the door.

"A good man," Mr. Hightower said after him.

"Seems like," Jim agreed. "He helped me and a friend of mine out."

"Well then," Charles said. "I can ask you questions all day, but it would be faster if you just showed me what you can do."

The small man led Jim into the heart of the building. They passed by a nearly-completed wagon.

"Is that a Conestoga?" Jim asked.

"No," Charles shook his head. "Conestogas are much too heavy for the plains. The wheels would cut through the soil and the team will fight it the entire way. We call this a Prairie Schooner. It's lighter and easier to pull."

They approached a man in a bright red shirt directing a crew as they assembled one of the wagons.

"Abe, this is Jim Heston, he's a newcomer," Charles introduced them. "Have him help out and let me know how he does."

Charles turned to Jim then. "Work here the rest of the day. Don't worry about showing Abe what you can do just do as he says. See me tomorrow morning and we'll talk."

"Right boss," Abe nodded then looked Jim over head-to-toe. "Big fellow huh? Well let's get you to work."

Jim spent the rest of the day with Abe's crew, lifting planks and then holding them in place while one of the other workers fitted them in tight and hammered them down.

The work was heavy and tiring, but Jim was no stranger to that kind of thing.

At the end of the day he regrouped with the Sides, the apple pie proved every bit as delicious as he'd imagined. When they were done eating Lily moved near the fire.

Her young face shone in the firelight. She licked her lips and started in.

"Pa said you built a wagon today. How do they get the wheels on without tipping it over?"

"THAT'S IT," David Barton announced. "Independence. Gateway to the west."

The city was still on the far horizon, barely visible as more than a few rising columns of chimney smoke. Ellen watched her father standing in his stirrups. Mile-after-mile his excitement had only built as they rolled along.

This trip is changing him.

In his soul her father carried the pioneering spirit. He always had. A hardworking man, intelligent too, but one who never seemed to catch that extra bit of luck needed to truly prosper.

They'd done well in Illinois. Her father had owned a piece of good land, healthy crops, a few cows, but he wanted more. He did not want to pour out sweat and labor just to make ends meet. He wanted to thrive. He'd talked of going west for years, and the tragedy of Ellen's marriage had given him the perfect excuse to go.

"Sit down David before you break your neck," Abigail said. She turned to Ellen and whispered. "Fool man will catch cold at the very least."

"He's just excited Mama," Ellen laughed and wrapped her own coat tighter. Normally, she didn't like wintertime, but the snow had been a blessing. It began within days of their departure, stacking up deeper and deeper, and there wouldn't be any tracks to follow. Not even the powerful Wilson family could change the weather.

"Not so fast Colton," Ellen's mother cautioned. She reached across Ellen's back to tap Colton on the arm. "Just because your father has lost his mind doesn't mean we need to."

Colton scowled but slowed the team down. He took too much

after their father, and Ellen had been sure to place herself between him and their mother.

"I'll be glad when we finally get there," Ellen's mother said.

Abigail Barton wasn't happy with their situation. She'd argued for Ellen to stay with Clive and work things out. No amount of talk changed her mind either. Two years of Ellen explaining to her mother just how bad living with Clive was resulted in nothing. Finally, Ellen showed her the bruises.

The change had been immediate. One look at the bruises and her mother swore if she ever got the chance she'd horsewhip Clive Wilson.

Ellen believed it. When she was roused her mother would confront a full-grown bear.

It was not wise to anger Abigail Barton.

"What do you think we will find in Independence?" Abigail asked.

"A thriving city, the likes of which you've never seen," David answered. "They call it Paris on the plains."

Paris on the Plains. Ellen doubted that very much. Independence was a young city, and nothing built quickly could be compared to one of those grand old European cities.

In Independence they found a spot down out of the cold wind to park their wagon, just at the edge of town. Ellen and her parents set up their little camp.

Ellen had hoped they could avoid another cold night in the wagon, her father had a friend here who might be able to get them a place out of the weather.

When the camp was ready, Ellen, Colton, and their father went into the town proper. Abigail and Martha stayed with Walt preparing an evening meal.

The day was late, the sky an iron-gray blanket. *More snow tonight. Good for covering tracks, not so good for travel and sleeping out in.*

"Father, we should get a few more blankets before we return," she said.

"A good idea," he agreed.

"I'm going to look around for a bit," Colton said. His eyes were eager and bright. He'd done a man's work on the journey west and now wanted some time for himself as a reward.

"Meet us back at the wagon," David said.

"I will," he nodded and smiled.

Ellen watched him head off along a busy street.

"He's growing up," her father said.

"Some, but he's still so very young."

"You all are," David laughed. "Come along, I know a man here. You remember Charles Hightower?"

"I do." Mr. Hightower and her father had been business partners in a general store back in Ohio before her family moved on to Illinois.

"He's set himself up with a business in town making wagons. He knows everyone out here."

"Everyone?" Ellen said. She looked at the hundreds of people in the streets. She doubted anyone knew everyone here.

"Excuse me?" Her father approached a passing man wearing a coonskin hat. The man ignored him completely and kept walking.

"Excuse me, I'm looking for someone." Her father tried again, this time with a rough-looking freighter.

The freighter only scowled. "No time to talk. Now get out of the way I've got to get these barrels to Tim Baker." Then the freighter slapped the reins on his mules, and they lurched forward.

Ellen's father opened his mouth to ask another man, this one an older man with a wide-brimmed hat and riding chaps. Ellen interrupted him.

"Hello," she said and stepped directly in front of the cowboy.

He stopped up short and eyed her up and down. "Hello, pretty lady."

"My father and I are looking for a Charles Hightower. Would you know where he might be?"

The cowboy swept off his hat. "You are in luck. I know Hightower. I'm headed toward his place now. If I could escort you?"

He offered his arm and Ellen hesitated before taking it. The last man who'd escorted her anywhere was her monster of a husband.

After an uncomfortable pause, she swallowed and took his arm. If the cowboy noticed he did not mention it.

The cowboy talked as they went.

"My name is Jarod Taylor," the man said.

"Ellen...Ellen Barton," she responded after a second. This was the first time she'd used her old name. Coming west they had traveled quickly, talked to no one, and she hadn't given her name. Ellen smiled. She suddenly felt lighter as if Clive's last name were some great weight she'd finally cast off. Despite the cold, even the air seemed a little clearer.

I will never use that man's name again. Walt too, will be a Barton from now on.

"You are going west miss?" Jarod asked.

"We are," she nodded over her shoulder at her trailing father.

"It's a good, fine land out there."

"You've been?" Ellen said.

"I surely have. I've got a ranch in California. Hard work, but it shows promise."

"Ohh, and what are you doing back here?"

"Came east to buy a few shorthorn bulls for my herd. I think they'll do very well out there."

Ellen looked over his clothing. It was well enough but showing a lot of dirt and wear. The hat in particular was battered and had a round hole near the crease.

He smiled. "Renegades in Nevada. Almost had us."

"Us?" Ellen hadn't noticed anyone with him.

"I've a few boys with me. They wanted to see civilization again."

Across the street, Ellen saw a man sleeping in an alleyway. "Is this civilization?"

Jarod followed her gaze and laughed pleasantly. "Well ma'am you surely cut to it. Independence is a rough place, but a month into those plains you'll remember it like one of those big towns back east like a New York, Philadelphia, or Charleston."

"It truly is that empty?"

"And then some," Jarod nodded. "No one for miles and miles."

"What about the Indians?"

"There are those," he agreed. "Some people go over the trail, never see a one. Some see a few too many. But they're out there and you'd best plan for them."

He brought them up in front of the largest wooden building Ellen had ever seen.

'HIGHTOWER'S' the sign above the door read.

The rancher opened the door and bowed. "I'll escort you inside, and then I've got to be along on my way. If I may call upon you later?"

"Call upon me?" Ellen's voice betrayed her shock.

Jarod smiled. "Of course ma'am, we don't get many women like yourself out here."

"I'm afraid I am spoken for Mr. Taylor," Ellen felt her face warm. *When was the last time anyone asked to come calling for me?* Certainly not since Clive made his interest known.

"More's the pity. I hope the fellow realizes how lucky he is." Jarod's smile was undiminished.

Charles Hightower met them at the door.

"Jarod," he said. "I was just locking up for the evening."

"Charles, I was just bringing these folks to see you."

"Oh," Charles gave them a second look and grinned. "Why David Barton. I haven't seen you in an age."

Mr. Hightower was just as Ellen remembered if a little older and maybe a little shorter. *Or is it that I have grown?*

"It's great to see you Charles," Ellen's father shook hands with his old partner.

Mr. Taylor patted Hightower on the back. "I'm on my way over to the Palace. I'll see you tomorrow to talk about a special wagon for my journey back."

"Of course Jarod," Hightower nodded. "Stop by anytime."

"I hope to see you folks again," the rancher said, but he had eyes only for Ellen.

"Thank you for your help," her father offered.

"Yes, thank you Mr. Taylor," Ellen echoed. Her face felt warm and bright.

Jarod waved and then was gone.

"Seems like a good fellow," Ellen's father said.

"He is. He's done quite well for himself," Hightower answered. "And who is this lovely lady with you?"

"You remember my daughter, Ellen."

"Ellen, of course," Hightower said. He stepped back to appraise her. "You were a child the last time I saw you. All grown up now though into a beautiful lady. I bet you've already driven half of Independence mad over you."

Ellen blushed again. "Who was that man Mr. Taylor? I thought he was a cowboy, but he mentioned a ranch in California."

"A ranch," Hightower laughed. "You might say that. Jarod Taylor owns the largest ranch in southern California. He's got thousands of cattle."

"Really," David said. "I never would have guessed by the sight of him."

"This isn't the east David," Hightower's tone was serious. "Out here you cannot judge a man by his appearance. A man in simple buckskins might own a gold mine or a freight company or a sprawling ranch like Jarod Taylor."

Hightower closed the door and wrapped his hands around his body.

"I know a restaurant nearby, let's find a warmer place to talk."

"Lead the way," David said. Hightower offered his arm to Ellen and for the second time that evening she found herself escorted by gentleman.

The restaurant was warm, just as Hightower promised, and the Barton's helped themselves to coffee and cake.

"What brings you to Independence?" Hightower asked.

Ellen and her father exchanged a glance. They'd worked out a story, but Charles was an old friend.

"Illinois didn't turn out like we hoped," her father started. "The farm just couldn't turn profit and I decided to come west to try again. I heard California was a rich land, a good land to start over."

Hightower gave him a long look and said nothing. "You've never been any good at hiding things, David."

"What do you mean?"

"What aren't you telling me?"

"Why Charles, I can't imagine what you're—"

"We came west for me," Ellen interrupted. She'd always liked Charles Hightower and right now they needed his help. "I had some trouble in Illinois and we had to leave."

"You?" Hightower's brows lifted. "What sort of trouble could you have?"

Ellen told him. She didn't go into the most horrific details. He didn't need to know about the bruises, the broken bones, but he was a sharp man and she told him enough that he would guess at them.

When she was done they sat in silence for a time.

"You have a problem." Hightower began. "There is nowhere to go. Not now at least. The trails aren't open yet."

"What? How can that be?" David said. "If Clive Wilson finds us here." The fear showed in his eyes. Her father was not a coward, in fact in his own way he was the bravest man she'd ever known, but he could not match Clive legally or physically. The law would be on Clive's side. Ellen was still his legal wife, Walt his son. Worse, Clive was a violent man, prone to terrible rages. He would not hold back even against her father.

If he finds us there will be nothing anyone can do.

"If we can't travel, what should we do?" Ellen said.

"I can put you up in a place I own, south of town, where you can wait out the winter. No one will know you're there," Hightower said.

"What about going west?" Ellen's father said. "We'll need to get supplies and then join up with a group at some point. We can't hide the whole time."

"I know a man," Hightower said. "One who can help."

"A trustworthy man?"

"I would trust him with my life or that of my own daughter if I had one," Hightower said and took Ellen's hands in his own. "If you explain things to him he will make sure you arrive in California safely or as safe as the dangers of the trail allow."

"We aren't looking for someone to fight my husband. We just need to escape where he will never find us," Ellen said.

"That is exactly what this man will do. When the winter breaks he'll be leading the first caravan west," Hightower smiled. "His name is Donovan."

8

Jim Heston couldn't hear the crowd roaring around him over the pounding in his ears.

A teamster from Minnesota, Jim's challenger, threw a wild haymaker at his head. Jim turned aside just enough to miss most of the punch, allowing it to graze him across the back of his shoulder. The teamster's follow-up landed on Jim's chest, but there was little power in it.

Jim responded with a pair of right jabs and a left hook that each connected solidly.

The teamster swayed for a few seconds; he refused to go down. Jim had already battered the man's face into a pulpy mess of blood and swollen flesh. Every punch felt like he was hitting into a sponge. Still the teamster would not fall.

Jim stepped in for a haymaker of his own, something to put this to a merciful end, but the teamster whipped a wicked left to Jim's face that rocked him to his heels.

Then the teamster grinned and started forward with both arms, pounding away.

Trying to weather the storm, Jim tucked his elbows down to protect his body and covered his face with his fists. The blows struck like hammers. His ribs hurt. His chest hurt. His face hurt. He too had taken a terrible beating.

Finally, the teamster tired. His punches slowed and lost their pop.

Jim took a breath, lowered his hands and snapped off a left and right to the other man's jaw. The teamster's hands dropped completely, and Jim put everything he had into one final right.

It struck hard. The teamster's whole body shuddered. He froze for a long second. He took a half step back, shook his head once, and then fell forward into the dirt and sawdust.

Only then did Jim hear the roaring crowd around them. Jim's eyes swung to the audience. There were hundreds packed into the warehouse. Despite the fact that he'd cost some of them money, none looked angry. They'd come to see a fight and he'd given them one.

"What a fight," Donovan said and clapped him on the shoulders. "I thought for sure he'd have you with that last flurry."

"It was close," Jim managed through swollen lips. "Let's get out of here."

"I've got the money," Donovan waved a stack of greenbacks. "Come on."

Jim donned his heavy coat and then followed Donovan out into the bitter Kansas cold across town to the Union Hotel. Normally, he stayed in a cabin at the edge of town he rented from Charles Hightower, but after fights he wanted a room close-by and a scalding hot bath. The Union had both, and as he'd made James Chaney—the Union's owner—a great deal of money betting on his fights they took good care of him.

Chaney was waiting for them when they arrived.

"Hell of a fight. I thought he'd get the better of you with that burst at the end. I don't know how you stood up to it," he said and lead them down a short hall to an open room. "Everything is ready."

"For your safe," Donovan said and handed Chaney the greenbacks.

"A good night's earnings for you two," Chaney said. He thumbed through the bills.

"He had a lot of friends who made their brag," Donovan said. "They paid for it."

"This will be waiting for you when you're ready." Chaney started out the door. "Should I send for the Doctor."

"Not tonight," Jim said. The words came thick and rough.

"I'll come by to check on you tomorrow," Donovan said. Then he and Chaney left.

Painfully, Jim stripped off his clothing. Then he eased down into the steaming tub. Jim bathed and sat soaking in the tub afterward until the water grew tepid, then he dressed and went up to his room.

The bed was soft and inviting, but though he tried to sleep, his mind was still keyed-up from the fight. He replayed it over and over in his thoughts. Unlike most of his opponents, the teamster had been both tough and experienced. The fight could have gone either way. A stray punch here, a misstep there.

He held up a fist, flexing the knuckles. Stiff and sore. Two days to recover just wasn't enough.

I'll have hell building wagons for Mr. Hightower on Monday.

After tonight he'd won eight fights since coming to town. He'd lost a couple early on, but Abe—Hightower's right-hand man—knew a great deal of boxing and had showed him a few things, how to roll with a punch to rob it of its power, when to wait an opponent out, what to watch for when you needed an opening, how to set your feet to maximize your own power.

With Abe's help he'd gone undefeated, and he'd built up a nice pile of cash. It couldn't last. The fights were getting tougher. Tonight proved it. If he kept going sooner or later he'd fight someone better and there would be a setback. He couldn't fight forever.

"There is always somebody stronger or quicker," his father had always said. One of the few things Jim remembered of the man.

Jim rolled onto his back and stared up at the wooden ceiling. In the dark outside the wind howled and moaned. Snow pattered against the window in gentle rhythmic taps.

Since coming to Independence time had passed slowly for Jim Heston.

Working for Charles Hightower had gone well. He now had his own crew of men working to assemble the Prairie Schooners. There were six crews in total, cranking out a new wagon every seven days. Charles Hightower raised his salary twice. He was making double what he'd been hired on at. Between that, the fights, and a couple other jobs he had significantly more money than he came out of Texas with. Preferring a quiet life, he had spent very little of it.

Stiff and sore, Jim rose later than usual. He studied his chest and back in the room's mirror. His left side wasn't so bad, but purple and yellow bruises colored his right side from hip to shoulder. Jim reached across and ran his hand along his ribs. None felt broken.

He dressed gingerly. This morning, even the light squeeze of the fabric sent shimmers of sharp pain through him. For the most part, he could ignore it; the real pain came when he leaned down to pull on his boots.

Donovan was waiting in the dining area, plate scraped clean and holding a half-full mug of coffee.

"You look like you went eight rounds with a grizzly bear," he said.

"Feels like it too," Jim replied. From face to knuckle even down to the soles of his feet, he hurt all over. *I can't take many more fights like that one.*

Jim eased down just before a dark-haired waitress came around to take his order. "Coffee, strong and black, and a plateful of eggs, ham, and beans."

She gave him a long piercing look. Jim gave her his best smile and she recoiled into the kitchen. *No doubt last night didn't make me any prettier.* Jim had wisely avoided looking at his face too closely in the mirror.

Donovan sat in silence staring out the window and Jim wondered what was worth seeing. The street outside was empty except for a pair of teamsters struggling to unload a barrel. Both men were bundled up in thick hides and steam came from their labored breaths. Most everyone else seemed to be staying inside where it was warm. More snow—fresh and at least a foot deep—lay piled up against the buildings and gnarled icicles reached down from the slanted roofs. The sky overhead was a dingy gray and threatening.

Would spring never come?

The food came and the waitress hustled off to other customers. Jim packed away the food and when he was finished leaned back in his chair. "What are you doing here so late? I figured you'd be off doing...well...whatever it is you do all winter when you aren't collecting my money."

"Waiting to see you," Donovan gave him an offended look. "I had to make sure you hadn't given up and died after last night. That was a powerful beating."

Jim flexed his hands. His knuckles were red and swollen and hurting, of course.

"And I wanted to give you the news firsthand."

"News?" Jim reached for his coffee.

"First caravan meeting is scheduled for tonight. I've got twenty wagons lined up already. More trickling in by the day. Come spring-time it'll be the biggest group I've had."

When Jim didn't speak, Donovan gave him a long look.

"Second thoughts?"

"I've got a good deal here. When I left home I just wanted a little farm to myself, but now...now I've got a real job, good money, enough saved by to set myself up pretty well here."

"Jim," Donovan leaned in and lowered his voice. "I wouldn't say this to just anyone, but you are a friend, so I'll spill it. None of this is going to last."

"None of what?"

Donovan swirled his cup to encompass the room. "None of this. The hotels, the wagon-making, the money from the men going west. None of it is going to last. It can't."

"You're sure?" Jim scoffed. "You were just telling me about the biggest caravan you've ever had."

"It will be." Donovan nodded and sipped his coffee. "And next year's might be bigger, but within five years all of it will dry up and be gone. The rail is coming west and with it the end of the wagon trains."

"They'll come through Independence. The town will be fine."

"The town, yes, but it won't be awash with money like it is now. Only the established places will survive."

Jim's brows lifted. "And what will you do then? If the trail dries up."

Donovan laughed. "Don't you worry about me. I've got aplenty put by. I might take a few more folks west and then settle out there somewhere. Maybe haul a little freight for one of the gold mines. But we were talking about your plans weren't we?"

Jim studied his coffee and sat silent for several moments. "Truth is…I just don't know. I want to see California for myself, but between Hightower's and what I've put by I'm doing well enough. I've got a little place at the south end of town. Not much but it's dry and warm, most days, anyway."

"Hightower is selling out."

"What?"

"Spoke to him this morning, said to tell you congratulations by-the-way. He's taking offers from a couple of men back east. He sees the signs just like I do."

"That changes things," Jim said.

"Yeah. Besides you can't keep taking a beating like you did last night."

Jim lifted his battered hands. He curled the fingers and winced in pain. "No, a few more of those and then I'm out."

"Don't wait too long. I've seen more than one man killed in brawls like those." Donovan looked him in the eye then. "And several maimed."

Neither spoke for a long time. Jim sipped at his coffee and went back to looking outside. The wind was picking up now. Loose snow swirled down the street in cyclones of white.

"You've been practicing your shooting?" Donovan said.

"Yes."

"Good. There are some bad men in town."

"They aren't hunting me," Jim shrugged.

"Of course not. Why would they?" Donovan snorted. "But several are mean as a shedding rattler. They'd go out of their way to kill a man who offended them."

"Nothing to do with me."

"No?" Donovan's eyebrows lifted. "If you buck their bets, they might decide to take their losses out on you. These men are just that type."

Jim studied his friend in silence. If Donovan wanted an argument this wasn't the day for it. *I am just too tired for one.*

"Anyway," Donovan scowled "I need you?"

"What?"

"I need you dammit."

"The great Donovan, explorer of the west, Indian fighter, guide of a hundred caravans, needs me?"

"I do." Donovan nodded. "I need a steady man along with me, more than one, to take this group over the trail. It's too many for one man."

"Too big for Donovan?" Jim said and grinned.

A sour look passed over Donovan's face. "Yes, too big even for me. A man with your skills would be a help. There's always wagons breaking down, oxen or horses needing care."

"Are you offering me a job?"

"I am," the guide nodded.

"How would it work exactly?"

"I'll pay your way west, including meals, and fifty dollars at the end. I'm going to bring an extra wagonload of supplies with the group. Pack it full of timber, spare wheels, axle grease, a little food and the like."

"And you want me to drive it?"

"No, I've already got a man for that. I want you to keep the wagons moving."

"I don't know the way."

"I'll take care of the trail," Donovan held up a hand. "Your job will be to fix any wagons that break down, keep an eye out for trouble, help manage the spare stock."

"What about a horse?"

"What about one?"

"Are you going to provide me with a horse to ride?"

Donovan gave him another scowl. "A horse to ride. Next you'll be wanting me to buy you clothes."

"A new rainslicker might be nice."

"Fine, stay here then or pay like everyone else. Damn proud Texans every one," Donovan started to rise.

"Easy now," Jim laughed. "Just seeing how desperate you were."

"Very. I've got a lot riding on this."

"It's settled then. I'll go."

"You're sure?"

"If the great Donovan needs me how can I refuse?" Jim smiled.

He and Donovan shook on it.

"Texans." Donovan shook his head. "Be at the meeting tonight and make sure you practice with your shooting. Rifle and pistol both, you may need both before trail's end."

"That sounds like fighting wages."

"Too late now my friend, you already shook on it," Donovan wagged a finger and laughed.

DONOVAN HADN'T LIED. By Jim's count there were forty-three men and women gathered into Hightower's back warehouse. He didn't try counting the children. Every family seemed to have at least three and they moved and shuffled around like puppies in an empty sack.

Jim scanned their faces. There were good men out there. A few hard ones, each eager in their own way. All seemed strong and healthy. It took strength to journey west. In the end the strongest survived and those who were soft either grew hard themselves or fell. He considered which ones might fall, those who would succumb to the dangers, and those who would press on. Would that strength be seen on the surface though, or shine through only when tempered?

His own second thoughts bubbled up. He didn't fear the danger.

Life was full of risk. Avoiding danger completely was an impossible task.

But is this the right thing for me?

Jim swallowed and forced away his doubts. If he meant to back out he should have done it sooner. He'd given Donovan his word to go through with this; Jim Heston did not break his word.

The Sides family was not among the others. *Mack must not have heard about the group.* They lived out east of town and were doing well last time he'd visited them. Mack too had been promoted several times at the farm, and the owner had given the family a little house to live in. They too had prospered. Sarah sewed canvas wagon tops for Hightower; Jim brought them back himself.

Jim frowned to himself. How long had it been since he'd seen them last? Two weeks? Three? He was overdue but there had been a lot of work at Hightower's and then the fights on top of that.

I'll head out there tomorrow for a visit. Mack and Sarah will be excited. Lily will hound me with a thousand questions. Jim snorted. That girl had to be part bloodhound.

Donovan's voice rose up above the others and jarred him from his thoughts.

"Thank you all for coming," Donovan held out his hands. He stood in the back of a wagon Jim and his men had put together only last week. "My name is Donovan, and I will be your guide out west."

Jim surveyed the crowd again and saw a girl looking at him from across the crowd. She was near his own age, tall and slender, with an older man—her father judging by his look—standing next to her, alongside a young man who could have been her brother. They were one of the few groups without children scurrying around.

The girl kept staring and Jim met her look. She had a confident look about her that he admired right off. He offered her a grin before tipping his hat.

She grimaced and then her cheeks flushed.

Jim noticed the conversation had died and Donovan was pointing at him with one hand. Suddenly the girl wasn't looking at him anymore and everyone else was.

What had Donovan been going on about?

Jim smiled and waved his hat to the crowd with an awkward little bow.

"As I said folks," Donovan took over. "He's a man of few words, but Jim Heston is first-rate at repairing wagons. He'll keep us on track."

"Looks like someone took a two-by-four to his face," someone in the crowd hollared. There was laughter all around.

Jim remembered his battered face then. No wonder the girl had been staring. He must look like a mess.

"You should see the man he whipped last night. Best fight I ever saw," another voice answered.

"I won ten dollars on that," a third voice added.

Donovan took control of the crowd before they started retelling the fight. Some of them might be sore if they lost money. "I can assure you Jim knows his way around the ring and a wagon. We'll be glad to have him before the end."

Jim crammed his hat back on, thoroughly embarrassed. *I smiled at her like a damned fool.*

Normally, what some girl thought of him wouldn't have made a difference. But for some reason this one did. He couldn't explain the difference; he couldn't deny it either though. He snuck a sidelong look her way.

She was talking to her father now and he was nodding. Jim liked the look of her, standing there honest and sure of herself.

Donovan finished speaking and climbed down out of the wagon back. He worked the crowd, shaking hands, patting backs, and exchanging smiles and words with men in turn. Jim remained alone in the back, leaning against one of the columns that held up the roof. Everyone began to shuffle out except the girl and her family.

They waited until everyone else was gone and then spoke to Donovan privately. The older man did most of the talking. The son looked bored, studying the ground or scratching at it with his boot toe. The girl held Jim's attention though. She clung to Donovan's every word—nodding at the right times—and Jim noticed she asked more questions than her father. Judging by Donovan's reactions they were the right kind of questions too. The caravan leader paused to consider before answering each one.

After a good half-hour Donovan shook hands with the older man and started toward Jim. The girl paused at the door and gave the room one last look before stepping out into the cold Kansas night.

"Who was that?" Jim asked.

"Friends of Hightower. Used to be partners on a store at one point. He's had them living in his home place south of town since before Christmas," Donovan said.

"Seemed a little skittish."

"I suppose they did," Donovan eyed him and cocked his head a little to the side.

"How long before we leave?"

"You didn't listen to my speech?"

"You bellow and bluster enough that I gave up listening to you months ago."

"Most people find my speeches entertaining. Not enough Texas twang for you?"

Jim snorted and stepped away from the column.

"A month. Maybe less. You weren't so eager this morning," Donovan grinned. "I wonder what's changed."

"Ready for fresh country," Jim answered quickly.

"I'm sure that's it," Donovan chuckled. "Tomorrow I want you to find Captain Neill and get him roused up."

"You're taking that drunk with us?" Jim couldn't believe it. For months Donovan's longstanding friendship with Neill Patrick had baffled him. At least once a week Donovan was taking him to dinner or slipping him a coin or two, and during that span the Captain had only been sober twice.

"No better man on the trail."

"He won't survive without a bottle," Jim said.

"Four times," Donovan held up his fingers. "Four times that man has been over the trail with me. He and I fought Indians, battled storms, blazed our way all over that country. No better man to have with us."

"If you say," Jim shrugged.

Donovan gave him a wide smiled. "A week out of town and you'll be amazed. I promise you."

"Will he bathe?"

Donovan laughed. "First condition of him riding with me." He wagged a finger. "Remind him of that when you see him."

"I didn't see Mack Sides," Jim said.

The guide's smile faded. "I think he's decided to stay on."

"Mack? Stay?" All Mack and Sarah ever talked about was going west. "I don't believe it."

Donovan shrugged. "Ride out and ask them. Mack told me himself just last week. I tried to talk him out of it. I think they're eyeing a farm near the river."

"Too late this evening. I'll ride over there tomorrow morning," Jim said.

"Make sure you find Neill for me."

"I'll do it this evening," Jim said. "Any idea where to look?"

"He was bunking on Hill Street last I heard. One of those old shacks. Try asking after him at the Marquis. The bartender knows him."

"Every bartender in town knows him."

"Trust me, we'll be glad to have him before the end."

On the Ohio River, at the end of a long, looping bend, twenty miles downstream of Louisville, Captain Clive Wilson waited in silence on the deck of his barge. He wasn't alone. Fifteen men, all trusted, all armed to the teeth, waited with him.

Clive held his breath, listening for even the slightest sound over the lazy water. The night was pitch black—not even the hint of a moon—with enough clouds to block all starlight and cold enough to keep men close to their fires, huddling tight against the weather and reminiscing over warmer days.

Clive smiled to himself. *Perfect weather for piracy.*

An owl that was not an owl called from the dark shore. Clive answered with a call of his own.

Chet Walker, his second-in-command stood nearest to him, quiet and calm as a stalking tiger.

"Take the row and fetch back Beau," Clive said. "He has news for us."

Without comment, Chet pointed to two of the better rowing men and all three set off in their little boat. The men knew their work well. Their oars were quiet, gently caressing the river before driving down and propelling the boat forward. Briefly, the orange glow of a lantern shone against the shore and Chet corrected his course.

In his head, Clive ran the calculations. Five minutes to shore, six or seven more back against the current, and then he would have to hear whatever news Beau had. That wasn't the end of it though. Beau would have spent ten minutes already, crossing overland to outrun their prize. Twenty minutes to a half-hour all told. Twenty minutes more to get the barge into position.

Clive smiled to himself. *Plenty of time.*

Beau's assignment had been to scout the river for their target, the Southern Queen. On the far shore a man in good condition could run overland in a fraction of the time a steamship could sail up and around the river's looping bend.

His return meant the Queen and her cargo, fourteen hundred and thirty-seven bales of high-quality cotton, were close.

"Ready to cast off," Clive instructed his men.

This particular shipment was unusual. Cotton typically went upriver to factories in the north, but this load was headed for a new textile mill in southern Illinois. The mill's owner—a friend of Clive's from the war—had told him of the shipment's arrival and together they'd agreed on a price—one much cheaper than the owner had agreed to—if Clive could *acquire* the load.

The deal had been too good to pass up. A prearranged buyer, few guards, and the owner would claim the insurance which meant there would be few questions.

Everyone makes money, and me in particular. Clive's smile widened. The only losers would be the men guarding the load.

The gentle slapping of oars came over the water and he could barely make out the shadowy rowboat on its return leg.

Chet secured the smaller boat against the barge and brought Beau over. The pair made an odd contrast. Where Chet was tall and lean, Beau stood barely over five foot and was built like a cannonball. He wasn't fat exactly, just solid. Still, of the two, Beau was by far the more dangerous. Chet was not a thinking man. A man of action, he left the planning to others and stuck to his knives and pistols.

Beau though. Beau had imagination. Beau had intelligence. Beau had ambition.

The combination was dangerous but only to a limited extent. The rest of the men disliked Beau. He did less of the work and reaped more of the reward and everyone knew it. Clive made sure of it. Without the support of others Beau would always lack the muscle to set into motion any schemes he might harbor against Clive. Clive knew well enough how to manage Beau, and he needed the man's intelligence. Dumb scouts were useful only as ballast.

"How close?" Clive asked.

"Not too much longer. I saw their lights. Then I made sure it was them," Beau nodded. "They're sitting nice and low in the water."

"Hmm," Clive said. *Maybe they have a few extra bales or something more valuable.*

Not that cotton wasn't valuable. Since the war production had plummeted and accordingly prices skyrocketed. There was even talk about bringing in great loads of it over from Africa until the South could recover.

The thought amused him. The finest cottonland in the world on their doorstep and they'd have to import it all the way from Africa.

Such were the fortunes of war. *The Rebels should have fought harder.*

Though he cared little for either side, Clive had served in the Union during the war. The South simply could not have won. They lacked the manpower and, more importantly, the firepower. That made the choice easy. He'd joined the winning side with thoughts of glory and advancement. With a little luck he could turn himself into a war hero. War heroes were respected and well-regarded. They are not accused as river pirates. Not that he'd been idle during the war. He'd looted more than one mansion during Sherman's march to the sea. After the whole thing ended he had carried home a few small, valuable pieces, more, far more, had been smuggled back through his contacts, and someday he'd return to Atlanta, buy up the old, empty lot at the end of Eighteenth street and quite unexpectedly discover a cache of loot he'd buried beneath the northwest corner.

"Anything else?" Clive asked.

"Didn't see but a pair of men on deck," Beau licked his lips. "And the captain of course. I heard the rest. It sounded like they had a dice game going."

"Dice game?"

Beau nodded.

That might make things harder. On the one hand, men gambling were apt to be drinking and distracted. On the other, they shouldn't have been awake at all. Sleeping men were the easiest of all to rob and murder.

Beau shifted his feet and looked at Clive expectantly.

"There's more?"

Beau nodded. "They've already hired men to unload."

"What?"

"I saw at least thirty men aboard. I heard one of them talking about the extra hired help for when they arrived."

Clive scowled. *Thirty men aboard. Three times the expected crew. They'll have us outnumbered two-to-one.*

Still, his men were armed and armed well with two revolvers apiece and a long rifle. Moreover they were killers, one and all. Those on the Southern Queen weren't. They also wouldn't be expecting trouble.

Despite their numbers, he held the edge in surprise and firepower. Clive's eyes ran over his waiting men. They'd heard it all of course—no way to prevent that—and now they were waiting for him to decide if they attacked or if this had all been a waste of time.

Some of them will die. Half? Likely.

Clive did not care, so long as he himself wasn't among the dead. If anything more losses was to his advantage. The shares for those surviving would only grow.

Men could be replaced. They always had.

Still, he needed to tip the odds in his direction. *A distraction. Give them something to stare at while we slip in close.*

"Load the rowboat with wood and whatever else you can find. Then set it to burning out in the channel," he said. He saw the relief in his men. They knew the score as well as he.

Live and profit. The creed of pirates and highwaymen the world over.

Chet and his selected two brought the rowboat around to the side of the barge and loaded it down with wood and tar and a bit of coal. When it was done they poured lamp oil over the top. As two of the men shoved the rowboat off toward the center of the river channel, Chet lit a torch and tossed it inside.

The current soon caught the little boat, carrying it downstream and into the river's center.

The fire was a mile away when the lights of the Southern Queen swung around the bend. The Queen was a big vessel, one of the newer steamships with paddles on either side instead of the wide single paddle at the rear. Easier to steer— according to what Clive had heard.

Unfortunately, the Queen would never survive to find out.

A cry came up when the night watch on the Queen saw the burning rowboat. Shadowed figures ran forward to lean over the railing. The Queen's Captain did what anyone with a wooden ship would do upon spotting fire. He slowed and brought his ship into slower waters. Waters where Clive and his men waited. The pirates, Clive included, brought their rifles up.

Clive held his fire until the Queen was right on top of them. The one man looked their way. The distance was short enough that Clive saw his eyes widen in shock. His mouth opened to shout a warning. Clive's rifle bucked and the man fell dead.

A sudden storm of gunfire lit the night. Outlined against their own lamplight, the men aboard the Queen made easy targets.

"Hooks," Clive roared. His men lobbed hooks and lines all along the length of the steamer.

Now aware of the new danger, the Queen's Captain tried to speed up and put water between them, but Clive had planned well. His prize wasn't going anywhere. The clawing hooks weren't secured to the barge itself, but on long lines to trees along the riverbank. That much rope had cost a fortune or would have if they hadn't stolen it from a warehouse in Louisville last week.

Chet used a small hand-axe to cut away the lines securing the barge in place.

"Pull," he said, and most of the men hauled on the newly thrown lines to bring the barge in quickly.

"Protect the lines," Clive ordered. The only danger now was in the defenders hacking the lines clear. Out in open water the steam-driven Queen could easily outrun the lazy barge.

A man came out on the Queen's deck with a rifle. Clive fired his revolver, but the distance was too great. The rifleman took aim, fired, and one of Clive's men fell.

A select group of Clive's men, the best shots, had already reloaded their rifles. Three bullets took the man in the chest and sent him falling. Another of the Queen's crew ran on deck, waving a short axe. He hacked at the nearest line cutting it clean through. He started for a second one. This time Clive's shot struck true.

Another man emerged on deck, this one with a revolver of his own. He began shooting and managed to wound one of the pirates, before another shot him dead.

The two boats were close now, a few feet separated them.

"AT THEM," Clive said. His men roared and scrambled up and over the Queen's railing.

He waited for Chet and the men to clear the fighting away from the deck, and then he and Beau followed them. A black man emerged from a hatchway. He carried a wicked looking knife and raised it to chop at one of the rope lines. His eyes widened when he saw Clive.

"Little late for that," Clive said and shot him.

The knife fell from the man's hand, and he pitched over the railing and into the inky water.

Screams and more gunfire came from all around as the pirates cleared away the crew.

"Let's go see the Captain," Clive said. He and Beau climbed the stairwell up toward the pilot house. When they reached the top, Clive slowed. He peered around the corner where he could just peer inside. He could see the pilot house when a shot rang out. He ducked back in time to avoid an explosion of splinters just inches from where his face had been.

Clive ducked and darted around the corner quickly then, firing away into the pilot house with both pistols. Beau ran behind him, cursing and screaming. A pair of shots answered. None struck close. Clive's left revolver emptied. Smoke blinded him. A man's form appeared from the smoke and he put the last bullet from his right pistol into the center of it.

Clive entered the little house. One man was down, bleeding from his stomach and shoulder. Another rushed forward with a long skinning knife in hand. Clive batted the knife aside with one pistol before splitting his attacker's skull with the other.

A third man, older than the others—the Captain by his appearance—sat propped up against one wall, bleeding from a gunshot to the chest.

"Who are you?" the Captain said.

"Does it matter?" Clive answered. In two long strides he was across the room and caved the Captain's skull in with his pistol.

More gunfire echoed from below. *Chet is still fighting then.*

Clive turned to Beau. "Tell Chet to finish up and then get those lines cut away. We need to be moving downriver. And Beau..."

The smaller man paused in the doorway.

"You know what I think of survivors."

Everyone knew Clive's thoughts on survivors. Survivors meant stories told to authorities. Stories that might describe himself or one of his men. That could not be allowed.

Beau grinned and nodded. "Of course, Captain."

Clive moved to the steamship's controls. He smiled to himself. He'd always wanted to be a steamship Captain. Pity it wouldn't last. A few days from now, just after offloading their precious cargo into Clive's warehouse at Shawneetown, the proud Southern Queen would be aflame and aimless. Then the poor girl would go down with all hands aboard.

Clive clucked his tongue. A tragedy to see such a beautiful ship burn, but that's what it often took to cover one's tracks.

Besides, they can always build more. Maybe I'll buy one.

JIM RODE EAST THROUGH CLEAN, white drifts of the prior night's snow. The drifts weren't deep, luckily, most less than a foot and narrow. The ground was bare in patches, covered in dead gray grass, and frozen hard like iron. Jim barely noticed the wintery landscape. His thoughts were on his friends, the Sides.

Mack's family had settled into life on a small farm east of Independence. Mack worked at a larger farm nearby, raising hogs to slaughter and then smoke or salt for sale to travelers going west.

Jim skirted wide around an iced-over pond. Then he brought his horse through a copse of leafless trees. The sky was clouded over, gray and dull.

The wind picked up and Jim drew his coat tighter. *More snow late today or tonight.*

Jim could feel it. How long since he'd seen his first real snowstorm. There had been snow in San Antonio, very rarely, and never lasting more than a few hours. But this far north the snow fell for hours—days even—and sometimes it stayed around for days before finally melting away. That first big storm he'd kept himself huddled around a fire for two days while it piled up in drifts deep enough to lose a horse in.

This was no fit country for a young man from South Texas. He needed heat, the sun on his face, a warm breeze blowing over him.

California has to be warmer.

The little cabin came into view, and Jim could see a face staring out at him. Lily, he smiled. She always looked forward to his visits. Early on he'd visited once a week but with the short days and colder weather he hadn't been out this way in over a month.

She might be angry at me now.

When he was closer she waved emphatically, and he gave her a quick nod. Jim secured his horse in the barn and then rapped his gloved hand on the cabin door.

"Come in," Lily said, and the door swung open.

"Howdy," Jim answered. "Are all the girls in Missouri so pretty?"

Lily blushed and for what might have been the first time in her life had nothing to say.

"They are in this house," Mack laughed. "Get in here you Texican scoundrel."

Jim stepped in and took off his hat.

"What happened to your face?" Lily said.

"It got in the way."

"Got in the way of what?"

"Someone's fist."

"That looks terrible," Sarah said from the kitchen. There was a look of horror on her face.

"Thanks," Jim grinned.

"Did you win?" Mack said. He shook Jim's hand and leaned in for a better look at his battered face.

"I did. But it sure doesn't feel like it."

"I'll bet," Mack said.

"Did you bring me anything?" Lily tugged on his coatsleeve.

Her brother, Matthew elbowed her shoulder.

"I mean us. Did you bring us anything?" she corrected herself.

"I might have," Jim offered. From his pocket he produced a packet of tightly-wrapped paper.

Lily and Matthew's faces both lit up with the promise of sweets. Sarah coughed and Mack laughed under his breath.

"Which I will, of course, give to your mother," Jim said.

Matthew and Lily's faces both slipped a notch.

"After dinner, you may have some," Sarah said.

"I thought I smelled something good after I rode around Castle Hill. I could barely keep my horse from running all the way here," Jim teased.

"Ham stew again," Matthew said with a roll of the eyes.

No doubt the Sides family had eaten their fill of ham stew this winter. Sarah ladled out a helping for Jim, the two children, Mack, and finally herself. Jim waited until everyone was seated before diving in.

After their meal, and a mouthful of the promised sweets, Mack sent the children to their rooms.

"What brings you out, Jim?" Mack said.

"Donovan is putting together the first train of the year. He's planning on leaving in another month or so."

Mack eyed his wife as she put away their dishes. "Sarah and I have decided not to go."

"Not to go with Donovan? There's no one better," Jim said. "It's shaping up into a big train. It'll be safer than most."

Mack licked his lips and straightened in his chair. "We've decided not to go west at all."

"I'm going," Jim said. "I almost convinced myself not to, but Donovan talked me into it."

"It's a good move Jim. Good for you."

"But not for you?"

"No. We're buying this place. Sarah has a dozen wagon tops ready for spring and I've been doing well with the hogs. Hope to start with some of my own soon. Maybe plant some grain in that west field you rode in across."

"You're sure?" Jim said. "This was your dream. You and Sarah both wanted to see California so much."

"It isn't for us," Mack shook his head.

"We've found a home here," Sarah offered. "It isn't much, not the promised riches of California, but this is real."

"California is just as real. I've spoken with men who've seen it."

"They say a tithe of those who start the journey never see the end of it. There's Indians, storms, Cholera. We have two children, Jim. We can't risk their lives like that, not when we have a real opportunity here," Sarah said.

Jim sighed. He listened to Lily and Matthew laughing as they played. He supposed if he had children of his own he might see it the same way.

"I understand," Jim said.

"If you find a gold nugget to spare you can send me one back," Mack laughed.

"I will," Jim grinned. He stood and moved to the door. "I'd better be getting back to town before it gets dark."

"You're welcome anytime Jim." Mack said and they shook hands.

Lily and Matthew came from the other room. Quiet Matthew shook his hand just as Mack had. Lily wrapped herself around his leg and squeezed him tight.

"When I'm all grown up, I'll come west to California to see you," she said. Her eyes filled to overflowing.

"No need to cry. I'll wait for you by the ocean with a basket of those great big oranges they talk about," Jim smiled and wiped away her tears with his thumb.

He buttoned up his coat, tugged his hat down tight, and started out.

"Good luck to you Jim," Mack said. He had one arm wrapped around his wife, and Sarah seemed to be almost as upset as Lily.

"Good luck to you all," Jim said and eased the door shut behind him.

9

The first day out of town did not bode well for the caravan. The sky was overcast with a dishwater gray and the wind howled out of the cold north. Tiny white flakes flew in its breath, flashing like so many diamonds.

From the top of his horse, Jim Heston watched the long lines of wagons lolling along and wondered if they weren't leaving a month too early.

West of Independence mile-upon-mile of flat, barren grassland waited for them. The Great Plains. Out there would be no shelter from the wind, no refuge from the blustery cold. The forty wagons of their group would be completely exposed to the elements.

A flake stung Jim's eye. He wiped the back of his glove across his face and looked up to regard the low rolling clouds.

What if a blizzard catches us out here?

Contrary to his expectations, Jim had not ended up driving the supply wagon. At the last minute, Donovan decided that he would be better served roaming about, riding alongside each wagon in turn, offering advice to their drivers, checking their teams. It made sense. He could spot problems and correct them quickly, before they grew into real trouble.

Jim swung wide around the Barton wagon and several others. More than a few men had spoken up against him coming. "A fighter," they'd argued, "would cause nothing but trouble."

Donovan laughed off their fears. "Jim Heston is one of the finest men I've ever met. He only fights if you pay him," the caravan's leader answered. "And I don't think anyone on this trip has enough left over to do that."

His fighting wasn't the only objection of course. Unlike the rest he hadn't paid to be on the trip but was in turn paid by each wagon. These were strong, brave men. Proud. Anyone willing to make the journey west had to be. These men thought they could do for themselves, and they resented Jim's oversight. His youth didn't help. Nor did his lack of experience. Whatever he might know of wagons, he himself had never been over the trail.

Jim saw Donovan in the distance, near the train's head.

The big wagon leader had been over the trail. No one had been over it more, and if he believed in Jim Heston then who could argue?

The first day—despite the terrible weather—they made good time.

"Ground's frozen," Donovan laughed and huddled over that first night's fire. "Little cold but awful easy to roll over."

The third day Jim could ignore those other wagons no more. Obviously several of their drivers knew nothing of oxen and struggled against their teams.

Jim took a breath and approached the Adams wagon. Milo Adams, a tall, proud man from Cumberland Tennessee, had been one of the most vocal against his coming.

"Having trouble with them?" Jim asked.

Milo scowled and took a corncob pipe from his mouth. "Slow, these beasts are just too slow."

"Mind if I take a look at them," Jim offered.

"If you want."

Milo stopped the wagon and Jim dismounted to examine the oxen.

"Let's see if they pull better if we switch them around," Jim offered.

"That can't make a difference," Milo said. "I've driven teams all my life and they don't care which side they're on."

"Horse teams usually don't," Jim unhitched the first ox and led the huge animal to the side. "But oxen care very much about such things. They're raised together almost from birth and they are creatures of habit."

Milo gave him a skeptical look.

"Might as well try it," Lisa Adams said from Milo's elbow. She was a pleasant woman, sturdy, with an easy smile

Jim reversed the animals, then rehitched them, checking the straps and yokes each in turn. He didn't like how the yoke sat across the left-hand ox and adjusted it tighter to fit.

"That should be better," he said and led his horse clear.

Milo shrugged and climbed back up into the driver seat.

"What I wouldn't give for a good set of horses right now," he said.

"Horses wouldn't last long where we're going," Jim offered. "Faster yes, but a good ox team will beat horses over the long haul."

Milo popped the reins and the wagon ground forward.

With Milo off and going Jim moved to the next wagon having trouble, the Bartons. Ellen, the young woman he'd seen in the warehouse, sat in the seat next to her father. She gave him a studying look.

"Mr. Barton, Miss Barton, how are you today," he said with a doff of the hat.

"These animals just don't respond. I'm trying to get them moving faster, but what am I supposed to do with this?" he held up the quirt.

"The quirt is only to help them out. You have to talk to them," Jim answered.

"Talk to them?" Barton gave him a crossways look.

"You didn't learn the commands?"

"Commands?"

Jim smiled and wheeled his horse so he was little more than an arm's length from the wagon.

"Get up," he said, and the oxen picked up speed.

"Gee," he said, and the team turned to the right.

"Haw," Ellen said, and the team swung back to the left.

Jim gave her an appraising look.

"Some of us paid attention," she gently scolded her father.

"Keep them moving easy and they'll do well today. They aren't like horses, you can't rush them," Jim said.

"Gee and Haw," the older man repeated. "Get up."

"You've got it," Jim laughed and moved on to the next wagon.

By noon he had spoken to each of the struggling wagons front-to-back. Later in the day, riding up through the column, each satisfied him with signs of improvement. Even gruff Milo Adams waved his hat when Jim started by.

"Doing better?" Jim asked and swung closer.

"Night and day," Milo said. He grinned around the stem of his pipe flashing his white teeth. "I never seen anything like it. All from switching sides?"

"They have their habits just like people," Jim answered.

"How many miles you figure today?"

"Donovan thought seventeen, a good day overall."

"Seventeen," Milo answered. "Slow as they are I would have said ten."

"Over a few weeks a good ox team will walk a set of horses right into the ground," Jim said. "Slowly of course. Very slowly."

"Of course," Milo grinned.

Jim ranged afield in the afternoon. He startled a deer but did not shoot it. The meat would have been poor after the long winter. Once he thought he'd seen a buffalo on the far horizon. He was late to the fire that evening. Remy, the young man Donovan hired to drive their supply wagon, and Captain Neill were already fast asleep.

Over their evening fire, he asked Donovan about it.

"It isn't likely," the guide said. "They like to hide down out of the wind or in the trees with the weather like this."

"Trees?" Jim said. "Out here?"

"There are some," Donovan laughed. "The land may look flat, but there's hills and breaks deep enough to hide Lee's army."

Jim shook his head. "I don't believe it."

"We've been keeping to the flattest parts, the wagons make better time instead of climbing up and down, in another week though we'll have to cross the Kansas river. Water should be low this time of year, but cold. We'll have to watch everyone closely. Maybe build fires on each bank to warm up anyone who gets wet."

Jim looked up at the darkened sky. It had grown warmer while they traveled, but the days were still short and always the clouds threatened snow.

"This weather going to hold?"

Donovan shrugged. "Shouldn't for too much longer."

"That river you mentioned. What if it's iced over?"

"It won't be," Donovan said. He took a hunk of sizzling meat from the pan and popped it in his mouth. "I heard you were back with the Barton wagon today."

"David hadn't learned the commands."

"David is it?" Donovan gave him a sideways glance.

"That is his name."

"And that daughter of his? You saw her I'm sure."

"Ellen usually rides up front with him," Jim said.

"David and Ellen both. Getting awfully familiar are we?" Donovan chuckled.

"You angling at something?" Jim said.

"No. Not me. Nothing at all," Donovan laughed. "If Jim Heston, model of propriety, wants to court one of the young women on the trail then that's his affair. Entirely his."

"I'm too young to hitch myself up with some useless girl," Jim said.

"Ohh, I can think of some uses for one like her," Donovan hooted.

Jim felt his face redden. He took a bite of meat to keep himself from talking. Ellen Barton had laughed at him, been horrified by him that first evening. She wouldn't want to see anyone like him, and he wouldn't want anyone like her.

"Well I'm all done in," Donovan said and started for his bed. "Wish I had me someone like Ellen Barton to warm it up for me. I had me a Shoshone squaw like that one time. Yessir. Pretty as a prancing pony."

The big man laughed then and rolled under his buffalo robes.

Jim glanced at the older man's sleeping form. What would a caravan driver know about women?

He sat in the dark alone staring at the fire. Captain Neill snored lightly, and Remy rolled over in his sleep. The young man had a boyish face though he claimed to be seventeen. Jim had seen little of either of them so far. Neill rode ahead most of the time and the wagon kept Remy hopping busy. Jim took the last bite from the pan and started for his own bed. *The last thing I need is a woman to take care of. Especially one like Ellen Barton.* A woman like that would want fine things. Home things.

Jim Heston knew little of such a life. When his mother and brother lived, and even further back when his father was home they'd never had much more than a broken-down farm. What did he have to offer anyone?

He held up a big fist, clenched it tight. *I have only these.*

They said in the west a man willing to work, willing to learn, could do well for himself. A year or two in California, five at most, and he'd carve out a place for himself. Something he could be proud of. Then, if he still wanted to, he might see about finding someone to share it with.

He doubted very much it would be someone like Ellen Barton.

CLIVE WILSON WAS NOT in the pilot house when the Southern Queen docked. Much as he'd enjoyed his time steering the grand vessel, now he had work to be done. Work that required his presence at the railing.

Frank Simmons, his partner in this venture stood at the end of the dock with a skinny cigar clenched between his teeth.

"Glad to see you made it, my friend," Frank said.

"Of course," Clive answered. He gestured to Chet standing beside him. "If your men will follow Chet we can get our haul unloaded quickly."

"You heard him," Frank said. "Let's not keep them waiting."

Dockworkers and crew alike sprang to their work, leaving them to themselves.

"Come up to the pilot house?" Clive said and led the way.

"I've never seen inside one of these," Frank said. He ran a hand over the controls. "The levers control it?"

"One for either side," Clive nodded. "You just press them forward to move."

"Fascinating," Frank took a lever in each hand,

"Let us discuss price," Clive Wilson said to his old friend.

"Price?" Frank raised an eyebrow at him. "We already agreed as to that."

Clive gave the man a flat glare.

He had met Frank Simmons near the war's conclusion on the long march south. Simmons was a respectable soldier, not so effective as Clive but still serviceable. They'd been of equal rank during the war. Both cavalrymen. Now that the fighting was over though, such was no longer the case. Whatever name he had made for himself in the army, Frank Simmons grew up the son of a poor farmer and he was Clive Wilson, scion of one of the State's leading families.

Time to remind my former comrade of it.

"I figure you owe me a little more that we agreed on. I figure you had this load insured, and you'll get a nice profit from that," Clive said. "Buying these bales at anything less than market prices would only increase your part of the split."

"If I pay you market price then I would have been better of just accepting delivery instead of arranging for you to take them," Frank protested.

"Either way I am the one with the cargo now." Clive ran a hand over the railing. "A cargo you need to get your new factory operating."

Frank's eyes flared. "There are other ways to keep the mill running. I could send you on your way."

"That would be difficult after you've been implicated in the theft of the Southern Queen and the murder of her crew."

"Theft? Murder?" Frank laughed. "I think you have the two of us mistaken. I am no pirate."

Frank's voice held little conviction and Clive knew it was time to end this. "Do you know who Nathan Stanley is?"

"He's my foreman. He was just here. The man I sent below to direct the unloading of the bales."

"He was."

"Was?" John's tone betrayed his lack of understanding.

"He was your foreman." Clive looked out the window to the deck below. He waved to Chet and the big thug brought a barrel rolling out onto the deck. Chet set the barrel upright and popped the lid open. The bloody and mangled corpse of Nathan Stanley was stuffed inside.

"My god," Frank covered his mouth.

"You were a gallant soldier Frank, a tough one. How tough would you be though if I put your wife, your children, in such a barrel? I think they'd all fit the same one. Might be a bit snug though." Clive paused. He took off his gloves and laid them in his left hand. "Now Frank, I have just discovered that you had your foreman murdered. Maybe he was stealing. Maybe he was having relations with your wife. I don't know. I don't care. I also found out that you and a gang of your men committed an act of river piracy resulting in you acquiring this load of cotton and the Southern Queen. During this robbery you murdered all hands aboard. My uncle—Bill Wilson—the Illinois State Attorney General, will receive testimony to this and he will execute his duties to the letter of the law. You will lose everything, Frank, your beautiful mill, your home, your family, and then you will hang. Unless of course..."

Frank's fists clenched tight. He looked down to the men gathered on deck on either side of Clive. None of his dockworkers were there. Clive hadn't ordered them killed. Not yet anyway. Only the foreman's death had been necessary to send the right message.

"I'll pay your price," Frank said. He had spirit, he'd been a good soldier, but today he'd been completely outmaneuvered.

"Good," Clive smiled. "See it was easy, you got your cotton and a new partner."

"Partner?"

"Of course, you'll be signing a nice contract with my own shipping company to haul all your goods to market. I won't charge you much of course. Need to keep your mill going so you can buy more of my cotton."

"I didn't agree to—"

"Now Frank, no need to hedge on our little deal," Clive said, "Like I said. I'll give you my best rates and terms."

Clive leaned out to speak with Chet. "Escort my new partner to his property. Take the barrel with him."

When they were gone and the cargo offloaded, Clive, began issuing orders to take the Southern Queen out downriver. With business brought to a profitable conclusion he needed to make sure there were no loose ends. He patted the Queen's handsome railing. Fine ship that she was, she would be far too recognizable for him to use. Pity. She'd go out in flames, like one of the Viking vessels of old. He thought of the crew's bodies stored below decks in the aft hold.

Only this won't be a burial for just one man.

ONCE THE SOUTHERN Queen and her crew were nothing but ash and sunken remnants drawn down into the long belly of the big muddy river, Clive Wilson gathered his men twenty miles downriver, on the Ohio side, ready to divvy up the money from their venture.

The moon hung high and bright. Clive sat at an improvised table made by a set of planks laid across a pair of empty barrels. Each grinning man lined up, laughing and joking with their fellows. Clive handed out small bags of money to each in turn as they shuffled past.

Chet, as usual, came up last in line.

"Well-earned as always, Chet." Clive handed the big man a heavy bag of coin. Chet hefted it, squeezed it tight, and grinned. Next to

Clive's own share, Chet's was always the largest, and if anyone grumbled about it they kept it to themselves.

At least the wise ones do.

Chet said, "Any idea when we'll have the next job?"

Clive lowered his voice. "I might have something lined out soon. Smaller—fewer men needed—but still highly lucrative. We can discuss it later."

"Good," Chet smiled.

"Have you seen Beau?" Clive asked.

"Not since this morning."

"This morning?"

"He took one of the rafts and headed downriver. Said he had something to do. Said he'd pick up his share from you later," Chet said.

Odd. Beau isn't a trusting man.

Just as Chet always picked up the last share, Beau was the first. Beau's share was only slightly less than Chet's own. Paying the scout well kept him focused on the richest prizes.

The men were starting to disperse, laughing even more now, clapping one another on the back, each going their own way. They would not go far. The pay was too good, dangerous, but too easy. Clive knew how to reach them when the time came again.

He stood, stretched, and started toward his boat. Chet followed him like a shadow. When they weren't pirates, the big man worked for Clive's legitimate freight business as dockmaster and did well at it.

Not nearly so well as a pirate though.

They were nearing the boat when a shout came from the south, followed by the report of a gun.

What was that about?

His men knew the rules, disputes among themselves were to be settled away from their gatherings. More gunfire started further inland due east this time. Clive saw bluecoat soldiers creeping along one of the footpaths to the north.

His men fought back but were vastly overmatched. The soldiers were organized, well-armed, and possessed training for this sort of thing. His men were pirates, skilled at ambush and river fighting. They were not used to this kind of action.

Clive and Chet took out for their boat at a run. The river. The river would carry them away to safety.

They emerged onto the shore and ran along through the darkened trees and scattered rocks. Clive stopped and looked out over the moonlit water. This was the place. The rope loop still hung around the stump he'd secured it to. Someone had cut it free.

Where is my boat?

Behind them, men were shouting. A pair of hound dogs brayed. Torchlight spilled out on the water.

Clive ran on toward the north, Chet following along after him. The river was wide here and without a boat to carry them they were boxed in. Maybe someone had heard the commotion and took his boat upriver.

I'll flay them when I catch them.

Clive saw it then. A dark silhouette on the water. *My boat.*

He dove into the water and swam as fast as he could. An instant later he heard Chet do the same.

Always a strong swimmer, Clive covered the distance quickly. He grabbed the boat's low railing and dragged himself over the edge onto the deck. His lungs, legs, and arms all burned with the effort of his swim, but he'd made it. Somehow he'd made it. Now he could escape.

Steps thumped on the deck. He was not alone. Clive rolled to his stomach and started to rise.

"Might as well just stay down Captain," a voice said.

Clive knew that voice. Beau. But how? The scout must have arrived late, heard the soldiers, and started out on the boat.

Lights shone back ashore. The shouts of the soldiers carried out over the rippled water. It was lucky the boat had already been out in the current, beyond rifle range.

"Beau," Clive said. He started to rise. The scout stood off to his left, near the rudder.

A pistol clicked and Clive froze. "I said stay down," Beau threatened.

"Beau, this is my boat and I'll damn well—"

"Not anymore. Move again and I'll put a bullet in your brain."

Keeping his movements concealed, Clive opened his coat, searching for his pistol, the one he carried at all times.

"Doubt that pistol of yours will fire after a nice, long swim like that," Beau taunted. "Not that it matters, I'll have you shot dead long before you draw it."

Clive's mind searched for a way out. There had to be something. Chet would help him. Where was Chet? Clive had it then. If he could keep Beau talking the big enforcer could sneak up on him and end this.

"You know Beau, I didn't drop your share. It's right here in my—"

Chet emerged on the deck beside him then, dashing Clive's plan, ruining any chance to catch Beau by surprise.

"Took you long enough," Beau said.

"You moved the boat," Chet growled and stood without hesitation.

"Search him," Beau ordered.

Clive did not understand. Why didn't Beau shoot Chet? Search who?

Chet rose then and put a hand on Clive's back, pressing him against the deck. His hands ran over Clive's coat. He grabbed the pistol from Clive's belt, then the bag of gold.

"Got it," Chet said.

"Toss it over," Beau answered.

"Not a chance," Chet growled. "You moving the boat wasn't part of the deal."

Deal? What deal?

With a flash of insight Clive understood then. Beau and Chet. The soldiers arriving at the meet. They had arranged all of this.

"It's a good thing I did," Beau said. "The army showed up earlier than I expected. I warned that fool Major of theirs."

"Either way, I'm holding onto the money for now," Chet said. "We'll settle up back at the warehouse after we open the safe."

Clive's mind raced. He couldn't believe it, betrayal by Beau was one thing, he'd always known the scout would one day press his luck, but Chet. After everything they'd done together. Clive had to escape this. He had to find a way to survive and then he would pay back their betrayal.

"Get on with it and let's get moving," Beau said.

"Sorry Captain," Chet said. Clive knew what would happen next, the knife would come. Chet would stab down at him with that knife of his, the one he loved. How many times had Clive seen him murder men in just that way? How many times had he ordered it?

Chet took a breath and his hand lifted for just a second. Clive had been waiting for it. Before Chet could stab down, Clive swung himself around and kicked the big man as hard as he could. Unstable, Chet fell back, knife falling away with him, and before he could recover Clive rolled off the boat and into the cold, black water.

Keeping below the surface and heading for shore, Clive cut across the current. He held his breath and pumped arms and legs for a long minute; rising too soon would be a death sentence. He needed to be far enough away from the boat that Chet and Beau wouldn't see or hear him.

When his lungs ached, and he could swim no farther he turned up for the surface. Slowly, he stuck his head just above the waterline, treading in place for a moment, trying to get his bearings. The black shadows of shore lay to his left, a hundred yards off, and he started swimming for safety.

The current dragged him ever south, but Clive had always been a strong swimmer. Soon enough he pulled himself up the cold, muddy bank and lay panting from exertion. Beau and Chet both betraying him. How could they even consider getting away with it? They would pay for this.

I will make them both suffer.

He lay there for several minutes, then heard trashing in the brush off ahead. Then a man's voice rang out.

The eastern bank. He was on the eastern bank. The soldiers were still out searching for the remnants of his men.

Like a wraith, Clive pulled himself farther up the bank, deep into the dappled shadows, out of the sticky mud where he could gain a measure of footing.

Whatever else he might be the man nearby was not a woodsman. He crashed through brush, making more noise than an entire cavalry troop.

Clive hefted a thick branch almost two feet long. He stood tall and still beside an old tree trunk. The searcher passed by just a few yards to the south. He held a small lantern in one hand and, in the other, a pistol. Clive waited until he was just past, looking the other direction. Then he hurled the branch up through the treetops angling it east where it landed with a thump.

"Who goes?" the searcher yelped.

Clive crouched down into the deeper shadows. The searcher's lantern flared out when he lifted it higher. Clive could see him better now. A young man in a blue coat, carrying a new Colt pistol in one hand and the lantern in the other. The pistol shook unsteadily.

Finding a large stone, Clive tossed it off to the east toward where the stick had crashed. The soldier spun to follow it. He took three steps forward. Clive was now behind him out of the lamplight.

Clive smiled. His situation was improving. He glided forward on cat's feet to get closer. Though he had to be careful now. A shot, even a miss, would draw more soldiers.

The young man took another hesitant step forward. His foot came down on a stick. It broke and shattered the night like a gunshot. The soldier turned then, just in time to catch Clive in the lamplight.

"Wha-"

Clive drove his knife through the man's soft throat.

"Shhh," he said and clamped one powerful hand around the pistol while the other twisted the knife free.

The young man tried to yell, tried to call out, but only blood came from his throat. He grabbed at it, pistol forgotten. Clive slammed him over the head with the Colt's butt.

The dead soldier was smaller than Clive, so much so that he couldn't exchange his soaked clothing, but at least the pistol would be useful.

He searched the man's pockets, found a little money, flint and tinder, a silver pocket-watch with an older woman's picture inside— his mother, no doubt—spare cartridges for the pistol, and a full canteen.

Clive took a drink and considered his next move. The night air was cold, and he did not want to go for another swim. He also couldn't start a fire with so many men out searching.

He needed to put more distance between himself and pursuit.

Further upriver there was an old ferry. The man running it was known to many who worked the river. Clive made good time, passing between trees and shadows silent as a shade. Jeremiah Bridger, the man who ran the ferry, lived in a hardscrabble shack on the river's eastern bank.

As Clive drew closer he slowed. He stopped completely in a bend in the path where he could peer around toward the ferry. Apparently the old ferry was known to the soldiers as well. A pair of them stood hunched over a small fire, warming their hands.

Clive drew his newly-acquired pistol. Shooting these two would make noise—no help for it. He still had the knife though. *Two men at once with a knife.* The odds would be against him. Unless he could find a way to change things in his favor.

An idea struck him then.

He tucked the pistol into the back of his pants and stepped out into the open to approach the fire. He blew into his hands and rubbed them together.

"Good evening," he said.

"Evening," one of the guards stood quickly and stepped back away from the fire to regard him.

"Is Jeremiah around?" Clive said amicably.

"Little late to cross the river isn't it," the second man said, and squinted at Clive across the fire.

Clive kept working his hands. "Not looking to cross. He and I have other business."

"Did you come from the south?" the standing soldier's hands moved toward his holstered pistol.

The first man, still seated, was close now. Clive kept a warm smile on his face.

"Came from the north actually. Walked right by this place the first time. Everything looks a little different in the dark."

The nearest soldier was within arm's reach. Clive held out his hands to the warm fire. He shifted off to his left, toward the shore, putting the seated man between himself and the other soldier.

Clive's move was both quick and unexpected. He took a long step around the fire, grabbing the nearest man, spinning him around, and bringing the knife up to his throat hard enough to draw a bead of blood.

"Drop the gun," Clive ordered. "Or watch your friend bleed to death."

The second man eased his pistol out and dropped it at his feet.

Clive smiled. He sliced the first man's throat and shoved him into the fire. The second man froze for a split-second, then started down for his dropped pistol. Clive was on him then. Three times, the knife took him in the ribs.

The second man stood and screamed, he slapped at Clive but there was little strength left to him. His eyes reflected the light in horror.

Clive left him standing and ran beyond the dead men then, to the cabin's door. He knocked twice.

"Jeremiah," he said. "This is a friend of Willis."

"From the war?" The question, like Clive's greeting was code of course. A 'friend of Willis' meant he might have something to sell, discretely.

"From before," Clive answered.

The door opened. An old man peered out, shotgun in hand. "The soldiers gone?"

"Dead, not gone." Clive answered.

"Makes things complicated. What do you want?"

"A simple crossing. Warm clothes if you have them. Some food."

"Stew on the fire and there might be something that'll fit you in the corner."

"Should I dump the bodies?" Clive asked.

"No, I'll deal with them," the ferryman said. He stepped clear of the cabin and began rifling through the dead men's pockets. "I'm off in five minutes."

Clive found an overcoat big enough to fit him and a battered hat of western style. He frowned at it. He never wore a hat. It might help to conceal his identity. The stew—squirrel by the taste—proved awful but Clive was hungry enough not to complain.

The ferry was a simple raft of lashed-together timbers with a heavy winch and tackle on either end. Jeremiah worked the winch alone. The ropes stretched and groaned as he pulled them across, but everything held together.

Midway across Jeremiah left the winch long enough to dump both soldier's bodies over the side.

"Current will take them miles downriver by morning," the ferryman said.

"What do I owe you?"

"Plenty in their pockets to pay the fee," Jeremiah spat and took back to his work. "And I didn't like them watching my place."

A cabin matching the first waited on the far shore along with a horse.

"How much for the horse?" Clive asked.

"Five dollars and he's yours," the ferryman grinned toothlessly.

Clive took the money from his pouch and paid gratefully. The horse wasn't one he would have ever chosen for himself, but that would only improve his disguise.

Somewhere ahead of him Chet and Beau would be heading toward his warehouse and the riches they believed to be inside.

Clive smiled to himself.

And won't they be surprised when I meet them there.

10

At the morning campfire Jim Heston downed a cup of scalding hot coffee and studied the fog his breath made.

Remy Biles, the youth Donovan hired to drive their wagon, sat beside the fire, eating the last of their breakfast. Scarecrow skinny, the boy had to have a hollow leg by how much he could eat.

"Going to be another cold one," Jim offered.

"Just like the rest of them," Remy answered and drew his coat tighter.

Jim grinned. He liked the younger man. Tall, thin, and quiet, he spoke rarely, usually only after being spoken to. He worked hard—with no complaints—and though uneducated in writing or cyphering he had smarts in the practical sense. He'd proven a very capable hand whenever a wagon broke down and Jim needed materials or help. Even better, Remy made a strong cup of coffee. A need Jim had underestimated setting out.

Jim took a last swig, poured out the dregs over the fire, and saluted Remy with the empty cup.

"Have a good one," he said.

"Same to you Mister Jim," the young man said.

Jim mounted a tall roan he'd taken a liking too, and then circled wide around their cluster of wagons until he came to where Donovan was speaking with Milo Adams.

Holding up a respectful distance away, Jim did his best to ignore their conversation. After he'd proved his point about the oxen, he and Milo had reached an accord of sorts. Nothing formal of course, but an understanding that allowed for them to be respectful of each other. Jim meant to preserve that. Unless there was an item needing correction on Milo's wagon or team and there had been a few, Jim kept a distance between them. Each problem had taken only once to correct, and Jim hoped each one built up a bit trust on Milo's part.

Jim looked out over the cold empty plains and waited for Donovan to finish.

The vastness of it all still moved him. Texas was a big place of course, but not so flat or open. There were trees and valleys and rolling hills where he'd lived. Out here a man on horseback could stand in his stirrups and see for miles and miles.

The group's progress over the first few weeks seemed encouraging to Jim though he couldn't say why. Mostly it was Donovan that gave him this impression. The frozen ground proved rough on the wagons —Jim replaced a pair of wheels and a busted axle—but it had been quick to travel over.

There were other worries besides speed though. Namely the food situation. With no game to speak of, the wagon train was eating through its supplies at an alarming rate. Normally they would have an occasional deer or buffalo to stretch their supplies.

Aside from his duties repairing the wagon, Jim went out hunting often enough. At times Donovan accompanied him. The older man often shared his wisdom. Donovan knew a hundred small tricks to make trail life easier. How to string up a blanket beneath the wagon to gather firewood or buffalo chips in. How to tell the safest stream crossings. How to make camp where smoke from the campfires would stay out of everyone's faces.

Donovan finally finished talking to Milo and both motioned Jim over. Neither man looked pleased.

"Jim," Donovan started. "There's been some hard talk about you in camp."

"Why? I haven't done anything." Jim gave Milo a glare. What had Milo told him? *I thought we'd moved past this.*

"I realize that," Donovan held out his hands. "Milo just came up here to let me know what's being said."

"You being some kind of fighter and all, I was against you coming. I was more against it when I learned we were chipping in to pay you for it," Milo started. He paused for a moment, swallowed, and then went on. "But I'm a big enough man to admit when I'm wrong. I've seen the work you've done for us. I want you to know I'm grateful for your help, and I don't think it's fair for the others to speak about you in the wrong way."

Jim was taken back. *This puts things in a new light.* But why did Donovan say there was hard talk about him?

"Sir, I don't want to cause trouble," Jim said. "I only want to get to California same as anyone else. I fought to put a little money together for a stake. That's all."

"It's nothing you caused, young man," Milo said. He pointed his pipe stem toward the wagons. "Only some of those men riding with us lost money after they bet against you."

"I can't help that."

"No, but you should know of it. The men that lost have been trying to poison the others against you," Milo said. "Don't get me wrong, you've done a passel of work getting us all in shape. And I seen you fix the Faulkner's wagon axle. Never seen it done better or quicker. You're a good man to have along and plenty of the others know it too. I've spoken with them."

"I'm not sure what should I do different then," Jim said.

"Nothing," Donovan barked. "Just keep on at it. Helping out, offering advice respectful-like. I only wanted you to know. That way you can avoid trouble. We have some good men with us, but in every bunch there's a few bad ones. Watch yourself with some of those. They get a chance to put you in your place they'll surely do it."

"I can take care of myself."

"I know," Donovan eyed him. "That's the problem. I don't want you whipping anyone with a bunch of women and children watching. And don't think they'll come after you with fists only."

Milo gave Donovan a long look then spat a wad of tobacco on the ground.

Jim eyed his friend. *There's more to it than this.* Donovan was chewing his lip and looking toward the wagons. "There's something else?"

"Some of the men are nervous with you around their women."

"What?" Jim felt his mouth drop open. "That isn't—"

"I know. I know Jim," Donovan held out his hands. "But look at it from their perspective. Most every man in this group is married. There's less than a dozen single men all told. And there's a lot of talk among the womenfolks about getting you married off to one of their daughters or sisters."

"What? I'm not marrying anyone." Jim couldn't believe it. *Of all the half-brained ideas.*

Milo grinned, eyes shining. "I once said the same thing myself. I've got seven kids now."

"Long way out there," Donovan said and nodded toward the west. "Not too many women out that way yet."

"I've got time," Jim said.

Donovan gave him a sidelong look. "I used to think that. Used to think another year, two at the most, I'll settle down and make my fortune. Only time has a way of slipping by. Before you know it you're an old man with nothing but a worn-down saddle, broken bones that ache when it gets cold, and hard times far as you can see."

"I've got the get back to the missus," Milo said and excused himself.

Donovan and Jim watched him go and, for a long time, neither spoke.

Jim eyed his friend warily. *This isn't like him.* Donovan was good-natured and cheerful to a fault. *Today something is bothering him.*

"Might as well get them started," Donovan said. "Go check on the Martin outfit. They've been slow the last few mornings."

The Martins. Jim sighed. He'd been hoping to avoid this.

Lane Martin and his wife Viv were good, solid people. "Salt-of-the-earth," Jim's mother would have called them. They had three children, a girl and two boys, none taller than Jim's waist. Quiet kids who seemed to be doing well over the trail. Unfortunately for Lane, his father-in-law, Moses, had come along to see California. The man was old, tough, and stubborn enough for any two men, and he very much enjoyed his whiskey.

"Moses snuck a couple bottles in," Jim said.

Donovan gave him a sideways look. "Does Neill know?"

"Can't say for sure," Jim said. "But he's been spending time back there."

Captain Neill Patrick was the party's official scout, and despite all of Jim's earlier misgivings, the man had proved to be a good traveling companion. It hadn't started out that way though. Two days out of Independence, Jim had found him shaking one morning so bad he couldn't hold onto a cup of coffee with both hands. The third morning was worse.

How a man could survive such a thing seemed impossible.

But true to Donovan's word, by day five Neill had become a different man. Mainly he kept ahead of the column, scouting the land, bringing back an occasional deer to supplement their dwindling rations. He'd even taught Jim a thing or two about scouting, despite their troubled history.

"You've got to keep him away from the whiskey," Donovan scowled. "Otherwise he'll be right back to the shape he was."

Jim shrugged, "Not much I can do."

"No, I suppose not," Donovan's voice was hard. "Tough day today, crossing the river. I'll be needed up front."

"Keep Neill with you. Have him help everyone crossing."

"He won't do it," Donovan shook his head. "Not if he knows that old man has whiskey."

"Maybe I can get him to show me some more about scouting."

"Can't spare you either. There's rocks and boulders on either side of the river. We're bound to have at least one wagon needing repairs."

With that Donovan climbed up into the saddle. "I'll think about what to do with Moses and his whiskey."

"He's not the only one carrying some," Jim said. Half the wagons had at least a bottle with them, either for cleaning wounds or easing coughs.

"He's the only one with enough to be drinking it openly." Donovan said. "And it won't be long before he's sharing with Neill and we'll be back at day one again."

Donovan started off after the lead wagon. The Webbs, as usual. The young couple had been the first ones ready every morning, rising early, packing quick, and making good time.

Jim had talked with them on occasion. Never over their team. Paul Webb knew his business, and he never needed help. He had worked as a wagon driver back in Philadelphia before California called.

His wife, Hannah, was a pleasant woman. Always ready with a warm smile and quick laugh.

Climbing up on the roan, Jim circled back toward the last wagon in the camp. The Martins were up and packing quickly, but not recklessly. Their children were pitching in, carrying pots and plates. Everyone was moving. All except Moses. Snores came from the old man's tent. An empty bottle lay on the grass outside.

Probably a full one inside, cradled beneath the old man's arm.

"Morning," Jim saluted.

"Good morning," Lane answered. "We're just about ready." He tried not looking at his father-in-law's tent but couldn't help a quick glance.

Viv's face reddened in shame.

"Of course," Jim agreed. "Is there anything I can do to help?"

"We've just about got it," Lane said.

"I understand."

Lane was a proud man, and he wouldn't ask for help. An impulse struck Jim then and he took off his hat and turned to Viv. "If it's alright with you ma'am I'd like to ask your father to go scouting with me today."

"Scouting with you?" Lane said.

"I've a lot to learn and it might do him some good to get out and about, away from camp for awhile." The thought had come on him quickly. True, Donovan would want him up at the front for the river crossing but they wouldn't get there until noon. He could keep Moses in the saddle and sober until then, and then he could get the old man up the crossing and give him some sort of task to keep him out of trouble.

"He was a good woodsman back in Virginia. I think he'd like getting out to see the country some. Even if there aren't any woods out here." She smoothed down the front of her dress and then an uneasy look came over her. "We don't have a horse for him to ride."

"I've got a spare, and I can scrounge up a saddle," Jim offered. "I'll go get it."

A few minutes later he was riding as promised with the spare horse, a lineback mare, saddled and ready.

The Martins were the only wagon not yet rolling, but they seemed faster than yesterday at least.

Moses Jensen stood scratching at an old scar on his arm and eyeing his daughter when Jim returned. Evidently Captain Neill had arrived in Jim's absence and sat waiting on his own horse, one knee propped over the pommel. He and the older man were talking when Jim arrived, but he couldn't make out what either were saying.

"Neill, I thought I'd invite Mr. Jensen to ride up front with me to scout and help out with the river crossing this afternoon," Jim said. "Donovan suggested it."

"That's a good idea. Donovan's always a step ahead," Neill agreed.

Jim wondered if Donovan knew his forward scout was hanging back at the last wagon.

"I brought you the spare horse," Jim said to Moses. "Even found a decent saddle."

Moses squinted one eye against the rising sun and gave Jim a long look. "What's this about?"

"Just thought you'd appreciate a day in the saddle instead of bouncing around that rough wagon. Mrs. Martin said you were good on the trail, and I thought I could learn a thing or two."

"You could help him, Moses," Neill offered. "I've tried but he's a hard learner."

"You know what we called hard learners in my day?" Moses said with a toothless grin. "Injun bait."

Neill laughed and said, "I'll bet."

Moses stalked over and checked the mare over. He let out the stirrups and checked the cinch. "Young folks today don't know how to properly saddle a horse."

Jim ignored the comment. He knew how to saddle a horse well enough. He'd been doing it for years. The old man would find nothing out of order.

"Looks like you did it right this time," Moses said and climbed up in the saddle.

"He does know his way around a horse pretty well," Neill offered. "It's everything else he's struggling with."

"I'll line him out," Moses said. Then he raised his voice where his daughter and her husband could hear. "I'm riding out front today to help with the crossing and teach this young man a thing or two about surviving among the heathen injuns. I'll be back to camp when I'm damn well good and ready."

Then the old man spun his horse, slapped spurs, and shot toward the front of the wagon train like a bullet. Jim swore and booted the roan into a run. He did his best to keep up. Moses could not get far—he had chosen the most docile horse he could find—but the old man drove the mare like a thoroughbred. Captain Neill was in the rear; Jim turned around long enough to see the man bent low over the saddle, grinning like a madman.

When they were a half-mile ahead of the lead wagon, Moses finally slowed the mare to a walk. Jim reined in beside him.

"This isn't a bad horse," Moses said and patted the mare on the neck. "At first I thought you'd brought me some old used-up plowhorse to ride, but she did real well."

Neill pulled up beside them, still grinning. "Nothing like a brisk morning ride," he said.

Moses gave him a long look, leaned over his saddle, and heaved up his breakfast on the grass. He straightened up and wiped his mouth. "It's no fun getting old. Man can't hold his breakfast after a decent ride."

"Yessir." Jim fought to keep a smile off his face.

They spent the morning scouting around, Moses pointing out tracks and asking Jim about them. They talked about what type of animal made them, how long ago it was, and why the animal had come this way. Mostly, Neill seemed content to let the old man talk and kept to himself.

"The why is always important," Moses lectured. "With animals the why is very simple. Food, shelter, danger, mate." He held up four gnarled fingers. "With people the why is often the same, but not always. You can add in greed, fear, hate, and other feelings."

"Tracking people is harder then," Jim said.

"Harder and easier both. Harder to know the why but easier to figure out where they're going next. People generally want to go toward other people. That means cities, villages, forts. Even if they're running from the law they're generally headed toward other people. An outlaw might run from one settlement to another or to some abandoned place he knows of. If you know it too, you can outguess him."

At noon they ate from their saddlebags and then they came to the river. This early in the spring, with the snowpack still frozen, the water was at its lowest, a little over a foot deep. There were rocks and boulders strewn along either bank in a wide band. Most were small, but some would shatter a wagon wheel to splinters if they struck it.

"Best crossing is about a mile that way," Neill said and tipped his hat to the north. "At least it was last time I passed through here."

"Can a crossing move?" Jim said.

"All the time," Neill nodded. "A river, especially a wild one like this, is a living thing, cutting through the country like they do. A good crossing one year might be covered up in mud or brush the next."

The Captain brought them to a place where the boulders were few and bands of white sand stretched along on both banks. There was a decent grade on the approach though.

"Wagons will come down fast over that," Jim said.

"Something like this, we usually lower them down with a winch," Neill said. "Otherwise they'll shoot right into the current. But with the water this low..." He rode further down where rainwater had carved out a notch into the hillside. "A little shovel work here and we could bring them down the slope then skirt up the sand before crossing. Save us from having to winch them down."

The idea was a good one. With a task to do, Neill was a far different man from the aimless wretch he'd been in Kansas.

Jim thought back to his own father. The memories were dim now. He remembered Pa working around the place, but his heart had never seemed to be in it. He'd always done as little as he could get away with. He seemed to like owning a farm, but not working one.

Had he changed into a different man when he went off to war? He was a changed man when those Comanches came visiting. Jim had never seen him move so fast.

Neill turned his horse back toward the crossing. He smiled over at Jim. "I'm off to scout ahead of course otherwise I'd help with the diggin," he said and was soon gone.

Moses watched him go and then eyed Jim. "Don't look at me, I'm not digging. I'm an old man."

THE FIRST WAGON, the Webbs of course, rolled into view and Jim still had a half hour of digging left to do. Moses had been no help, preferring to sit on a blanket while staring off into the distance.

"Watchin for Injuns," he called it.

When the Webbs rolled closer, Moses rose and saluted them with a wave of his floppy-brimmed hat.

"Afternoon," he said.

"And to you," Paul Webb returned. "Looks like you two have built us a fine road to cross through."

"Indeed we have," Moses said. "Young Jim here is just finishing up."

Jim growled at the older man—he hadn't built anything—and got an amused look in return. He threw the last shovelful aside and stood back to admire his work. He didn't mind hard labor, in fact he enjoyed it, but Moses sitting there watching him while he dug reminded him of breaking rocks down in that dusty hole.

Webb walked down the embankment while Jim drank from his canteen. He eyed the bank from the bottom, nodding to himself, before approaching.

"It's good work," he said.

"The actual crossing is about two hundred yards upriver," Jim replied. Then he turned to Moses. "You want to show them where, or would you rather stay and admire 'our' handiwork."

If Moses was admonished he showed no sign of it. "I think I might stand right here and guide each wagon as it comes in. Where's Donovan?"

"Right here," Donovan said and rounded the wagon. He eyed the cut just as Webb had. "Good. This will save us from lowering the wagons down." He looked up at the sun, then back at the wagons strung out behind like pearls on a string. "Probably gain us three or four miles today. Neill found this?"

"He did," Jim answered.

Donovan grinned at him. "The man earned his money today then."

Jim started to complain about how he left Moses and himself to dig before riding on, but then he thought better of it. They all had jobs to do. Neill's was scouting, Donovan's was leading, Jim's was repairing wagons. If an afternoon of digging saved breaking out the hoists to repair a broken wheel or two then it made his job easier in the end.

"I suppose so," Jim only said.

Donovan's smile widened. "And you as well Jim." He turned to the Webbs then. "Paul, would you christen this new road our friends have made for us."

Paul Webb, smiled in return, and eased his team slowly down. The wagon creaked and tilted a little but made it down safe enough.

Jim mounted the roan. His back, shoulders, and arms all hurt, and it was good to be in the saddle again.

"Next wagon is just a few minutes back. Moses, will you do me the honor of guiding them in?" Donovan said.

"I surely will," the old man grinned and stood up a little straighter.

"Let's go scout out the opposite shore," Donovan said to Jim.

They left the proud old man on duty at the notch and followed the Webbs down toward the crossing.

"Good idea to get him away from his whiskey," Donovan said when they were alone. "Though he'll be angrier than a hornet when he finds out what I did."

"And what was that?"

"After you rode off with Moses and Neill, I decided to inspect the Martin's wagon. The old man had three more bottles hidden in his rucksack. I took them all in the name of culling dead weight off the Martin's load."

"You didn't put them in our wagon for Neill to find?"

"Course not. I divyed them up between some of the others. Men I could trust not to get drunk."

"I feel bad for the Martins," Jim said.

"Good."

Jim gave the caravan leader a sideways look. "Good? How is that good? That mean old man will give them fits."

"Yes, good. Because you'll need to keep Moses busy the next week or so until the mad wears off."

"Now wait a minute, Donovan. You can't..."

"You just said he'd raise hell with his kinfolk and you did good keeping him away all day. Might as well keep it on going."

"I didn't sign on to watch after an old cuss all day," Jim said.

"No, you signed on to watch after a whole caravan of people. And people are the hardest animals in the world to watch after. They'll stick their hands in a hole just to see if there's a rattlesnake inside."

Jim thought for a minute. "So this is what being a caravan leader is all about? Watching after people?"

"That's what a great many things are about. Ohh, to be sure there's more to it. You have to have some knowledge of the route, of how to survive in the wilderness, of when to run or when to fight. But mostly it's about herding men and women in the same direction."

"Did you herd me into taking Moses along today and keeping both he and Neill out of trouble while you ransacked their whiskey?"

Donovan smiled again and his eye gleamed. "Well I hoped you'd think of something, and after you did I decided to seize an opportunity."

Jim and Donovan crossed the river; the cold water rose to their horse's hocks at the deepest.

"Bitter cold, but usually the water is another foot higher," Donovan commented.

The Webbs had their wagon just ahead. It groaned as they climbed out of the river back up onto the flatland. Jim saw a few marks where someone—Neill it must have been—had done a little digging of his own to make the climb easier.

Jim frowned. It hadn't occurred to him that Neill might have ridden ahead to dig out an easier path out. *Maybe I underestimated him too.*

Neill himself waited at the top, rifle slung over his shoulders nonchalantly. "Something you should see."

Jim and Donovan dismounted and followed him ahead over a little rise into a charred area about an acre in size. In the center was a sad heap of black timbers and boards. Neill picked up a loose board, turned it over in his hands, then passed it to Donovan.

The caravan leader eyed the board carefully and handed it along to Jim.

Familiar with the making of wagons as he was, Jim knew exactly where this particular board went. It was the back of a wagon seat. This one had burned less than the others, it either fell clear of the fire, or had been protected somehow. There were two round holes in it, both together, both on one side, just where a driver might have been sitting.

Jim flipped the board over; the holes didn't go all the way through.

"Renegades," Jim said.

"Why'd you say that?" Donovan asked. "Could have been Indians."

"Two bullets, well-aimed," Jim said. "Plus I don't know why Indians would burn the wagon."

"Anger, hate," Donovan said. "We're killing the buffalo. Ending their whole way of life really."

"Maybe, but I'd still say renegades," Jim answered. He looked at the rest of the wreckage, picking up a few stray boards. "I don't see any arrows or scars where an arrow might have struck. No sign of anything but bullets."

Neill gave Donovan a slight nod and Jim felt he'd just passed some sort of unspoken test. *Both of them reached the same conclusion. They were wondering if I could figure it out for myself.*

Jim stepped away from the burned wagon. Nearby there was a place where the grass had been pressed out. There he found a porcelain doll head. A child's toy. He picked it up and wiped gritty dirt and ash from the doll's face with his thumb. The left half of the face hand been fire blackened. He saw more places in the grass where something lay. He stepped closer. Bones. Bleached-white bones lay scattered all over. Coyotes or wolves had gnawed on most of them. The bones were small, delicate...like a—

Jim's stomach turned. He dropped the doll in disgust.

Donovan moved beside him and gave him a pat on the back. He looked at the bones and his face grew hard and still. "Let's get back to the trail. We have to get our people across safely."

"Will you tell them about this?" Jim asked.

"Yes," Donovan said. He picked up the doll and held it in his hands. Then he tucked it into his pocket. "They need to understand this is a dangerous undertaking. This is why we press them to keep together. This is why we're hard on them at times. This is why we keep them armed at all times."

Jim eyed the wagon and thought about the doll again. He thought about his friends, the Sides and Lily. In all the excitement of heading west to start a new life he'd forgotten about the dangers. Now he understood better why they'd chosen not to risk the trip.

Men had done this. White-men, not Indians, judging by the signs. What kind of men could do something like this?

How could anyone harm a child?

11

A week after they found the burned wagon, the caravan arrived at Fort Kearny. Jim considered the Fort dubiously. There were soldiers for sure, plenty of those, but by their dress almost half the people were civilians. Kearny had no wall nor much by way of fortifications. Other than a scattered cannon or two, it looked more like a small town than a proper army fort.

Donovan led them to the edge of town and arranged the wagons into a loose circle. That done, he gathered the settlers all together and stood over them on the tongue of the Webb's wagon.

"Folks, it's good to be here in the state of Nebraska."

A cheer rose up from the crowd and Donovan took a moment to bask in it.

"We've made good time on the trail and although the first few weeks were hard I'm happy to say that was three days fewer than my normal pace. Take some time in town, replace any supplies you need. Feed your stock well to get them ready for the long haul ahead of us. We've still got the hardest part of the journey to go, but it will all be worth it when you top that last hill and see California shining out below you like a ray of pure golden sunshine."

Another cheer, this one twice as loud.

"Please do me one favor folks, remember the advice I've given. Tempting as it may be, do not load down your wagons with any weight you don't need."

Donovan was looking at the Martins when he said the last. Moses dipped his head and shuffled his feet.

"Thank you all for listening," Donovan said. He hopped down off the wagon tongue and shook hands with Paul Webb and Milo Adams.

Jim and Remy started off toward the Fort with their horses. Donovan had given them their own shopping list, replacements for the wood they'd used repairing wagons, extra canvas, food, oats for their stock, a few boxes of ammunition, and other miscellaneous items.

There were two general stores in Kearny, Donovan said to use the farthest as the prices were usually better.

After they'd purchased the supplies, Jim helped Remy load the two horses and they started walking back toward the wagons. They passed by a number of the caravan travelers on the way through. Moses gave Jim a shameless grin while entering the Royal Oak Saloon. To Jim's surprise Neill wasn't with him. Maybe the Captain had already gone inside. Most of the other families had taken Donovan's advice about which store to use, but several contrary souls had gone to the closest.

One of those was David Barton. He stood out front, struggling to load a supply horse, not having any luck. The skittish animal kept stepping aside whenever David tried to put the pack on him.

"Go on ahead," Jim told Remy and handed over the reins to his own horse. Then he crossed the street to where David was struggling.

"He's surely set against carrying that pack," Jim said.

Breathing hard, David lowered the supplies onto the boardwalk. "Yes, yes he is."

"Mind if I look him over?"

"Be my guest," David panted.

Jim moved up beside the horse, patting his neck and making soothing noises. He slipped the blanket off him and turned it over. He laid the blanket over the hitching rail and ran his hands over it. As he suspected there was an old sandbur buried near the center.

"Had a burr under here," Jim said.

"I didn't know. That blanket is an old one," David said.

"Couldn't see it. I had to feel for it myself."

He picked the burr out with the point of his knife and put the blanket back in place. Then he lifted the supplies up and set them in place. With the burr removed, the horse never moved.

"He should be fine now," Jim said. He moved up to pat the horse's neck again and, without looking, held the reins out to one side for David. Then he felt soft, smooth fingers brush over his.

"Thank you," a woman said and took the offered reins.

Jim turned then and Ellen Barton stood watching him.

"Ohh, excuse me ma'am," he said and removed his hat. "I was thinking you were your father."

"He had to run back inside for the rest," she answered.

"Should I stay to help?" Jim said.

"We can manage," she answered hesitantly, "but he is very tired from the trail."

"I'll wait then," Jim said. He glanced quickly at Ellen then away. She was a beautiful, young woman and he had no business thinking of such things. He'd done his best to keep well clear of her during their journey. He went back to scratching the horse along the jawline to keep his mind off her.

"You like horses?" she said.

"I do. All animals really."

"Father said you were good with the oxen. I heard several of the other men talking about it too."

"I should hope so. Otherwise I wouldn't be much use on the trip."

"Mr. Webb said you cut the trail with a shovel where we crossed the river."

"It was Neill's idea, not mine," Jim said. "I only worked the shovel some."

He glanced at Ellen then. Her eyes were clear and bright and staring hard at him. He remembered the way she'd looked at him that first time back in Kansas. Back when he had the battered face. For a moment he forgot himself.

"How are you holding up?" he said.

"Well enough, I am young. Father is doing well enough, but he's very tired each night. Colton had been helping but lately he's off with some of the others."

Jim had seen Colton Barton spending more and more time with Pat Robeson and some of that rougher crowd.

"You don't come around our wagon much. Not since that one day when you told father how to steer the oxen better," Ellen said. "Why?"

"Your father has the hang of it now. There are others who need my help."

"I wish you'd come around more," she said. Then she suddenly looked at her feet. "Father could still use some help I mean."

"I will try."

She was silent for a time, but he could feel her eyes studying him. "Your face has healed up. You looked terrible that night of the meeting."

Jim couldn't help but grin. "Not fighting helps."

"Why did you do it?"

"The fighting? I needed the money to come west."

"But Mr. Donovan said we were all paying you. Why would you need more money?"

"He didn't really say you were paying me. He only said *I wasn't paying him* to ride along. I'm working for my passage helping you all. That's the deal we made. When we reach California I'll only have the money I brought with me to get a new start."

"I understand," Ellen said and nodded. "And what is it you plan to do in California?"

"I've got the last of it," David Barton announced from behind another pack of supplies.

"I'll help you get it loaded," Jim said and took the supplies from him. He put the second pack on the horse, lashing it down. "That should hold you until you reach camp."

"Thank you," David said. He looked from his daughter to Jim questioningly but neither spoke.

"I'll see you all back at camp," Jim said and replaced his hat.

At the camp, Donovan, Neill, and another man were sitting beside a fire, drinking coffee while Remy made dinner. The newcomer was a rough man, dressed in skins and with a cannon-like buffalo gun laying on a log beside him.

"Jim, this is Black Anders."

"Nice to meet you," Jim offered.

"Same," Black said. "And whatever Donovan tells you about me is guaranteed to be only half-true."

"Half-true is bad enough," Donovan grinned.

"You were telling us about the trail," Neil interrupted.

"It's clear ahead until the Rockies. Some snow left in the high places—Devil's Gate and Splitrock—but the winter was mild."

"Indians?" Neill asked.

"Quiet so far. Quiet enough to make my scalp itch. I wintered with the Shoshone near Soda Springs. There's talk in the lodges about Sioux raiding down the trail. I didn't see any sign of it."

"What about other trouble?" Donovan said. "We came across a burned wagon near the Platte. Had bullet holes in it. No sign of arrows."

"Can't say much about one wagon. Late last year though a group of renegades wiped out a whole train west of Chimney Rock."

"That close to Laramie? The soldiers would have had patrols."

"Patrols watching the north. Like I said there's been talk of Sioux trouble for eight or nine months now. The soldiers are riding thick around the Cheyenne river country, not watching the trail these days," the mountain man swirled his coffee then took a sip.

"You know who it was?" Neill asked.

Black nodded and stared into the cup. "Bill Knight's train."

Donovan swore.

Bill Knight. Jim knew the name if not the man himself. Around Independence he had a reputation as a good man, solid, dependable, cautious. Regard for him was nearly as high as for Donovan and the pair had been friends.

"And who leads the renegades?" Neill said.

Black licked his lips, clearly not liking the question. "You know I don't go for giving names Captain. I'm a neutral party. I don't need enemies like that. The Sioux and the Utes and those other tribes are trouble enough."

"But you do know?" Donovan said. "Bill Knight was a good man and I remember that was a rich outfit he started out with. He knew the stakes. He was planning on hiring a few guards right here in Kearny. If the renegades could take him they could take anybody."

"And what if the trouble started from within? What if his hired men were with the renegades?" Black studied the cup's contents again.

"You're saying the renegades planted men inside his own camp?" Jim asked.

Everyone looked at Black then, even Remy.

"I'm saying there were several men off that train that made it out unscathed. Only they never made it to California, nor did they have any notions of doing so."

"That would take brains to pull off. More than most renegades have. Who did you say their leader is?"

"I don't recall," Black scowled.

"Of course you do, old man. You remember every mountain you ever crossed, every desert you ever smelled, every stream you ever drank from. You know exactly," Neill said.

"And I've lived long enough to know not to drop no names," Black said. "I'll give you this though. You know him." He looked from Donovan to Neill and back again. "You both do and he is a bad one. One of the worst."

The trail driver and scout looked at each other.

"Slade," Donovan said.

"I didn't say it," Black grinned.

"How many men does he have?" Neill said.

"I'd say there's at least twenty and more all the time. Money draws them like flies to dung heaps," Black said. He stood and stretched then took up his rifle. "It's been good to see you boys, but I'll be moving along now. Sold my furs and the market's plum busted, but I got enough to feed myself another year. That's all I need."

"Don't suppose you'd hire on to protect the wagons?" Donovan said.

The mountain man laughed. He looked around at all the wagons. "I haven't lived this long by painting a big ole target on my back and tying in with a big haul like this."

"Ride careful old man," Neill said.

"You too, Captain. You too," Black said and was gone.

"Slade Cooper is as bad as they come," Neill said. "We could hire on a couple more men."

"And how will we tell the good ones from the bad? You heard what he said. Some of Bill's own turned on him." Donovan shook his head. "No, we've got to do this with what we have."

Jim considered the problem. The outlaws were obviously smart. Strike a few trains, get them to hire extra guards, and then put your own men posing as guards inside the train. You could attack from within and without.

"We can train the men we have," Neill said. "Teach them how to fight in an emergency. Practice forming the wagons into a real circle."

"Doesn't have to be just the men," Remy surprised them. "The women will want to fight too once they know the stakes."

"Both good ideas," Donovan said. "When we've got a few days between us and Kearny we'll start. Every night I want the wagons formed up into a ring. We'll lose time, but I don't see how we have any choice."

"Might want some extra ammunition," Jim said. "A few rifles too?"

"Tomorrow I'll get each of us another rifle along with a spare pistol," Donovan agreed.

Jim considered the situation. The four of them plus the men from the train, forty or so, against an unknown number of enemies. Enemies who could strike at the time or place of their choosing. It wasn't a situation he liked. He remembered the burned doll, the scattered bones near the wagon. There were a number of children along with the wagons. Ellen Barton had a little one. They would have to keep a good watch. He would not allow any renegade to harm a child.

ELLEN BARTON WATCHED Jim Heston approach their wagon with trepidation. *What did you expect silly? You did ask him to come check on you.* He'd only shown himself to be a man of his word. She should have expected no less.

In a strange way, Jim Heston reminded her of Clive. They were of the same size and build, both large, powerful men. From a distance, they seemed similar enough, but closer up the similarities quickly dropped away. Both seemed to appeal to people. Clive was smooth and polished, winning people over with charm, while Jim was earnest and forthright. Men looked to him for guidance and quiet assurance. His complete unawareness of it only made his appeal stronger.

Still there were differences. Wide differences. Clive would never have lowered himself to anything so mundane as repairing a wagon, but Jim seemed to enjoy the work. He'd shoveled open a notch in a hill back at the river to allow the wagons easier passage. Milo Adams had praised him for it, and Mr. Adams did not seem the sort of man to praise lightly.

On his tall horse, Jim circled their wagon and, for a moment, Ellen felt a fluttering in her chest. Would he just pass on by?

He slowed then reined in near her father and climbed down from the saddle to walk beside him. Another way he and Clive differed. Clive never had the time of day for her father.

Walt was walking beside her father, as was his habit. Ellen's heart swelled with pride in her son. Since they'd left Illinois, he hadn't complained once. If anything he buoyed their spirits with endless enthusiasm for the grand adventure. Jim shook Walt's small hand, then scooped him up, and set him on the horse. Then he started talking to her father again. Her father listened close and then laughed, a sound they'd all heard far too little of these days.

Ellen quickened her pace to move around the wagon and catch up to them. If Jim was giving him some advice about the team or the wagon she should hear it.

Father can be so forgetful.

"The team is coming along," Jim said.

"You think so? They don't seem any faster."

"Probably not. But they're pulling easier and they act more comfortable working together. They're healthy and fat. Ready for the big haul west."

"How much further do we have?"

"I'm not sure. This is my first time over the trail myself. Donovan says over a thousand miles."

"A thousand miles...It sounds so...far."

"We'll get there father," Ellen interrupted. "One step, one hour, one day at a time."

Jim smiled at her and his eyes shined. She felt lightheaded for a moment and looked away.

"You daughter is right of course. Just gotta be like the oxen, keep plodding on," Jim said.

"Look at me, mama," Walt said. "I'm on a real horse."

"Yes you are," Ellen said. "You look like a regular cowboy."

"Not a cowboy, mama. I'm an outlaw." Walt puffed out his chest.

Ellen's breath hung in her throat and she missed a step.

Jim's arm caught her before she could fall. "Are you alright?" he said. "Lots of holes out here."

"Fine, I'm fine." Ellen brushed a lock of stray hair from her face.

"Maybe you should take a turn on my horse," he said.

"Really, I think the sun just got to me," she protested. Her father gave her a worried look.

"What are those?" Walt said. He pointed off to their left toward several scrubby trees. Something very black and round was on the ground below them.

Jim squinted and said, "Wild turkeys looks like."

"We have turkey sometimes," Walt said.

"I do to. Should we go see about rustling one up for dinner?" Jim asked. "Of course outlaws don't get to hunt turkeys."

"They don't?" Walt's eyes grew.

"Outlaws just eat beans and old leather boots."

"Old boots?"

"Yes," Jim nodded. "They don't get to eat very good when they're running from the law. Scouts eat better though."

"Scouts do?"

"Scouts get to eat whatever they can shoot. Buffalo, deer, elk."

"Even turkey?"

"Turkey too. If they can get one."

"Mama," Walt said. "I want to be a scout."

"That would be better," Ellen smiled.

"Scouts have to learn a lot," Jim said. "Even I'm still learning."

"Even you Mr. Jim?"

"Even me. But I know a thing or two about wild turkeys. Should I show you?" Jim stopped to look at her.

"I don't know about," Ellen's father interjected.

"You'll listen to Mr. Jim?" Ellen said.

"Promise," Walt said.

"I'll take care of him," Jim said.

"Well then bring back a turkey and I'll cook it for you both."

"My mom is a good cook," Walt said to Jim. "She can cook anything."

Jim swung up behind Walt. "We'd better bring her a turkey then. I'd hate for her to cook old shoe leather for dinner."

They rode out in pursuit of the turkeys and Ellen watched them go.

"Is that wise?" her mother said from behind the wagon. "We don't know him."

"He seems honest enough," Ellen said.

Both her parents were frowning at her, and she felt a hint of fear. Had she really let a stranger take her son off? She turned to call out and stop them. Jim had his horse at a gallop and Walt held an arm out on either side, flapping his hands, and screaming in a child's pure joy. *No, I'm worried about nothing.* She'd look like a fool calling them back now, both to her family and to Jim.

Biting her lip, she went back to walking beside the wagon. "They'll be fine," she said and tried to believe it.

When they were closer the turkeys retreated into the trees with Jim and Walt plunging after them. Then they were both gone.

Ellen watched the spot they'd ridden into. Surely they couldn't hope to catch a turkey.

Seconds ticked by, then minutes, and soon her son was a half-hour gone. Ellen's neck hurt and she rubbed at it. Had Walt ever been away for so long? There had been times with her parents or a nanny at the estate. Overnight stays even. But certainly not with anyone else. How much did she really know about Jim Heston? He was from Texas, well-mannered enough, but crude in some areas. She was learning that most western men were the same. He was kind and helpful, both to her and her father when he'd needed help. What was he going to California for though? What drove him?

She turned again to look over her shoulder.

"Your neck is going to hurt if you keep doing that," her mother scolded. "If you weren't sure about him going you really should have stopped them."

Ellen frowned. Her mother was right of course; that was the worst of it. There was nothing to do now but worry and hope for the best. Walt would be fine. Eyes front again, she noticed a rider approaching from ahead. For a minute she thought it was Walt and Jim, but the man was too wide and the horse a different color.

Donovan reined in beside her father and climbed down.

"David, have you seen Jim? Milo Adams said he saw him headed this way."

"He was here earlier. He took my grandson hunting after some wild turkey," Ellen's father pointed to the trees.

Ellen's heart jumped up into her throat. She glanced protectively around for Walt before realizing he was gone. "Is there something wrong?"

"Wrong, ma'am?" Donovan's bushy eyebrows rose. He shook his

head. "No. Not at all. Nothing for you to worry about. I just need to see him is all."

Donovan lowered his voice and moved in closer to her father to keep whatever was said between the two of them. Ellen strained to overhear.

She didn't believe the trail driver. Something was happening. Her son was missing and now their leader was here looking for the man Walt had ridden off with. There had been talk of renegades back at the Fort. Men who seized wagons and took what and who they wanted. Some of the others hadn't believed it.

"No, it must have been the Sioux," they argued. White men, civilized men wouldn't do such a thing. And now the danger was past. The Sioux were gone. All up on their reservation far away. Men who were otherwise perfectly sensible did not want to face the danger, to believe it was real.

Ellen understood them though. *Sleep comes easier if you believe the trouble is far away, instead of just outside a piece of stretched canvas.* She remembered the burned wagon. Someone had died there, never to reach the promised land of California. Sioux or not, an evil man had ended their trail. She knew all about evil men. She'd been married to one.

A whooping yell came from behind them then, and Ellen felt her heart quicken. She balled up her fists. If renegades came she would not go quietly, not ever again. They would have to kill her.

Only it wasn't renegades, it was a lone man with a boy riding ahead of him. The boy held a dead turkey by the neck and was screaming in triumph.

They slowed into a trot and fell in beside the wagon.

"Look mama," Walt held out the turkey.

"I see it," Ellen wiped a tear from her eye.

"No need to cry mama," Walt said. "We were respectful to the turkey's spirit. Jim taught me to...to..."

"Honor it," Jim said.

"I was just worried that's all," Ellen said. She tried to force a smile.

"Yes, your mama was just worried about you," Ellen's mother said. She patted Ellen on the back then squeezed her shoulders.

Jim swung down first, then lifted Walt and his prize clear.

"Why that must be the biggest gobbler I've ever seen," Donovan said.

"I shot it myself," Walt said. "Only Jim held the gun for me. It kicked though." He rubbed at his shoulder.

"His arm might be a little sore tomorrow, but he shot true," Jim added. He looked at Ellen and she could tell he was confused by her tears.

Donovan knelt down beside Walt to shake his hand. "Young man by the time we reach California you'll be leading this train instead of me."

"Walt, take him to Uncle Colton and have him help you pluck him," Ellen's mother said.

Walt scuffed his boot toe in the dirt. "Uncle Colton only wants to play with that new gun of his. He doesn't have time to play with me anymore."

"Then take it to Aunt Martha."

Ellen caught the end of a look between Donovan and Jim, something passed unsaid, it involved the news that Colton had bought a new gun.

"Thank you for bringing him back," Ellen told Jim.

Jim dipped his hat to her but didn't have any words.

"Let's go check on the other wagons," Donovan said. "I need to show you something."

"You'll come to our fire for dinner tonight?" Ellen said. "Both of you, of course."

Jim started to answer but Donovan jumped in. "Much as we'd both like to we have another matter to deal with."

They both mounted up then and walked their horses back toward the end of the wagon train. Neither looked back. Had something she said or done offended them? She'd only been crying with worry over her son, surely they could understand a mother's concern.

No, that didn't make sense. Something had caused Donovan to

come hunting after Jim, and whatever it was would keep them busy tonight.

THE EVENING after Jim took Walt to shoot the turkey, Donovan called an early stop and started forming their circle of wagons each night. He told the families it was a precaution against Indians, but that there were rumors of bad white men as well.

Several protested. The cost of caution, of delay was high and they knew it; taking time to form the circle meant losing at least a mile every day. It would take them a lot longer to reach California. When they were gathered up Donovan reminded them of the looted wagon. He took out the burned doll from his pocket. He held it out for them to see. None of them wanted to look too close at the charred toy. Jim saw mothers clutch their children just a little tighter. Their resolve steeled, though there were still grumbles about the army not protecting them.

A week out of Fort Kearny Jim was scouting ahead when he saw her. Just shy of noon, he topped a rise and saw someone walking alone towards him. He looked again. It was a woman. She was tall, maybe as tall as he himself was, built thick enough not to be gangly, and her long strides showed purpose.

Jim slowed his horse to an easy walk and studied the surrounding country. What was a woman doing out here in no-man's land? The flat prairie stretched for miles here. No sign of anything but grass swaying in the wind.

How did Neill miss her? The scout should have been miles ahead, and he would have seen a woman alone out here.

She looked up and saw him then, paused a bit and only watched them, then she kept on. She did not wave or give any sign that she'd seen him.

Jim started his horse towards her. The lead wagon would be less than a mile back.

Drawing closer, he saw she wore a man's plaid shirt, loose, but tucked into a pair of buckskin pants. Except for a menacing longknife in her belt, she seemed unarmed.

"Ma'am," he said when she was close. "Are you lost?"

"Water?" she said in a rough voice.

Jim took the canteen off his saddle and passed it to her. She uncorked it and took several gulps. The last one she swirled around in her mouth, closed her eyes, then swallowed. A few drops tricked down over her pale face and neck into her shirt.

"Might want to go easy on that if you haven't had any in awhile," Jim offered.

She opened one bright green eye to study him up-and-down, Then she took off her hat, shook her head once, and a cascade of flame-red hair swept halfway down her back. She was older than he'd first thought, a few years older than himself. When she spoke this time her voice was smooth as aged whiskey.

"I am not lost," she said.

"There's not much out here. Nothing except Indians."

"I haven't seen any of those. My brother and I started west and had some trouble."

"Your brother?"

"Jake, and I am Lou, short for Louise, we were bound for California and our wagon broke down. We could use some help." She smiled and her teeth were white and even. Jim felt his face redden. If she noticed her smile only widened.

Jim pointed over his shoulder "There's a whole caravan of wagons coming up behind me. We can help with your wagon. How far back do you think it was?"

She shaded her eyes with one hand. "Not far. Three or four miles."

"A long way for you to walk," Jim said.

"Not so far," she smiled again. "I have very long legs."

"Our caravan should make that before dark." Jim offered her a hand. "Climb up and we can ride back to the wagons for help."

"I wouldn't accept a ride from a stranger," she said.

"I am Jim Heston from San Antone."

"I am Lou Archer from all over."

Then she took his arm and sprang up into the saddle behind him. Jim felt her breasts against his back; her thighs around his own. Her legs were long. She slipped her hands around his stomach and the warm feeling in his face passed through his body.

He swung his horse around and started back.

Riding beside the lead wagon, Donovan spotted them first. Jim reined in between the wagon master and the Webbs.

"Mrs. Webb this is Lou Archer, she and her brother had some wagon trouble. Would you have some grub for her? She's probably thirsty as well."

"Of course," Mrs. Webb said, and their wagon rolled to a stop.

While Mrs. Webb started fussing over Lou, Donovan and Jim rode off to discuss the situation.

"Where did you find *her*?" Donovan said. He was watching the redhead with interest.

"Less than a mile ahead. She was just out walking alone, no gun, no canteen, no nothing. Said her brother is with their wagon ahead."

The Webbs were both fussing over Lou now. Mrs. Webb offering her a washbasin and a small towel. Paul was digging through a pack.

Donovan watched her rinse out her long hair, "That there is one fine woman. If you can find one of those every time you ride out ahead scouting I'll replace Neill tomorrow."

"Where is Neill anyway? He couldn't have missed her."

"Too true," Donovan rubbed at his chin. "I suspect he's back of the line again."

"The Martin's?"

"A-huh," Donovan said. The trail driver studied Lou like a mountain lion might study an injured doe.

"Should we go check on him?" Jim said. He could certainly see Lou's appeal. He remembered only too well the feel of her pressed up against him, her warm breath hissing over his bare neck. He moved his horse between Donovan and the Webb's wagon. "Both of us."

Donovan coughed and shook himself as if waking from a dream. "Both of us what?"

"Both of us should go check the Martin wagon for Neill?"

"No, I'll go. You ride ahead and see about her brother. Don't get too far ahead though."

Jim watched Donovan slowly turn his horse back toward the rear of their strung-out column. He spurred his own horse out toward the west.

12

Clive Wilson came home to a silent house.

"Ellen," he called through the doorway. "I am home."

Only silence greeted him. The place lay abandoned. Cobwebs hung in ghostly strands from framed pictures along the walls.

Room-by-room, he searched the house. The great old manor lay dark and silent as an abandoned tomb. His hired servants were gone. Where was Ellen? Where was his son? At her parent's house he was certain. *She must have taken Walt over there.* How long since he'd seen them last? He had been gone well over a month now. The Southern Queen's capture took far longer than he'd planned. It wasn't the first time he'd been gone for so long. It didn't matter. He would finish his business with Beau and Chet then swing by to collect Walt and her.

Clive frowned and looked down an empty hall. Ellen should not have left their home unattended. He would teach her the error of her ways after he brought his family home.

He returned to the front door, ready to head out for the warehouse where he was certain Beau and Chet would be. In the open yard, his cousin, Thomas, waited for him with a rifle.

"I thought it might be you," Thomas said and lowered the rifle muzzle.

"Where is everyone?"

"Gone. Near as I can tell they left out of here almost a month ago."

"Gone?" Clive's fists clenched until his knuckles cracked. "They aren't at Ellen's parents?"

"No one took them. The Barton place is empty too. Whole lot of them packed up and left, your wife and son went along with them."

"Ellen...leave me?" Clive laughed. Impossible. She couldn't. How could his little mouse of a wife ever leave him? What would she do? She had been nothing when he married her and made her the Queen of his growing empire. Why would she go back to her poor little family?

"She is gone," Thomas said.

Gone...Clive's vision blurred. He slammed his huge fists onto the door. The hinges rattled under the impact. He slammed them down again, again, again. *How dare she. How dare she take my son away.* Did she not know who he was? He was Clive Wilson. His family-owned Illinois. How could she think he'd let her take his son?

Finally, he gave the door a final slam and turned from the door to his cousin.

"Where is she?" he growled.

Thomas licked his lips. "They left here headed south. I tracked them down to the main road then lost their tracks."

"What did the neighbors say?"

"The neighbors—"

"You did ask them. Didn't you?"

"None of them knew anything. They might have been lying of course."

"Then arrest them," Clive said.

"Arrest them for what?"

"You're the Sheriff, think of something. But arrest them and bring them here, their neighbors, their friends, the shopkeeper who sold them supplies, my servants, anyone who might know," Clive said. He held up a fist. "I will ask them myself. We will see how much they know."

"That could draw attention," Thomas cautioned.

Clive sneered at his cousin. Thomas had plans—big plans—for his future. He wanted a position in the legislature, then the Governor's mansion, Senator even. None of that would be possible though if they knew about Clive's business on the river, a business Thomas took a healthy cut of in exchange for his protection.

"Listen to me, little cousin. I am going down to the warehouse to clear up a few matters of my own, and when I return I want someone here who can tell me where my wife took my son."

"That could be difficult."

"As difficult as your future might be if our business on the river came to light?"

Thomas's eyes narrowed. "You'd ruin yourself and me along with you over some simple girl? It would destroy the whole family."

"No, you not doing your job would destroy the family. You should have kept an eye on her while I was gone."

"I can't watch over your affairs," Thomas said. "That isn't my job."

"Then you should have hunted after her once you knew she left."

"Hunted where? There wasn't much of a trail. They were at least a week gone when I found out."

Clive grabbed his cousin by the shirtfront and dragged him close. "You will find out where they went or I will, and you can wave goodbye to your political future." He threw Thomas back and his cousin fell sprawling in the dirt.

Clive climbed up on his horse and spurred him into a quick run for his warehouse. He would finish his business with Beau and Chet, then he would return to see what Thomas found. After that he would have a long, painful reunion with his wayward wife. Her family would have to be punished as well.

I want this lesson to sink in deep, to her very bones even.

They would then return to the estate and all would be as it should.

THE WAREHOUSE AIR stank of dust and stagnant water when Clive arrived. With most of his men now jailed or scattered to the winds no one had aired the place out in weeks. Small waves lapped at the wood in a steady rhythm and a chorus of frogs sang in the deep of night.

Years ago he had hired a pair of old men to keep watch on the place. Mostly they drank and fished off the long dock. Clive had never seen them catch anything, but they performed their job well enough.

They were gone at this late hour of course. It was well after midnight.

There were several doors to the warehouse's interior. He took one of the smallest, on the north side. Inside, the warehouse wasn't much, a single long room, several stalls and bays, mostly empty, a few long aisles. The freight business, legitimate or otherwise, had been slow these last years. Shipments were quickly moving to the rail. The heyday of the river was at an end. The rails would take over. Oh there would always be some movement on the big muddy. Heavy cargoes, hard to move, hard to steal, and all of little worth.

Soon enough Clive would have to find other ways to turn a profit.

A pair of oil lanterns hung on pegs beside the door; he left them as they were. He didn't need the light. He knew his own warehouse like he knew his own face. He crept along in the dark toward the waterfront. His office was there, a walled-off section. A light shone inside where there should have been none.

Beau and Chet. Despite the delays and obstacles his timing had been perfect.

He still carried the pistol he'd taken along the river, plus a second one he'd picked up at home and tucked into his leather belt. Hoisting the first up to his shoulder, he crept closer.

"How do we open it?" Chet's voice, loud and blunt, came from ahead.

"I stole a look at the combination one day over his shoulder," Beau answered in his nasal tone. "I been waitin for this ever since."

Clive was at the doorway. His former employees had their backs to him. Beau was leaned down studying the shining dial on his safe. Chet stood behind him and a little to the left. Clive smiled. *I couldn't have asked for a better opportunity.* Slowly, he rose to his full height.

Clive drew the second gun and thumbed both hammers back with a pair of deadly clicks.

"You'll have to wait a lot longer," he said and fired.

Most of his focus was on Chet; the big man would prove the more serious threat. His bullet took Chet squarely in the back, an inch right of his spine and just above the waist. The big man jerked to the side and started to fall. The bullet intended for Beau took the smaller man along the arm, ricocheting off the safe, splintering the floorboards.

Like a frightened rabbit, Beau bounced up. He leaped through one of the framed windows to land in the warehouse proper. The crackle of shattering glass echoed through the office.

Clive's attention shifted back to Chet. His former lieutenant managed to draw his own pistol but was slow to bring the gun into line. Clive was not. He squeezed off another shot.

A round, black hole appeared in Chet's chest, and the big man's gun fumbled to the floor.

Footsteps, quick and running, came from inside the empty warehouse. Clive spared a second to put a third round into Chet, this one into the fallen man's face, and then he was out of the office running after Beau. The wiry man could not be allowed to escape. Judging by the noise he was heading for the back of the warehouse and one of the bigger cargo doors.

Clive's own steps rattled the floor like summer thunder. He heard Beau curse—the door had been barred for the night—and then the sound of the wooden bar being removed.

The door swung open then and Clive caught Beau's silhouette against the moonlit night. His guns stabbed flame. One shot missed completely, but the second landed with a telltale whump.

Beau cried out and fell.

Slowing his pace, Clive approached the fallen man.

"You shot me," Beau said. Blood ran from his side and the bullet burn along his arm.

"No more than you tried to do to me."

Trying to forestall the end, Beau raised a bloody hand. "Listen,

Clive, it was Chet's idea. All of it. He threatened me. Said if I didn't go along with him he'd kill me."

"I don't care." Clive raised a pistol, taking his time to aim.

"Please Clive, there's a big score down in—"

The gun roared and Beau's right eye exploded.

"No more big scores for you, Beau," Clive said.

He stooped down and took hold of the dead pirate and dragged him into the office with Chet. Clive opened the safe, withdrew the contents, four thousand dollars in total, and closed it up again. He took the lantern his former associates had used and smashed it on the floor. The oil lit instantly, flaring up, hot and yellow. Clive backed out of the office and headed outside.

The decision had been made quickly, but he trusted his instincts. The river was dying and with it his ability to steal what he needed to support his lifestyle. Perhaps his mousey wife had the right idea, head to California and greener pastures. The goldfields there were supposed to be rich. He wouldn't dig for it himself though. He didn't need to.

Gold will be easy enough to steal.

He could follow her out West, do business for a year or two, then return to Illinois with his son in triumph. All he had to do was find Ellen.

For his cousin's sake, he hoped Thomas had found something useful.

A LONE, white-topped wagon stood in a wide basin beneath the bright springtime sun. The wagon faced east, the wrong direction for California. So they'd become lost at some point. The wind blew warm, and it struck Jim suddenly that the weather had somehow crept up on them. The grass around the wagon shone the bright green of new spring.

Jim took a moment to watch the wagon before riding on down.

Other than the mules, there was no sign of life anywhere. White canvas rippled and popped taut in the breeze. The stock remained harnessed; they'd stripped the young grass—all of it within reach—down into bare brown dirt. Jim lifted his pistol clear, checked the cylinders, eased it back into the holster. He walked his horse up at a slow walk, keeping his eyes moving, searching for any sign of danger.

At his approach the team looked up. They were hungry—in good shape—young and strong and well-fed.

Still fifty yards out, Jim circled wide around the wagon. He paused when he could see into the covered back.

If Lou's brother, Jake, was concerned about Indians or renegades he showed no sign of it. The man's legs dangled over the back of the wagon while he lay sleeping in the shade.

Jim scowled. Lou's brother had stayed here resting while his sister walked for help. If trouble had come along and scalped him, the man certainly would have deserved it.

Jim stood up his stirrups and peered inside. There didn't seem to be much resemblance between Lou and her brother. Jake was dirty, with black scraggly hair, a sunburnt face, and a thin mustache. He wore a shirt that might have been blue once, but now seemed brown, caked with dust and dirt as it was. His pants had holes in them as did the sole of his left boot. Only his gunbelt looked new. The pistol within shone bright with polish.

Unsure of how to wake the man, Jim cleared his throat. Jake came awake with a start and the gun was suddenly in his fist but pointed in the wrong direction. Jim's own gun had him covered. He froze, looking at Jim and the drawn pistol with wild, angry eyes.

"Your sister sent me," Jim said. "You are John aren't you?"

"Jake, I'm Jake," the man said.

"My mistake," Jim let out a breath. The man had drawn that pistol almighty fast; he might have fired if Jim didn't have his own gun covering him.

"Lou found help then? A wagon train?" Jake licked his lips and lowered his pistol. His eyes never left Jim's own gun though.

Jim holstered his weapon, "She did. The train's a couple miles back but heading this way. They'll pass through north of here maybe a mile or two."

Jake smiled. "She's a good girl."

"Seemed awful tough. Walking like that."

"Tough?" Jake's smile widened. "You have no idea."

"What's the trouble with your wagon?"

"Yoke's busted in half. The stub end just plows the ground," Jake answered.

Jim grunted. He'd seen the marks and guessed as much.

"Let's see about a fix then you can roll north and meet up with the wagon train," he said.

Jake dropped down from the wagon while Jim climbed out of the saddle. He followed Jim up to the team. The break was clean through and near the front.

"If we take this end off and shorten the team it won't drag," Jim said.

"We'll have two less mules then?" Jake said.

"Yes, but making a short run like this won't be a problem. You aren't loaded heavy. You can also rotate the spare mules in-and-out to rest the others."

Jim set about repairing the wagon as best he could. Jake was little help. But for rolling the occasional cigarette, the man seemed useless with his hands. He carried and fetched whatever Jim asked for, but otherwise seemed content to stand beside the wagon, watch, and smoke.

If it hadn't been for the woman, Jim would have left the man to his own affairs. It was what he deserved. By mid-afternoon the wagon was usable. Jim tied the two spare mules to the back. He climbed onto his own horse.

"You should make it now," he said.

Jake squinted up at him, "You're leaving?"

"I'll scout ahead and get you pointed in the right direction."

With that he rode north at a quick trot, eager to put some distance between himself and Jake. He couldn't say why he didn't like the man, but he had a feeling about him. The only skill the man had showed was with the pistol. He'd been quick with it.

Very quick.

As soon as he cleared the little basin, Jim spurred his horse into a gallop riding northeast. The flatness of the plains proved misleading. Rolling hills and shallow gullies rippled the land, any one of which could be hiding wagons or enemies alike.

Jim topped a hill—one a little taller than the others—where he could see better. He saw a rising trail of dust to the east. Only wagons could have made so much. He could wait here. If Donovan kept them on the same heading they would pass the base of the hill he'd chosen. A single rider was off to his right.

Captain Neill.

Donovan must have found the man, likely drinking with his new friend, Moses, in the last wagon.

Something needed to be done about that. It was Donovan's problem, but where Neill was concerned the wagon master tended to step lightly and use others to keep him in line. What history held two men like Donovan and Neill together?

Donovan had told him they crossed over the trail together. Had several times in fact. Jim admitted that—when sober—Neill made a good outrider. The man knew his business. Twice he'd found easy river crossings. He brought back meat every two or three days, and Neill could track better than anyone he'd ever seen. None of that explained why Donovan put up with so much from the man. When Neill worked, he did a good job. But he only worked occasionally.

His condition wasn't helped by old Moses. Moses shared his liquor a little too freely with Neill. For a time, Jim's ploy had kept them apart, but after Fort Kearny, Moses had restocked his bottles and their evening friendship resumed.

Neill was close now. He waved and Jim returned it. The Captain swung right and joined him on the hill.

"Good view from up here," Neill offered.

"Not bad," Jim said. "Lou's brother is off toward the south. He should be heading our way."

"A-huh," Neill nodded. "Something odd about that situation. Did you learn anything?"

"He doesn't know a thing about wagons. He was sound asleep in the back when I showed up and his stock hadn't been fed or watered. Even had the wagon heading in the wrong direction."

"Sounds awful casual what with renegades around and all that," Neill said.

"I wouldn't push him," Jim cautioned. "He's touchy and quick with that pistol of his. Awful quick."

Neill said, "Good to know."

"Donovan found you?"

"I was helping the Martins."

"A-huh."

If the answer made Neill uncomfortable, the scout didn't show it. Downwind as he was, Jim smelled the whiskey on him. *The man must sweat the stuff.*

Donovan rode over a swale below and spurred his horse to join them. "Did you find her brother?"

"I did," Jim said. "He's heading this way now."

"You left him?" Donovan shook his head. "She's awful worried about him."

"He's a man grown, not wet behind the ears."

"Jim said he's handy with his pistol," Neill interrupted. "Said he was sleeping in back of the wagon when Jim found him. Not a care at all."

"I fixed his wagon for him. He's only got four mules pulling now, but it was loaded light. Should be here anytime," Jim said.

"You should have stayed with him," Donovan said. "Now I'll have to tell Lou you lost her brother. She's been worried sick about him."

The Webb's wagon rolled up below them.

"Start the circle here," Donovan bellowed. He regarded Jim and there was a glint of anger in his eye. "I'll go find her brother then. You can get these wagons into line."

Donovan spun his horse around then and rode hard for their own wagon. Lou sat on the front seat, that mane of red hair lifting in the wind. Remy was down, walking near the lead ox.

Lou waved to Donovan as he approached. Jim noticed how their leader suddenly sat up just a little straighter in the saddle.

"He's surely struck," Neill said. "The damned fool."

"He's just helping her out," Jim replied. He gave Neill a hard glare. "We all have our little problems."

"But not you eh?" Neill gave him a half-smile. "Young men always think they have all the answers. Someday though they'll know what it's like growing old, having nothing but broken dreams, a cold bed, and a few bits to rub together. That's if they don't come across some other hot-blooded young man first. One who draws a little quicker or shoots a little straighter. I suppose even the Sioux have their arrogant young men."

"Good thing we have so many old men along to guide and teach us then," Jim snapped.

Neill grinned. "Teaching young men takes time. They need experience. Reading sign out here for instance. If you think deep about your new friends, Jake and Lou, you could reach some interesting conclusions."

Neill started off then, heading toward the back of the train. *No doubt to find Moses and share a warm bottle.*

Jim had nothing to say. Nothing that would improve the situation. He watched Donovan swoop by their wagon, exchange a few words with Lou, and then trot off to the south.

Sighing, Jim rode down to meet with the Webbs and get them lined up in on a flat patch of ground. With so many wagons it took a large area to get them into a defensible circle.

By nightfall he was finally finishing up. Last once again, the Martins had fallen even farther behind. Neill was no help of course, but despite Jim's expectations, he wasn't with Moses. Neill had ridden off at dusk, alone and without a word or explanation. More confusing yet, Moses did not have a bottle himself tonight. The old man looked at Jim with serious eyes as he ran his hands over a long black Sharps buffalo gun.

Jim finished with the Martins wagon and by the time he reached his own Remy had dinner on. Potatoes, carrots, deer flank, a few onions all boiled up in a stew together. A pan of Dutch-oven biscuits sat off to the one side, cooling. Jim snatched one free. Fresh as they were, his fingers burned, and he blew on the biscuit to cool it.

"Hot," he barked.

"Serves you right," Remy grinned. "Those just came from the fire."

Deciding to risk it, Jim bit off a chunk. Immediately, he regretted it. His mouth burned like he'd bit into a hot coal; he puffed air around it, desperate for relief, and too hungry to just spit it out. The day had been a long one—every day out here was—but this one in particular had been bad. He drew a ladle of water from the bucket. The water, warm though it was, cooled the burning biscuit down almost immediately.

"That was entertaining," Remy's smile grew. "Next you'll be breathing fire."

"What?" Jim said around his second bite.

"My Pa took me to a carnival once. There was a man there who could breathe fire. He'd open his mouth and flames would shoot out. Must have been two or three feet long and blazing like a furnace."

Jim considered that for a moment. "I wouldn't say your cooking is that bad. In fact I like it just fine."

Remy laughed.

"How did he do it? Breath fire like that."

"Before he did it, he took a drink from a bottle of some kind. My Pa said it was some kind of spirit. Then he'd spit the liquid out over a flaming torch, and it would ignite." Remy shrugged. "Anyway it was just a trick he'd learned."

"What did you think of your rider?" Jim asked.

"Lou?" Remy said. His cheeks reddened. "Seems nice enough. Good to talk to anyway."

"Yeah?"

"Wanted to know all about us, the wagons, how many of us there were. Just making conversation like."

"Where'd she get off to?"

"She went to eat with the Webbs, I think. Probably sick of talking to a kid like me anyway."

"I doubt that," Jim smiled. "She'll be sore once she finds out she missed out on the best food in the train."

Remy's cheeks brightened again until even his ears were red.

"When we get there, to California, I mean. I'm going to open a restaurant. Right on the seashore. Hire me a few women to help out, serving food and the like. And some afternoons I'll close up early and just walk down to the water and watch the sun go down. They say it melts right down into the Pacific, slipping slowly away." He faced Jim squarely. "That's what I want. My own place where I can serve good food and watch the sunset."

"Sounds pretty good," Jim agreed.

A noise came from outside the circle. The rattle of a wagon and team approaching, horses too. Jim stood and saw Donovan, getting down. His face was haggard and dirty, but he smiled like he'd just won a thousand dollars.

Donovan spotted Jim. "Tell Lou I've brought her brother in."

"She's over at Webb's. Opposite side of the circle," Jim answered.

"What?" Donovan let out an exasperated breath. "I thought for sure she'd be here."

"Is that grub I smell?"

Jim recognized the voice as Jake's. After doing the man's work all day he was in no mood to share a meal with him. Before he could protest though, Jake was around the wagon and hunkering over the fire. He had two biscuits scooped up in his left hand and was eating them like a man possessed.

"You aren't going to see to your team?" Jim asked.

"Later," Jake answered around a mouthful.

Those mules had been hitched for a minimum of two full days. They'd have sores where the leather rubbed, he'd already seen several. They didn't deserve such treatment. It galled him. Still, he wasn't willing to do more of Jake's work.

Donovan joined them at the fire. He took his hat off and brushed at his hair. "She really isn't here?"

"Over at Webb's," Jim pointed.

Donovan's head swiveled in that direction. "I'd better get over there and let her know about her brother." He tugged his hat back on, eyed Jake in a brief moment of disgust, and then spun on his heels before marching off across the open space.

Jim could only stare after his friend. Neill had been right. *He has gone plumb loco.*

"No coffee?" Jake said and interrupted his thoughts.

"Just getting it on," Remy said.

"Not ready yet?" Jake said. "What kind of wagon train is this?"

Jim ignored them and went to his blankets. The sky was clear, the stars shone down bright, and he didn't see any chance of rain so he turned in as far from the newcomer as he could.

Laying down, he considered what Remy had said. *A restaurant by the sea. Sounds a lot better than me working myself to the bone out on some ranch or scratching gold up out of the ground.*

Still he would have his ranch and it would be his own. It might take time, but eventually he'd get there. Then he too could enjoy a sunset only his would be looking out over his growing cattle and horses. All he had to do was reach California.

With that, he slipped off into sleep.

What felt like moments later, the nudge of a boot woke him. Jim swore and rolled over to see Neill sitting on his haunches by the fire, sipping coffee.

"Did you just boot me in the ribs?" Jim said from his blankets.

"I did," Neill spoke over his coffee.

"What time is it?" The stars were still out and there wasn't so much as a hint of light in the east.

"Three hours to dawn," Neill stood then. "We've got a ways to ride today."

"We do?"

"Yes, I had a hunch and followed it last night. But now I need someone to watch my back. Too dangerous alone."

Jim tugged on his boots. "You cleared it with Donovan?"

The Captain shrugged. "More or less."

"And that means?"

"It means I told him what I was doing, and I told him you were coming with me and I told him it was important."

Fully dressed now, Jim stood. He looked Neill in the eye. For the first time in days, the man's eyes shone clear and bright, without a hint of whiskey.

Neill stood slowly and tossed the dregs of his coffee into the hot coals. "We're goin for a scout."

13

E llen rose early, as was her habit, and coaxed the fire alight. She filled a heavy pot with water for brewing coffee. Though early, she was far from alone. Several other women were up and, in the clear morning air, she heard the clanging of their pots as they too began their morning chores.

She wrapped her cloak tight around her. Though Mr. Donovan assured them the danger of snow was long past, mornings on the plains were quite crisp and her exhaled breath made a wispy white fog that the wind carried away.

The wind. There was always the wind. It was the one constant in their journey. Some days even the sun lost its way in the high clouds. But though it might change direction, the wind was always there. It ebbed and flowed. Sometimes powerful enough to whip and pop the thin canvas and cause her father to tie a strap around his hat, other times it gentled down to a whisper. There were no trees to offer relief; the short gently rolling hills did not blunt its bite.

By chance they'd ended up two wagons down from the one Jim Heston shared with Mr. Donovan, Captain Neill, and young Remy, their driver. Ellen smiled to herself. Perhaps it wasn't all luck. Remy had been making eyes at Martha the last few weeks. Ellen caught them walking together once or twice after the wagons had formed their nightly circle. He seemed like a fine boy, young, too young to be serious, but so was her sister.

Neither will be a child once this journey's done.

More and more she was appreciating how much the miles were aging them. Her father showed some signs of wear, but after a few tough weeks, he seemed to be improving. He walked with his head held high and his eyes on the far horizon. He spoke of California almost constantly now. He would open a store and trade with the miners. Ellen thought that a fine idea.

Her mother, solid and stoic as ever, could outlast a stone. Still even she had a gleam in her eye when father talked of his plans. Sheltered by her youth, Martha retained every ounce of excitement. Ellen would owe her sister a great debt when they arrived in California. She'd been such a great help with Walt.

The water was boiling hard and fast now, boiling away like a steamship's boiler. Ellen added the makings for coffee. She started on the biscuits and bacon. She'd always liked bacon, the sizzle and pop of it cooking, the way her mother sometimes poured a little molasses over it and her biscuits. Rarely, they even got a little honey with it.

A sound came from behind the wagon and Ellen saw a man approaching in the dark. The man's outline was tall and big and utterly silent. He came straight toward her and Ellen grasped the handle of a small derringer hidden in her skirt. She'd bought the gun in Kearney, never fired it though. She hoped it was loaded correctly, her father had done it. Nearer the fire the shadow cleared. Her breath caught.

How has he found us?

She froze, overwhelmed by icy fear, the gun forgotten.

Without even a word, Clive squatted by the fire and snatched up a strip of bacon. He blowed on it and stuffed it in his mouth.

"Are you alright sis?" he said.

Ellen blinked. She looked at the man closer. Clive vanished and was replaced by Colton. She let out a long sigh of relief. Colton didn't resemble Clive in any way. Why had she thought he was Clive?

"Where were you?" Ellen asked.

"Card game with a few friends," her brother said and poured himself a cup of coffee.

"All night?" Ellen's tone betrayed what she thought of Colton's new friends. One in particular, Pope Robeson, made her uncomfortable. The way he looked at her reminded her all too much of Clive's leering.

"Yes, all night," Colton said. "Are you my mother now?"

"Someone needs to be." Ellen eyed the gun hanging on his hip. "The further we go, the more your judgment has declined."

"Nothing wrong with my judgment," Colton snorted

"No? You're staying up late every night, playing cards or getting drunk, and your new friends why they—"

"That's saying a lot given why we are here," Colton shot back.

"What do you mean why we are here."

"We left because of who you married. That was what your judgment brought us *little* sister."

Little sister. Ellen gasped. Clive had called her his *little mouse.* How dare he say that to her?

"Maybe I'm not the one with a judgment problem," he grinned.

Ellen scooped up the closest thing at hand, a pot of cold water, and threw it at him. Water and pot alike struck him in the chest, and he fell back off his heels.

"Why you—" he started to rise.

"I don't think that's a good idea," a voice from the dark said. To Colton's left, Jim Heston stepped into the firelight. He stood tall and straight, holding a rifle in one hand; Colton seemed to shrink back at the sight of him.

"Why she—"

"Doused you pretty good," Jim said. "Be a good idea to walk it off."

"Walk it off?"

"Sure," Jim smiled a little. "Take a walk around the camp, it'll keep you warm."

"It's freezing," Colton protested.

"My friend Remy has a good hot fire going. See if he'll get you some coffee while you're over there."

"And if I don't," Colton's hand inched a little closer to his pistol.

"That'd be a shame," Jim said, and his eyes were suddenly still and hard. His rifle hung loose and pointed in Colton's general direction.

Looking from one to the other, Ellen fought down a scream.

Why are they acting like this?

She moved between them, facing Jim. "My brother had an accident with the water," she said.

Jim's look shifted to her. "That's what happened?" he asked. She felt those eyes, weighing and measuring her. It was not a feeling she liked, but there was also more to it, a sense of desperate searching.

He wants something from me.

"Sis, I don't need you to—" Colton said.

With a sharp glare over her shoulder, Ellen cut him off, "There's a spare shirt in the wagon, Colton, one of father's, get changed out of that wet one before you catch pneumonia."

Colton rolled to his hands and knees then got to his feet and went to the wagon.

Ellen regarded Jim again. "Now if there's nothing else you need."

"Need?" he said. Suddenly he was a young man again, polite to a fault, and more than a little tongue-tied. "No, I didn't need anything. Only heard raised voices."

"Well then, I've got to get back to finishing breakfast," Ellen said and turned her back to him.

Jim went off then, muttering to himself, walking toward his own campfire.

She paused to watch him go. How long had he been listening? Had he heard Colton's talk about her husband? Another thought crossed her mind then. He'd been carrying a rifle. Why was he out prowling the camp?

Come to think of it, she'd seen Remy last evening making a loop of the camp. He too had been carrying a rifle. He'd stopped long enough to talk to Martha a moment then moved off.

Trouble, they were expecting trouble. But from whom? The store-keeper in Kearney said the Indians were all north on the reservation. Who else were they watching for?

Ellen noticed that woman, Lou and her brother, rousing and starting their own fire. Lou watched Jim as he moved through the near-dark, following his every move like a lioness laying in the deep grass while flicking her tail in anticipation.

What is she looking at?

She was too old for him. Much too old. Ellen frowned at her. By the way she leered after Jim, Lou did not agree. The woman had no sense of decency. Her brother, Jake, shifted near their fire. Ellen felt her skin crawl just looking at him. Last night she'd seen him moving off toward the wagons where the rough crowd gathered. Where her own brother now spent his nights.

"Good morning," her father said. He and mother were just rising.

"Good morning Papa," Ellen answered. Already she could see he was moving around better, not nearly so slow and stiff.

"Is the bacon burning?" he said.

Ellen swore under her breath and rushed to the fire. The bacon was popping and sizzling, but already well browned along the edges. Ellen hated burned bacon.

Serves you right though. Too much thinking about that woman and Jim Heston.

Ellen sighed. Jim Heston was a grown man and if he wanted to spend time with that woman then he certainly could. It wasn't her place to say anything one way or another.

Not my place at all. Even if she's far too old for him.

JIM FINISHED his rounds and looked down at the sleeping Neill. Most men had aged during their journey west, broken down by mile-upon-mile. The women were worse. Their hands were bony thin, weathered and dark by hard sun. Neill though seemed to be better by the mile. His skin took on a bronze color, his eyes shone clear and sharp.

Neill's scouting the prior night produced little. Nothing really.

They followed the trail of Lou and Jake's wagon to where they'd broken down and then far beyond.

As Jim suspected, they'd come from the west. Jake—fool that he was—had gotten turned around somehow and blundered his way to help.

Dumb luck saved him and his sister in the end.

He went to rouse Neill. The older man came awake with a touch, wide eyed and alert.

"Trouble?" he said.

"No, it's quiet. The rough bunch is settled in around the Watkins wagon."

"I don't expect the trouble to come from them," Neill said and shook out his boots. "Our new friend Jake?"

"I think he spent the night with that bunch, playing cards."

"Hmm, something to consider then. His sister?"

"No sign and no sign of Donovan."

Neill scowled. "He's probably prowling around looking for her, but she's not the type to give in easy." Neill looked him in the eye. "He's liable to be sore as a young buffalo bull today. Best to stay clear of him."

"Easy to say when you're out scouting," Jim said.

"Anything else?"

"Some trouble over at the Barton's."

"Ohh."

"That boy's spending his nights with that same lot."

"He's not a boy. He's wearing a gun. Sooner or later he's bound to draw on someone," Neill said.

It occurred to Jim then that this was the most he'd ever talked to Neill. When had the change occurred? He'd become a different man since leaving Independence, but more so the last few days. Since Fort Kearney. Since the whiskey was gone.

"What has you spooked?" Jim said.

Neill grinned. "Askin for advice now?"

"Forget it," Jim snorted.

I don't need this today.

Neill looked at him for a long minute then shrugged. "I can't explain it, but I feel like we're being watched. Someone has his eyes on us, whoever burned those wagons. And now we find this Lou and her brother out here."

"We didn't find anything last night," Jim said.

"We didn't go far enough," Neill said. "We should have followed them back further."

"If there are renegades out here when will they hit us?"

Neill poured a cup of coffee. "No idea. Could be the next few days, if not, then they'll wait until we clear Fort Laramie. We'll start seeing patrols soon."

"Will it be that Slade the old man warned us about!"

"He's a canny one. Smart. Ruthless. He's got a bloody reputation."

"Why doesn't the army go after him?" Jim said.

"Better things to do. The Sioux are the real threat. Renegades might take a train or two, but the Sioux would close the trail completely."

Neill went to his horse then, saddled up, and rode off with nothing more to say.

After breakfast Jim and Remy packed up the wagon. They left a few biscuits, the coffee, and some sausage out for Donovan, and the man himself showed up just after daylight. He looked haggard and worn.

"Didn't get much sleep," he said.

"Ayuh," Jim offered.

Wolfing down breakfast, Donovan ignored them. Jim watched his boss with concern. The man's eyes kept darting around, searching, seeking, always returning to Lou's wagon.

Twice, Donovan started to ask something, but then he must have decided the better of it. When he finished eating, he sat by the fire; his eyes kept searching.

Paul Webb finally came over. Jim could see the young farmer's confused look.

"We waiting for something?" he said.

Jim waited a moment and when Donovan didn't answer he

cleared his throat. *Someone had to say it.* "Boss, we're ready to roll out today."

Donovan stood then, and he seemed to see Paul for the first time. "Paul, please lead us out then," he said. "I apologize. Too much on my mind today."

"Of course," Webb said. He gave Jim a questioning look.

Jim shook his head. He could not explain it.

When Webb was gone, Donovan looked at Jim and Remy. "Do you two plan on sleeping all day? Let's get going,"

"Just waiting on—" Remy started. Jim stopped him with a quick look though.

"Time to go," Jim said. No need to let the young man catch Donovan's anger.

Remy hitched up the team, and Jim started for his horse, "I'll ride through and make sure everyone's ready."

"No need," Donovan said. "I'll do it. You ride on ahead with Neill."

"Neill's been gone for an hour, rode out before daylight. He's expecting trouble."

That took Donovan back. "Trouble? He didn't say anything to me."

"He wasn't real specific," Jim said.

"Imagining things," Donovan snorted. He was looking toward Lou's wagon again. "Doubt there's any trouble within a hundred miles."

Two hours later, Jim saw the first column of smoke rising ahead, and then he learned just how wrong his friend had been.

AFTER RIDING AHEAD of the wagon train, Jim sat on a rise and surveyed the wreckage. This wasn't like before. This wasn't a single wagon, but over two dozen. Smoke curled up from their sad hulks in fat, gray clouds. Debris littered the ground between them, scattered clothing, smashed boxes, broken kegs, sacks of flour or salt or sugar, fallen pack animals—mostly dead or dying—and mixed in among it all there were the bodies, over a hundred Jim estimated.

Neill walked among them, stooping to study the ground occasionally, muttering to himself. He paused over one man and rolled the
body over to examine his back. Seemingly satisfied, he mounted up
and rode over to Jim.

"The Sioux?" Jim asked. He knew the answer. From where he sat
he couldn't see even a single arrow. The Sioux wouldn't bother
burning the wagons nor would they have killed the pack animals or
left so much food behind.

"No, not them," Neill shook his head. "Nothing but bullet
wounds."

"Bastardo," Jim said.

"Yeah. I've seen worse, a few times—Indians mostly—but this is
bad. Whoever did this had no hesitation at all. Even the little ones..."
Neill's voice trailed off and he studied his hands. He took a deep
breath and lifted his eyes skyward. "Makes a man wonder if it's all
worth it."

"California?"

"Livin'. Just knowing I draw the same breath as whoever did this."
Neill regarded Jim then; there was a haunted look in his eyes. "There
isn't a hell hot enough, deep enough, or black enough for whoever
did this."

"Should we bury them?" Jim asked.

"We should," Neill agreed. "How far back is the lead wagon?"

"An hour, maybe two."

"Ride back and get more help. Six or seven of us can dig a lot
faster. Tell Donovan what we found. Maybe that will snap him out
of it."

Jim turned his horse and was about to go when something caught
his eye. Away from the wagons, the wind blew a bit of blue balled-up
cloth up the side of a gentle hill. The grass there was tall, rippling in
slow waves. But in one spot, near the cloth, a gap was visible. Something had mashed down a flat spot. Jim spurred his horse toward it.
Likely it was another body, someone who'd escaped the carnage
below and made a run for it, only to be shot down from behind.

The cloth was a thin strip of tattered ribbon, shiny, like a little girl might have tied up in her hair. Jim had seen Lily Sides with one just like it. She'd been proud to wear it.

The place where the grass was mashed down was to his left and he rode up slow. Each of his horse's steps felt like gathering thunder. If there was another body it needed to be buried. He wasn't about to let the buzzards or coyotes have anyone.

Over the edge of the grass lay a small girl—no more than seven or eight—curled up tight into a ball. Her face was an ashen gray. Jim's stomach turned. Who could have done this? Then, closer up, he saw she was shivering against the cold. Faintly, her lips moved, and he thought he heard bits of prayer.

"Neill!" Jim was off his horse in a heartbeat. He scooped up the girl and held her close against himself. *Cold, she is so cold.* He ran his hands over her back and arms, trying to warm her. Her eyes fluttered open then shut tight. Moments later, Neill was beside him. The scout drew an old shirt out from his saddlebags and wrapped it around her.

"I'll hand her up to you," Neill said. "Get her back to the wagons and get a fire going. She'll die of cold otherwise."

Once they were on horseback, Jim ran his horse for the wagons. The Webbs were not the first in line for a change. He wasn't sure who was. Then he recognized Ellen Barton walking out beside her father's wagon.

She looked up when she saw him. Her father ran to the wagon and took up his rifle.

"Get a fire going," Jim said when he drew closer.

David Barton leaned forward and stared out over the horizon. He held the rifle close and ready.

"Injuns? Are they coming? Where are they?"

"A fire," Jim yelled. "No Indians. Need a fire going."

Ellen must have heard him. She spoke to her father and they soon had the wagon stopped, and then she set about gathering fuel for a fire. When Jim reached them David was trying to coax it to flame.

"Is that a child?" Mrs. Barton gasped from the back of the wagon. She, her youngest daughter, and Ellen's boy, Walt were gathered there.

David held up his arms and Jim lowered the girl down. She'd warmed some by the trip and blinked up at him with a pair of brown eyes.

Ellen took the girl from her father and brought her near the fire. "Mother, can you bring me some water?" She turned to Jim. "How long was she out there?"

"I don't know. Neill said the wagons were attacked at least two days ago. I'd say since then," Jim answered.

Mrs. Barton brought a canteen from the wagon and gave it to Ellen. Ellen lay the child back a bit and poured a trickle of water into her mouth.

The girl spit up the first swallow then drank a few more down. The shivering had stopped. She regarded Ellen and drew tight against her. Then she closed her eyes.

"Is she?" David said.

"She is tired, very tired," Ellen said. She bent her head down against the girl. "But she is still breathing."

"Anything I can do to help?"

Jim looked up toward the voice. Another wagon had rolled up. Lou sat on its seat, beside her brother Jake.

"No, I think we've got it sorted best we can," Jim said.

Jake's eyes narrowed and he licked his lips. He stared at the girl lying in Ellen's arms. "You sure? My sister has had some experience with this sort of thing."

"Experience with survivors of a massacre?" Jim said. "Seems like a strange thing to have experience with."

"Well now mister," Jake smiled without warmth. "She's cared for young uns a time or two is all."

"I have," Lou nodded. She too looked only at the weary child. "I can sure take care of her."

"Has she said anything?" Jake said. He struck a match to light a slim cigar.

Ellen started to talk; Jim laid a hand on her shoulder. "Not a word," he said. "Not even sure she speaks English."

"Ohh?" Jake said.

"Lots of languages headed out west. We've got two Swede families with us, along with a Czech and Russian. Most of them don't speak more than a word or two." It was true. Jim had communicated with them via hand signals unless one of their children could interpret.

Jake was about to reply when Lou elbowed him in the side. "If you need any help we would be happy to help," she said. "Plenty of room to ride in our wagon."

"We'll keep that in mind," Jim said.

Jake and Lou started their wagon on by then, and Jim noticed Ellen watching after them.

"It would be better if she stayed with you. I'd trust a little girl to a shedding rattler before leaving her with that Jake," he said.

Ellen's look shifted to him. "I was just thinking the same thing about Lou."

"Lou doesn't seem so bad," Jim shrugged. "I feel mostly sorry for her always having to look after her brother like that. She walked all those miles for help while he just slept in the wagon."

Ellen scowled. "Men are blind where a pretty face and a pair of hips are concerned."

She took the child over to her mother and they wrapped her in wool blanket and laid her in the back of their wagon. The youngest Barton, Martha, Jim recalled, took the girl in her lap while Walt looked down at her.

"I never seen anyone sleep so sound, Mister Heston," he said.

"Neill—Captain Neill—that is, figured she'd been out there for several days."

"Wow," the boy said. "All alone."

"Alone the whole time," Jim said.

"Poor thing," Mrs. Barton said.

"We will take care of her," Ellen announced. She gave him a look that would have withered a pine tree. "No need to involve anyone else. Especially that woman friend of yours."

Jim paused, trying to decide who she might be talking about. *Lou. She thinks me and Lou are friendly like.* He flushed and climbed back on his horse.

He did feel sorry for her is all.

"I'll come by to check on her," he said and fled back toward the safety of his own wagon. He didn't know what he'd done to draw Ellen's wrath, but it was better to steer clear until it passed. That was one lesson his father had passed on.

"There's just no accounting for women," he told his horse.

14

A week after they found the girl Jim first sighted the purple Rockies. Though still many miles distant, the jagged peaks rose high above the prairie in soaring snow-crowned spires.

To his eye the line of mountains formed a solid barrier. How could they hope to climb one of those and reach the other side?

A speck of movement on the far horizon drew his attention. A rider. Jim drew his rifle from the scabbard. Was this the attack Neill had long feared? The scout had been withdrawn and morose the last few days, spending more and more time afield away from Donovan, away from all of them. He still did his share of guard duty over the camp, but Jim barely saw him, or when he did the scout only barked out a few sharp words.

The rider turned toward him. It was Neill. The scout reined in and gave him a rare grin, the first Jim had seen in days.

"Come along with me," he said and swung around. "We'll eat well tonight."

Putting the rifle away, Jim fell in behind him. They crossed two miles of wind-swept hills down into a sandy creekbed. Neill rode upstream until they reached a notch embankment, then dismounted. Jim followed suit.

"What are we—"

Neill cut him off with a hiss and a finger to his lips. Then the scout half-walked, half-crawled his way up to embankment's edge. He peered over the rim. With a sigh, Jim did the same.

He heard them first. The deep sound of huge breaths and cropping grass. A heavy hoof, rock hard, stomped at the ground. Creeping up another inch, Jim could just see their shaggy backs.

Buffalo.

Donovan promised we'd see some, but we haven't found so much as a track this entire time.

He rose up higher. At least fifty of the animals were in front of him, some lying in the sun, some munching on tufts of spring grasses. A pair of old bulls stood fifty paces apart eyeing each other with their shaggy heads high. One pawed up a shovelful of dirt and flung it over his back. The other lowered his head, shook those gleaming black horns from side-to-side. Seeming uninterested, several younger bulls fed closer to where he and Neill lay hidden.

Neill cupped his hand to Jim's ear and whispered.

"Take the closest bull. Put the shot right into his armpit. I'll shoot that one." He nodded toward a cow on their right.

Jim nodded. Slowly, he lifted the rifle to bear, sighted in on his target, and let out a slow breath.

He brought back the hammer with his thumb. His heart hammered in his chest. They were big. So much bigger than he'd thought. In his mind he'd pictured shaggy cattle, but the animal he sighted on was huge. It would outweigh the biggest longhorn he'd ever seen by five hundred pounds and it was not the largest buffalo out there. Not by a long shot.

Jim's finger tightened on the trigger. He glanced at Neill once to see if the scout was doing the same. With a final breath, he squeezed. The rifle bucked. He heard the bullet strike home and in the same instant Neill's rifle fired.

The herd exploded into action. As one they spun away from the sound and tore out at a run. Dust and debris, knocked loose from two hundred thundering hooves, flew until the air was cloudy. The bull

Jim shot had taken off with them. Five steps later, it collapsed. Another one dropped close-by.

Neill's, he thought.

The scout had backed down out of the dust and was feeding another round into his rifle. Jim followed his example and reloaded his own. Then he and Neill climbed back down to the horses.

"There's an easy way up a few minutes that way." Neill nodded upstream.

Soon they were up on the prairie again, standing over the two downed buffalo. Neill looked at them almost reverently and removed his hat.

"I can't help but admire them," he said.

"I can see why." They were beautiful creatures, proud and fierce. *We needed the meat though. Otherwise I'd like to just sit and watch them for a time.*

"Most tribes revere them. We thank you for the gift of your meat, brother buffalo," Neill said.

"This will feed the wagons for a week," Jim said.

"Five or six days I'd say," Neill put his hat back on. "But fresh meat will lift everyone's spirits some."

"How's the taste?"

"Better than beef or deer meat if you ask me. Not so good as an elk though."

Neill took out his skinning knife. "Help me with mine first then we'll tackle yours. When we're done you'll wish you'd missed."

The Captain's words proved true. By the time they'd skinned out the pair, pulled off the meat, rolled it all up and secured it, Jim's hands and forearms ached. On the farm he'd done a lot of work with his arms and hands. He'd done more breaking rocks in that prison quarry and later in Independence building wagons, but those two buffalo wore him out.

"We'll have to walk to camp and then come back for the rest," Neill said after they loaded the horses. They managed to load only the choice cuts.

"Any idea where it is?" Jim asked. The day was just about ended, the shadows stretched out long and willowy.

"Due south, maybe a mile or two," Neill said. "They wouldn't make it much farther than that. First wagons should be setting up now in fact."

"Still think there'll be trouble?"

Neill gave him a long look. "I do."

"Isn't the Fort close?"

"Yes. But I haven't seen signs of patrol yet. The Yanks are either tucked in tight to Laramie or..."

"Or?"

"Or they're sending their men mostly north. Toward the Sioux."

"They said in Kearney the Sioux were staying on the reservation."

"Maybe they were an maybe they aren't now," Neill said. "Either way I expect trouble. Between Indians and renegades there's plenty to go around. That Lou and her brother. There's trouble in those two for sure."

"Donovan can't see it."

"Donovan isn't thinking straight. He's all hung up on that mane of pretty red hair. She's liable to get him or someone else killed."

Jim wanted to defend his friend, but he could see Neill's point. The wagon master wasn't in his right mind. He hadn't been in days. A sickness had come over him. One named Lou. When he wasn't riding out front of the wagons, trying to look gallant, Donovan spent every waking moment chasing after her like an old bull on the prowl. In many ways Jim didn't blame him. Half the camp wanted to join him, even some of the married men.

Not that Jim hadn't had his own thoughts about the pretty redhead. A man couldn't her way without a few.

Only Neill seemed unaffected. And why might that be?

"What did you do in the war?" Jim asked.

Neill's step faltered and a far-off look came over his face. "My father owned a number of warehouses in Atlanta. I was at West Point when the fighting began, half a year from graduation with honors."

"Only you left to fight for the South?"

"I did. A lot of us did in fact. Instructors too." Neill's eyes were haunted. "We had to sneak out and make our way down to Virginia to join up with General Lee. Strange...riding south past all those fine homes and quiet little towns. Mile-after-mile of green fields. We'd come back later and fight among them. Buildings shrouded in smoke from our muskets, cannon fire echoing off their walls like God's own thunder, blood— both ours and the Union's—soaking into that rich black ground."

The Captain grew quiet then.

"My father and brother both died in the war," Jim said. "My brother at Gettysburg."

"Gettysburg. I remember the place. Bloody. So very bloody. That was the end you know."

"The end?"

"It broke our backs. Lee lacked the troops to invade the North. He'd hoped to capture Washington and force an early end. From there on it was mostly downhill."

They said little over the walk, each alone with their own thoughts.

DONOVAN RODE out to them when they came into view of the wagons with the meat.

"Buffalo?" he said.

"A pair," Neill agreed. "Should be enough here for a meal or two. More back at the kill."

"Good, I'll send someone for it." Donovan's eyes turned to the looming mountains. "I'm worried we're too early."

"There will still be snow in the high places, binding them up tighter than a banker's vault," Neill said.

"I agree. The grass is good here, though, plenty of water, and now we have meat. Tomorrow we'll let the stock catch their breath."

"Shouldn't we get closer to the Fort?" Jim said. "What with the renegades and all?"

"The risk is small. There are too many of us."

"That might be what the last train thought," Neill said. "Before they got killed anyway."

Donovan's face flushed and he glowered at Neill. "Laramie is close enough. I'll risk renegades over the snow ahead. A late season storm catches up there and we'll be in for a time. We are stopping."

He wheeled his horse about and headed for the Webb's wagon, and minutes later Webb had the circle started.

"At least he's keeping us ready for trouble," Jim said.

"Trouble from outside," Neill squinted after Donovan. "Not so good at handling trouble on the inside though."

Word spread quickly through the wagons. The families were pleased with the early stop and the promise of a day spend at rest. Donovan gathered up some of the steadier men and sent them back for the rest of the meat. They rode eagerly, acknowledging Jim and Neill with smiles and waves. Everyone was ready for fresh meat.

Still angry with Jim and Neill, Donovan set them to work. A number of wagons had gathered small problems, groaning axles, loose spokes, a hub that needed patching. Neill was relieved of his normal scouting duties and assigned to assist Jim and Remy, though the Captain did little more than observe and offer useless advice.

Just after noon, they were finishing a new wheel on a wagon when Lou appeared.

She stood with hands on her round hips and watched them for a time before speaking. "The women of the camp would like to invite you all for a pot-luck supper followed by an evening dance."

"Sounds fun," Remy said, but Lou's eyes remained fixed on Jim. If she noticed the young man at all she didn't show it.

Jim felt himself blush. Her look was level, direct, and carried an unspoken challenge in it.

"When you're all done here I could use a few things fixed over at my wagon."

"Donovan's already got a list made up for us," Jim said. "We've got three more to go between now and nightfall."

"Can't you make an exception and move me up?" She laughed then, low and soft. "I'm sure he wouldn't mind."

With that she turned and swayed off toward her wagon.

Jim watched her go. That sway could stop a man's heart.

"He'll damn sure mind," Neill said. "Foaming after her like he is, he'll kill anyone she lays hands on."

"You seem immune to her charms," Jim said.

Neill looked at him askance. "I had me a pony one time. Pretty little thing. Pretty enough to win the state fair. Could prance and show like you wouldn't believe."

"Not sure what that has to do with—," Jim said.

"Thing about that pony was, no one could ride her. Just fine in a halter but try putting a saddle on her back and you might as well try to ride a tornado," Neill said. "She killed a man. Friend of mine who thought he could ride her. Threw him off then struck him dead center with one of those pretty little hooves. Caved the front of his skull right in."

"What did you do with her?" Remy said.

Neill started to speak, paused, then seemed to think better of it. "Another time," he said.

Ellen Barton came from around the wagon then. The little foundling girl held her hand and in the other had a doll squeezed tight against her chest.

"I've come to invite you to our pot-luck dinner tonight," Ellen smiled.

"We heard. A dance too. I'm looking forward to it," Remy grinned ear-to-ear.

"Who told you?"

"Lou was just by here," Jim answered.

Ellen turned in time to see the woman returning back at her and her brother's wagon. "That woman—"

"Miss Barton. We would love to come," Neill said with a sweep of his wide-brimmed hat. "Be honored in fact, but I'm afraid there will be no dancing for us. Guard duty you see."

"Ohh, are we still in danger? Mr. Donovan thought the trouble was past."

"There'll be danger all the way up to California I'm afraid," Neill said. "Thieves and murderers, war parties of wild Indians, sickness, floods, grizzlies, and the like."

Ellen paled visibly with every word.

Jim gave Neill a hard look. Why frighten the poor woman? *Every time I decide he's a decent person he does something like this.*

"No need to worry though," Jim said. "We'll be out watching and keeping everyone safe."

The girl looked up at Ellen then with wide eyes. Had she understood the dangers?

"Has she said anything?" Jim said in an attempt to change the subject.

"What?" Ellen looked at the girl then. "No, she hasn't. Martha tried guessing her name, but she didn't have much luck."

"Probably Swedish or Finnish or something by her look," Neill offered. Now that she was clean the girl had very fine almost-white hair and bright blue eyes.

The girl let go of Ellen then and scampered over to Jim. She held up the doll for him to see. The doll was stuffed with down—one feather stuck from a seam along its shoulder—and had black buttons for eyes with a band of red ribbon in its hair.

"Yes, I see your pretty doll," he said and knelt down to her. She looked at him, then the doll, and then wrapped him up in a hug.

Jim became conscious of how small she was. Compared to him she was just a slip of a thing. Tiny and frail. Then he smelled his own sweat. They'd been working hard and he must stink terribly, but the girl didn't seem to mind. After a time she backed away and went to take Ellen's hand again.

Jim stood. Remy was packing up their tools and Neill was studying him closely. Ellen too was doing likewise.

"That's the first time she's done that," she said.

"What?" Jim said.

"It's the first time she's gone to anyone but me or Martha."

"She remembers Jim pulling her out off the prairie," Neill said.

No one spoke for a time. Jim wiped his greasy hands on a rag.

Ellen broke the silence. "So you don't think any of you can spare guard duty for even a single dance?" Her question was aimed at the group in general, but she looked to Jim for the answer.

"Well, I'd sure like to—" Remy said.

"I don't think we'll have time," Jim interrupted. "Like Neill said. We have guard duty."

"Ohh, I see," Ellen said. She glanced down at the ground and it seemed like the air went out of her.

The wind stirred and again no one spoke.

Finally Ellen said, "I've got to get back." Then she and the little girl went off.

Jim stared after them for a time, struck by the moment. She had been sad that they couldn't go? Why, they were just the hired help? They weren't truly part of the caravan. He felt the weight of Neill's eyes on him, studying, and turned to the man. "What?"

"You are a fool," the Captain said and walked away.

15

W ith the wagons finished, Jim took up a plateful of hot buffalo steak, white potatoes, and a cold biscuit, picked up his rifle and walked out away from the group. The wagons were circled up in a small basin, and he wanted to watch from a grassy knob a few yards away.

To his left he saw Neill, riding out toward the south. The scout had planned on making a long loop around the camp while Jim and Remy each kept lookouts on either side.

Jim settled down on his blanket roll, ate, and then began cleaning the rifle. The evening breeze was cool and low, rolling over the grassy prairie in gentle waves. The sunset hung behind the mountains for a long time, sending out red and purple rays.

Neill passed by below him without comment, slumped in the saddle, singing a sad tune about some lost love from long ago.

Jim couldn't imagine the Captain as a young man in love, but even as he thought it he could hear the regret in Neill's voice. "That man carries his demons close," Jim's mother would have said. No wonder he preferred to drown them in bad whiskey.

The moon rose, pale and faintly blue and distant coyotes lifted their own songs. Music—happier music—came from the wagons.

Milo Adams had brought along a fiddle and Paul Webb banged away on an overturned pan. Pat Robeson stood with the rest his usual crowd, and for once they were all smiling. Even Pope—the most troublesome of them—seemed to be happy enough. Pat's wife, Sally, started to sing in a language Jim didn't recognize, her voice ringing out clear and strong.

Jim faced outward again, toward the deepening night. The swaying grass caught moonlit beams reflecting thousands of ghostly shimmers. There were trees in the distance, stunted little things that bucked and swayed in the evening wind. He watched the far dark mountains. They were still miles away.

How could they be so large?

The click of a stone startled him. Jim swung around, rifle flying up to one shoulder, searching for a target. Someone had snuck up on him. He found himself looking down his rifle barrel at a frightened Ellen Barton. Ashamed, he lowered it.

How close did I come to...no use thinking of that. What was she doing up here?

Ellen held a plate in her hands, draped with a red-and-white checkerboard napkin; the little girl stood close behind her like a shadow.

"Sorry," he offered and quickly lowered the rifle. "I wasn't expecting company."

Ellen hesitated and looked at the rifle. She gathered herself and lifted the napkin off the steaming plate. "I brought you dinner."

"Nice of you," he said.

Then she saw the empty plate resting beside him. She gave it a dark scowl.

"You've eaten already," she said and started to go.

"No, that's alright," Jim said. "It wasn't much. Just a lump of undercooked buffalo."

Slowly, Ellen turned back around. He took the plate as she moved closer, and he offered her the blanket roll to sit on. He started to rise.

"No need to stand on my account," Ellen said. "There's enough blanket here for both of us."

"No Walt tonight?" Jim asked. He settled back on the bedroll leaving a bit of space between them. Without pause, the little girl scrunched up her coat and squeezed in tight between them.

"Fell asleep beside my mother," Ellen smiled. "I swear he's getting bigger by the day. I know that sounds silly."

"This country will do it," Jim said and looked again to the mountains. "Plenty of open ground out here to spread in."

Down below, the campfire was starting to die, and Mrs. Robeson sang another song. This too was in a language he didn't understand —slow and sad—holding the entire camp enthralled. Jim held his breath and listened.

"I'm not sure what she's singing but it sounds lonesome," Jim said.

"It's French," Ellen offered. Her eyes were big and dark in the moonlight. Deep as midnight pools.

"You understand it?"

"Most of it," Ellen said. "My father used to deal with French Canadian traders, and I learned a bit of it."

"Traders?"

"We lived in New York. Up on the very border. He traded for furs and skins. Beaver pelts too. Mostly those old trappers liked teaching me swear words. Those I learned quite well," Ellen grinned.

"Swear words? You?" Jim said.

"Oh yes," Ellen nodded. There was a mischievous light in her eyes now. "I learned them all. But they taught me others as well."

"What's she saying now?"

"A woman is walking on the shore, calling to her husband out on the sea. He's been away for years now and she is lonely."

"Years? That would be a long time away from home," Jim said.

"How long have you been away from your home?"

"I don't know that I've ever been home. I was alone after the war. After that it just wasn't home anymore. I used to think it was."

"What about your mother? Your father?"

"Do you believe a person can die from a broken heart?"

"I do," Ellen nodded.

"My mother died after we got word that my brother and my

father were both killed in the war," Jim said. "Ohh, it took awhile. She was a strong woman, but the life just slowly sapped out of her and she was never the same after the news came. I tried to keep her going but..."

Ellen and the little girl and he sat quiet then. In the distance a wolf howled. All at once the coyote chorus dropped away.

Jim grinned and leaned in against the little girl. "Showed em who's boss didn't he?"

"I haven't seen any wolves out here," Ellen said and shuddered.

"Donovan said there weren't many left. Used to be packs following the buffalo herds."

"What was the buffalo like?"

"Big, beautiful animal. Proud and strong. I felt awful sorry, but we needed the meat."

"We did," Ellen said. "Papa said one day the buffalo will be gone."

"Maybe," Jim answered, not liking the thought. The buffalo were the Lords of the plains. What would all of this be like without them?

Empty. Not that it wasn't already. The Indians had been driven off —placed on reservations—and there were already far fewer buffalo than there once were.

Ellen shifted beside him. She was looking down at the little girl again. "She's asleep."

Jim looked down at her. The girl had laid her blonde head against his shoulder, and one hand was wrapped tight around his arm.

"Seems like," he agreed.

Jim turned his attention back away from the camp. He'd been negligent on watching for trouble. A shadow approached from the right and lower down, one rider, head tucked down against his chest against the night's coming chill. Neill.

"I can't get over how quiet it is and how fast the temperature drops," Ellen wrapped her shawl tighter.

Jim started to respond when someone screamed from inside the camp. A woman. In an instant he was on his feet, rifle in hand. "Stay down with her," he said.

Hoofbeats came from the right and Neill reined in beside him. He took in Ellen and the little girl at a glance. "That came from the camp," he said.

There were no shots, no further screams. Was this the attack Neill had been expecting?

"Nobody came from this direction," Jim said.

"Keep watch here and I'll ride in," Neill said and was gone.

Jim scanned the horizon in all directions. But for the wind the grass was still. Nothing but swaying grass and moonlight. The trouble came from Remy's side or started within the camp itself.

His attention swung to the camp. Men were shouting down below. Someone had thrown more fuel on the bonfire. The flames rose up high and bright. Neill quickly disappeared into the circle of light. At least one woman was sobbing. Figures were shifting around the campfire, throwing odd shadows.

A man-shaped shadow slipped between a pair of wagons and started out into the deeper night. Jim raised his rifle for a shot. But who was he shooting at? Who was this slipping out into the empty night?

The shadow turned slightly. Whoever it was their path would take them just twenty yards from Jim's position. Lowering the rifle, Jim took off at a run.

Closer now, he could make out a man's hat, the glint of a gun barrel. The fleeing man's attention was on the wagons though. Those and getting away clear. Jim was less than ten yards away and still unseen when he spoke. "Stop."

Very slowly, the man's head turned toward him. His pistol was held in one hand, low and ready.

Jim cycled the rifle. "I wouldn't."

"I'm tossing it," the man said, and Jim knew the voice. Jake. Well, he'd expected trouble from the man. Jake tossed his pistol out into the high grasses.

"Walk back toward the camp. Hands held high," Jim said.

Jake started forward. They were at the edge of the camp when Neill and Donovan came out to meet them. Both held lanterns.

"Got him did you?" Donovan said. The Wagon master's face was flushed.

Jake paused and Jim imagined he was reconsidering his decision to come in peaceful. He'd tossed his weapon aside though and Jim didn't plan on giving him a choice.

"Go on in," Jim said and pressed the rifle barrel against Jake's back.

Donovan and Neill fell in on either side of the prisoner, both armed with drawn pistols.

"Take him the rest of the way," Jim said. He needed to get Ellen and the little girl back down here. Out away from the wagons alone was no place for them. "I've got to—"

"She's already on the way," Neill said.

Turning, Jim saw Ellen and the girl coming down off the hill. Ellen was carrying his gear except for his bedroll. The girl struggled with that. Jim intercepted them and took up his gear.

"What's all this about?" Ellen said when closer.

"I don't know," Jim answered. "I caught Jake trying to slip away from the camp."

They crossed into the circle of wagons and the firelight. The men of the wagons stood in two distinct groups. Pat Robeson stood at the head of one. Milo Adams at the other. Jake and his escorts were between them, Donovan and Neill on either side. Remy had come down off the hill as well. He held his rifle in both hands hanging down across his legs.

"Hang him and end this tonight!" Paul Webb shouted from Milo's left. He gave Jake a look of hate hard enough to startle Jim. A number of the men around Webb nodded in agreement.

"Hang him now," one said from further back.

"He didn't do it," Pat Robeson said. His faction was the smaller of the two, but their faces were stone hard.

"My boy caught him." It was Ellen's father who spoke. He stood beside Milo Adams, ash-faced and with tears shining on his cheeks.

"Father," Ellen said. "What's happened?"

"Ellen!" he answered, and his head whipped around toward her. "Ellen. Thank God you're alright. Your brother's been shot."

"Shot," Ellen gasped.

"Shot by that coward over there when he was caught molesting my wife," Paul Webb pointed to Jake and spat.

"She wanted me to touch her," Jake grinned. "Practically begged me for it."

"You son-of-a..." Webb started forward, but Adams and several other men held him back.

"He admits it Robeson," Milo said. "You heard him just admit it."

Pat Robeson looked at Jake. "Did you do it? Did you set upon Mrs. Webb? Did you shoot young Colton?"

"No, no I-" Jake started.

"He's lying," Webb said. "You all heard him. My wife said it was him and the Barton boy interrupted him."

"Colton hasn't said anything. He's unconscious. When he comes around we'll ask him."

"Unconscious? Colton?" Ellen said.

"Go to the wagon, Ellen," her father said.

Girl in hand, Ellen raced off toward their camp. Jim watched her go. Her brother had been spending too much time with a rough crowd, Jake included, but surely one of them wouldn't shoot him.

"My brother is innocent," this time it was Lou who spoke. She was pushing herself to the front of the Robeson group. "He wasn't anywhere near that woman."

"He just admitted he was," Webb responded.

"Now now," Donovan said. "Everyone needs to just calm down."

"We will not," Webb said. "Not until he's up and dancing to the Devil's tune."

"We are not going to hang a man tonight," Donovan said.

"Search his pockets," Webb said. "He stole a locket from my wife. There's an inscription inside."

Before Donovan could stop him, Neill rifled through Jake's pockets. He drew out several gold pieces and a round silver locket on a long shining chain.

"That's mine," Jake said.

Neill tossed it over to Jim. "You say it's yours, Jake. Then tell me what's inside."

Jake licked his lips. His eyes darted around nervously, finally landing on his sister. "There's an inscription. It says, 'love always'."

Jim flipped the locket open, tilted it where it caught the light. He read the words.

"No," he shook his head.

"It says 'Hannah'," Paul Webb said.

"It does," Jim nodded.

Remy came running into the firelight then. "Colton's awake. He said Jake shot him when he caught him molesting Mrs. Webb."

Jake's face took on an ashen color and the air seemed to deflate out of him. His sister melted away into the crowd behind Pat Robeson.

Pat Robeson looked at Jake for a long moment. Jim felt a trickle of sweat on his back. The rifle in his hands was cold and ready. The men on either side of Robeson shifted uneasily, waiting to see where their leader landed. If Pat started something he had plenty of men with him. Outnumbered they might be, but those were hard men. They would fight.

Robeson's jaws clenched, he glared at Jake, and he spat on the ground.

"Hang him," he said in disgust. Then he turned and pushed his way through the others and back toward his own wagon.

Jim didn't see Lou leave with them, but she must have. When they cleared out no one but the Adams group remained.

"You heard him," Paul Webb said. "Hang him."

Several in his group nodded and shouted support.

So cocky before, Jake now looked like a beaten man. His head hung low and the fire had gone completely out of him. With his friends abandoning him, he'd aged ten years in half a minute.

"Nobody's getting hanged tonight," Donovan said. "In the first place there's no trees tall enough for the job. In the second I'm not letting anyone in my caravan get hung and I'm not—"

"He's not in *our* caravan," someone in the back shouted.

"And I'm not going to let anyone in my caravan hang anyone. We're going to turn the matter over to the soldiers at Laramie. Let them deal with him," Donovan continued.

"You're just protecting him for his sister," the same voice said. "You been chasing after her like a dog."

Jim saw Donovan's nostrils flare and his face grow instantly red. *That one stung.*

"Enough of that," Donovan barked. "Yes, I don't want this man's sister to see him swing. Do you? Any of you?"

Silence.

"Paul? Do you want that? Will you hold the rope yourself? Hoist him up?" Donovan took a step forward and held out his gun. "No trees out here. Better off shooting him. You'll have to look this man in the eye and then shoot him. Are you ready for that? Is that justice or vengeance?"

Paul Webb licked his lips, his mouth opened, and Jim held his breath. *Calling him out like that was a mistake.* The man's wife had just been attacked. He would likely take that offer. *I would.*

"No," Paul finally said. Something had gone out of him. "Sarah is unharmed. The soldiers can handle justice."

He started to go then turned back. "But I want him tied up and watched and kept far away from my wife!"

With that he left, followed by everyone but Donovan's little group and their prisoner.

Jake let out a long breath in relief. He gave them a half-grin. "Thought they were going to get me gents."

Donovan slugged him across the face, hard enough to send him down sprawling. "Take this trash to our wagon and tie him to one of the wheels. Tie him tight"

Jake rubbed at his face. "Ooh jest roke my raw."

"Lucky I didn't cave your skull in," Donovan said. He held up a finger. "One time. Test me one time and I'll shoot you."

The big man stalked off.

"Remy, you and Jim pick him up and I'll keep him covered," Neill said. "We'll get him tied tight."

JIM WOKE to a string of Captain Neill's most colorful curses. Sober, Neill cursed only rarely, but when he did the words came hard and free like water bursting from some great earthen dam. Jim opened his eyes and kept his hat low enough to blot out most of the coming light. The scout held a short length of rope in one hand. He waggled it at Donovan.

"Did you do this?" Neill said.

"I can't believe you'd even ask that," Donovan said. "You of all people."

"Well who did?" Neill said.

"What happened?" Jim groaned. His head ached; he stuffed his hat on and shook a brown scorpion out of one boot. The vicious little thing snapped a claw at him.

"Someone," Neill eyed Donovan, "cut our prisoner loose."

"What? Jake escaped?" It was Jim's turn to swear. There'd be hell to pay. How could any of them face the Webbs or Bartons after this? "What do you mean cut him loose?"

Neill tossed him a length of rope. "End's sliced clean through. Knife cut. Somebody cut him free."

Jim looked at the wheel they'd tied Jake to. "Where is Remy?"

Neill "Gone. Along with Jake."

"Why would Remy set him free?" Jim said. "He didn't like him anymore than the rest of us."

"Three sets of tracks heading off to the west. Remy, Jake," Neill paused to glare at Donovan. "and Lou."

"Lou's gone?" Donovan said. "Why would she go off with them? Why would she leave their wagon and belongings like that?"

"Tracks don't lie," Neill said. "Go see em for yourself, if you aren't still blinded by a head of pretty red hair."

Donovan flushed. He shot Neill a dangerous look and said nothing.

"So do we ride out after Remy? Do we know if he went willingly?" Jim asked. He looked to Donovan for guidance—he was in charge after all—but the big man turned away.

"Why don't you ask the Captain?" Donovan said over his shoulder. "He seems to have all the answers already. I'm going to get the wagons started out."

Again Neill swore. He tore off his hat and slapped it against his thigh. He studied the retreating Donovan's back.

"Damn him," the scout muttered.

"So, what do we do?" Jim asked.

"We don't do anything. You get the wagon ready, loaded, and started out. I will ride out and see about where they went," Neill said.

The scout jammed his rifle in its scabbard and set out at a brisk trot. Jim watched him go. His friends were falling apart, and they still had half the distance, the worst half if the stories were true, yet to go.

How are we ever going to get there?

16

Clive Wilson entered Kearney well after sunset. He'd ridden hard after crossing the river into Kansas, searching for Ellen and his son.

The Barton's neighbors had known little—unfortunately for them —but after he'd taken his knife to Carl Sampson, the owner of the general store, his wife suddenly remembered Mrs. Barton asking about the road south toward St. Louis.

With that revelation he'd slowly pieced together their journey from Illinois, down to St. Louis, then west toward Kansas. It was painfully slow. Too much time had passed, months, and few remembered the Bartons. He spoke mainly with the men operating ferries though and learned just enough to keep going.

Almost four months had passed since they'd gone. Their month-long head start had grown significantly while he sussed out the trail. The winter had been deep though, and he did not think they would have made good time.

His luck had turned at a small town in Missouri though. The storekeeper's wife remembered Walt and Ellen. Ellen had asked about what clothing they might need on the trail to California.

That had been all he needed.

Despite the size of the country there were only so many places they might start overland from. The exact details of their trail were unknown. Too many people coming and going, all strangers to one another, all headed west. But he knew the broad strokes. The safest trail west started in Independence. From there it wound up through the plains like a vine, passing a limited number of forts and ferry crossings. Clive had trusted his luck and ridden out alone to Kearny, one of the main stops along the way. Here, no matter where they started from, the trails all merged into one. Given their head start and his delays, Ellen and her family were almost certainly ahead of him. Several trains had already come and gone, and it made sense that if Ellen were running she'd be with the first one to take them on.

Kearney wasn't much of a town. The streets were wet and muddy, churned under so many hooves and wheels. The air stank of manure and sweat.

Clive stopped at a saloon and swung down. His horse had made good time and come far, but it was showing signs of wearing down. He should get another. With two horses he could push harder.

There were—he believed—at least three wagon trains still ahead of him. An old man in Independence had told him five set out so far. He'd passed the first two days later, riding along slowly, making conversation with a few of the men.

"Looking for my wife," he explained. "I was captured during the war, presumed dead you see, and when I got home she had gone with her people west. Missed her by less than a month."

"Bad luck," most of the men had replied with a shake of the head. Their women had thought it terribly romantic how he'd come home from the war and was riding after his love. They promised that they'd keep watch for his beloved wife and son, and did he need any supplies?

Clive smiled to remember them. People were fools, especially women and their romantic notions. Braying sheep to be sheared and slaughtered.

The bartender stood wiping down the bar with an oiled rag. "Get you something?" he said.

"Whiskey," Clive responded.

The bartender drew down a glass, produced a bottle, and then poured.

Clive took it down all at once. "Another."

The bartender refilled it and this one Clive sipped slowly. To his surprise the whiskey was good, not that vile stuff he'd heard they served further west. He turned his back to the bar and leaned against it to survey the room.

Several men sat at scattered tables. Two older men argued about the weather nearest to the door. At the next table, closer to the window a pair soldiers—apparently off-duty from the fort—played cards with a third man Clive couldn't see very well. One soldier looked up, noticed Clive's cavalry hat, and gave him a quick nod.

Clive dipped his hat in return, but it wasn't the soldiers or their companion that held his attention. They might have seen Ellen of course, anyone could have, but he recognized the two men at the next table or rather he recognized their type.

Both were dirty and wet from riding in the rain. Most of their gear was old and worn. Holes showed in the elbows and cuffs of coats and the knees of their pants. Only their guns were clean and cared for. Their tanned faces each had a long, lean look to them, the look of hunters. They sat very still, waiting on something or someone. Only their eyes seemed restless, darting from person to person, to the windows, then the door.

Clive turned back to the bartender. "I'll take a bottle and two more glasses," he said and flipped out a gold piece. The bright coin rattled and spun on the mahogany.

As he'd expected, when he turned back to toward the two hunters they were eyeing him carefully. The ringing of gold had a tendency to draw their kind of attention.

Clive picked up the bottle, then the glasses, and walked to their table. He set them down and pulled back a chair. They were watching him carefully now, stealing glances at the cavalry hat, then the gun he wore on his own hip.

"Join me?" Clive smiled and poured the glasses full.

One of them, the smaller of the two, looked at the other who shrugged. "Why not?"

Clive lifted his glass and clinked it against theirs.

"We toasting something?" the smaller man said.

"New friendships."

"Of course," the man said and drank.

Clive refilled the glasses. "I'm looking for a woman."

"Aren't we all?" the small man smiled. Two of his bottom teeth were missing. "There's a house two streets back."

"Not that kind," Clive said. "One on the trail. She has a young boy with her, my boy."

"What would it be worth to you?" the second man finally spoke. His voice was rough, raspy like an old file.

"A good deal."

"Would that good deal involve a few more of those gold pieces?"

"It might," Clive allowed, "but it might involve more."

"More?"

The saloon door opened, and Clive turned. The old men had gone. The soldiers too, both scowling, were leaving. Their companion, the third man, sat at the table with his back to Clive, counting out their money.

"Did you hear that, boss?" one of Clive's companions said. "He said there might be more."

The small man on Clive's left drew a knife and laid it on the table. "I'm interested in the gold."

"I'll have no trouble in here," the bartender said.

"You'll shut your mouth, Frasier, or I'll burn this place down and you with it," the gambler said. He folded the money neatly then tucked it into a vest pocket.

Clive sat very still, watching the two in front of him. He was not afraid. They had no idea who they were dealing with. His own knife was close. His pistol too. He could kill both of the sitting men at any time, but that third man to the right. He would be trouble.

The third man came around the table, slow and confident, not holding a gun precisely, but with one thumb tucked into his belt so his fingers hung loose near his holster.

Momentarily, Clive shifted his gaze off the seated men and up toward the gambler.

"Well I'll be...Clive Wilson," the gambler said.

"Slade," Clive smiled.

Slade Parsons had been a scout assigned to his unit during the war. He'd been a rarity, a southerner who'd sided with the Union. Clive heard he'd lost a plantation to some bank in Atlanta and ridden north to use the Union troops for revenge. Slade burned that same bank to the ground under General Sherman's orders, after he and Clive had stolen the gold inside, of course. No need to burn up all that money for nothing. "These two are with you?"

"You know him?" the more talkative of the two said.

"I do," Slade grinned. "Gentlemen this is Captain Clive Wilson of Illinois and formerly the Union Army."

"So can we rob him?" the man with the knife said. He was eager, Clive saw it in his eyes.

"I doubt it," Slade said. "He'll likely kill both of you, but I'm pretty sure I can drop him."

"Pretty sure?" Clive said.

Slade shrugged. "Fifty-fifty I'd get lead into you before you killed them both."

"Not my kind of odds," Clive said.

"Mine neither," Slade agreed. "Put the knife away Billy. There'll be no need for it today."

The man with the knife took it off the table. His partner only stared and said nothing.

"This is the Tollivers, Billy and Trent," Slade gestured to the pair.

"Pleasure," Clive smiled coldly.

Slade flipped a pair of coins onto the table. "You two go find some fun for awhile. I'll collect you when I'm done here."

Billy Tolliver scooped up his coin like he'd never see another while his brother took his slowly, without his eyes leaving Clive. "You know where to find us," he said.

"I'll follow the smell," Slade said. "Now I believe you were saying something about a missing wife."

"I was. She's with one of the outfits traveling west."

"Lots of outfits going west," Slade said and poured himself a drink.

"Three have gone through Kearney so far. She's with one of them."

Slade gave him an appraising look. "You have good information. So why ask about her here? Why not just keep riding?"

"I've come to collect her, and she might not come willingly."

"Really?" Slade sipped at the whiskey. "Taking a woman out here, even if you are married to her, is a serious matter. Westerners take offense to such."

"So I understand. Her family might also be with her."

"Ohh?"

"Her parents, an old man and woman, a brother, a sister, and my son."

"Son is it?" Slade's eyes shifted. "Now it becomes clear."

Clive felt his jaw tighten. He did not like anyone knowing his business, necessary though it was. Slade had always been a canny one. A good ally if he could be won over, and a source of information even if he wasn't. With him in Kearney he'd know everything about those wagon trains ahead.

"They stick together," Slade went on, "those fools heading west. It might not only be the family protecting her."

"Of course. It might be very lucrative though, to retrieve her and my son and then remove any witnesses."

"Lucrative," Slade smiled. "You always had a way with words Captain. I figured there was more to it than a woman."

"My son wouldn't be harmed of course."

"Of course," Slade smiled. "The three groups that have passed through are well-armed though. Several dozen men who know how to fight with each, but there are ways of dealing with that. I know a few people who could help."

"So long as I get what I want," Clive agreed. "And a share of course."

Slade smiled. He raised his glass toward Clive. "To a lucrative association."

"ELLEN."

She heard him calling and her heart raced. *Clive.* Where was he? Somewhere behind her and she was…was…where exactly? A maze of some kind. It looked vaguely like the interior of their house only the corridors were strange, branching off in a dizzying set of directions, endless, and there were no windows only doors.

She tried one. Locked, just like the last and the one before.

The hallway just ahead ended and split in either direction. She paused to consider. Left or right?

"Ellen," his voice rang out again. It came from both directions. It came from the walls, the floor, the high ceiling. He was both everywhere and nowhere.

She felt Clive's fetid breath on her neck and spun around. Nothing.

"Not there, Little Mouse," he laughed. "Not yet."

Ellen ran then. He could not be everywhere. Not truly. A new thought came to her then. Walt? Where was Walt? Did Clive already have him?

Oh God…please no. Please let him be safe.

He had to be safe. She had to find him and then free them both from this wicked place.

Suddenly more choices confronted her. More empty hallways branched off to the right, six in total, and all identical. Which one to take?

"Mama," Walt's voice this time. The note of fear stabbed into her heart. He sounded so very young. "Hurry mama. Help me."

"I'm coming dearheart," Ellen screamed. "Hold on."

"Help him Ellen," Clive said. "Help my son."

"He is my son, not yours," she snarled.

"Ohh, Ellen. When you look at him all you see is me. My eyes, my face. He is my son. Why do you think you've abandoned him?"

"I haven't abandoned him. You took him."

Clive laughed. The walls shook with it. "Lie to yourself if you wish, but you have abandoned him. When did you hold him last?"

The words hit her with hammer blows. He was right. When was the last time she held him, kissed him, loved him? She had abandoned him.

Ellen sank to her knees.

"Mama," Walt pleaded. A cry then. He was here. There was a door between them, locked like all the others, but her son was here. Behind this very door.

Ellen twisted the handle with all her strength. Nothing. She slammed her fists on the door, but the wood was strong.

"Unlock the door dearheart. Please let me in."

"I can't. It's dark. I can't see."

"He's right there, little mouse," Clive taunted. "All you have to do is get through that one door. Can't you do it? Don't you love him enough?"

Ellen beat her fists against the door until they bled. She sagged slowly down, face pressed against the cold wood. "Walt. My beautiful boy."

A hand fell on her shoulder and Ellen jerked. A man loomed over her, reaching down.

"NO! I won't let you have him." Her breath came fast and ragged. She would fight him. Walt was her son, not his.

"Ellen." *That voice. It isn't Clive's.*

"Ellen," it repeated. Her father's voice. She saw his face then, lined with worry.

"Ohh, Father," she said and wrapped him in a tight hug. The tears came then. "Father, he had Walt and I couldn't reach him."

"I know dear," her father said and stroked her hair just as he had when she was a little girl. "It was only a dream."

Ellen stared up at him. The lines around his eyes were deep.

When had he become old and worn? "Have I neglected him on our trip west? I feel as if I've cast him off on Martha."

Her father said nothing and drew her close.

"I just see so much of Clive in him," Ellen sobbed. "I hate him for that. More than anything. More than the lies. More than the beatings. I hate him for putting his mark so deep on my sweet boy."

"Walt won't turn out like Clive. You'll raise him to be a good man." He stroked Ellen's hair again.

"Mama," Walt's voice called. "Mama, are you sick?" Rubbing the sleep from his eyes, he came over and leaned on her shoulder. "Don't cry mama. It will be alright. Uncle Colton will be fine. Aunt Martha said so, and she never lies."

"Uncle Colton will be fine," Ellen agreed. She looked at her father over Walt's small shoulder.

His face was gray, but he nodded.

Colton would recover then. Doctor Mims had been up with him all night. Ellen had stayed awake with them as long as she could, but she was so very tired.

"Help me up dear," Ellen said.

Walt took a step back and helped her climb to her feet. The little girl still lay sleeping in a thick roll of blankets. Ellen took her son by the hand and led him over to the girl.

"What do you think of her?" Ellen said.

"She's awful quiet," his eyes were big and dark.

"Do you think you'll be friends."

"I don't know." Walt scrunched up his nose.

"She's all alone in the world," Ellen said. "Imagine being lost and alone with people who you can't even speak to. That would be tough wouldn't it."

"Tough," Walt nodded. "Tough like Mr. Heston."

"Yes," Ellen smiled. "Tough like Mr. Heston."

"Did you see how his face was all mashed up when we left Kansas?"

"I did," Ellen nodded.

"They said he punched the other man and knocked him out cold. They said he looked twice as bad."

"Who said?"

"The other boys," Walt said "Some of them saw the fight and they said there was blood and spit everywhere. They said Mr. Heston almost killed that other man."

"I'm glad he didn't," Ellen said and vowed to keep a closer eye on who her son was talking to.

"Me too. Then he couldn't be with us teaching me how to track and hunt."

"Those are good things to know," Ellen said

"Things a man should know." Walt's chest puffed out.

"Now back to this girl. I want you to treat her like your sister."

"She's not my sister."

"No, but I want you to take care of her like she is."

"I don't have a sister," Walt said.

Ellen sighed. How to explain this.

"This girl is all alone with no family and it's our duty to take care of her and keep her safe. I want you to help me keep her safe."

Walt considered her for a second. "Okay. I will keep her safe, but she isn't my sister."

"Good enough," Ellen agreed. "Now let's go see what's for breakfast."

"Bacon and biscuits, mama, it's all we ever have anymore," Walt said. "Except for that buffalo Mr. Heston shot."

Ellen's mother was pulling the last strip of bacon off the fire. She too showed signs of worry. Her face was drawn and tired.

"Let me help," Ellen volunteered and started on the coffee.

"Thank you," Abigail said.

"How is he?"

"Sleeping now," Ellen's mother said and stole a glance at the wagon. "The Doctor said he'll be alright. A scar of course, but the bullet went through without hitting anything."

"Martha is with him now?" Ellen asked.

"He was lucky," her mother nodded. "So very lucky."

"Lucky, Abigail?" Ellen's father shook his head. "If he was lucky he wouldn't have been there at all."

"Honestly David, do you hear yourself?" Ellen's mother started.

"If he hadn't been there Mrs. Webb would have been alone with that animal," Ellen said. She had a better understanding than most of how that would have gone. More than once Clive had come home drunk and forced himself on her. *I should find Mrs. Webb and offer some comfort. She shouldn't be alone at a time like this.*

Ellen's mother surprised her then. "Colton brought some of this on himself. I've seen those men he's been spending time with. I've seen the way he's always practicing with that gun of his. David, when he recovers from this, you need to get our son back into line before something worse happens."

Ellen's chastised father threw a biscuit and two strips of bacon on his plate, and then he shuffled off toward the wagon. "I'll switch out with Martha." He said over his shoulder. "You'll have something ready for her?"

"Of course," Ellen's mother said.

"I'll do it mother," Ellen volunteered and set about making her sister a plate.

"Thank you again." Ellen's mother sat on a barrel of salt they'd unloaded for a chair. She rubbed at her eyes.

Ellen dished up a plate for Walt and sent him along after his grandfather. That done she stood and looked at her exhausted mother. It was just the two of them now; Ellen couldn't remember the last time they'd spoken alone together.

"Have I done the wrong thing, mother?"

"What do you mean?"

"Dragging all of you out here? Out in all this...this," Ellen gestured all around, "vast emptiness?"

Ellen's mother sighed. She looked Ellen in the eye. "For a time I believed this was all an overreaction. I thought Clive was a gentleman. I thought you were wrong to leave. Wrong to take Walt from his father. Clive Wilson came from a good, respectable family."

"For a time?"

Ellen's mother, Abigail Barton, one of the toughest, proudest women, Ellen had ever met suddenly looked into the fire. When she spoke again her voice cracked. "For a time. But one day—a week before we left—Walt was staying with us and he told us how his mother cried," Abigail brushed at a tear. "He told us how his mother screamed when his father got angry and hit her."

The tears came faster now and when Ellen caught her mother's gaze again it was full of shame. "Walt asked me why his father made his mother cry," Abigail sobbed. "I didn't believe you. Ellen. I didn't believe my own daughter and I was wrong."

Ellen went to her mother and embraced her. "I understand." Then they were both crying.

After a time, Ellen felt a set of small hands wrap around her. The little girl was holding both of them tight.

Ellen's mother patted the girl on the head and smiled. "Such pretty gold hair. You are a sweetheart. I can't imagine what you've seen. Poor thing."

"I wish she'd tell us her name," Ellen said. "We can't keep calling her 'girl' can we?"

"We should pick a name for her, even if it isn't the right one," Ellen's mother said.

"How about we call you Alma?" Ellen asked. Then she touched her own chest and said, "Ellen." She touched her mother's shoulder and said, "Abigail." She touched the little girl and said, "Alma."

The little girl looked confused and Ellen repeated the whole thing again.

"I think it's a nice name," Ellen's mother said.

Then the little girl said, "Alma."

17

Clive followed Slade several miles north, out of Kearney, and into a camp down in a hollow on a fork of the river. There were over a dozen men there, milling around in battered tents or lean-to shelters, all with the same hungry look the Tolliver brothers had. Looking at the gathering, Clive was reminded of his former crew. If they had practiced their trade on land instead of out on the water they would have looked much the same.

Slade reined up beside a small log cabin and dismounted.

"It ain't much, but there's no law," Slade drawled and went inside.

There were two men waiting there, one tall—taller than Clive himself—and wide across the shoulders. He wore a fringed deer hide jacket and curly red hair poked out in long tangles from under his coonskin cap. The second man was seated at a table near the back of the room, covered in shadows. He held a deck of playing cards in one hand, several were turned face-up before him, and a pistol lay on the table.

"Clive, this is John Mears," Slade nodded to the big man, "and this is Syd Boyle."

"Boys, this is Clive Wilson. Clive commanded the cavalry troop I scouted for back during the war."

The big man grinned. "You look like you can fight."

"He's not going to fight you John," Slade said. "Clive has a wayward bride he wants us to help him find. She ran off with his boy and he wants them back."

"We in the business of returning lost women now?" Syd asked and moved a card from one hand to the other.

"No, but our goals lie in the same direction. Do you remember that first big train that came through? John there was a family with them that you noticed."

"Two women, both pretty, one young man, an old man with grey hair at the temples, his wife, stern-looking like a schoolmarm, and a boy that didn't fit. Too young to be theirs," John rumbled.

Clive's breath caught. That was them. Ellen and Walt were close.

"Don't let his size fool you, John here has an excellent memory," Slade said. "How many in that group?"

"Forty-three men, thirty-seven women, fifty-eight children. Donovan and Neill were leading them."

Donovan. Clive smiled. That was one of the leaders the old man in Independence had told him about. It had to be Ellen.

"Ahh, it seems our new friend has found his missing wife," Slade said with a grin. "John, how long since they left?"

"Two weeks and three days," John said.

"And why didn't we hit them John," Syd said.

"Too strong," John shook his head. "Too many guns and Donovan."

"Donovan?" Clive asked.

"Their wagon master is a good one, maybe the very best. Him and his friend Neill."

"Neill can sniff out a trap with the best of them," Syd said. "And Donovan is an old wolf from way up in the high country."

"You have a dozen men outside," Clive said.

"And they have forty-three, plus the women, most of them will fight as well," Slade said.

"A flock of sheep compared to your men," Clive said. On the river he'd taken longer odds and always come out ahead.

"Lot of those men survived the war. Even those that didn't, a man with his family and everything he owns all tied up in one place. They'll fight. Every one of them. But if we had someone on the inside. Someone to help us out."

"We already have Lou and Jake for that," Syd said.

Slade scowled. "Jake's an idiot. He'll get caught doing something stupid. I only sent him to get him out of camp for awhile. He kept picking fights and killing the new recruits."

"He's good with a gun though," Syd said.

"And that's why I sent Lou to keep an eye on him."

"So you'd planned on attacking this Donovan anyway?" Clive said.

Slade grinned. "Not necessarily. Might be they get waylaid by some other outfight. Or Injuns take a hand. Maybe not enough to wipe them out, but enough to lighten the odds. We like to keep our options open and that group is loaded down. Donovan's always are. We could eat for a year on what they have."

"And the women," a grin split John's granite face.

"John likes his women." Slade patted the big man on the shoulder.

Syd laughed and flipped over another card.

Clive did not like the situation. He knew Slade and trusted the man, to a measure. They'd worked together well enough during the war and both had prospered, but with Slade and every other endeavor Clive had always been the one in control. This was Slade's outfit. His men. His experience.

Clive would have to force himself to be patient. There would be an opportunity here. And if what Slade said of this Donovan were true Clive would need help to retrieve what was his. Slade or Syd or this John fellow would betray him of course. They were not the type to share.

Well, he'd been playing that game a long time too. Only once had he been caught unaware, and even then it was more a matter of timing than being truly blindsided. Chet and Beau both paid the price for that betrayal. He could play along, for now, and see where this went.

"What would you need me to do?" Clive said.

JIM WALKED beside the team and looked ahead into the high mountains.

The 'Rockies' men who'd been west called them, always with a sense of awe and wonder in their voices and a far-off look in their eyes. Seeing them, passing among their foothills, crossing their streams, Jim understood why. With their jagged peaks, barren of trees or other life, snow-covered, showing streaks of stone-gray, these were not the gently rolling hills of South Texas. These were mountains. These were proud towers of stone and ice.

How will we ever cross them?

But cross them men had. Given incentive enough and time enough every obstacle placed in man's way fell. Burning deserts, thick forests, raging rivers, broad oceans all crisscrossed with as the country met its expanding destiny.

Even these wild, beautiful Rockies can't hold men back.

Donovan, morose of late, rode back along the column to their wagon; he paused beside Jim.

"Trouble ahead. Slow your pace to tighten the wagons up and be ready."

Jim looked past his friend to a rising plume of dust.

"Indians?"

"No. Indians wouldn't give themselves away like that."

"Then who?"

"Just be ready," Donovan growled and rode for the next wagon. Jim's eyes followed him. He hadn't been the same man since Lou disappeared. The other men of the wagon train had noticed both his new mood and how he'd behaved when she was in camp. There was talk. Loud and bold enough talk for Jim to have heard it.

Of Captain Neill Jim saw little. The scout returned every couple days, sullen and bitter, for supplies or to pass along a word about the trail ahead. He did not speak to Donovan—only Jim-and then only the barest of words.

He had found Remy. Lou, Jake, and Remy had all walked away from the wagons and then followed a streambed along south. Neill said there had been horses waiting. Two horses. Remy had died with Jake's bullet in the back and they'd left him, mounted up, and ridden east.

"Took advantage of the boy to get away and then murdered him," Neill said. He did not share any of it with Donovan. That task fell to Jim.

"Why would they have horses waiting?" Donovan said when Jim told him. "Neill's drinking again. He can't have the right of it."

Donovan had been spending time with Pat Robeson. He was not welcome among Paul Webb or his friends, not anymore. Donovan forced Jim to relay the directions to that group; Webb and his group tolerated him but after Jake's escape there was no warmth from them.

The dust plume was closer now and Jim saw mounted figures at its base, dark against the backdrop of green hills.

Jim stopped his team. He eased out his rifle, laid it just inside the wagon, out of sight, but within easy reach. He shaded his eyes for a better look at the approaching men.

Their coats were dust-covered but dark blue, light glinted off sabers rattling at their hips.

The army. Must be a patrol.

Their commanding officer dismounted and approached. He was a young man, straight-backed, dark haired, and with a tightly trimmed beard and mustache. *Probably grown to make him look older,* Jim decided. He was very young for a Lieutenant. There was a depth in his brown eyes though that spoke of experience.

"I am Lieutenant Wells, Sixth Cavalry, out of Fort Laramie."

"Jim Heston out of San Antone."

The Lieutenant looked at Jim askance. "You're a long way from home aren't you?"

"Right now home is this wagon," Jim said. "Headed to California."

"Another gold-seeker," Wells said.

"Maybe, maybe not. I had a farm in Texas, but all it grew was white rocks. Thought I might try again out there."

"A better path than treasure hunting."

"Perhaps."

"How many in your group?"

"Just shy of forty wagons. Men, women, and children."

"And you are in command?"

Jim shook his head. "I work for..."

"He works for me, Sean," Donovan said and swung down. He and the Lieutenant met in a back-slapping embrace.

"Donovan," Wells smiled. "It's been too long. You're early this year though."

"We left ahead of schedule. Wanted to see if it could be done."

"And?"

"Good time for the first few weeks while the ground was still frozen. Slower after the thaw, but overall a success so far."

"It's been unseasonably warm. The passes are clear to Salt Lake," Wells grinned. "Father will want to see you."

"I wouldn't dream of disappointing the General."

"Good. I'll ride back and tell him to expect you," Wells climbed back into the saddle.

"Any trouble with the Sioux?" Donovan said.

"None. The treaty holds so far."

"And other trouble? We've seen sign."

A cloud passed over the Lieutenant's face. "Bandits everywhere. Two of them for every Sioux we've run off. Two caravans were lost last year. Father will tell you more."

Wells and his troop swung off then, riding back in the direction they'd come from.

"You know him?" Jim said.

"Him and his father," Donovan replied. "Both good men. I pulled a Ute brave off his father once down in the San Juan country. Almost cost me my own scalp. If they're worried about bandits it must be bad."

They stretched their travel into the night to reach the Fort and in the dying light it did not look like what Jim had expected. He'd seen the Alamo, along with a few army outposts along the border with the Indian territory. Obviously, he was familiar with the one he'd been imprisoned in.

Fort Laramie looked like none of these nor did it look like Fort Kearney back in Kansas. The Fort lay within a deep bend in the Laramie river with log buildings laid out in an orderly grid. The barracks were the largest. Several long, two-story buildings with white plaster walls and a covered balcony. The Fort proper consisted of several other buildings, the Commandant's quarters, the supply house, stockades, a post office, stables, and an armory. Then there were the civilian's places, several trader's shops, a few scattered houses, two general stores, and a saloon.

With the snowy mountains rising high and proud in the distance, the great sweep of plains stretching out all around, and the river coursing round the fort and then journeying east, it struck Jim just how terribly small their presence was in this empty land.

Men have been crossing this trail for twenty years and we've barely made a mark on it. Only a tiny wooden Fort in the wide wilderness.

Donovan led the wagons just south of the Fort and circled them up. To this there were grumbles. The day had been long enough already, and the Fort was near enough to protect them.

"Good habit to stay in," he said when asked. "Even near the soldiers like this."

Jim set their little camp up alone. He wished Remy were still with them and wondered for the hundredth time what he had been thinking going off with those two.

"Jim, come with me and meet the General," Donovan said when he was done.

"What about the wagon?"

"Neill can watch it," Donovan nodded across the camp and Neill was walking his horse in. "He's coming in now. He doesn't care much for the soldiers."

"They don't care much for me either," Neill said. "Killed too many of them at Shiloh."

Jim mounted up and followed Donovan across the river into the Fort. The river's spring runoff came up high on their horse's legs, full of angry froth and bitter cold. They were up on the bank and Donovan brought them to the Commandant's home.

Lieutenant Wells waited for them there. He snapped to attention and Donovan threw him a quick salute. "I never was an officer, just a battered old scout," Donovan said. "You met my friend Jim Heston earlier?"

"I did. Father said if it wasn't for you the Utes would have wiped out the whole command," Wells answered.

"He exaggerates. He and his men shot their way out of there. I only pointed them in the right direction."

Jim studied Donovan. He'd never seen his friend downplay his accomplishments. In Independence, Donovan always played up his every act to an audience of men eager to pay him for a journey west.

"The old man's waiting inside. Injured his ankle two days ago," Wells said.

"Fell off his horse again," Donovan laughed. "Man has a knack for choosing the tallest horses and then falling off."

The Lieutenant's face reddened, and he stifled a laugh.

The Commandant's quarters were spacious and open. There were stuffed heads of animals on the walls, elk, deer, antelope, wolves, even a buffalo. A home the building might be, but Jim noticed how thick the walls were and how the shutters had holes where a defender could close them and still shoot out. Lanterns hung at regular intervals, lighting the house with a warm glow.

"Unfortunately, I drew the night patrol," the Lieutenant said as he led them inside.

"The General can't get you out of it," Donovan said.

"Being the Commander's son comes with its burdens. I draw the dawn patrol twice as often as the other Lieutenants," Wells gave a rueful grin.

"In that case I will see you tomorrow," Donovan said.

"Nice to meet you Mr. Heston," Wells said and shook Jim's hand before leaving.

"And you," Jim responded.

A woman came out to greet them then, older but Jim could see the resemblance between her and the Lieutenant, the same look about the jaw and mouth. Different eyes though, hers sky-blue against his brown.

"Donovan," the woman said.

"Myrtle," Donovan said and scooped her up in a great hug. "It's been far too long."

"It has," the woman smiled. Her look turned to Jim then. "You've brought a guest."

"Jim Heston from San Antone," Donovan gestured with his hat. "Came with me over the trail."

"Captain Neill won't be joining us?" she said with a crestfallen look.

"Not tonight," Donovan said. "He sends his best, as always."

"Honestly the war is over. Eustis enjoyed his talks with the Captain," she said and seemed to mean it.

"He's not the man he once was," Donovan said. His hands tightened over the hat.

"I remember him from home. I was there the day he and my brother rode off to war. They were so gallant. Dashing and brave and strong," her voice slipped. "It seems an age ago now."

The room grew suddenly quiet. Donovan shifted his feet nervously. Jim had never seen the man at a loss for words, but he seemed utterly lost now.

"You were from the South?" Jim said into the silence.

Mrs. Wells looked at him and a fierceness came into her eyes then, "Though my husband fought for the North. *I am* from the Commonwealth of Virginia."

"My apologies," Jim said.

Her face softened but only by a degree. "There is no need for that. I am not ashamed of where I came from and neither should you be Mr. Heston. I know many a Texas man who died for what they believed in."

"I lost my father and brother," he said. "My mother too...in a way. After we got the news she never recovered."

"I understand," Mrs. Wells voice held compassion and he found himself believing her. She reminded him much of his mother in fact. *Unbending, hard as steel, but always courteous, always compassionate.*

"Myrtle are you going to hold our guests out there all night? See them in woman. See them in."

"Of course," she said and brought them into the dining area.

Jim's first impression was light. There were candles burning everywhere, on the table, on the shelves, on the mantles. Jim marveled at so many. Ma would never burn more than one or two over their evening meals. On the table were plates, each with a pair of forks, a knife, spoon, and white linen napkin. Light flared off the silverware like sunlight off a rippling stream. The chairs were high-backed and ornate, carved with leafy scrollwork.

Jim eyed the room and shifted uncomfortably. *Where to sit?*

"No Captain Neill?" a man with salt-and-pepper hair asked.

"He sends his best," Mrs. Wells said.

"Pity," the man said with a scowl. "I had another theory to run by him and I do so love hearing his thoughts."

"You know how these Southerners are," Donovan said and winked at Mrs. Wells. "Too proud by half."

"Of course," the Commandant laughed. "I've often said that myself to Myrtle."

"Only every day," she said.

Donovan gestured to Jim. "This is my friend Jim Heston from Texas."

Jim dipped his head. "Nice to meet you."

"And you as well sir," the General said. "Please excuse my infor-mality. I've injured my leg and the doctor doesn't want me putting weight on it."

"Fell off your horse again," Donovan said.

He pulled out a chair beside the General while Mrs. Wells took one at her husband's other side. Jim settled down next to Donovan.

Food was served on silver platters. Heaps of potatoes, squash, and fresh tomatoes. "All from our local garden," Mrs. Wells said. The meat was a small fowl called a sage hen, seasoned with salt and butter. There were hot rolls and dessert was a cake with molasses icing.

During the meal little was said, aside from bits of small talk. General Wells asked about conditions on the trail. Donovan answered and responded with his own questions about the land ahead. How clear were the passes? How much snow had fallen during the long Wyoming winter?

Mrs. Wells asked about their group. How many women had come along? Did they bring their children?

Donovan told her most of the men were married or traveling with their parents, and this seemed to please her. "The West needs her men, but she also needs her women and children to really grow."

Jim found himself liking the pair. Given their respective backgrounds, his and theirs, he wouldn't have expected it.

When the meal was done the General eased back his chair and lit a thick cigar. "So tell me Donovan. How are things really?"

Donovan sighed. He responded with a question. "How much have your scouts found?"

"Too much. Burned wagons and more than a few. We had two trains wiped out last year. I'm expecting more this year."

"More?"

The General nodded, "They've grown bold. And the winter has made them stronger, not weaker. There are many Southerners who've lost their homes and are desperate."

Mrs. Wells cleared her throat.

"Yes, yes dear," the General amended. "There are Northerners among them too."

"I believed as much," Donovan confided. "We had a couple not return in the fall. They were good men. Too good to be taken easily."

The General nodded. "As I said, the renegades are strong, and they've proven resilient."

"You can't do anything?" Jim ventured.

"Too much ground to cover," the General answered. "If I had a dozen more scouts, and fifty more troopers, I might be able to round them up. But my area, my responsibility, is two thousand square miles running South to the edge of Denver and North up to the Sioux reservation. Patrolling the trail isn't even my primary assignment. This Fort exists to watch the Sioux." He waved his cigar at Donovan. "And yes my friend, I know it's a bit more than that, but the fur trade —buffalo especially—is dying out."

"We passed a small herd a few days east," Donovan said.

"Remnants of the past. Soon they will go. The hunters will follow. And what will happen of the trail I wonder?"

Donovan leaned back in his chair, "I have this trip to finish... maybe another...then I'm getting out. I've saved up enough to find a good place of my own."

"Don't wait too long," Mrs. Wells said.

"There's still a few wild places left for an old mountain man. A hidden spot or two that few people know about."

Jim the twinkle in Donovan's eye. *He sounds sure of himself and what of my own future? Where will I call home?*

Truthfully, he hadn't given it much thought. The idea of California sounded grand, growing green fields, clear streams running wild and free, mountains soaring up into wispy cloud tops. A land of hope. *But how do I fit in? Am I to be the treasure-seeker, diverting those streams and sifting through gravel for a few ounces of gold, or am I the farmer, tilling the earth and planting something new?*

Seeker and grower, Jim held no judgments of either. No doubt men good and evil alike were found among both.

"Have you come alone Mr. Heston?"

The question startled Jim for a second. Mrs. Wells was staring at him expectantly.

"Yes, ma'am," he nodded.

"Is the trip difficult for a man alone?" she said.

"I suspect it's more difficult for those with families," Jim said. "I've no one to share the work with true, but with only myself there's much less of it. It takes little for a man alone to survive on the road."

"I envy you young man," the General waved his cigar. "To travel and see such marvelous country. Most men live and die within thirty miles of where they're born. I understand it's even less than that in Europe. But you...you'll get to see all the Lord's grandeur."

"You should come along after us," Donovan said.

"Someday I shall," the General said.

"Eustis," his wife said and patted his hand.

"Someday we both shall," the General corrected himself. "Someday I'll be done with the army and we will go see this great land for ourselves."

"Someday," Mrs. Wells smiled. Her eyes said she didn't believe it though.

They talked for another half-hour, Donovan and the General mostly. Jim's mind went back to San Antonio. *I've covered so much ground already since then.*

The candles burned low when Donovan finally pushed back from the table and stood. "We have to be going. If I don't get this youngster back into bed he's cranky in the morning."

"More like a tired old man is needing his sleep," Mrs. Wells laughed.

"That too," Donovan grinned.

The General stood to shake hands. "She talks to me the same way old friend. She forgets though that I am but two years her senior."

"I forget very little, husband. Two years makes all the difference," Mrs. Wells smiled.

Jim followed Donovan's lead.

Mrs. Wells took his hand and said, "Travel safe Mr. Heston you travel with good people. Stop in and see us if you ever find yourself here again."

"I will," Jim promised.

The General shook his hand next and said, "Mr. Heston, thank you for joining us this evening. I wish you all the luck in the world out there."

"Thank you," Jim said.

"Godspeed, young man," the General said.

Donovan led the way outside and back to the horses. Lieutenant

Wells waited for them there. Gone was the easy talk from earlier, his face was serious.

"How's guard duty?" Donovan said.

Wells shrugged. "Quiet, as usual."

"With Indians it's always quiet, right up until they're slitting your throat."

"How did he look to you?" the Lieutenant's gaze locked with Donovan's.

"How long does he have?"

"Six months. A year," Wells shrugged. "You know how it is."

"I do," Donovan nodded. "I knew a man lived with it for three years. Cancer didn't get him though. A Sioux arrow did."

The Lieutenant gave them a rueful grin. "He must have known the same man. He tells mother the same story. But the doctors say it's bad."

"Damn all doctors," Donovan spat. "Lawyers too. World would be better off without all that."

"I'll see you in the morning?"

"You will," Donovan said. "We might rest up a day or two. Stock could use it and I wouldn't mind seeing him a bit more. I might even get Neill to come in."

"He would enjoy that."

Donovan mounted up and Jim followed suit. They rode for the camp.

"How did you know?" Jim said when they were across the river.

"Know what?" Donovan said.

"How did you know he was sick?"

"I rode with that man for five years, fighting Indians, renegades, blizzards. Living by rules and regulations. Orders from fool politicians who never had to look down a war lance or see their best friend scalped bloody. Through it all Eustis held firm. Never once has he talked about leaving the army. He loves the army. It's all he's ever known."

The night was cool. The wind, so harsh out on the open plains, lay still and quiet, resting for what would surely be another blustering day tomorrow. They made their way toward camp and dismounted at the circle of wagons. Several of the rough crowd were keeping watch, smoking, and talking among themselves.

"There they are," a cigarette-smoking man said. "Riding back from dinner with the big man himself. Damned Yanks."

"Why don't you find another one of those women to chase around after wagon master?" another said. This one Jim knew. Pope. One of Pat Robeson's brothers. A big man and tough.

Donovan gave Pope a sharp look. His hand fell to the butt of his pistol.

"Easy now," Jim said. "Nothing to shoot anyone over."

"Looks like you've upset them, Pope," the smoking man said.

"They ain't so high and mighty now," came another voice. "Specially now that that woman and her brother are gone."

"I remember you boys being friendly with that pair," Donovan said. "Especially the brother. Pope, I remember you siding with him over Mrs. Webb and now here you are full of big talk."

"Donovan..." Jim said. "Keep on walking. No need for this." He saw though that Donovan was full of vinegar and in no mood. *No way we're getting away without a fight.* And where the hell was Neill? The scout should have been watching for them. An extra gun would back this lot right on down.

"You stay out of this," Pope said to him. "You're just as bad, slipping around with that Barton girl. There's a nice piece. Why I've got a few dollars and I might give her what that Webb woman got—"

Pope never finished. Jim's right fist took him in the jaw, spun the big man's head around like he'd been shot. Pope came back around, and Jim hammered him with a left. Then a wave of anger came over Jim and he was swinging away, time and again, both fists driving hard and quick.

If Pope countered, Jim never felt it. He knew only white-hot rage. What seemed like hours later, he stood triumphant over the remains of a broken man, glaring down, head hammering like cannon fire, fists clenched and blood flowing free from his knuckles. He couldn't see from his left eye, and he felt blood trickling from his cheek, nose, and mouth. There was no pain. There was only joy in seeing this man lying beaten and still. This hadn't been a fight. It had been a massacre.

When he was down, Pope's friends rushed to him. Donovan and two more men from the camp hauled Jim back by the shoulders.

"Jesus, you damn near killed him," one of Pope's friends said. "When Pat hears about this he'll string you up."

"You tell Pat his brother is a dog and if he barks like a dog again I'll just shoot him," Jim said.

"Jim, come on," Donovan wretched at his shoulders.

They were away from the fight then into the ring of wagons and their own little camp. Milo Adams eased Jim down on a small stool.

"Let me look at you," he said and began feeling over Jim's face. "Does this hurt?"

"No," Jim said numbly.

Webb touched Jim's nose, "And this."

"No."

"It should. It's broken."

"It's been broke before."

"Go get the Doc," Milo said, and Donovan turned to go.

"Donovan," Jim called, and his friend paused. "I'm sorry."

Donovan grinned. "If you hadn't done it, I would have. He surely needed it."

"What set this off?" Milo said.

Jim suddenly found that he was too tired to answer. Moreover if he told anyone what had been said about Mrs. Webb the man would likely shoot Pope at the next opportunity. "Private matter," he mumbled.

Milo eyed him suspiciously. David Barton, Ellen's father, was there suddenly. "I just heard someone beat that man, Pope, half to death," he said. "Donovan needs to—" He cut off when he saw Milo working on Jim's face. "Ohh, ohh, I see."

"Get me some water boiling," Milo said.

"I will," Barton said and looked around for a pot.

Just then Captain Neill staggered into camp. He held a whiskey bottle loose in one hand and had an arm wrapped around Moses Martin's shoulders. Moses had a bottle of his own, less than half remained.

"Hey, I heard sssomeone put that Pope in hisss place," Neill slurred. "He said something about Mrs. Webb and then that Barton girl..." He looked at Jim and then laughed. "What happened to your face?" Then he blinked. "Ohh...Ohh...Nice work then."

Milo snatched the bottle from Neill and doused it on a rag. He held it out a few inches from Jim's face. "This is going to hurt."

"I doubt it," Jim said and was immediately proven wrong. Milo might as well have set Jim's face afire for how much it hurt.

Donovan arrived then with the Doc in tow.

"Hey Doc," Neill said. "Someone bashed Jim's face in."

Moses started laughing then. "He's going to have a hard time chasing after that Barton girl with a face like that," he said. "Course some women like that sort of thing."

For a brief instant, Jim caught a strange look from David Barton and then the Doc was between them.

"What have you done so far?"

"Dabbed away the dirt, as best I could," Milo said. "I also doused him with whiskey."

The Doc nodded. "Alright, all of you stand back a bit then and give me some light. What a mess you are."

"Is Pope dead?" Jim asked. His lips were numb now and swollen.

"I don't think so," Donovan said. "They took him back to his wagon and Mrs. Robeson was working on him."

"She has some skill," the Doc said. "I'll check on him after I'm done here."

It took the better part of an hour before he was done stitching up Jim's face. There had been cuts above the left eye and a deep gash along the cheekbone. The lip and nose he could do nothing about.

Jim never remembered Pope throwing a punch.

When the Doc finished and left to see about Pope, Donovan helped Jim into his blankets.

"Lay here and rest," he said. He pressed Jim's pistol into his hands under the blankets. "I don't think it will come to it, but you'd better be armed just in case."

Jim squeezed the pistol tight. His left eye was swollen shut. He felt like someone had hit him with thrown bricks. He didn't want to sleep. What if Pope's friends came for revenge while he was down? He felt the warmth of the pistol's wooden butt. He had that at least.

His mind grew heavy and slow until he dropped off.

18

They rested at the Fort for the better part of a week. Jim recovered, day-by-day, and he saw no sign of Pope or any of his kin. Though he was not afraid of the Robeson clan he did not want to force the issue either. There were rumors of a split between the wagons—that Pat Robeson would lead his people off on their own—but when Donovan finally sounded the muster they all pulled out as one long single column.

Donovan hired an older man named Stewart in Laramie to drive the wagon, the General had vouched for him, and Jim was able to resume his old job of seeing to the other wagons. Overall he found little was needed. Most of the families had learned to heed his words and were doing a good job keeping both their wagons and stock in shape. That was not to say they were without problems.

The third day out of Laramie, after repairing a broken spoke for the Talon family, Jim rode up past the lead wagon and was surprised to see Milo Adams.

"Hello Jim," Milo offered. Milo was one of the few men who seemed undisturbed by his fight with Pope.

Jim dismounted to walk beside him. "I'm surprised to see you up here."

"Don't think my team is good enough to lead?"

"It's not that but," Jim looked all around, "I'm used to seeing Webb up front."

Milo's look darkened and his eyes narrowed. "He's struggling. Didn't break camp until well after the rest of us. I waited a few minutes for him to break trail, but we had to get moving."

"I might check on him," Jim said.

"Careful Jim," Mrs. Adams cautioned, "He's a proud man."

"And he's on the prod," Milo added.

"Thanks for the tip, ma'am," Jim dipped his hat.

He mounted up and rode slowly back along the column. Webb's wagon wasn't second in line, nor the third, nor even the tenth, he'd fallen all the way back near the center, just ahead of Pat Robeson's.

Jim climbed off his horse and watched as Webb's team came along. Paul Webb walked out beside the head of the team, guiding them along, eyes down and looking only at the ground ahead. His wife was nowhere to be seen.

Must be in the wagon. Perhaps she'd taken ill.

Right away Jim saw something he didn't like. One of the oxen on the right side didn't seem to be moving right.

He waited until Paul drew close then spoke.

"Everything alright Paul?"

"Fine, we're all fine," Webb said without slowing or looking up.

Jim thought for a minute on what to say next. "I think one of your team is coming up lame. Mind if I take a look?"

"Ohh," Webb said and looked up for the first time.

The man looked like he'd aged a decade. His eyes were bloodshot with deep bags beneath and his skin had a sickly gray cast to it.

Jim circled the team. The ox he'd suspected had a nasty cut on its lower leg, near the foot. Jim ran a hand over it and the beast stamped his annoyance.

"Hurts does it?" Jim said.

"How did that happen?" Webb asked from over his shoulder.

"Cut it on something looks like. Maybe when we passed through that brush at the last creek," Jim said. That had been the first morning out of Laramie. Two days ago. Webb hadn't noticed his animal was injured for two days.

"I'll get the medicine," Webb said and started for the wagon.

Jim unhitched the injured animal and brought him around to the back of the wagon. For now at least, the ox would do better following than pulling. If they could keep the wound clear of infection he'd be ready to work again in a few days.

When Jim had the ox secured, another wagon creaked past.

"There he is," he heard a woman's voice say. "Brute."

Jim looked up to see Pat Robeson and his wife. The long-faced man gave him a hard glare, but kept walking, saying nothing. His wife looked down at Jim from the wagon seat. She spit in his direction and then pointedly turned back to the trail ahead. Several of their children walking beside the wagon copied their mother's gesture.

For a time Jim watched after them. He supposed he'd started the fight; whatever Pope had said. In their eyes he was the one who'd beaten their cousin half to death.

"Here it is," Paul Webb said and handed a leather bag over.

Jim dipped out a bit of paste and smeared it on the injury. Then he bound it with a strip of clean linen.

"Want me to come by and change it tomorrow?"

"If you think it best," Webb shrugged.

Jim studied the man's face. What had happened to him? The old Webb would have been offended at the offer. Of course the old Webb would have noticed the injury immediately and taken action.

What has broken him?

"I'll be by this evening then when we make camp. Your team should make a little better time now with this one only following."

Webb turned without another word and took up his old place beside the lead ox. Soon he had the team rolling along and Jim was left alone with his doubts.

Still standing he heard the creak of another wagon approaching. He looked up to see the David Barton and his family. David, to his surprise, did not give him so much as a hello. His wife too was silent. Ellen paused for a moment, opened her mouth to speak, but closed it at a hard word from her father and then ducked her head before falling back in alongside.

Young Walt and his new sister both stopped walking to wave at him.

"When we going to do a scout again?" Walt asked.

"Soon as I can," Jim said.

"Walt, come along," Ellen said and took him by the hand.

"I was just saying hi to Mr. Heston."

Ellen gave Jim a quick look then took Walt by the hand and dragged him along.

Colton and the younger girl, Marsha, he thought her name was, were riding at the back of the wagon. Colton still wore a bandage around his middle and he scowled at Jim.

Jim stopped to watch after them.

What had that been about? Did they believe some of the lies the Robesons had been spreading? Jim looked down at his big, scarred hands.

No, they are afraid of me. Like everyone else.

The thought cut him to the bone. He couldn't ignore what had just happened though. Ellen had deliberately walked past him, saying nothing, and looking at him like a rabid dog.

Remounting, Jim circled a half-mile to the south then swung west toward the front of the column. He supposed he couldn't blame them. *Brute*, Mrs. Robeson had called him. *Perhaps I am. But no more than her nephew, Pope, or her husband even.* Pope and he had fought, and he'd beaten their man. He supposed everyone played the villain to someone.

According to Donovan they were just shy of the midway point in their journey. Soon enough he could say goodbye to all of them and go off on his own way. Soon enough he could be alone again.

CLIVE WILSON WAS NOT a patient man, but he was practical.

He waited alone on a ridge overlooking the remains of a wagon train, thinking about how many miles might lay between him, his son, and the woman who'd stolen him away.

There was loot among the broken wagons, and Slade's men picked through it like vultures feasting on fresh carcasses. Slade himself walked toward Clive, a bottle of whiskey in one hand and a blooded knife in the other. The renegade took a deep draw on the bottle and wiped his mouth with the back of his hand.

"Not to your liking, my friend?" he said.

"Ready to be on after the next one," Clive answered.

"We'll be on our way soon enough. And you'll have your wayward bride," Slade said. "The boys needed a little release is all. They been cooped up all winter and they're hungry."

Clive's fists clenched. His hand shifted, slightly, toward the grip of his pistol. *I should just kill him now. Who does he think he is telling me to wait?*

A scream came from the wagons, a woman's, and Clive's thoughts shifted. Abruptly, the scream cut off and a shirtless John emerged from the back of a wagon with a smile splitting his big face and a smear of blood across one cheek.

Slade laughed. "Enjoying yourself John?" he yelled.

The big man only grinned wider and headed for the next wagon. Syd stepped around a wagon then, stuffed a small leather pouch into his saddlebags, and came up to join them.

Clive considered the surly gunman. For all the gunman's threats he at least seemed in control of his appetites. *I could use a man like him, if he doesn't try to kill me.*

"And you, Syd?" Slade said. "Are you enjoying yourself?"

"I've got what I wanted," the small man said and patted the bags.

"You don't split it equally?" Clive asked.

"We split the loot, the goods, the food, and all that. But every man keeps whatever gold money he finds."

"If he can keep it," Syd said.

"If he can keep it," Slade nodded.

Another woman screamed.

"And John gets the women," Slade added.

"Most of them," Syd said.

Two newcomers rode into the destruction, a thin man who slapped one of Slade's men on the back and then hopped into the nearest wagon. The other was a woman, tall with a mane of red hair trailing out behind her. She rode straight for Slade and Syd.

"Slade," she said with a nod. "Who is this?"

"I didn't expect you here," Slade said. "You were supposed to stay with that first group."

"Then you shouldn't have sent Jake."

"Got into trouble did he?" Syd laughed.

"When isn't he?"

"Lou, meet Captain Clive Wilson, a friend of mine from the war," Slade said. "Clive this is Lou, John's little sister."

"Captain is it?" she said.

"It was," Clive shrugged. "Though I'm quite out of favor with the government just now."

"Out of favor," she smiled. "I like that. The west seems to be overrun with Captains these days. There was one in the wagon train I was just with. A rebel, I believe."

"Rebel Captains are hardly real Captains I assure you," Clive said. He decided he liked this woman. There was a challenge to her that he hadn't encountered before. She thought herself strong. He would enjoy seeing just how strong.

"Clive is looking for his lost family. A wife and son. He'd be about eight or nine. They are traveling with her younger brother, sister, and parents."

"A wife, pity," Lou said and stuck out her lower lip. "Does she have a name?"

"Ellen. Ellen Barton," Clive said. "And I'm afraid an accident might soon befall her."

Lou gave him a sulky smile. "You're in luck. I've seen your missing wife, and your son. A handsome boy who favors you." Lou moved closer until less than a foot separated them. "Why don't you tell me more about your wife's looming accident."

"Of course," Clive smiled. "We've got all day."

19

Morning dew beaded the grass in fat clear drops that scattered like so many clear pearls when Jim approached the Webb's wagon. Paul Webb stood out front, staring into the distance, scratching at his chin, oblivious to everything.

His oxen idled around back, picking at the damp grass, tails swatting away a cloud of tiny flies.

"I've come to see about that ox," Jim said.

Without looking, Webb raised a hand. "Have at it."

Jim found the particular animal quickly enough. He removed the old bandages, dabbed on more of the poultice medicine and rewrapped the wound with fresh linen to protect it. The wound was coming along nicely. It would take another week, maybe two, before the ox would be ready to pull again. In the meantime the Webbs would not be able to match their former pace. Though with Paul in this condition even if the team had been whole they wouldn't be capable of maintaining the pace.

"Coming along nicely," Jim said.

Webb grunted in response.

Mrs. Webb appeared then, climbing down from the back of the

wagon awkwardly. She saw Jim and immediately cowered like a frightened rabbit.

"Mrs. Webb," Jim dipped his head.

She said nothing, only kept her eyes low, and retreated back into the wagon, drawing a curtain down to shut the world away.

"My wife," Webb started as Jim moved toward his horse. "My wife...she is sick. Very sick."

"I'll be back tonight," Jim said.

He mounted and rode on toward the next wagon. Someone needed to do...what exactly? Something. Jim was out of his depth. He had no experience with this sort of thing. He knew livestock, horses, oxen, mules. He knew wagons and a bit of farming and he'd come a long way as a scout. Still he recognized that the Webbs, both of them, needed help of some kind.

Is it my place though?

No, it wasn't. All he could do is make the situation worse. Maybe the women of the caravan could do something.

Ellen. He would ask her. She'd nursed the little girl back to health. She could do the same for Mrs. Webb.

Whatever she or her family may feel about me it won't extend to Mrs. Webb. All I need to do is ask.

The Barton's wagon lay two down from Webb's. Jim was there in a moment. He hesitated, remembering the look her father and brother bore toward him. Before the fight with Pope, the Bartons had been nothing but friendly to him, but whatever had happened, whatever had changed they would not greet him as a friend now. Still he only had to see Ellen for a moment. Long enough to explain the situation with the Webbs.

They were still gathered around the fire, eating their breakfast and talking low among themselves. Ellen's father said something; the rest of the family laughed. Colton turned his head enough to see Jim then. He leaned over and said something in David's ear, and then they were all quiet and looking at him. David rose as he approached.

"We don't need you to look at our wagon," he said. "Pat Robeson sent one of his boys over to check it this morning."

"Actually sir, I wonder if I might have a word with your daughter."

David scowled. "You may not."

"He may not what?" Ellen said from the wagon.

"I would speak with you for a moment," Jim said before her father could answer.

"Very well," Ellen said. She walked to her father's side.

"Alone would be best," Jim said.

David's face hardened. "Now see here—"

Ellen took her father's arm and cut him off.

"Whatever you have to say to me go ahead," she said.

Jim licked his lips and glanced at her father. "I am concerned about the Webbs. Mrs. Webb she..."

"You're concerned about Mrs. Webb now," Ellen said. A fire blazed in her eyes now. "Mr. Heston, the women of this group, myself included, do not need your concern. We do not need your attention. We do not need your protection. We are perfectly capable of seeing to matters ourselves."

Taken back, Jim fumed inside. What had happened to turn her so completely? What lies had the Robeson's been spreading?

"Ellen, I only—" Jim started.

"I have nothing more to say to you," she said and spun away.

Jim could only watch her go.

"Leave us be," David said. "We don't need help from your kind."

Jim took a big breath. "Obviously not. I won't trouble you again."

He turned and stomped back to his horse. Swearing under his breath, he made his way back to Donovan's camp. Of all the times to be pig-headed... Ellen had seemed so different from other women he'd known. But no, she was just like the others. Just like Nancy back in San Antone, using him whenever it was convenient.

Stewart, the new man Donovan had hired in Laramie, was packing up when he arrived back at his own wagon. Donovan and Neill were nowhere to be seen.

"Coffee," Stewart offered. "I was just about to pour it out."

"Thanks," Jim held out his cup. "I will never understand women."

Stewart smiled. "Then you'll be just like every other man since Adam."

Jim liked the man well enough. He was older than Remy by a full ten years at least, but he could cook well enough and he was better at caring for the wagon and stock. Jim had no concerns about him wrecking the wagon. More than once, he'd needed to correct something Remy did before he turned the wagon over.

Mounting up, Jim rode to the West, well away from the column. The horse he'd chosen for today was quickly becoming his favorite, an Appaloosa, Donovan had called him. He was a handsome animal, brown on the head and chest turning more to white on the rump and with gray freckled spots all over.

More importantly, he could run all day without tiring and he'd shown a burst of speed when called upon. Neill hadn't much liked the horse—called him a man-killer in fact—and Jim had to admit that he had a wicked temper.

Much like my own.

They bought him back in Laramie, and the first time Neill tried to ride him the horse had immediately planted the cursing scout in the dirt.

The Captain was an excellent rider-even Jim would admit that-but he wanted no part of the Appaloosa. Jim had spent hours with the horse afterward, feeding him a carrot or apple occasionally. Just being around him and getting him used to Jim's presence had calmed the horse considerably, and his patience and persistence had been rewarded.

"He'll buck you one day," Neill warned. "The time you need him most he'll toss you into a pile of cactus. Better off shooting him now."

So far Neill had been proven wrong, but time would tell.

Jim was well out ahead, and he dismounted to walk for a time. He did not hear Donovan approach until the man was right beside him.

"Decided not to see to the wagons today," Donovan said.

"I've been told my help isn't wanted anymore."

"Told you that did they?" Donovan said. He eased down beside Jim and led his horse. "That's the way of the world."

"What?"

"Jim, there is a time when people need men like us. First, they need us to break their trails, to explore the land, to find the path forward and make it safe. Then they need us to show them how to make it. How to survive the journey."

"And then?"

"And then the journey is done. The frontier is tamed and quiet. There are no more Indians, no more renegades. No wild rivers to cross or mountains to climb. Then our day is done, and they don't need us anymore."

"I don't believe that."

"No, I suppose you don't," Donovan said. "I didn't, not at your age. Jim you are unfortunate in that you were born too late. Years ago men like you went West and sought their fortunes. Some, a lucky few, came out rich. All of them got to see a vast new country, wild and untouched by civilization. Men like you, like us, were needed to tame this great American West."

Donovan stopped then. He breathed deep and looked at the mountains rising to the South and North.

"I caught the end of it, that last great exploration. But I'm afraid you missed it entirely."

"I'm going West to build something," Jim said. "A farm, a ranch, a life. Something."

"As did I. But then the wind came calling and the mountains offered their challenge and I had to know and see what lay on the other side. I see that in you. That's why I asked you to come. You would have labored away in Kansas, making wagons until no one needed them, fighting until someone bigger or faster or better came along. There is always someone better."

"My father used to say that," Jim said. "He said 'there's always someone bigger or stronger, but you can always be tougher.'"

"Sounds like a wise man," Donovan grinned.

"My mother did not agree."

"Women can't understand what it is to be a man. They can't hear the wind. They want home and family and safety. But men like us,"

Donovan tapped Jim on the chest. "Men like us want the mountains. We need them."

"Maybe," Jim agreed. His mother would not have been frightened of the mountains. She'd faced down more than one Comanche over a rifle barrel.

"Give them a few days," Donovan said. "Pat Robeson doesn't know a damn thing about wagons. He'll have them all broke down and they'll be begging you for help."

"It's not so much that as..." Jim couldn't finish. What was bothering him? Was it Webb? The change in the man and his wife had been dramatic.

No, that isn't it. It's her. Ellen Barton. What turned her so firmly against me?

"It's the Barton girl," Donovan grinned. "She's a pretty thing. Pretty enough to give a man all the wrong kind of ideas."

"I suppose," Jim allowed.

"Something odd about her situation though. Notice how they never talk about that boy's father? Whole family dances around it. Like they're hiding something."

"They say he died in the war."

"A-huh. Where? What battle? What regiment was he with? People talk about such things, but not them. They don't give up a single detail. And they came to me under strange circumstances."

"Strange?"

"They were in Kansas for months, but they barely made the cutoff. In fact I'd decided against taking on more wagons, but Charles Hightower begged me to see them through." Donovan looked at Jim them. "Begged me. Charles Hightower never begged for anything in his life. He said there had been trouble for them back in Illinois. Trouble for her."

Jim considered it. He didn't know Hightower as well as Donovan did, but he too couldn't imagine the man begging.

"What kind of trouble would there be for a young woman who'd lost her husband in the war?" Donovan said.

"That doesn't make sense," Jim said.

"No it doesn't," Donovan climbed back into the saddle. "But there it is all the same."

"What do I do in the meantime?"

"Take it easy," Donovan rested his hands on the pommel. He took in a deep breath. "Enjoy the rest and the view. Spend some time with Neill. I know how he is—I know better than anyone else—but the man has a lot to teach."

ELLEN SQUINTED at a lone rider approaching on the far horizon. She held a hand up to shade her eyes, trying to decide who it was. It looked too big to be Captain Neill and moving too quickly to be Donovan. Jim Heston then. It had to be. Over the last week he had been gone a lot, riding out ahead of their little column, spending time with Captain Neill, and keeping close to the camp he shared with Donovan and their new driver.

The day had been a hot one, beating down on them without mercy. She'd been warned about getting a sunburn at altitude, but she didn't heed it and her bare arms would take the brunt of it. Luckily, her oversized hat shielded her face somewhat.

"A real scorcher," her father said from ahead.

Walt and his new sister, Alma, walked beside her while her mother and Martha were on the opposite side. Colton was off somewhere. His recovery had been quick, and he proved eager to be away from doting sisters and his parents.

Alma still spoke only rarely. Ellen saw her shading her eyes and studying the approaching rider. She took Ellen's hand, tugging it, and pointing.

"Jim," she said.

"What?"

"Jim," Alma repeated and pulled harder.

"She wants to see Mr. Jim," Walt said.

"Not today. We won't see him today," Ellen shook her head.

Alma's face slipped a notch, and she went back to studying the rider. Then she waved to draw his attention. Soon Walt was following suit.

Keeping his distance, Jim swung wide around them and on toward the next wagon in line.

Ellen didn't think he saw the children, but then he gave them a wave and made his speckled horse rear up on its hind legs.

Alma laughed in glee and Walt cupped his hands to hollar 'ye haw'. Then he too was laughing.

Jim waved his hat once and passed by.

Ellen turned to watch him go. He was a strange young man. He was older than her of course; in many ways though he seemed younger and so very carefree.

"He's a killer," a voice said from behind her.

"Where have you been Colton?" Ellen answered.

"Over at the Robeson's. Practicing my draw," he said and then demonstrated. One instant the gun was in its holster and the next it was out and pointed in Jim's direction. "I've gotten faster."

"You're going to get yourself into trouble with that," Ellen said.

"No, I'm going to get myself out of trouble with it. If I'd been faster Jake never would have gotten away. He'd be buried in the ground."

"Or you'd be," their father interrupted. "You should take that off and set it away."

"I won't," Colton said. "Someone has to protect our family."

"That is father's place," Ellen said. "He will-"

Colton looked at their father and seemed to consider his words. "I'm not talking about protecting us from debt collectors or taxmen. I'm talking about stopping real killers like that Jim Heston. He nearly beat Pope to death. Would have if they hadn't pulled them apart."

"And what did Pope do to cause it?" Ellen asked. She knew Pope. She'd seen him. She'd felt his eyes on her often and the wicked grin that went with that attention. It made her skin crawl.

"He didn't do anything," Colton protested. "He said something about where Jim and Donovan had been and then Heston jumped him. No warning at all."

"I've seen this Pope fellow. He's a lecherous thug. I see the way he looks at your sisters," Ellen's father said.

"After the way she's acted with that Heston-" Colton started.

"What do you mean the way I acted?" Ellen couldn't believe it. What did they think she'd done?

Colton's face flushed red but there was anger in his eyes. "You went out after dark the other night to be with him."

"What?" Ellen said.

"The night of the party, the night Jake attacked Mrs. Webb, the night I almost..." Colton's voice trailed off. He rubbed at his wounded side and then steadied himself and went on. "You were with him weren't you. With him alone in the dark."

David looked at Ellen and she saw the hurt in her father's face. "Is this true Ellen?"

Ellen clenched her fists and thrust them into her pockets. "I took him a plate of food. I thought it would be nice. Alma went with me."

"You were out there a long time," Colton charged. "I was headed out to check on you when I saw Jake force himself on Mrs. Webb."

Ellen whirled on her brother and jammed a finger into his chest. "You were out spying on me."

"I was concerned. Pope said you and Jim were out there—"

"Your good friend Pope again. Wasn't he good friends with that Jake fellow before what happened to Mrs. Webb. Seems like they were drinking together a lot."

"See what she's doing, Father," Colton said. "Deflecting attention from Heston again. That's why Pope said-"

"What exactly did Pope say to set Mr. Heston off Colton?" David said, voice raising. Ellen had heard that tone before, though not for a long long time. Most people thought her father meek or weak, but there was an iron core deep within him. She'd seen him become quite strong when roused; more of that core had been showing on the journey West. "I am suddenly ashamed of how we've treated Mr. Heston the last few days based only on your word and that of this Pope. Now it comes out that Pope accused your sister of wrongdoing.

And it seems Mr. Heston came to her defense and you convinced us to shun him based on that."

"Well I-" Colton started but their father cut him off immediately.

"No son," David said and moved close into Colton's face. "You've been running with a bad crowd, son, and I have failed to put a stop to it. You're wearing that gun around and you're going to get hurt. You did get hurt."

"But Father I—"

"I am grateful and proud that you were able to prevent Mrs. Webb from anything worse, and I know if you hadn't been armed you would likely be dead, but it's time you grew up. It's time you learn that you will be judged by the company you keep."

"And what about her?" Colton pointed to Ellen. "What about the company she keeps? We had to flee our home because of her. Because she wasn't happy being married to the richest man in town. Because she wanted to run away from her troubles. Where are your lessons for her? Where is your wisdom there? Now she's doing it all over again spreading her legs for any—"

David Barton struck his son then with a hand across that face that knocked him down into the dirt. "Do not speak of your sister that way. Not ever. You didn't see the bruises from the beatings that man gave her. You don't know about the broken bones. We shielded you from that, your mother and I, and now I regret it."

Colton's gun was suddenly in his fist, pointed at their father. His face was drawn into a wild snarl.

"Colton, no," Ellen screamed.

For a long, long moment she thought her brother would actually kill their father, but he got up, dusted himself off and walked back toward the wagon. Their mother stood there, horrified at what she'd just witnessed.

Colton kissed her cheek and said, "They're right. Pope and all the Robeson's. My sister is just a common whore."

Then he picked up his bag out of the wagon, gave a stunned Martha a quick hug, slung it over his shoulder, and walked back down the line of wagons.

"Where is Uncle Colton going?" Walt's little voice said.

Ellen sighed. She'd forgotten about Walt and Alma standing behind her. They had heard everything. "I don't know."

20

J im Heston rode out into a vast carpet of bright spring. Donovan told him the greenness would soon end, that further west the great sweeping plains would wither into high desert, that the grass would fade into clumps of purple sage, that even the mountains would trade forests of leafy aspen for stunted and scattered pines.

On the far horizon Jim could just see the first ragged signs of what lay ahead.

"This has been the easy part of the journey," Neill said. He and Donovan were just a few paces behind him.

"Easy?" Jim said. "Blizzards, constant threat of Indians, rivers swollen with icy runoff, renegades on every side-including among us-that's been the easy part?"

"Well yes," Donovan said. "In blizzards you seek shelter, for Indians or renegades you stay vigilant, rivers you find a good crossing or wait them out, but in a week we'll be at the desert."

"And for the desert there is no answer," Neill chimed in.

"No answer but to plow on ahead," Donovan said with a nod.

Jim looked back at snaking line of wagons behind him. The group continued to use the advice of Pat Robeson, leaving him free to roam ahead. In many ways it was a relief not to be needed and he'd learned a great deal. He'd gone out with Neill often, bringing back fresh meat, deer or antelope.

But more and more he went off by himself. Neill, of all people, supported the idea. "A man's got to try it for himself. You can only learn so much by watching others."

Jim spurred his horse along and left the others behind. He crossed over a long sweeping ridgeback and downslope among stunted cedars and scattered sage. This early there was still grass of a sort, long-stemmed and pale looking. Sickly, he might have called it. He turned a little north, following a shallow creek toward a range of mountains. On the opposite range of mountains lightning flashed from a growing cloudburst. Jim never heard the thunder. It had to be miles distant.

He paused on the hill, watching the storm, breathing mingled scents of rain, sage, and pine.

Can California be so grand as all of this?

Then, on a whim, he brought the Appaloosa up a draw. There would be more mountains beyond. What would they look like? Before the horse reached the top he heard brush pop to his left and saw a startled elk bull.

The bull bounded away, and Jim followed after him. The Appaloosa was a good horse, strong and quick, but no match for a running elk.

Jim brought the horse up short. The ground was littered with broken rock and fallen branches. Dangerous to be racing across. Drawing the rifle from its scabbard, he dismounted to walk and decided to follow on after the elk for a ways. If the big bull stopped he might be able to get off a decent shot.

They didn't really need the meat, he and Neill had taken deer the last few days, but it would always be appreciated.

The junipers grew scarce until he came to the edge of a clearing maybe a hundred acres in size. The bull stood at the far edge, nose tilted up and sniffing the air in great huffs.

Jim knelt down and steadied the rifle.

He squeezed off the shot and heard the bullet strike home with a deep thunk. The bull ran a short distance, seemingly confused of what had happened, and then fell. By the time Jim reached him the elk was dead, and he set about with his skinning knife.

The blade was sharp, and he made quick work of the bull. Then loaded the meat on the Appaloosa before setting off back toward the wagons.

It was dark by the time he reached them, the moon not up yet. Instead of taking the meat to his own camp though he snuck his way up to the Barton wagon. Young Colton hadn't been traveling with his parents for several days. He'd moved entirely over to the Robeson group. For all his faults, Colton had gone hunting a few times and sometimes brought meat to his family. Without him they'd be reduced to salted meat alone.

Despite what they thought of him, he'd brought Alma to them and felt somewhat responsible for her. Growing kids like her and Walt needed fresh meat from time to time. *It's only right that I leave a little to see them through.*

He hung the elk's hindquarters on a strip of leather beside the wagon. He started to slip away when he heard someone sobbing. Whoever was sobbing suddenly cried out in their sleep. Something about a man named Clive. It sounded like Ellen.

Missing her fallen husband, no doubt. It must hurt to be so young and have a spouse taken from you. Especially with a youngster to care for.

Young Walt would remember almost nothing of his father. Jim's memories of his father, his brother, had faded over the last few years, but he remembered their faces, their voices, what they were like. *How much have I forgotten though?*

How much did anyone forget over the course of a lifetime?

A lamp came to life inside the wagon then. Jim saw Ellen's outline, sitting up and obviously crying.

"Are you alright dear?" her father said.

"Of course. Just another nightmare."

"Was it him?" Ellen's mother this time.

"Always," Ellen said as Jim walked away.

. . .

THE WAGON TRAIN lost six head of stock that night, four oxen and a pair of horses. Jim joined Donovan and Neill at the Walston's camp where they'd been taken.

"Indians," Neill said after examining where they'd been taken. "No one else could have snuck in so close."

"Utes?" Donovan said.

"Or Blackfeet," Neill pointed. "They slipped up without being seen but didn't make much effort to hide their trail."

"Might be trying to put miles between us and them. Figure we're tied to the wagons and can't pursue," Donovan said.

"I'll trail them for a bit and see," Neill said.

"Take Moses with you."

"I'll go," Jim offered.

"Not this time," Donovan said. "Neill and Moses can handle it. You keep close to the wagons and keep your rifle handy."

"You think they're trying to draw us off?" Jim said.

"Possibly," Donovan shrugged. "Strong as we are I can't see them making an attempt, but I also wouldn't have expected to lose stock like this."

"What about the Walstons?"

"Gather an ox each from Webb, Adams, and a few of the others. They're traveling lighter now-they've eaten a lot of the weight-and giving up an animal each won't slow them."

"Some of them won't like it," Neill said. "Especially if you send him."

"Nathan Walston has a wife and four kids. Sacrifices have to be made."

Neill held up his hands. "I'm just sayin'."

"Yeah," Donovan shook his head. "Damned fools think we're just a hill or two away. They'll learn soon enough, once we get into the alkali flats. They'll quake for sure at the sight of the Sierras."

Neill gathered his horse's reins and collected Moses and the pair set out after the missing animals while Jim and Donovan got the Walstons sorted and the rest of the wagons moving west.

An hour later Donovan dropped back to speak to Jim.

"Up ahead there's a canyon that drops off to the left. It's deep but sloped shallow so a group of mounted men could ride out. If there's Blackfeet after us they'll likely attack from there."

"What do you need me to do?" Jim said. He wiped his hands on his pants. His palms were suddenly damp. Pistol or rifle, he was a good shot, but other than the Comanche attack back in Texas he'd never been involved in anything like this.

"Get on that Appaloosa of yours and be ready," Donovan said. "Fall back around the tenth wagon. If the shooting starts don't bother with a circle, we won't have time for it, just roll them up beside the first wagons and make a pair of lines. That way they can cover each other's backs."

"Can't we swing wide around the canyon?"

"I plan to, but there's hills opposite. They pinch us into a narrow place."

Jim dropped a handful of extra rifle cartridges into his pocket and saddled up the Appaloosa. Then he slowed until he was at the Barton's wagon, the tenth one in line today.

He took a breath and approached David Barton.

"Jim, good I wanted a chance to speak with you," David said. "Jim, I feel awful about what-"

"Donovan is expecting an attack."

"What?"

"Donovan is expecting to be attacked by Indians in the next hour," Jim began. Then he outlined the plan for David.

"He wants us to roll up beside the first wagon? How much space should I give them?"

"Several feet. The point of it is to watch each other's backs and not let anyone squeeze in between."

"Alright," David said.

"You'll want the women and children all up in the wagon where it's safer."

"Mother, get everyone up in the wagon."

"Your son isn't with you?" Jim said.

"He's not," David said.

"Make sure anyone who can shoot has a rifle or pistol ready," Jim said.

"We will," David said.

"I'll stay with you, riding on your right. If anything comes at us from that direction I'll handle it," Jim said.

The first shot caught Jim by surprise. It came from ahead and he thought it sounded like Donovan's gun. He exchanged a quick glance with David Barton. "Like we planned."

David slapped the reins and picked up his team's pace into a run and led them to the right into a parallel line beside the lead wagons.

Jim waited long enough to get the next wagon moving along behind then spurred the Appaloosa toward the front.

Rifle raised, Jim slowed alongside the Barton's wagon, watching the hills to their right and the flat area directly ahead. In a brief moment he saw Ellen, her mother, and the youngest girl all holding the children tight. Ellen held raised pistol.

Where had she gotten that?

Gunfire was coming quick now, both the quick snap of pistols and the deep boom of rifles. In the background to the gunfire a chorus of shouts and whoops rose up. A mounted warrior wearing red and white painted streaks across his face and chest appeared ahead of them. Jim's rifle jumped; the warrior fell.

"Stop here," Jim yelled when the Barton wagon had pulled close to the lead.

Dust and grey smoke obscured the battle. Jim caught glimpses of Indians, fired where he could snap off a quick shot. An arrow struck the side of the Barton's wagon and lodged itself there.

More whoops came then. This time from the hills directly to their right.

"Watch the right side," Jim roared. He raced the Appaloosa along the line of wagons pointing to the hills. The ambushers had planned well. With Donovan skirting wide of the canyon he'd brought them close to the hills where the Indians could shoot down at them.

Rifles barked as more attackers appeared above. Arrows plunged down from the heights. Women and children were screaming. Men shouted their defiance.

We have to break free. Otherwise they'll pick us to pieces.

Jim swung about and ran his horse ahead, past the lead wagons; he wheeled right up the nearest hill. War club in hand, a brave rose up to challenge him. Jim shot him in the forehead.

More braves turned to face the new threat and Jim was riding through them, screaming, cursing, shooting. His rifle came up empty; he hammered the barrel into one warrior's neck then slammed it down into the scabbard. Smoke rose from his pistol as he cut down two, three of his enemies. The Appaloosa swept through the ambushers like a black stone skipping over a pond. Too many. There were far too many for him alone. He'd broken their attack though. Every bullet, every arrow sent at him was one less that struck the families below. It would buy them time to break free. All around more guns fired.

Jim's pistol clicked on an empty cylinder. Had he already fired all six? An Indian loomed ahead, holding a war lance. The warrior heaved the lance and Jim ducked low beneath it. He brought the pistol down and slammed the barrel into the Indian's temple. Then the fighting was suddenly behind him. The Appaloosa ran down into a draw and Jim wheeled around. He slammed new cartridges into his pistol first, then the rifle. he would need every shot. He cycled the action as hoofbeats sounded through the smoke.

He lifted the rifle, finger tightening, then stopped as Neill emerged.

"You wounded?" He said.

"No," Jim lowered the pistol as Neill began reloading his own weapons.

"Wait up a minute and we'll ride in together," Neill said.

Jim scowled. He didn't have time to wait for an old man. He'd left the Bartons in a vulnerable position. They could have Ellen or those children even now.

"We've got to get them off the wagons. They'll be shooting down on them again."

"No," Neill said and shook his head. "You broke them."

"What?"

"Your charge," Neill said. "It broke them. They've given up the fight."

"But what about the—" Jim tilted his head. He didn't hear anymore firing.

"It's over. We'll have wounded of course and a few dead, but not so many," Neill replaced his guns and started back at a steady walk.

The wagons were a mess. Several draft animals had broken loose in the confusion. They milled about in torn harnesses. A number of dead Indians lay scattered around, and there were men of the wagon train lying with them. Some had been scalped. Wives, mothers, and children cried over their fallen. Several wounded men and women were being seen to by the Doc. Most of the wounds looked trivial, shallow cuts or bullet burns, but one of the Robeson men had an arrow stuck through his lower left side and a young woman Jim didn't know had a nasty wound on her leg.

Mercifully, he didn't see any injured children.

Donovan was up near the wagon's head, speaking to Milo Adams, David Barton, and a few others.

"Horsehead spring is two more hours on. Once the wounded are ready we'll travel and camp there. Anyone able-bodied needs to help the others gather their teams and get moving."

"How long will we stay there?" Milo asked.

"That depends on the wounded," Donovan said. "I'll not leave any family behind though, not here."

"You think they'll be back?" Paul Webb asked.

Jim noticed the man seemed to have recovered himself after the attack.

"I don't, but there are other dangers out here. A clever gang of renegades might hit us while we're licking our wounds."

Donovan paused for a moment and looked up toward Neill and Jim.

"Gentlemen, nice work today. A lot of us owe you our lives. I didn't expect them to hit us from both sides, but you reacted well," Donovan said.

"I just followed him," Neill pointed to Jim.

"What can we do to help?" Jim said. He didn't feel like he'd done enough. The dead and their families wouldn't have much to be grateful for.

"Round up any loose stock and get these wagons rolling. We need to reach that spring tonight before resting up. In this country it's best to camp on water."

Jim started back along the wagons.

"A word Jim," Donovan called.

Jim paused and waited while the other men dispersed. Neill gave him a clap on the back and left him alone with Donovan.

"You did well," Donovan said.

"Tell that to the widows," Jim nodded to the crying families. "I should have acted sooner."

"And I should have sent a scout or two up into the hills at the first sign of trouble," Donovan answered. "But we're here, we're alive and so are most of our people. That's what counts."

"If Neill hadn't followed me I'd likely be dead myself," Jim said. "I should have—"

"Maybe, but Neill did ride along after you. You both survived and you pulled them off us. Take this as a victory. People die. It's a part of the journey, an unfortunate part, but a part of it none-the-less."

"I'll go help Neill," Jim said.

"Thanks," Donovan said. "Don't let this wear on you. This won't be the last time we face danger, and if we don't lose anyone else we'll be lucky beyond belief. I will need you. We will all need you again."

21

Ellen Barton gathered a heap of laundry into her arms and set out to do the day's washing. After the battle with the Indians— Utes as Captain Neill called them—Mr. Donovan had brought the wagons through a broad cleft carved deep into the shoulder of an old gray mountain. After winding along, the cleft widened out into a grassy park just large enough to hold all the wagons. There was a pool in the center, maybe a hundred feet across, fed by water spilling from a crack in the granite wall of the mountain. Overflow from the pool spilled out into a narrow stream full of moss-covered boulders and gravel. The stream ran on for about fifty yards, twisting and turning around clumps of bright stalky grass before sinking into a flat, sandy area like water into a hungry sponge.

Ellen went to the end of the stream with the laundry. There were other women there, knelt down over washboards and buckets, lathering their clothes with soap before wringing them out. The day was clear and bright, but not so hot. The walls of the canyon rose up around them in towering spires of smooth gray and crimson rock. Ellen found a spot further down from the rest and set about with her chore.

Most of the women were smiling and talking. They and their

CARSON MCCLOUD

families had survived the attack. Not everyone had been so lucky; several families mourned their fallen. If not for Jim Heston and Captain Neill it might have been worse.

Martha had been doing most of the laundry, but since the Indian attack she'd refused to go off anywhere alone. Her sleep had been troubled and restless broken by occasional screams or sobs. Ellen pitied her younger sister. During the battle, Ellen had sheltered in the wagon with Martha, their mother, and the children. She shuddered, remembering the fear she'd felt when the shooting and screaming started.

They'd huddled in terror as gunfire erupted outside. The battle seemed to last for ages until the air grew rank with smoke and sweat and the scent of blood.

Once, near the end of the fighting, an Indian had tried to enter their wagon. It wasn't the first time she'd seen one—Fort Laramie had been full of them—begging for money or sleeping against one of the Fort's walls, clothed in little more than rags. But the man coming into their wagon was not one of those broken souls. This was a wild, strong warrior, eyes fierce and dark as onyx and with lines of red and white paint on his face and along his tanned arms.

Martha had been closest to him. He'd grabbed a handful of her hair, trying to wretch her out of the wagon. Martha screamed and batted at the warrior's hands and face until he'd slapped her with his other hand. To her shame, Ellen had simply frozen at first, too shocked to move. Where was father? Where was Colton? Why hadn't they kept them safe? Then she'd remembered the pistol hidden in her skirts.

She'd drawn it and when the Indian saw it he'd smiled at her. Smiled and wretched all the harder on Martha's hair. Ellen lifted the gun, sighting down the long barrel as she'd been taught and squeezed off a shot. A miss. The bullet struck the top of the Indian's ear, spraying a fine line of blood on the canvas. Ellen cocked the heavy pistol again; the stunned warrior released Martha and vanished. Martha yelped once and then her eyes rolled over white as she went limp.

Ellen had moved to follow him, but her mother caught her by the hand. "No. Help me with your sister."

Unconscious, Martha had fallen awkwardly, and Ellen helped lower her down into the wagon bed.

By then the fighting outside seemed to be moving away. Ellen peered out from the canvas and saw the Indians riding away. Her father stood near the front of the wagon, rifle in hand. There was a dead warrior at his feet, not the same one who fled the wagon.

"Father," Ellen said.

When he turned she saw the gash on his forehead and the line of blood trickling from it.

"Ellen, thank God you are alright," he said.

"Father you're wounded," Ellen pointed to the gash.

Her father ran a hand over his forehead and then looked at the blood. "I am," he agreed. "How is your mother? How are the others?"

"Martha feinted, but we are well enough," Ellen said. "One of them tried to get her and I...I...I shot him."

"You shot him?"

"I did," she nodded.

"Is he dead?" her father's jaw set.

"No, I only clipped his ear."

"A good lesson for him then," her father grinned suddenly. Then his face turned grim. "It was a near thing Ellen. They almost had us until Heston rode up behind them. He broke them Ellen. He and Captain Neill broke them and sent them running. Otherwise...otherwise..." He trembled then, bowing his head, and running a hand through his hair. "Otherwise I don't know."

Afterward Ellen overheard some of the other men talking. They'd all agreed. Jim and Captain Neill had been heroes. Even Pat Robeson had admitted it.

Ellen set the laundry beside her pail and about scrubbing. Soap bubbled up to her elbows as she dunked each garment in turn. More women came down from the caravan. Some set their wash near her. Most were young, younger than herself by a few years, and soon they were talking.

"I heard his father owned a big plantation down in Texas," one said.

"I thought he was a soldier for the Confederacy," another answered. "You saw how he rode his horse. He had to be in the cavalry."

"He's too young," the first woman said. Ellen thought her name was Elise, some cousin to the Robesons. She was young and blonde and pretty with emerald eyes and a full figure.

"Captain Neill said he killed at least six of them up on that hillside. Rode right through them. Rifle and then pistol. Even killed one with his bare hands," one of the older girls added.

"I wish he'd ride back beside my wagon more often. Papa asked him to repair a broken axle a few weeks out of Kansas. Even bundled up against the cold, I could see how strong and handsome he was. Made me tingle warm all over," a dark-haired girl giggled.

"I wonder what he's going to do in California," Elise said.

"I heard he lost his love down in San Antonio to a bandit. And he rode out after them," the dark-haired girl said. Jolie was her name. Her father was a blacksmith back in Missouri.

"Did he find her?"

"He did," Jolie nodded. "He found them and fought the bandit but his love..."

"Of course," another woman said with a sigh. "I wish my husband would ride out after me like that. He'd be too busy scratching his butt."

The women all laughed then.

"I'd help him forget her," Elise said. "I'd twist him around until he plumb forgot about her."

"Your Pa might shoot him."

"He might try," Elise nodded. "Though Pa said it was a brave thing he did. Even Cousin Pope had to admit that, and he hates Jim."

Jim. Ellen's mind raced. They were talking about Jim Heston.

"Says something that does," another woman said.

"He rode up there against all those Indians, alone, except for Captain Neill of course, and he charged right in," Elise said. "My Pa went up there later and studied the tracks. He said there had to be two dozen Utes on that hill and Jim riding in all alone."

"A brave man," Jolie said. "I wouldn't mind helping him forget his lost love either."

"Not if I do it first," Elise grinned fiercely, and the women laughed again.

Ellen scooped up her laundry and set out back for camp. Her eyes stung and she walked quickly. She heard them talking though.

"What's wrong with her?" Jolie behind her asked.

"I heard she set her own cap for him," a woman said. "He's been over to her wagon often enough."

"Isn't she a little old? And what about those kids of hers, the one they found?" Jolie said.

"The one *he* found," Elise said. "Rescued from renegades."

Ellen walked faster to put their voices firmly behind her. Her breath was coming quick and hot. How dare they talk about her like that. And Jim. He was not some prize bull to be auctioned off. How could they be so catty?

Returning to the wagon she dropped the clothing in a heap near the fire. Her father had set up a pole with a line running between it and the wagon and Ellen practically threw the clothes at it. Where was Martha? *Martha should be doing this.*

Martha was sitting by the fire, staring blankly into the flames.

"If you're going to sit around you might as well help with the laundry," Ellen snapped.

Martha jerked as if stung.

Her father gave her a long look and took the pipe from his mouth. "Ellen—" he started.

"She's moped around long enough," Ellen said. Tears ran down her face now, hot and bitter. "She has to pull her share. I had to go down there and listen to those...those...women and their talk."

Ellen retreated to the back of the wagon. She took out a handkerchief and dabbed at her eyes, but the tears didn't stop. She stared at the damp marks in frustration.

Why am I crying. I don't understand.

"It's alright," her mother said beside the fire, holding Martha and rocking her gently. "Ellen didn't mean it. She's just frustrated that's all. We were all scared. We understand."

Walt and Alma emerged from the wagon where they'd been playing.

"Mama," he said.

"Walt, I'm alright."

He looked at her eyes and frowned. "But you're crying," he said.

"Sometimes I just need to cry. That's how girls are."

Walt stole a look over at his new sister. "All girls?"

"Sometimes," Ellen said. Then she wrapped her son and daughter up in a fierce hug.

JIM HESTON WAS RELIEVED to be moving again. Three days resting at Horsehead spring left him restless and eager to get the journey done. From what Donovan and Neill said they still had weeks of desert to go and after that the final and most formidable obstacle in the journey, the crossing over the High Sierras.

Both the older men spoke in reverent tones about those raw peaks.

"They rise up like daggers into the sky, huge slabs of pure rock and passes so high it's hard to draw breath," Donovan said.

"Nowhere like them," Neill would nod along. "Treacherous and poison mean."

"The timing has to be just right. Too soon in the year and there'll be snow and thawing runoff choking the creeks and canyons. Too late and you could get caught in an early snow. Ask the Donner Party how that turned out," Donovan said.

Beyond the Sierras California would all be worth it. First though, the desert with its bitter alkali hardpan and blinding white desolation. Donovan said they would lose stock during the crossing, especially in the dreaded Forty-Mile stretch.

"Everyone pays the tithe there. At least one wagon down, several draft animals. It's a gruesome march through the hottest, driest country on earth and then to the foot of that great gray wall of gran-ite," Donovan said. "I've seen more than one man broken by it."

For now though they were headed to Fort Hall where the trail forked north for Oregon or south for California. They followed the Bear River, going round the north end of the Wasatch mountains.

Ranging a few miles ahead, Jim noticed a group of wagons at the base of a steep incline. A few wagons were already at the top and men were leading teams down those below.

Some of the men saw Jim and picked up their rifles.

Jim lifted a hand in greeting riding slowly closer. "I'm friendly," he said.

"Most men are when they've got a half dozen rifles aimed at them," a tall man in a gray shirt said. Jim took him for their leader.

"I'm Jim Heston out of San Antone."

"San Antonio Texas? Son, you are a long way from home."

"Figured to head west for California, like you folks," Jim gave them his best smile.

"Alone?"

"Wagon train behind me, a few miles. We're out of Independence."

"Who's leading it?" Gray shirt asked.

"Donovan along with Captain Neill."

The man in the gray shirt smiled. "I know Donovan. A good man, slim fellow with almost-white hair. I saved him from a band of Apaches one time who wanted that hair awful bad. That's why he shaves it now."

Jim grinned. "Well I never met anyone who called Donovan slim. Seems to me built more like a grizzly bear with a shaggy mane of brown hair."

Gray shirt squinted at him and lowered his rifle. "Alright so you at least know what the man looks like. Doesn't prove you aren't a rene-gade or some such."

"I suppose not," Jim agreed. He rested his hands on the pommel, moving slow and deliberate. These folks were taking it awful careful.

Something has them spooked.

"This the 'big hill'?"

"It is. Have to rig up double teams to pull up and the descent is worse. Steep, narrow, full of switchbacks. Hell on wheels and axles."

"And a man's nerves," one of the others said with a laugh.

"Sounds like," Jim nodded. "Mind if I climb down? Coffee smells good."

"Suit yourself. I'm Rodney Tate," the gray shirted man offered a hand.

"I thought we were the first outfit out of Kansas this year," Jim said.

"You might have been," Rodney agreed. "We started in Nebraska near Fort Kearney. Gathered wagons there all winter."

"Wagons coming in," one of the other men said.

Rodney looked over Jim's shoulder. "Yeah, that's Donovan alright. Even at this distance I recognize the man."

"He's a hard one to miss," Jim said. He looked around at all the men, still holding their rifles and watching the wagons rolling up. "Seems like you folks have had some trouble."

"You don't know the half of it," Rodney said. "Stolen stock, Injuns, bandits. You name it, we've had it."

"We just had a little run-in with the Utes ourselves," Jim said. "I'd heard they were more peaceful than some of the other tribes."

Tate eyed him, "Indians get odd notions at times. Even if the old men want peace the young want honor and glory. To a warrior just one of our wagons would make him a wealthy man."

Donovan was within shouting distance then and offered greeting.

"Leslie Tate is that you?" Donovan's voice boomed like a cannon.

One of the men snickered and Rodney scowled at him. "He knows I hate that name."

Rodney turned back and cupped his hands. "It's me you damned old buffalo; now come on in before you bring the whole mountain down on us."

Donovan laughed and spurred his horse into the camp. Neill followed, while the wagons formed up.

Donovan climbed down and shook hands with Rodney. "How the

hell did you get here before me Rodney? It was still snowing when we started out. I thought for sure I'd be the first along."

"Started in Kearney," Tate said. "And only a damned fool like you would try crossing the plains before spring."

"Kearney?" Donovan shook his head. "Cost a fortune to winter there. Besides the ground was nice and frozen. Crossing was easy before the thaw."

"And after?"

Donovan's cheeks reddened a little. "We managed." He spotted Jim setting by the fire, "I see you met Jim."

"We did," Jim saluted with his cup. "And the coffee is better than it smells."

"Why all the guns though?" Donovan looked around.

"We've had trouble." Tate said.

Tate spent the next few minutes outlining the problems they'd encountered. The Sioux had attacked them twice. Renegade whites once. A number of spare wheels and axles had been lost after one of the oxen was attacked by a mountain lion. Wild with fright, the team raced over a steep cliff in the mountains and lost everything down in a deep ravine.

"Have you replaced the spares?" Jim asked.

Tate shook his head. "We haven't stopped long enough for that. Every day we fall further behind. At this pace we won't make the Sierras before the snow flies."

"We could join up," Donovan suggested. "We've a few spares and I would welcome more guns to hold off the Indians."

"Where you bound for?" Tate said.

"Going to drop down toward Sutter's Mill."

"My people want to swing south. Plan on settling down in the Stockton area."

Donovan looked up toward the 'big hill' where they continued to hoist wagons. "I could loan you a few of our wheels and a couple axles."

"I'd be obliged," Tate said.

"Jim here knows a good bit about repairing them and shaping

new ones," Donovan said and pointed his hat. "Jim, how's the timber here look to make a few replacements?"

Jim studied the trees on either side of the trail. They were tall and healthy. Wood from one of them would be awfully green. *Probably wouldn't last long.* If he could find a one or two blown down by the wind he could trim them into axles easy enough. He didn't see anything promising nearby—no doubt travelers had loaded up with firewood against the cold desert nights ahead—but there would be some further off the trail. Shaping wheels would be harder. *I'll have to make my own tools to bend them.*

"It's possible," Jim agreed. "I'd need a few men to help. Some to guard and some to help with the wood."

"We'll keep what we have then while Jim here stays with you for a few days and gets you set with a few spares."

Tate rubbed at his jaw and studied Jim. "You think you can do it young man?"

"Axles shouldn't be hard. Planks either if you need those. The wheels will take time and a bit of luck. Did you keep any of the busted ones?"

Tate gestured over his shoulder toward a heavy-set man in a dirty red shirt. "Clyde's hauling three with missing spokes."

"That will help," Jim said. "I can replace the spokes easy enough and get them ready."

"It's settled then," Donovan said. "We'll help you get over the hill here and once we're over Jim can stay with you. After he gets you situated, he can ride along after us."

"Dangerous for a man riding alone," Neill said.

"You're welcome to stay with him then," Donovan said. "I think the two of you can handle yourselves."

22

J im spent four busy days repairing the wheels and cutting axles. Captain Neill helped, much to his surprise, the older man rolling up his shirtsleeves and setting to work with little comment.

Despite their help, Tate's people kept their distance. Only Tate would share their food and fire.

"They're a clannish lot. Not welcoming of strangers," he explained. He gave them a half-smile. "Barely tolerate me, truth be told. Always going on about that strange religion of theirs."

"We understand," Jim said. "It is much the same in our own camp."

"I believe it," Tate said and looked into the flames. "It's different for us. Those of us bound to the trail. We're needed sure enough, but we aren't really wanted."

In the deep dark, Neill would slip off away to be by himself. Jim didn't know what ailed the Captain. He spoke little, and it seemed like all the emotions had been drained out of him. Jim couldn't seem to get more than a word or two out of him. He'd been out of sorts since the battle with the Indians.

Jim went to sleep thinking of Ellen and Alma, the little girl he'd rescued. A fine thing he'd done. One fine thing, saving her like that. His mother would have been proud no doubt. Aside from that, he couldn't recall the last good thing he'd done. In Independence his only aim had been saving money to come west. He'd fought. He'd beaten men senseless and been beaten himself just for a little handful of gold.

It took money to reach California though, and once there he'd need more money to settle in. *Settle in on what though?* He didn't think farming was his future. Gold mining held little appeal. What was it Remy had gone on about? Owning a little restaurant down by the sea.

Somewhere ahead of them Donovan would be sitting beside a fire, staring into the flames and thinking...thinking what? About a home. About a life that might have been. All he'd given up for a life spent on a cold and lonely road. Their work was needed, Jim knew that. Men like Donovan, Tate, and Neill tamed the west as much as the settlers they led.

Jim didn't want that life though. He wanted something better. A man needed a place to call home. Not an endless series of cold, drafty cabins, waiting all winter for the next group of settlers to escort across. Waiting and wondering if this was the last year there would be a trip.

When the wheels were done and the axles loaded, he shook hands with Tate.

The older man looked over his shoulder at the line of wagons rolling along. "They won't say it so I will. Thank you."

"We don't hold it against them," Jim said. "Our folk might do the same."

Tate's jaw tightened and he dipped his hat. "See you next time then," he said and followed along after them.

Neill and Jim sat a moment and watched them go.

"He's a good man," Neill said, the first words he'd spoken that day.

"Seems like," Jim agreed.

"Without the wagons we can save time cutting across," Neill said and led the way.

They rode for a full day, skirting mountains, passing over an arid landscape of rock and brush and dry creek beds. They saw rabbits, coyotes, pairs of desert quail. They went quietly over the land, not shooting, not drawing attention to themselves in any way.

Generally the Utes and Shoshone were friendly enough, but as the earlier attack proved, any Indian could be a threat. Several of the tribes along the Snake river hated the white man. They did come this far south at times. Moreover Tate's earlier words rang true: any brave looking to impress his tribe would want their horses and their guns.

They made a camp in a gully while the wind howled overhead, and the sky was clear and bright. Jim settled down over their meal across the fire from Neill.

"You've been quiet," Jim said.

"Thinking too much."

"Thinking about?"

"Thinking I'm getting too old to do this anymore." Neill poked at the fire with a long stick.

"Donovan said the trail's days are just about done. People will ride the rails soon. The trip will take no more than a week. They'll sit in the comfortable little cars and look out the window at all this and they'll miss it."

"Miss it?"

"The struggle. The land. Everything. They'll wonder at how easy it is going west and why everyone made such a big fuss out of it. They won't appreciate what we've faced."

Neither spoke for a time. The fire popped and a few sparks took flight.

"What will you do?" Jim asked. He knew Donovan had some sort of plan, but he couldn't imagine Neill doing anything but drinking himself to death.

"Do you know what I did during the war?"

"Cavalry, I always figured."

"Started out that way," Neill chuckled. "Then I got hurt during a night raid. Busted my leg right here." Neill gestured to his knee. "Still hurts like the devil anytime the weather changes. And since I couldn't ride they sent me to another outfit. We were raiders. Blew up railroad bridges. I got pretty good at it."

"I'd see a Yankee bridge. Just sitting there pretty-as-you-please. Beautiful bridge, all fresh lumber and covered trestles. And I blew them up." Neill sniffed. "That was the job. Most times no one got hurt. One time though the railroad didn't realize the bridge was gone. I watched one of their smoking locomotives steam hard and fast around a corner and then down it plunged right down over the side into the river below."

Neill swallowed. Jim saw the flames reflecting in his eyes.

"I killed more Yankee soldiers that day than I ever did riding a horse."

"What will you do when this is all over?" Jim asked.

"I don't know." Neill went to his blankets and laid down.

They rose early while the air still held night's chill. Following the trail as the wagons had to, Donovan and the group couldn't be more than a day ahead of them. They skirted a range of dry mountains crossing several empty creeks and drainages. This far west there was little more than skeletal sage and rare clumps of withered grass.

"Dry country from here until the foothills of the Sierras," Neill said.

"How far is that?"

"Five hundred miles or so." Neill shrugged.

"Surely there's water," Jim said but to his eye he could see none.

"We'll follow the Humboldt west. Water's a might foul—lots of minerals—but plenty of it. Then there's the hard stretch."

"Hard stretch?"

"The Forty-Mile."

Donovan had talked of it, and Jim had heard of it before, back in Kansas. Everyone traveling west had heard of it. Forty miles of white, choking alkali dust. Totally empty. Not even enough shade for a bird to hide in.

"It's as bad as they say?" Jim ventured. Donovan had said as much but he wanted Neill's version as well.

Neill gave him a look and a wry smile. "Worse. We're early too so we'll have high-summer heat. Nothing but hardpan, poison dust, bad water, and blinding sun. Abandoned wagons. Lots of those along with the bones of anyone who didn't make it."

They rode past noon, seeing little, not even an antelope or mule deer.

Neill reined up suddenly when they crossed over a long ridge.

"Riders," he dipped his hat to the north.

Jim saw them then or rather the dust rising from their passing. The group looked to be a large one by the size of the cloud.

"Army?" Jim said.

"Could be." Neill squinted. "Or could be something else. They're riding awful hard. Don't know why the army would be riding so hard and so far from the nearest Fort."

"Indians wouldn't leave so much dust," Jim said.

"You're learning," Neill smiled. "Unless they were in the middle of a fight, no Indian would raise that much sign."

"We'd hear the gunshots if they were attacking the wagons."

"I think there's a trail south of here that sweeps around that peak ahead. It's longer, but we'll come out ahead of them. Might even be ahead of Donovan. Let's avoid whatever trouble this is."

Neill set a quick pace and led the way. They climbed up the shoulder of the mountain, rising up from sage country into scattered pines and rocky outcroppings. Purely by accident, they found a seep where they watered their horses and refilled their canteens.

As they climbed higher the air cooled. They topped a high ridge of granite and discovered a valley full of lush grass and white-trunked aspen. A herd of elk lounged in the distance.

"Never would have guessed this was here," Neill said.

"Where are we?"

"The Ruby mountains," Neill pointed to a stream running down toward the desert below. "We can follow that right down into the Humboldt."

"The wagons will be there?" Jim said.

"Should be by now," Neill said. "I want to be there before that group of riders. Something about that don't sit right. Why would anyone be running their horses out here?"

"More renegades."

"That's what I'm thinking. We need to let Donovan know."

They were off again, this time riding north along the stream. The sun dipped down to touch the horizon and still they rode. More streams merged together from the mountains and the water grew dark and cloudy green with minerals.

Just before dark they saw the sun-bleached canvas of a wagon top. Then there were more, all arranged in a circle, near the river.

Jim noticed a single rider approaching the wagons from the east. *One of the earlier group or someone they pursued?*

He pointed the newcomer out to Neill. "Someone riding in."

"It's dark, but that doesn't look like anyone I recognize," Neill said. "You find out who while I warn Donovan."

Jim swung south where the rider had gone behind a boulder bigger than a house. He dismounted and took the riding thong off his pistol. Then he picketed his own horse near water and a sand bar covered in fresh grass before walking to the boulder on foot.

The light was almost completely gone now. Only a slit of red shone in the far west. The shadows were cast long and deep.

Jim drew his pistol and crept to the boulder's far side. He heard a horse stripping grass and eased around. The rider had left his horse here. Jim's concern grew. An honest man or any of their own people would have ridden into camp and not left a horse out here.

Moving quickly, Jim headed for the camp. Fires flared up inside the circled wagons as the settlers prepared their evening meals. There was the low chatter of voices. Jim stayed outside the wagons and their light. He would need his night vision.

Somewhere out here was a man who did not want to be seen.

Ahead, a shadow moved from the dark toward one of the wagons. Jim recognized this one. David Barton's. Jim crept closer. A man, tall and wide across the shoulders, stood less than six feet away, pressed up against the wagon, peering toward the fire.

"Why don't you just walk on in," Jim said.

Faster than Jim would have believed, the man spun and leapt for him. Jim's gun fired, a miss. How could he have missed at that range. Then the man closed in, punching away with both hands, strong powerful blows.

Jim struck back with the pistol. He felt the barrel hit the man on the shoulder, but there was little power in it. Worse, the man slapped at his hand and the pistol went flying. Jim took a hard left to the chin and threw a hook in counter that set his attacker back on his heels.

They met again, each punching wildly. Jim's head rang with the blows, but he kept hitting. His knuckles hurt. The man's ribs were iron bars. He landed a blow to his attacker's kidneys that sent him reeling back. Pressing in, he was met with another vicious uppercut that snapped his head back.

The man came at him in a bull rush and Jim met him with a left hook that whipped his head around. Jim followed up with a pair of blows that seemed to do little. The man was tough to hold up to such power.

Jim caught a right to the body that almost doubled him over and narrowly bobbed aside from another uppercut that would have ended him. He threw a quick jab back, trying only to put some distance between them. He followed the jab up with a strong right that hit nothing.

His attacker struck again, and Jim countered. Both blows landed. Both men fell. Rising, Jim saw a long gleam in the night. A knife.

Suddenly, then there was light all around them and men with guns drawn.

"Don't move," a voice boomed. Donovan's voice. "What is the meaning of this?"

"I caught him sneaking around the wagons," Jim said between breaths.

He could see his attacker now, a dark-haired man, a little older than himself, with hard eyes.

"Were you?" Donovan said.

"I was just looking for someone," the man said.

"Funny way of doing it," Donovan said, "poking around the

wagons. Someone might think you were a scout for those men riding after us."

The man smiled coolly. "I am alone, and I know nothing about any men riding after you. I am Captain Clive Wilson, and I am merely looking for someone."

"Who?" Neill said.

Jim saw David Barton break into the circle of men surrounding them. One look at the newcomer and he drew back and began to cry.

"Ellen Barton," the newcomer said. "My dear lost wife."

ELLEN BARTON HEARD the crowd gathering outside the light of her campfire. She followed in her father's wake as he pushed his way through to the front. First she thought it might be Colton or that awful Jake had somehow returned.

She heard the voice then. The one that haunted her darkest nightmares and deepest fears. His voice. The one that sent chills through her like daggers of the wicked ice.

With those words Ellen Barton, free woman, died and Ellen Wilson, a pale ghost of a thing stood in her place. Ellen Wilson was woman condemned. Condemned in this life to be forever chained to a monster.

"A chain you yourself forged," a voice said. His voice. His voice now inside her head. She'd never be free of it again. Had she ever been?

One last flare of defiance remained. She had to take care of something before he found her. *I have to save what I can.* Ellen turned and ran back to the wagon.

"Mama," Walt cried at seeing her. "What's wrong?"

"Nothing dear," she said between tears. "Only Alma has to go to live with Mr. Heston again. I'll explain when I return."

It was the least she could do. She'd never forgive herself if that little girl became trapped in Clive Wilson's world.

She packed Alma's things, few though they were and took her by the hand. The girl looked at her with big, soulful eyes. She took her by the hand and led her to Donovan's wagon.

The new man was there lounging by the fire and sipping a cup of coffee, Stewart, she remembered his name. When he saw her he stood quickly.

"Ma'am."

"This is Alma. I need you to watch her until Mr. Heston returns. You have to keep her here away from my wagon from now on," Ellen said. "Do not let her near my wagon."

She turned to Alma and knelt down to eye level.

"Alma be a good girl and wait here for Mr. Heston. Jim. He's the one that found you. You remember him?"

She nodded and a tear formed in the corner of her eye. "Did I do something bad?"

Ellen's heart broke in that moment and she drew Alma close and held her tight enough to feel her the beat of her pattering heart. *I have to be strong now and so does she.* "No. No you didn't do anything wrong, but there is a bad man coming to live with me and I can't let him hurt you. I love you and I have to keep you away from him."

"Stay with me then. Bring Walt too."

"I would, but I can't escape him," Ellen said.

"Ms. Barton," Stewart said. "If there's trouble I'm sure Donovan can sort it out. He's a good man I assure you. He wouldn't let anything happen to you. Jim too, I don't think he could stand it."

Ellen dabbed away the tears and looked at him.

"They can't save me from my own husband," she said.

"Husband?" Stewart's mouth fell open. "I thought he was killed in the war."

"Evidently not," Ellen said and stood. "If Mr. Heston and Mr. Donovan wish to help me they can take care of Alma here. She is a good girl and keep everyone well away from my wagon."

"I don't understand," Stewart said.

"I know," Ellen said. "Just promise to keep her safe and tell Mr. Heston..." Tell him what exactly? Clive Wilson was a jealous man. If he thought that Jim had any interest in Ellen it could only end in bloodshed. "Tell Jim to please stay away from me and my family. It will be for the best."

She rose then and walked slowly back toward her father's wagon like a woman facing the gallows. With every step a piece of her withered and died. She did not look back. She considered for a moment the gun hidden in her skirts. She could end it all. She could walk out alone into the grass and end it all. Where would that leave precious Walt though? Her feet carried her toward the fire.

He was there then, looming in the growing dark and smiling a crooked little smile. The one he always gave her just before he punished her. Ellen's knees felt weak

"Dearest wife," Clive said in that oily voice. "I am so relieved to find you."

He came to her then and started to wrap his arms around her. She stood stiff as a post.

"I know it's been some time," he laughed. Then lower he whispered in her ear. "Little Mouse, we have much to discuss."

Oh God. Ellen broke then. She started to fall, felt Clive holding her upright, then gently lowering her to the ground.

"She's overcome with joy," Clive said aloud. "It's not every day your husband returns from the dead." Then he scooped her up and carried her back to the wagon.

Ellen's mind swirled into blackness and she knew nothing more.

23

J im Heston knew nothing about raising a small child, especially a girl child. Alma, fortunately, seemed to know what was required, and Stewart had evidently had younger sisters.

Alma spent most of her days with him, riding the wagon and always on the lookout for bad men or Indian attacks while Jim went about his usual tasks.

The men of the wagon train knew their business by now. They could mind their own teams and repair most of the minor problems with their wagons. Jim helped, of course. He replaced broken spokes or set bent hubs back into shape. By this point even the Robeson clan accepted his help.

He and Pope might not be friendly, but after the battle with the Indians, the man did seem to offer him a measure of grudging respect.

Pat Robeson himself pronounced Jim Heston a good man to have alongside in a fight; that ended any lingering hostilities.

A number of the young Robeson women had invited him to their wagons for supper. Jim had declined, politely, but several didn't seem to take no for an answer. They grew creative. Asking him to look at their team right as supper was on and wouldn't he like to stay for a bite?

The miraculous return of Captain Clive Wilson was on everyone's mind. "Wasn't he gallant," they said and "Ellen—Mrs. Wilson—must be so relieved to have her lost husband back."

Jim fixed a pleasant smile on his face even as his stomach twisted with every word.

He brought Alma along on most of these visits. The ladies of the camp made a fuss over her. They braided her hair or gifted her with a dress that no longer fit. They said that he was a good man to adopt a lost little girl.

Jim wasn't sure if Alma's presence made things better or worse, but she needed to be around girls and children of her own age. His own days on the farm had been lonely, with only his older brother for company.

After a meal with Elise Robeson and her parents he and Alma returned to their own campfire. Though barely more than a girl, Elise was by far the most persistent of the camp's young women.

"Back awful soon," Donovan said and laughed.

Jim said nothing, only tucked Alma into her blankets in the back of their wagon. It was cool enough now and she'd be free of the bugs and critters that liked to prowl around at night. He still didn't understand why Ellen had brought her to him. *And why warn me to stay well away? Well, I've been doing that almost since the fight with Pope.*

"Didn't feel much like talking afterward," Jim said and sat down.

"I've seen that Robeson girl. She isn't interested in talking," Neill said. "That's a woman with her mind made up on a man."

"Not me," Jim grunted.

"You wouldn't be the first young fellow to say that," Donovan said into the fire. "You could do worse though. The Robesons will do well out here."

"They're looking for a big swath of farmland. Thinking about planting orchards or vineyards," Jim said.

"There were several already starting last year. Big valley on the other side of the Sierras runs north and south, and there was talk of digging canals to water the fields. Could do well there," Donovan said.

"And what about you?" Stewart asked Jim. "Donovan here says he's retiring after this run. Got some secret place up in the mountains. Neill doesn't seem so certain—"

"I'm going up to Oregon," Neill said. "Got a sister there with a pack of young uns, and I'd like to see her. Maybe get a little house by the coast and mend nets or fish or something."

Jim eyed the rangy Captain.

Neill, mending nets?

"That still leaves you," Stewart looked to Jim. "Little girl like that needs a proper home if you plan on raising her."

"I've been thinking about a ranch. Maybe raise a few horses. No cattle. Not unless I can find a few thousand acres. Doubt I can afford that," Jim said. He took a swallow of scalding coffee. "What about you Stewart? What are you planning on?"

"It's the mines for me. Gold. I'd like to run my hands through a stream and pull up a few nuggets."

"Lots of men have tried," Donovan said. "Some succeeded."

"I aim to be among them. I've a partner with a claim near Sutter's Mill. He's been there for over a year while I traveled." Stewart patted his shirt pocket. "He wrote and said he sunk a shaft, and that the vein is as wide as his thumb and clear."

"Sounds pretty good," Jim said.

"You lot are welcome to join me," Stewart said.

"Not for me," Donovan said. "I tried my hand at mining years ago. Found a little color but mostly just a sore back."

"Think I'll try to find a place first," Jim said. "But if it doesn't work out I'll look you up."

"Good," Stewart said. "We'll need good men."

Jim looked out into the distance. Three wagons down he saw lantern light from the Barton wagon. He'd seen the Bartons only from a distance the last few days. Rather than being excited at the return of Ellen's husband, they were a downcast lot. Maybe it was the travel finally getting to them. David in particular looked to be taking the trail hard. Their son, Colton, kept away. Jim saw him around the Robeson wagons, usually hanging back, always wearing his gun loose and ready.

What had happened between young Colton and his family? The split had been before Clive's return so it wasn't that. An argument of some kind? Over what?

Alma cried out in her sleep, and Jim turned his thoughts away from the Bartons and their troubles. He had enough of his own.

"No sign of that group we saw all the dust from?" he asked. He and Neill had explained what they'd seen to Donovan. The wagon master had doubled the guard, but so far they hadn't seen anything. He'd also sent Neill riding back behind them to keep an eye out; so far nothing there either. Whoever followed had vanished.

"Haven't seen anything," Neill said with a huff. "I know they're back there, but I can't seem to catch sign of them."

"How do you know?" Jim said.

"A feeling. An itch right between my shoulders. I can almost feel them watching. Whoever they are they've been able to keep themselves hidden though."

Jim did not like the sound of that. He'd ridden with Neill enough to respect the Captain's abilities. If they could remain hidden from Neill they could hide from anyone.

"If they are renegades is there a likely place to try us?" Jim said.

"Too many places," Donovan said. "If they circle around us they could lie in wait a dozen likely spots. These won't be a few warriors with bow and arrows either. Not if our suspicions are right. They'll have rifles."

"And we'll be strung out one wagon after another," Neill said.

"Send a scout ahead?" Jim suggested.

"Neill is watching behind and whoever rides up front will likely ride right into their trap. Best we can hope for then is a few warning shots," Donovan said.

"I'll do it," Jim volunteered.

Donovan and Neill exchanged a long glance.

"You'll be painting a target on your back," Donovan said. He looked at Jim doubtfully. "If we're right you'll be a man alone riding into hostiles. If you see them, get clear and ride away to warn us. Don't try fighting on your own."

"He can do it," Neill said. "He's ready."

That seemed to settle Donovan. "Tomorrow then. But don't get more than a few miles ahead. You aren't riding out to look for a way through. From here on the trail is clear enough. Wagons have worn ruts into the ground."

"Tomorrow then," Jim said and finished his coffee.

"I'VE GOT to stretch my legs Little Mouse. Not to worry though I'll be back soon enough," Clive said and climbed out of the wagon. Ellen's only response was a hard glare. Clive ignored it, much as he had everything else she and her family said or did.

A man does not concern himself with the affairs of his lessers. And make no mistake, the Bartons were certainly beneath his concern.

Ellen's father had protested whenever Clive reclaimed his wife and son, but a stern look followed by a strong slap across the face put the old man down in the dirt and out of the way. Ellen though, had been the biggest surprise. She'd struck him when he faced down her father. His Little Mouse had actually struck him. A matter she paid for soon enough. A swift backhand for her and then the continued threat he held against her parents and sister had kept her toeing the line.

Clive raised both arms and took a deep breath. The air was blessedly cool compared to the stifling daytime heat. Clive felt good. Things had progressed as he'd planned. He had his son and soon-to-be discarded wife both well in hand.

Ellen's father came around the wagon then, saw him, lowered his eyes to the ground, and scurried back around to the opposite side.

Clive laughed. *Ohh yes, I am truly in command here.*

"I'm going for a little ride," he announced.

The horse was eager to be away from the camp. It seemed he held

Clive's distaste for the plodding wagon. Clive smiled to himself. They would not have to endure it much longer.

He rode back along the trail, keeping his trotting horse in the worn ruts of the wagons.

Clive saw them first, four riders approaching with the evening skyline behind them. When they were close he held up and struck a match to light his cigar.

"How's married life?" Slade said.

Clive looked at Lou and grinned, "Quite dull."

"Do they suspect anything?" Slade said.

"No. But they've kept one man scouting ahead and another out behind."

"We've seen them," John said. The big man rubbed at his rough jaw. "Captain Neill is the one in the back. He's a wily one. I don't know the one up front."

"He's of no concern," Clive said. "Some half-grown fool." He rubbed his jaw and remembered the power of Heston's punches. He'd been a handful, but only the intervention of the others had kept Clive from cutting him wide open.

"I know him," Lou said. "Jim Heston. He is a dangerous man."

"I want him," Jake said. "He's the one that caught me after I had some fun with the Webb woman." He turned to Clive then and grinned. "At the time it seemed like he was awful friendly with your wife."

"He's been put in his place now," Clive growled.

Jake cackled. "He is huh. I'll bet he's over at her wagon right now, laughing about how her husband rode off and left her all alone."

John Mears joined in with the laughter, his big voice booming.

Clive's hand fell toward his gun and suddenly Jake wasn't laughing. His mouth was curled up into a grin and his own hand hovering just inches from the butt of his pistol.

"Anytime you're ready," Jake said.

"Don't speak that way about what's mine," Clive growled.

"Make me," Jake said.

"Enough," Slade interjected. "A shot now would alert the wagons. Anything else we need to know?"

Clive slowly relaxed. Much as Jake's insults galled him, he would deal with the man at another time.

"No," Clive said.

"Good," Slade said. "Tomorrow, we make our play. Expect us around noon. They'll be hot and tired by then out on that hardpan. Slow to react. They'll still get into their little circle and then Clive will get us inside."

"I'll be ready. Remember though my son is not to be harmed and I will deal with my dear wife." Clive gave Jake a final look; then he started back for the camp. He ran his horse for several minutes, putting distance behind him.

When he reached camp again, his wife's family had finished eating. Without asking, he helped himself to what remained while they retreated to their blankets. He heard them whispering—about him no doubt—but ignored them. What could they do? Nothing. And tomorrow this charade would all be ended. Then he could ride on with Walt for the coast. Maybe he'd take Lou with him. He'd kill Jake first of course, for the insult the man had given him. Slade too would likely die. He knew too much about Clive and besides...fewer heads meant bigger shares for the survivors. Lou's brother, John, might be willing to help.

Clive smiled and rolled into his blankets away from the others. He hadn't forced himself on Ellen, not yet at least, she'd cry and scream and draw too much attention. Tomorrow though. Tomorrow after the men were all dead he'd indulge himself one last time.

24

Jim rode with the sun beating down overhead. He looked out into the alkali choked Forty Mile desert. There were ranges of mountains rising up in the distance, brown and desolate, but the basin below shone blindingly white. Heat shimmers rose off the hardpan in taunting waves.

Sweat trickled down Jim's back, gathered along his spine, and caused his shirt to stick.

The Humboldt was miles behind them now. Much to his surprise, he found himself missing that stagnant, green water.

At least it had been cool. Out here nothing is cool. Even night brings little relief.

He got down off his horse and walked ahead. No need to wear him down in this heat. Why had he volunteered to scout ahead? There was nothing to see. Not another soul. Not a hint of vegetation. Not even a good place to attack from. Jim scuffed his boot over the cracked ground and thought back to the rocky fields of his South Texas farm. Not even a rock out here.

His canteen hung over his saddle and Jim paused to get a drink. Though it was just past midday, the water was hot and unpleasant. He drank just the same. Tepid as it was, it would keep him alive.

The bleached bones of a wagon lay off to his right, close to the shoulder of a mountain. There was a small pool just beyond, surrounded by tawny grass, its water clear and just a couple inches deep. Poisonous too, no doubt. He kept the Appaloosa well back. A pair of oxen had given in to their thirst. Jim saw their bones and bits of dried hide. A long-legged bird stalked through the water, plucking snails from below.

Jim looked east. Single file, the wagons were coming up along behind. Though dulled by the shimmering waves, the oxen stood out against the too-white landscape. He moved back to his horse, started to climb into the saddle, and then stared at the wagons for a long moment. Something was wrong with them. Streams of dust rose from their wheels. The oxen were moving too fast. Way too fast. Something had frightened them.

A group of men on horseback rode into view then, rifles lifting, then firing into the wagons.

Jim was suddenly on the Appaloosa. He spurred the big horse and raced back toward the wagons. He was supposed to scout ahead and watch for the renegades.

How did they get past me?

More riders appeared. They came from between a pair of low hills just off the trail to the north. Jim had noticed those hills; he had ridden up a ways then passed on by. He couldn't check everywhere.

The Appaloosa ate up the distance. Jim drew his rifle from its scabbard, levered a round into the chamber. The renegades were swarming all around now, like wolves circling a wounded elk. Shots came from the wagons, but few and far between. Donovan should have had them fighting back by now.

The nearest renegade was watching inward, toward the wagons. A mistake. Jim's bullet struck him between the shoulders and sent him crashing down.

Alerted by the noise, a pair of men turned to face him, but Jim had already sighted in on the first. He squeezed the trigger and a second man fell from the saddle. The third man got off a frantic pistol shot. Jim heard it whistle by. He took his time, aiming deliberately, slow. More bullets whistled around. At that range the pistol was a poor weapon. Jim's rifle was not. Only a stumble by the man's horse saved him, as Jim's shot struck him in the shoulder and sent the pistol flying and the man running.

Jim was at the wagons then. He goaded the Appaloosa on, and the horse leaped between a pair of oxen and the next wagon and he was inside. One of the defenders must have taken him for a renegade and he felt a shot burn along his left side.

"Friendly," he yelled and leapt down. He ran toward the nearest wagon just as a huge bear of a man wearing buckskins drew a knife and climbed inside. Jim heard screams and jumped in after him.

The big man filled the canvas frame. He was laughing, and a pair of young girls screamed from the wagon bed. The big man turned as Jim's weight shifted the wagon and he raised the knife.

Jim slapped the weapon aside and tackled the bigger man hard enough to drive both of them through the canvas and out onto the ground below.

With Jim's weight on top, the big man caught the worst of it.

Jim rolled free and started up. He drew his pistol, but the huge man lanced out with a kick and sent him rolling back. Jim landed on his back. He felt for his pistol. Gone. He saw the knife's glinting edge in the dust nearby. The huge man rushed at him with a roar.

Jim felt the knife's handle. He brought it in close, ripped upward with the blade, felt it tear through the buckskin. Felt the edge bite. Then the huge man bowled him over again.

They fought in the dirt. The big man ended up on top.

Reversing his grip on the knife, Jim slammed the blade between his attacker's ribs. He struck once, twice, a third time.

The buckskin man growled. He sagged down. His eyes were frantic. Spit flew from his mouth in a fury, but even as he fought the strength died out in him.

"I think this is yours," Jim said and slammed the knife home a fourth and final time.

A light went out in the bigger man's eyes and Jim rolled him aside.

He stood then. There was another man inside the circle with him.

Another big man. Jim recognized him, Clive Wilson, Ellen's husband. Even as he watched Clive ran toward the nearest wagon. Donovan stood alone there, using the wagon for cover, firing out toward the renegades.

Coolly, Clive leveled his pistol. Smoke flew from the barrel and he shot Donovan square in the back.

"NO," Jim said.

Clive spun and turned in Jim's direction. Suddenly Neill was in the circle, standing up in his stirrups and firing.

A bullet struck the wagon beside Clive, sending splinters flying. Clive slipped beneath the wagon, rolled clear, and was then lost in the swirl of dust and powder smoke.

Neill paused long enough to look at Jim and the giant man lying dead beside him. "You hurt?"

"Not really," Jim answered. He looked at Donovan lying against the wagon.

"Then pick up a gun and get to fighting, before they overrun us," Neill ordered.

Jim found his pistol covered in dirt and ran a hand over it. The giant wore a gunbelt and he drew the man's own pistol with his other hand.

A rifle would have been better, but it was on the Appaloosa somewhere.

Jim ran to the nearest wagon and looked out. There was still a swarm of men out there. He fired two quick shots. Neither scored a hit. More shots sounded from the wagons around him. One of the renegades fell. Then the renegades and retreated back out of range.

Both pistols ready, Jim watched them go. He looked to where Donovan had fallen against the wagon. He knelt down over his friend. The wagon master's eyes were blank and expressionless. Shot in the back by Ellen's husband.

"Killed on the final journey West," Jim said to himself. Donovan had been so close to riding away into his hidden valley. How many scrapes with renegades and Indians had the man survived only to be gunned down by a man he'd been hired to protect?

"He'll pay for it," Jim said. "I won't let him get away with it, Donovan."

A horse approached from inside the circle of wagons, Jim spun and brought his pistol up. He thumbed back the hammer. Wilson. How had the man gotten behind him?

"Easy now," Captain Neill said. "Found your horse."

Jim holstered his pistol and stuck the extra into his waistband.

"Donovan didn't make it."

"I saw," Neill let out a long breath. "He was my friend for a long time. My only true friend."

"Not your only," Jim said.

Neill gave him a half-smile. "No, I suppose not."

"What now?"

Neill looked toward the distant renegades. They sat their horses at the base of a long scrub-covered hill. "They don't seem to be in a hurry, and they aren't giving up. Try to wait us out most likely."

Jim studied the wagons. Several men were wounded, even a few women. The doc had set up a litter and was treating those he could. *We have wounded and the women and children, not to mention the stock pining us down. They can ride to water whenever they want.* The wait wouldn't be a long one.

"We have to break free somehow," he said.

"I agree. But I don't know how."

"We could leave the wagons. Put everyone on a horse or ox. Maybe keep one or two for the wounded."

"I don't think they'll be satisfied with just the goods and wagons," Neill said. "They want it all and...we'll still be too slow to outrun them."

Men began to gather in twos and threes then formed up into a larger group. They saw Neill and Jim and started over. Milo Adams and Pat Robeson walked in the lead, side-by-side. Paul Webb was just a couple steps behind. He had blood on one ear, but Jim hadn't seen him wearing that look of determination since his wife had been attacked.

Milo and Pat looked at Donovan's fallen body then at Jim and Neill.

Milo spoke first. "What do we do now?"

AN ANGRY JIM HESTON stomped toward the Barton wagon. No one from the family had come to the gathering—cause enough for a visit —but more than that his friend had just been killed by Ellen's husband.

And I want to know why.

Mrs. Barton was the first to see him. She ran to the back of the wagon and her husband soon appeared. He had a deep gash on his temple, blood showed through heavy wraps of bandage.

"What happened here?" Jim said.

Husband looked at wife and then back at him. Neither spoke.

"I asked what happened here," Jim tried to keep his voice calm and steady; he only partially succeeded.

"My husband happened." It was Ellen who answered. The words didn't sound right though they were garbled somehow. She emerged from the wagon slowly then. Her movements were stiff and deliberate. Her face was hidden by her loose hair. She swept it out of the way and Jim caught a glimpse of her. Someone had beaten her and badly. Her right eye was swollen completely shut and a purple bruise colored her cheek. He saw too why her words had been slurred, her lips were broken and busted. Bloodstains ran down the front of her dress.

She paused long enough to help Walt down from the wagon. The boy's eyes were red-rimmed, and his shirt was damp from crying.

"He murdered Donovan. Shot him in the back while he was defending all of us." Despite her obvious injuries or because of them, Jim felt his anger rising. "Why?"

"I can only guess that he was in league with the outlaws," David said.

"What?"

Ellen spoke this time. "My husband is a monster. It comes as no surprise to me that he would help such men."

"I thought he died in the war. That he was a hero."

Ellen wrapped an arm around her son's head and drew him close. "My husband was a riverboat pirate and murderer after the war."

"Why didn't you warn us? We might have—"

"Might have what?" Ellen's voice rose. "Might have sent him away? He is my husband. He is Walt's father. You could not have cast him out without him taking Walt too."

"We might have watched him," Jim said. His anger subsided. He looked at her battered face, then the boy's tears. *These people are as much that man's victims as Donovan was, and for far longer.*

Jim started to say more when he noticed a group of men leading another man from one of the Robeson wagons. Someone had draped a swath of dirty canvas over the prisoner's head. It billowed and puffed with the man's every breath. They had also tied a noose tight around his neck and his hands were secured behind his back.

"Please no. He had nothing to do with it," a young woman pleaded. Between the distance and dust Jim couldn't see who she was. But he did know the man holding the noose. Pope Robeson. The girl had him by the arm and was pulling with all her might.

"He's got to answer for what he did," Pope said and shrugged the girl off.

She collapsed to her knees, sobbing hysterically.

Then she noticed Jim and Ellen, climbed to her feet, and ran over. Jim recognized her then. Ellen's young sister.

"Martha. Martha what's wrong," Mrs. Barton said.

"It's Colton," the girl said between sobs. "They're going to kill him."

"No!" Mrs. Barton screamed. "Not my baby."

"STOP. There'll be no killing anyone," Jim said and stomped his way toward the gathering crowd.

Pope Robeson stepped between Jim and the hooded man, crouched and ready. Jim slowed and for a moment they eyed each other.

"You aren't going to interfere with this. He's getting hung," Pope growled.

"For what?"

"He helped those men out there. Him and that Clive Wilson."

"What's this all about? Who is that?" Pat Robeson said. He, Neill, and Milo Adams had approached.

"Colton Barton," Jim answered.

"We're gonna hang him," Pope grinned.

"Why?" Pat said.

"He was helping that Clive Wilson. I saw him," Pope said.

"So did I," someone in the crowd added.

"Pull that off him," Milo said.

Pat Robeson didn't bother with words he yanked the hood off of Colton. The young man had taken a beating. Blood dripped from his crooked nose and both eyes were almost shut.

"Colton," Ellen gasped. Jim felt her hand reach out to take his own.

"You did this to him?" Jim said.

"Not us," Pope answered.

"Then who beat him?" Milo asked. He turned to Colton. "Who did this to you."

The young man tried to speak but the words didn't come. He gasped for a ragged breath.

"Get that rope off his neck, he's choking," Jim said.

Pat Robeson drew his belt knife and cut through the rope. Colton gave out a rasp and then slumped. He would have gone to his knees but for the men holding him upright.

"Clive," he said with a rasp.

"This young man was beaten by Clive. He didn't help him," Milo said in disgust.

"He's lying," Pope said. "He has to be. They're in it together all of them." His eyes narrowed as he turned to Ellen.

"No they aren't," Jim said. "Look at them. Look at her."

The crowd seemed to see Ellen and her family for the first time then. David's bloody bandage. Ellen's closed eye and bruised cheek.

The dried blood on her dress. Young Walt's tears. Even Marsha had an ugly bruise on her forehead. Everyone stood silent.

"He beat all of them," Jim said. "Then he killed Donovan before Neill drove him out."

"You tried to stop him?" Jim said to Colton.

The young man could only nod.

Pat Robeson gave Pope a hard look. "You tried to hang this young man for defending his family."

"Sir I-" Pope started.

"No. You've been nothing but trouble this entire trip Pope," Pat's voice rose. "I'm done with it. I'm about done with you. I've a mind to shoot you down for the trouble you've caused."

"This is pointless," Jim interjected. Then he gestured out toward the renegades. "The enemy is out there. We can't afford to be fighting among ourselves. That's what they want. That's why they put that man in here with us."

"He's right. Jake was out there," a new voice said. The crowd parted a little to reveal Paul Webb. "He and his sister. I saw them. Jake came right for my wagon. He rode close enough that I could hear him. He said, 'he'd come back for more'. I shot at him and he laughed. I'm no gunfighter. Got lucky when Captain Neill arrived and drove them off."

"We have to stick together," Jim said. He could almost see the crowd's growing resolve.

"So what do we do?" a voice in the background called out.

"First, we stop fighting ourselves and defend the wagons. We've got too few people looking out right now. They can hit us at any moment."

"And then what?"

The crowd was looking at him now, Jim realized. Paul Webb, the Bartons, the Robesons, Milo Adams, even Neill. He'd taken charge without even knowing it.

"And then we fight our way out of this," Jim said.

25

Night fell over the desert. The wind stilled and the alkali flats glowed a faint blue beneath the falling moonlight like shimmering water.

"Ready?" Jim asked.

"Yes," Colton answered. Jim hadn't wanted the young man to join them. His face was still a battered mess, though the swelling had gone down. He'd insisted on coming though. He said he needed this and... he was right. Pope and some of that lot still didn't trust him. Many of the others probably had at least some doubt.

Jim looked at him and sighed. *I was wrongly convicted once; I remember how desperate I was to prove my own innocence. At least he'll get a chance to.*

Jim leaned closer to the wagon. The Appaloosa stomped impatiently. "You're up to this?"

"I'll be fine," Colton nodded. He wrapped the reins around his hands. "All I have to do is keep them going."

"Leave the shooting to us," Jim nodded. "Neill, if I don't make it through see that Alma gets to Ellen."

"I will," the older man agreed. "You boys take care."

"See you at the river," Jim said. He nodded to the men waiting just ahead. "Let us out."

Quiet as they could manage, Milo Adams and three other men rolled one of the wagons back to create an opening. Not a very wide opening, just enough to allow a single wagon out.

"Slow at first," Jim said and led them out. He and Stewart each rode horses, one on either side of Colton's wagon. To the north a campfire burned where the desert touched the shoulder of the mountain.

Jim thought he knew the place. Near that poisoned pond. *Must be using that old wreck for fuel.* That would put them a good quarter mile from the circle of wagons.

The wagon wheels hissed as they rolled out over the sandy ground. They'd secured everything down. No loose metal or wood to give them away. The sideboards had been raised and reinforced with added planks and thick buffalo hide. They'd even switched out the slow oxen for a team of horses.

Speed would be essential if this worked. *We have to keep ahead of them.*

The distance between themselves and the fire grew to a half mile.

Jim frowned and reined in. Stewart fell in beside him.

"Go ahead," he told Colton over his shoulder and the silent wagon continued west.

"Did too good a job," Stewart said.

"I guess so. Whoever they have on watch must have fallen asleep."

"Or we caught them flat-footed," Stewart's grin flashed in the moonlight. "How far should we let the wagon get ahead."

"I don't—"

One of the renegades began yelling in the direction of the campfire. Far as they were Jim couldn't make out the words, but the voice was angry.

"Looks like it's time," Jim said. While Stewart rode after Colton, he drew his rifle and fired toward the campfire. Only the luckiest of shots would hit; the distance was too great. But it would give the renegades an idea of where he and the others were.

Jim refilled the rifle and jammed it into the scabbard. He swung the Appaloosa around after Stewart and the wagon. The plan, so far at least, had worked. Now he had to lead them far out into the desert.

Shots rang out behind him. They were firing blind, and none came close.

Jim snapped off a pair from the pistol he'd taken off the giant, then tucked it back into his waistband. *Can't have them getting lost now.* Dimly, he saw dark shapes and rising dust on the horizon. They were following.

Colton had the team moving now. They weren't running full tilt. Even if they were, they couldn't match the outlaws speed, and they didn't have to. They only needed to draw them along from the wagons on a good long chase. Neill would take care of the rest.

"Unless we fail," Jim muttered.

They ran on into the desert. Jim lost track of time. He caught the wagon and fell in beside Colton and Stewart.

"They're still back there," Stewart said.

"Good," Jim answered. "How far do you think we've come?"

"Couple miles, maybe three. How far away do we need to get them?"

"We need to make ten before they figure it out. At the rate they're running the horses they won't be able to turn and make it back to the others then."

"Dawn's still a ways off," Stewart said. He pointed to the dust rising from the wagon's wheels. "With all the dust they won't see us clear until then."

"Keep him running straight," Jim said and nodded toward Colton. "I'm going to make sure they stay on the hook."

Stewart nodded back and Jim veered the Appaloosa off to the south. He dismounted and poured most of his canteen into his hat so his horse could drink. Remounting, he drew his rifle and waited. They shouldn't be much further behind.

He heard them before he saw them. Heard their horse's hooves drumming on the sand and the rattling of their gear. Vague shapes appeared against the white emptiness of the flats. Aiming high and leading his target, Jim fired at the nearest. A horse screamed. He fired three times more, each time snapping off a quick shot. One of the bullets struck and made a thumping sound, the other two seemed to hit nothing.

Then he replaced the rifle, and the Appaloosa was off and running again. He kept the horse heading slightly south of Colton's wagon where if the outlaws followed him they might lose a little ground.

Gradually, he swung back north toward the others. The renegades were close—Jim saw them at the very edge of his vision—but none of them seemed to be riding the equal of the Appaloosa.

Stewart slowed enough to speak to him.

"Got to be ten miles by now," the older man said.

"Should be," Jim agreed. The first gray rays of dawn rose in the east now. Their pursuers would be close, though with the dust and dim light he couldn't make them out. *Soon they'll see we just have one wagon. Will they give up or ride all the faster?*

He'd done what he could, drawing them off, giving the others a chance at escape. If Neill could get the settlers back to the river they stood a far better chance now than they had trapped out on the dry, empty desert.

They continued on, the sun peered over the mountains a little higher, coating the highest peaks first with purple and then red. Jim saw them then. They were not where he expected. They'd bitten hard on his diversion south and were off in that direction, no more than a quarter mile away and riding hard straight for the wagon. The lone wagon. They would see that at any time.

One of them stood in his stirrups and yelled at the others. The renegades slowed their horses first to a walk and then to a full stop.

Jim imagined the anger and confusion they must be feeling. He stopped the Appaloosa and took aim with his rifle. *Maybe I can goad them into more delay.* His shot splattered against the chalky hardpan. He chambered another round and sighted in higher.

His bullet must have burned a horse. One bucked and sent his rider flying.

One of the outlaws seemed to take charge then. He gestured with his pistol and then turned back toward the east. The outlaws split into two groups. Most headed east but four fanned out and came on for the wagon.

Jim booted his horse into action and soon caught up with Colton and Stewart. "Turn the wagon around," he said.

"What? I thought you said keep going west no matter what."

"And now I'm saying turn it around. There's four coming up after us. The others headed back."

"You want to charge them?" Colton said.

"I do," Jim nodded.

"When we pass through keep the wagon going. Stewart and I will handle them."

Jim lifted the canvas aside to look into the back of the wagon. "You ready?"

Paul Webb worked the action on his rifle. "Ready enough. You damn near rattled me to death though. A man can hardly sleep."

"No time for sleeping now," Jim said. "You heard what's coming. We'll keep them looking our way before you open up.

Stewart gave Jim a grim nod and swallowed. "We sure will," he said.

Colton slowed the team and spun the wagon in a tight circle. Jim took up a position on his left, Stewart rode on the right.

The four were just ahead now. Not two hundred yards away and coming on hard.

Stewart let out a wild cowboy yell and they sprang into action.

If their attackers were surprised, they hid it well. All four drew their pistols and readied to fire.

Jim palmed his own pistol. The two men bearing down on him were somehow familiar. He swore he'd seen them before. They smiled and raised their pistols each taking a shot. One bullet missed entirely, but the other whizzed by Jim's ear like an angry hornet. Jim held his fire, waiting as the range quickly lessened. He leaned forward, closer to his horse, to give them less of a target.

Two more shots whizzed by. More firing came from Stewart's direction.

Jim took aim. The Appaloosa's stride was smooth and strong. He waited until the instant the horse was between strides, and then fired. The leftmost man jerked back but remained in the saddle. Jim adjusted his aim to the second attacker. He fired quick this time— they were close now—the bullet flew true and the second man dropped his pistol with a hoarse scream.

The outlaw jerked his horse hard to the right, directly into the wagon's path.

With the weight of eight horses, plus the speeding wagon, they collided in an audible crack. Dragging one leg, the outlaw's horse staggered free. The rider went down under a cloud of drumming hooves and wheels. The wagon rolled on, slowing only a fraction.

Jim looked for the first man he'd shot. Saw him several yards back, sagging in the saddle, head resting against his chest. The outlaw's horse took a step and slowly the rider slumped further and further forward before falling out of the saddle completely.

Despite all the shooting, the one outlaw on Stewart's side had come through unscathed.

From the back of the wagon, Paul Webb opened up with his rifle then.

He hit the last man with his second shot, knocking him from the saddle. All four outlaws, his and Stewart's, were now down.

Stewart? Where was he?

A riderless horse passed Jim then, one he recognized immediately. Stewart's.

He rode the Appaloosa back. Stewart lay face down on the desert. He'd been shot at least three times. The fourth outlaw lay just beyond him. Dead.

"You took him with you, my friend," Jim said.

Jim looked back toward the east. Dust rose from the renegade's horses. They were pushing hard. Hard enough to catch Neill and the others though?

He didn't think so.

Young Colton brought the wagon around in a long circle. He rolled to a stop nearby and Paul Webb sprang down out of the back, eyes searching around for more enemies. Following Jim's gaze, he stared long and hard into the east.

"I don't think they'll catch them," he said.

Jim heard the hope in his voice but also the fear. His wife had remained behind with the others. One of Milo's older sons had volunteered to drive her.

"They'll kill their horses if they keep it up," Jim answered.

Colton dismounted and joined them. His hands shook.

"I didn't even manage a shot," he said.

"You didn't let the wagon tip over and that was the main thing," Jim said.

"I'll say," Webb agreed. He looked down at Stewart then adjusted his hat back. "He was game all the way through."

"He was," Jim agreed. "Let's load him into the wagon and water the horses. Catch up these loose ones if you can. They'll be thirsty too and we can use them."

The wagon had a barrel of water inside, enough to survive on for several days, despite the heat. It had been lashed down tight against the side to keep it from spilling.

"What about these others?" Colton asked.

"Leave them for the buzzards," Webb said, and Jim agreed. They didn't have time for proper respects for these kind of men. Not when their families remained in danger.

"Strip them for bullets and guns," Jim said. "We've got to push east to catch up."

CLIVE WILSON GROUND his teeth and raked his horse's flanks with his spurs. The beast ran faster. He would die in this heat soon. So long as he caught the wagons, Clive did not care. He could steal another horse easily enough. How could this have happened? How could they have been tricked so thoroughly?

We had them. We had them trapped and cornered and then we fell for a

stupid trick. The Tolliver brothers. It was their fault. They had fallen
asleep on watch and allowed that wagon to break free.

One of them had evidently roused enough to see the fleeing
wagon and wake everyone. They'd assumed several wagons were out
on the flats, making a run for it. In the dark and dust there had been
no way to know it was alone.

Despite the loot and plunder promised the other wagons offered,
Slade wanted everyone dead. Clive agreed. There could be no
witnesses to his involvement. Besides, they could always ride back to
collect the rest.

Slade's gang had ridden hard until the rising sun finally revealed
how they'd been fooled.

Riding out front, Clive was the first to come to the wagon's former
campsite. It was empty. Only the gray coals from their fires remained.

Slade reined in beside him.

"They've gone back toward the river," Slade said. "It's the only
thing that makes sense."

Clive grunted. He could see the line of tracks easy enough.

"You let them get away," Clive said. There was an abandoned
body laying off to one side. A big one. Clive used his boot to roll it
over.

"No," Lou gasped when she saw it. "John." She climbed down to
see about her brother.

Clive snorted. The man was obviously dead and likely had been
since their initial attack. Lou had held out hope that the defenders
had only captured him.

Lou knelt beside the body. She bent her head and brought both
fists down on her dead brother's chest. "You should have waited. Why
did you have to be the first one in?"

So he could have the first choice of loot and women. To Clive the
answer was obvious.

"How far back to the river?" Clive asked.

"It will take them most of the day."

"Can we catch them?"

Slade squinted into the distance. "No. They'll get there before—"

He never finished. Clive's first shot tore out Slade's throat; his second struck dead-center on his chest.

Gun drawn, Clive looked at the others.

"I am in command now," he said. "You will take your orders from me...unless there are any objections?"

Syd Boyle sat his horse to Clive's right. The gunman casually rested both hands on his pommel. He and Clive watched each other for a long moment.

Finally, Syd spoke, "And just what are your orders?"

"We ride after them. I want those wagons taken. It will be harder now, especially if they reach water," Clive nodded to the fallen Slade. "You have him to thank for that."

Syd paused to look at the others. "You all heard him. Let's ride."

Lou approached Clive's side. Her eyes were red and there were tears on her cheeks. Clive hadn't thought her the crying kind. "I want the man who killed my brother."

"Then you will have him. As it happens, I know just who you want."

26

Two men lay dead on the sand where the wagons once stood. Jim recognized one of them immediately, the giant he'd killed during the first attack. But who was the second?

Jim dismounted for a closer look.

The unknown man lay face-up; someone had shot him through the throat and chest. He was a stranger, not one of the men from the wagon train. He'd died after the giant, quite a while after. The blood was fresh and blowing sand hadn't covered him nearly so much. The stranger wore two guns, both used often, the grips worn smooth. He'd filed the front sights down smooth as well. *An outlaw then.* But how had he died here?

"Who's that?" Stewart asked.

"Not one of ours," Jim said. He rifled through the stranger's pockets. Tobacco, a few dollars, no papers of any kind, nothing to identify him.

Jim stood and stuffed the money into his pockets. Despite their best efforts, men had fallen on this trip. More likely would. Their widows could have what little he'd found.

"Nothing on him," he said. Then he unbuckled the man's guns and handed them off to Colton. "Might come in handy."

"I'm not sure I understand," Colton said.

"Neill took our own dead in the wagons and left the big man here," Jim said. "Then this other fellow died sometime after. He's one of them, the renegades."

"Who killed him though and why?"

Jim shrugged. "Either he decided to come check on the wagons after we led the rest away or he was killed afterward by his own."

"Killed by his own?" Colton looked as if he couldn't believe it.

"Maybe he was the man on watch," Webb interjected. "They killed him for letting us trick them."

Jim squinted off into the distance. He couldn't see far. Under the noonday sun the heat shimmers were at their greatest. Had Neill got the wagons to water yet?

"Water the horses," Jim said. "Then we'll press on for the Humboldt."

The horses drank greedily. After the chase ended they hadn't pressed them hard, killing the animals wouldn't catch up to the others any faster.

With that in mind, they set out at a steady walk. They followed the ruts of the wagons. The tracks of horses, many horses, were mixed among them. The renegades hadn't given up then.

The sun bore down, hot and bright. Sweat rolled off Jim's brow. Mixed with the salt laden dust, it stung his eyes. Wiping at them brought no relief. Everything was coated in the poisonous white dust. Twice more they stopped for water and then pressed on.

No one talked. They were too tired and too thirsty to talk. Webb switched from the wagon to one of the outlaw's horses.

Finally, the sun sank into the west and the light grew mercifully dim. They were still on the flats, but a brown line of sagebrush lay a mile or two ahead. The Humboldt wouldn't be much beyond that.

Jim cast his mind back over the route. Would Neill stop at the edge or go on east into a more defensible condition?

The Humboldt had carved a notch down from the surrounding land, in some spots it lay almost twenty feet deep, but there was a place where the land around the river flattened. The grass had been good there, enough to last the stock for several days. It would be the place he chose.

He slowed enough for Colton to catch up.

"Let's go over the wagon again and make sure everything is tied down. I think they're just ahead."

Quickly, they checked the wagon for loose buckles or straps or anything else that might make noise.

"Have you given any thought to how we ride in?" Webb said.

"No, I haven't," Jim admitted.

"If we just go charging up our own people will likely shoot at us," Webb said.

"And if we don't ride in fast enough the outlaws will find us," Stewart added.

Jim considered the problem. He studied the setting sun. "We wait for dark then. Sneak up close and call out to the camp."

"Those men might hear us," Webb said.

"If you have a better idea I'm all for it," Jim said.

"Not really," Webb shrugged.

"They'll mostly be watching the east side," Colton volunteered. "It's where help would come. Another wagon train. They know our people won't go out into the desert again. They might not have anyone on this side."

"What about the wagon?" Stewart said.

"What about it?" Jim asked.

"Why do we need to take it? We could leave it out here and ride in. The horses would make less noise and be harder to see."

"Not bad thinking," Jim said. Then he had another thought. "We could use it as a distraction."

"How?" Webb said.

"Unhitch the team and then all of you ride south to the edge of that mountain." Jim pointed. "I'll meet you there in a few minutes."

With his belt knife Jim set about cutting slivers of wood away from the wagon planks. Then he cut several strips out of the canvas and wrapped them around the slivers. He set the bundle into the back of the wagon and struck a match.

After waiting to make sure the bundle caught, he rode quickly toward the others. When he reached them a long column of smoke lifted from the wagon and flames roared along the canvas.

"They'll see that for sure," he said. "Now let's see about reaching our people."

Slowly, Jim led the way. The outlaws would surely see the smoke and fire. If they went north around, where he thought the wagons would be they were safe. South though and things could get tricky. He needed to see them first, and then they could either hide and let them pass or race for the safety of the wagons.

Jim held his breath, ears straining for any trace of danger. He heard the clop of the horse's hooves, the whisk of sage brushing against their flanks, the whoosh of their tails. Then he smelled it. A fire. Something cooking. Between stalks of sage he glimpsed a tendril of orange flame. Then the curve of a wagon's top.

He drew his pistol and waved it forward. He quickened his pace. Fifty paces from the wagons he climbed down and brought the others to a halt.

"Hello the camp," he said. No answer. He called again, louder this time.

He heard the sharp click of a rifle's hammer being drawn back.

"We're friendly. It's Jim and Colton and Webb," Jim said.

"Jim," Neill's voice. "Come on in boy."

"We're keeping low, but we have horses with us." Then Jim and the others were running then, quick and silent.

They climbed between a pair of crossed wagon tongues and were suddenly in the circle. Webb's wife stood waiting for him. He wrapped her up in a long hug, lifting her and spinning her around.

Jim watched them for a moment. *One good thing then, since the attack whatever unease settled between them has been forgotten.*

Colton's family stood in a group; he ran to them without hesitation.

"You made it," Neill said and patted Jim on the back. "Stewart?"

"He took one with him," Jim shook his head. "You got them to water."

"It was a close thing," Neill said.

"Out there too," Jim said. He watched the Barton family and saw that Alma was back among them, clutching tight to Ellen's skirts. "What do we do now?"

"Wait them out. We've got water and food enough. Sooner or later another train will come along or an army patrol. I'm not much for blue-bellies, but I'd dearly love for a few dozen to come riding over that hill tomorrow."

"They're done then," Jim said. Relief washed through him and he sagged against the wagon. "All we have to do is hold out a little longer."

"You did it," Neill smiled. "You bought us the time we needed. Donovan would be proud."

Gunfire erupted from the north then, too many shots to count. Men yelled and horses reared and screamed.

"Keep them out," Neill said.

Jim was on his feet then, running fast. If Neill was right, the rene-gades had a single option left to them now. Desperation drove them. They had to strike hard and fast, destroying the wagons entirely before help arrived.

Using the corner of a wagon for cover, he studied the night. He could see little, but the sounds of their horses were plain enough. A muzzle flash to the left drew fire from several defenders. One of the attackers swore bitterly.

One of the outlaws began firing, slowly, with several seconds between shots. Jim raised his pistol. He waited for the tell-tale flash and fired three times. Several guns answered back, splintering the wagon as he ducked behind it.

They can't hope to win like this. We have the wagons for cover, and they're exposed. Sooner or later we'll land enough lucky shots to hurt them.

The first torch sailed into the circle of wagons then. Harmlessly, it struck the dirt just a few feet beyond him.

Fire. They are trying to burn us out.

More torches sailed through the air then. They came from the west. Jim ran to the westernmost wagon. Why wasn't anyone there?

Everyone must have rushed to the north to beat back the attack. Two riders were coming in fast, torches lighting their way. He shot the first out of the saddle. The man's torch fell when he did. The second man threw his torch in a high arc. It sailed up and then came down on the wagon to Jim's right.

The canvas caught quickly, lighting the sky. The heat was intense, and Jim shied away from it. More men rode up with torches, at least a half-dozen now. Jim fired. He winged one. Sent another veering away but the others launched their torches and whirled their mounts before he could hit more.

Most of the torches landed harmlessly. Two did not. One caught another of the wagons afire, and a second struck an ox, and the maddened beast screamed and ran toward the nearest wagon. Women sheltering in the wagon screamed as the ox collided with it at a dead run. More of the beasts began to bellow and snort and soon the interior of the wagons was a churning brew of frightened oxen and blinding dust.

The gunfire intensified off to the north, but Jim remained where he was. Somehow the outlaws had either drawn off or killed outright all of the defenders on the west side. He saw a body lying under the next wagon. Jim ran to it, keeping well away from the angry oxen.

Pope, Pat Robeson's kin. The man's throat had been cut clean.

While the defenders were distracted to the north someone had snuck in close and killed the men on this side in silence. Then the torches had started.

With a flash of insight, Jim knew who'd done it, and he knew where the man would go next.

JIM ROLLED BENEATH THE WAGONS, away from the angry oxen, and ran into the night.

He flipped open his pistol to reload. He cursed aloud as his trembling fingers betrayed him. They needed him. Ellen needed him, and somewhere out there Clive Wilson hunted her. The last shell fell into the chamber and he flipped the cylinder into place. Now to find them.

The night was dark, the only light coming from the burning wagons behind him. The scents of burning sage, gunsmoke, and alkali dust hung over everything. Jim stalked forward, pistol raised and ready.

Gunfire sounded sporadically from the north. The frightened oxen bellowed. Then somewhere ahead a woman screamed.

Jim sped up into a run.

Was that Ellen? Does he already have her?

He heard talking ahead, raised voices. Then the whap of a fist connecting.

The woman screamed again. "Let him go. He's done nothing."

Jim knew her voice. Ellen's mother.

He saw Clive then, just ahead, his features shone in the flickering firelight.

"I want my wife and I want my son. I want them now!" he roared.

"I am here, monster," Ellen said. She stood on the seat of a wagon, gun held in her trembling fist. "Let my father go."

Clive laughed. He dropped the unconscious man into the dirt.

Jim's position was poor. Clive stood between himself and Ellen. A miss might hit her. He shifted around to his right, trying to keep Clive in sight.

"I've come to take my son home," Clive said. "You won't shoot me, Little Mouse." He started forward and Ellen's bullet struck the ground in front of him.

"That was not nice," Clive scolded her. "You will have to be punished for that."

The wagon shifted then, and Ellen spun to her right, but not in time to stop Lou from knocking her gun clear. The fiery redhead's fist sent Ellen down off the wagon and into the dirt.

Jim moved quicker. He licked his lips. Just a few seconds more.

Clive was laughing again. He stood close to Ellen now, looking down at her. "Poor Little Mouse has her head all scrambled," he said.

Ellen, bleeding from a wound on her scalp, wobbled on her

hands and knees, reaching for the pistol. Clive bent down and picked the weapon up. He opened the cylinder and examined the gun for a moment.

"This is a very naughty thing for you to have," he said. He knelt down and grabbed a handful of her hair then jerked her head up. "I want you to look at me now."

"I have him," Lou said from the wagon. She held Walt by the arm. The boy twisted and tried to break free but she held him fast.

"Mama," Walt cried when he saw his fallen mother.

"Clive," Jim said suddenly. "Move away from her."

"Ahh, the protector," Clive turned and smiled. "I'd heard you were sweet on my dear Little Mouse. But I've never been very good at sharing."

"It's over Clive. Hear that?" Jim said. The last of the gunshots had died out. "The fighting is over. Your men are done."

"There's still time to take what's mine."

Holding Walt close, Lou climbed down from the wagon. Then a small shape leapt from the wagon, landing on the redhead's back with a flurry of scratches and kicks.

Lou swore and spun around and Walt broke free. He ran toward his mother. Clive stood and moved toward his son, but Ellen grabbed at his boot. Off balance, the big man went down in a heap.

Jim brought his gun up for a shot. Ellen was too close again.

A scream came from his right. Lou had torn free from Alma. She aimed her pistol.

Jim fired from the hip, striking the redhead with two shots. She spun. Her mouth fell open in surprise. She turned away, took two steps toward the desert and then fell.

Jim swung his aim back to Clive, but the big man was on his feet and close. Jim caught a fist across the jaw that rocked him to his heels. He pivoted back and away, just avoiding a powerful uppercut that could have ended him. He chopped down with the pistol. Clive caught it across the arm and the gun went flying.

Clive roared in anger and struck Jim two quick blows to the body. The man was unbelievably fast for his size. Jim took them hard. He countered weakly with a jab to Clive's face. The bigger man laughed and shrugged the blow off. Then he came in fast and low with a bull rush.

Jim hammered down with both fists, catching Clive on his shoulder and the side of the head. He felt Clive's arms wrapping around him, lifting, and then Jim was off his feet. Clive tossed him aside. Jim hit and managed to roll enough to soften the blow. Then he was on his feet, trading blows with the bigger man in reckless abandon.

Desperately, Jim threw a looping haymaker that took Clive in the mouth. The bigger man fell back a step, paused, and spat.

Jim used the delay to his advantage, closing enough to whip two rights to Clive's side then a huge left that caught Clive in the ear.

Clive ducked down then and shoved Jim clear. Jim bounced back quickly following up with a barrage of punches that sent Clive falling.

Jim staggered on his feet. He looked down at the big man. He ran a hand across his mouth. It came away dark with blood. Ellen lay where she'd fallen, Walt and Alma both kneeling over her and crying.

"Help her. Somebody help her please," they said.

Jim started toward her. His legs felt like lead and his thoughts were slippery like a greased pig.

Young Walt looked up at him then. His mouth dropped open in warning. Jim spun and lost his balance. The fall saved his life.

Clive's gun stabbed flame. The gun Jim had taken from the giant outlaw was suddenly in his hand. He fired once, twice. Two wounds appeared in Clive's chest, but the man didn't so much as jerk.

Clive sneered and adjusted his aim. A bullet spat dust just inches from where Jim had fallen.

Jim kept firing. Three more bullets struck Clive, but the man fought on.

"Kill you all," Clive said. His gun came up slow.

Jim aimed. One round left. It had to count. He fired. This one hit Clive in the left eye.

Clive's head snapped back and finally the bastard fell.

Jim lay panting. He rolled his head. Ellen's mother knelt over her. In the distance he saw Neill, Webb, Milo Adams, Pat Robeson all running over. He saw the triumph on their faces. Somehow they'd done it. The outlaws were broken. Ellen was safe. Walt and Alma and all her family were all safe. So were the rest of the settlers.

EPILOGUE

"This is it," Neill announced. He sat his horse at the end of a long, green valley high up on the western slope of the Sierras.

Jim pulled the Appaloosa to a stop.

"This is beautiful," Ellen said from behind him. Then she wrapped her arms tight around Jim's chest. "Where should we build the cabin?"

"That little bench there would have the best view. Maybe sink the house down a little to keep the worst of the north wind off," Neill pointed. "Donovan always got a wistful look on his face whenever he talked about this place."

"I can see why," Jim said. "It's perfect."

"A few cows or horses and a man could do well up here. Quiet of course. No neighbors for a few miles. Some people don't care for the loneliness."

Jim looked back at the wagon. Ellen, her parents, the two kids, her brother and sister. More family than he'd ever known. "I don't think that will be a problem."

Neill smiled and followed his gaze. "No, I expect not." He coughed to clear his throat. "You'll want to stock up well for the winters. Lots of snow this high up. Cut hay for the stock. The creek runs year-round, though it might freeze over in a few places. Donovan and I wintered here a time or two."

"You're sure you won't stay?" Jim said.

"Me? No, you folks wouldn't want me around."

"Of course we would," Ellen said. "You're family."

"Truth is, I've been thinking a lot about family. I'll see my sister up in Oregon first. Then I still have a brother down in Georgia. Thought I'd go back home and see him."

"Down the trail?"

"No, maybe catch a ship and sail round the cape. My father had a ship once and he'd take us out now and then," Neill said.

"You're always welcome here Captain," Jim moved the Appaloosa closer and held out a hand.

For a moment, Neill glanced down at it, then he took it. "You turned out good."

"You and Donovan didn't leave me much choice," Jim smiled.

Neill gave a sad smile of his own. "I'll see you." Then he swung his horse and rode south.

Jim and Ellen watched him go. The Captain topped a hill, waved once, then disappeared down the other side.

"I'll miss him," Jim said. "We spent half the trip fighting and arguing, but I will miss him."

"So will I," Ellen agreed.

Colton brought the wagon rolling up to a halt. He looked after Neill then said, "Where do we start?"

AFTERWORD

Thank you for reading To a Far Western Land. In terms of sheer scope this was one of the more difficult books to write and I hope I pulled it off to your satisfaction.

Please subscribe to my email list to avoid missing out on new releases.

Signup

If you haven't already please enjoy the first chapter of my previous western:
The Buckshot War

THE BUCKSHOT WAR

CHAPTER 1

Rainwater cascaded down in steady sheets onto the Plata saloon's slanted tin roof. Drops marshaled their strength then took a second plunge—this one at a height much nearer than the angry heavens—before drenching Abel Lang. An endless stream of water fell from the brim of his sad sagging hat, but despite the damp and cold, Abel enjoyed the rain. It felt clean and pure. He decided he was in need of a good cleansing.

Downpours like this were rare in El Paso, and the rain transformed the normally dusty streets into flowing rivulets and swathes of sticky brown. Only a desperate man or one without any sense would remain out-of-doors in tonight's weather. Tonight, Abel Lang was both.

Patiently, he waited in the shadowed alleyway between the Plata and Edmund's Mercantile Exchange. Through the saloon's thin walls, he heard the tinny piano playing while some local beauty sang on stage. Despite growing up near the border, Abel's Spanish had never been good—neither of his parents spoke more than a few words—and he could barely catch a word or two over the piano's notes. Her voice sounded lovely though, rich and full. Even without knowing the words, he could tell she sang of home and love and a sense of belonging. Home, love, and a sense of belonging.

Funny...that's just what brought me here, hunting a man.

Up the street, a door shut. Not slammed shut like some cowboy who'd drunk too much might do but shut gently like a businessman or a shopkeeper might. It wouldn't be long now. Slowly, Abel eased his Colt out of its holster. The weapon's familiar wood grip comforted him, a tangible feeling to calm his nerves and steady his hand. He wished he had a couple shells for the gun. Six full cylinders would have been greedy. But two? Two would at least make him feel better. He'd fired his last round two days ago, before swimming his horse across the Rio Grande ahead of a pack of enemies.

It wasn't too late to turn back. He was sure they thought him dead by now. He could let the man just walk on by, and then Abel could disappear into the night with no one the wiser.

He could pull up stakes, as the traveling men said, and start over somewhere. *I always wanted to see the ocean.* Father said the Pacific was the most spectacular blue. He could see it for himself in a few weeks. All he had to do was walk away. No one would know. No one but himself.

There...steps on the boardwalk. They grew louder by the second. Abel made his choice.

The Yankee's elbow appeared first. In vain, he held a folded newspaper up over his hat, shielding it from the dripping rain. He was a young man, not much older than Abel, short and thin. Renegade droplets dodged around both paper and hat though as several clung to the glass in his thin spectacles. Abel waited until the man stepped past. He placed his Colt's barrel against the man's curly black hair and cocked the trigger.

Mid-step, the Yankee froze.

"Not a word or the sound you'll hear next is Gabriel's trumpet," Abel said. Then he took the man's arm and jerked him into the alleyway. The dark-haired man splashed in the mud while Abel drew him deep into the shadows. Violently, Abel spun him around so that they faced each other. The captive's eyes were wide, full of fear and recognition. He began muttering a quiet prayer.

Abel couldn't blame him.

"Good, you remember me," Abel said. "Now you and I are going to have a little talk. I'll ask questions. You answer them."

Frightened, the man nodded quickly. Over the scent of fresh rain Abel smelled piss from the Yankee's pants. He suppressed a chuckle.

"What was your name again?"

"I...I...Isaac Goldberg."

"Isaac. And are you armed Isaac?"

"No." He shook his head.

"There's gold in the railcar?"

"Y-y-yes," Isaac nodded again.

"Good. You'll take me to it, past the guard. You'll count out fifteen thousand in gold. Then, my friend, you and I will leave the car and go our separate ways."

"Fifteen thousand?" Isaac's eyes bulged, "but the offer we made wasn't nearly so generous."

"Your low-ball offer wasn't worth considering. Fifteen is fair."

"We only needed to buy the acreage where the line should go."

"And cut the place right in half? No, it's all or nothing."

Isaac started to protest then remembered the gun when Abel jabbed it into his stomach.

"Besides right now you're also buying your life," Abel grinned. "Don't you think it's worth a little extra?"

Abel's captive nodded emphatically.

"Good, then lead the way."

Abel placed his arm over Isaac's shoulder as if he were helping a drunk weave his way home. His other hand pressed the Colt into Isaac's ribs. They crossed the muddy street together, and then they walked down toward the train station. An iron horse—sleeping like a silent giant without its cloud of white steam—waited on the tracks, a half dozen cars strung out behind it in a string of midnight pearls. Like the engine the cars lay dark and silent, all but the last, their destination. Yellow lamplight shone from its shaded windows cutting through the rain.

Abel took a moment to tug his ruined hat down lower then drove Isaac forward. The ladder up from the tracks was slick with the rain. Abel climbed up first, keeping his pistol covering Isaac at all times, and then he half-dragged his prisoner up behind.

On the little platform outside the car they resumed their places, Isaac ahead, Abel close behind with the Colt held tight between them.

"Go on," Abel whispered. "Steady now. The hard part is almost over."

Isaac hesitated outside the bolted door as if trying to decide how best to proceed. A strong prod from the Colt persuaded him to hurry. He knocked on the steel door. It gave a hollow ring.

"Sam, open up."

There was movement from inside and Abel thought he heard giggling. A man's shadow reflected in the lamplight onto the ground below.

"Sam, it's me Isaac. Open this door at once," Isaac said.

"Isaac. We're a—that is I'm a little busy in here. Can't you come back in the morning. Whatever it is will keep till then."

Abel heard more giggling inside. It sounded like a woman. *What have we stumbled into here?*

"He won't open up," Isaac said with a shrug of the shoulders.

Abel jammed the Colt a little tighter against Isaac's spine and the Yankee started to whimper.

"Change his mind," Abel said.

Isaac's face flushed red and his cheeks puffed with fear. "Sam, unless you open this door, I will have your job. The railroad can easily replace you. One telegraph back east is all it will take. Open this door now."

The bolt rasped as Sam withdrew it. The door cracked open and spilled a line of yellow light on Isaac. Sam peered from around the door's edge.

"Isaac please. Look I need a favor. Promise you won't report me to O'Massey for this," Sam pleaded.

"I...I won't. He need not know of it," Isaac said in obvious relief. "Now let me in."

The door opened further. Wearing only his trousers, Sam stood inside. He was a tall man, lanky, and with a greasy handlebar mustache. The loops of his suspenders dangled loosely near his bare white feet. Drops of sweat beaded on his forehead, and his cheeks were crimson. He retreated a step back as Isaac and Abel entered.

Rows of plush, red cushions lined either side of the rail car. A brightly colored carpet with dizzying patterns of interwoven squares and diamonds in reds, purples, and rich browns spanned its length. A pile of clothes, both men's and women's, lay on the floor. On the seat nearby was a rumpled gray blanket. At the car's rear, beyond a small wooden table, sat Abel's aim, a squat black safe. Bright gold letters and a numbered silver dial hinted of the riches within.

Sam fell back another step, holding his palms up, pleading with Isaac. Abel didn't think he'd even noticed that Isaac wasn't alone.

"Thank you, Isaac, thank you."

On the cushion the blanket shifted, followed by another giggle. A long lock of tightly-curled golden hair dangled from beneath it.

"What were you doing in here?" Isaac asked.

"Noth-nothing," Sam stammered.

"Who else is in here?"

"Calm down Isaac. Don't forget your promise now. Come on out Miss."

The blanket lowered a little to reveal a young, lovely girl. Her neck and white shoulders were bare, and a bright blue ribbon that matched her eyes held the tight curls hair in a ponytail. She clutched the blanket tight around herself and smiled widely.

"Why Sam, I didn't realize you were planning on having an audience," she smiled.

Sam blushed a bright red in embarrassment. So did Isaac.

"Evening Molly," Abel said.

"Abel Lang," the blonde cooed. "I thought a posse of railroad men shot you crossing the river into Mexico. I cried after hearing of it."

Sam must have recognized the name. The bare-chested man turned his attention to Abel. His eyes widened as if noticing the newcomer for the first time; he reached for his pistol, slapping at an empty thigh, only to then redden further when he realized his weapon wasn't there.

A sickened look spread over the man's face and his mustache drooped.

Abel smiled at his discomfort. He took a quick step before slamming his pistol barrel against Sam's temple. The bare-chested man collapsed in a heap atop his and Molly's discarded clothes.

This time Molly laughed outright.

"Isaac why don't you see about that safe now. Molly, bring me your friend's pistol if you would."

"Abel Lang, I am stark naked. I was just getting ready to entertain here."

"Nothing I haven't seen before Molly. I recall spending several afternoons in your Pa's hayloft last summer."

She grinned wickedly, shrugged, threw off the blanket, and then retrieved the gun and belt while Isaac spun the dial on the safe back and forth. The number clicked as he muttered them aloud. Abel took the sleeping Sam's gunbelt, opened the cylinder of his own pistol, and refilled it with cartridges from the loops.

"Robbing a train without any bullets," Molly grinned. "Pa always said you were too brave for your own good Abel."

Isaac stopped working. "No bullets?" he sputtered and looked around.

"Not to worry my friend. I have plenty now," Abel said as he clicked the cylinder shut. "You go on and finish up with that safe."

The little man went back to work on the dial.

Abel turned to regard Molly. Always a pretty girl she'd grown into a beautiful young woman. "Sorry to hear about your Pa. A bronc threw him?"

"He was trying to break in new batch of mustangs. He shouldn't have done it at his age, but we needed the money. Got thrown, landed on a rock, and broke his back. The bank took our farm. Me and Janey couldn't make it alone. I've been working down at the Line Shack ever since."

"Sorry to hear that." Abel meant it. Molly's father had been a close friend to his own.

"He always liked you. Said you were good help busting broncs."

"He might not have if he'd known about you and me in that hayloft."

"No, I imagine not," Molly flashed him a wide smile.

She reclined on the cushion again and draped the blanket over her long bare legs. She reached up into the mane of golden hair and twirled a stray curl around her fingers.

With her in the room, naked as she was, Abel had a hard time keeping his attention on Isaac.

Isaac finished working the combination, twisted the handle, and pulled the safe's door open. It squeaked in protest.

"Count out fifteen thousand. Then close it back up," Abel ordered. He tossed over a set of saddlebags.

"You don't want all of it?"

"No, just what's due me. I figure the land, water, and cattle are worth fifteen. I'll also want a Bill of Sale signed by you."

Isaac counted out the money and placed it in the bags. Then Abel and Isaac each signed two Bills of Sale, one for each of them.

"Molly, care to witness?" Abel offered.

"Why not?" she laughed and signed her name with a flourish. "It's been that kind of night."

"You know a Bill of Sale doesn't make this legal right?" Isaac said afterward. "Not when you held me at gunpoint."

"Maybe not, but I never stole nothing in my life and I ain't starting now."

"O'Massey will kill you for this. He's relentless."

"That the big shouldered man who drove the wagon?"

"Yes. He's a thug and a brute and he likes breaking tough men like you. He's very good at it," Isaac said.

"I'll wager he won't be too happy with you either for helping me with this," Abel grinned.

"Helping you but I—" Isaac stammered.

"Anyway, he'll have a hell of a time catching me first. Though I wouldn't mind a crack at him for what he did to me."

Abel draped the heavy saddlebags over one shoulder and held the gun on Isaac.

"Off with your clothes Yank."

"Wh-wh-what?"

"You heard me, skin em."

Isaac stripped down to his small clothes. His face colored just as Sam the guard's had when they'd first entered. Molly giggled again.

"Toss them outside. And the guard's too."

"What?" Isaac's eyes bulged. "Why?"

"Because if you don't, I'll shoot you," Abel answered.

"Abel, you could take me with you," Molly said eyeing the saddlebags. "I'd be awfully awfully good to you. You know I can."

"I'm headed into Mexico, Molly, and as lovely and tempting as you are tonight I'm traveling fast and alone. You've been paid for the evening?"

She nodded in response.

"Good, since Sam here won't be enjoying your company, Isaac will take his place. I'll make a contribution to the cause as well," Abel said. He tossed Molly a shining gold coin. "Think you can keep this young man occupied all the way until dawn?"

She nodded, turned to Isaac, and laughed again. "I'll think of something."

"Well then friend Isaac, I leave you in Molly's most capable care."

"O'Massey will kill me for this and then he'll kill you," Isaac said.

Abel raised a finger to his lips. "No more talk now." He glanced over to Molly then back to Isaac again. "You'll thank me later."

He left the car and wedged a block of wood under the door with his boot to prevent their escape. *Not that he'll want to*, Abel thought. Molly Mills was full of charm enough to keep a man plenty busy.

With that Abel plunged into the night. Fifteen thousand in gold richer and free and clear of El Paso, he retrieved his horse from a nearby barn and headed south toward the river and old Mexico beyond. The water was cold and swollen with rainwater runoff, but Abel made the crossing without incident.

He rode on without stopping until just after midnight finally taking refuge for what remained of the night in an abandoned adobe at the far western edge of Paso Del Norte, or Juarez as the locals were starting to call it.

Setting the saddlebags and then a rolled-up blanket beneath his head, he bedded down for the night. It was cold and damp, but he dared not risk a fire. Not this close to El Paso.

He felt a moment's envy for Isaac.

Maybe I should have taken Molly up on her offer. A warm woman sounds a lot better than a cold wet night sleeping out of doors. Having a few miles between himself and the law by sunrise sounded even better though.

A ROOSTER CROWING in the distance woke him. The bird was a little early. Sunrise was just a band of light gray on the horizon. Wary of scorpions, Abel shook out his boots, pulled each on with a tug, and rolled up his bedding. One corner of the abandoned adobe's roof looked to have caved in years ago and in minutes an orange sunrise peeked in at him over the opening.

His side ached. Abel lifted his shirt to check the bandage. The wound looked clean, no bleeding, no signs of deadly inflammation. The bullet had burned along one rib. He'd been lucky. It tore out a good swath of hide, painfully wide, but didn't come close to any organs.

O'Massey and his men had come awfully close to killing him.

Abel set out cutting west, directly away from El Paso and continued on through the Chihuahuan desert until noon. Last night's downpour hadn't fallen this far out in the desert and his horse stirred small clouds of fine brown dust with every step. Low dry sagebrush—broken up only by the occasional faded green cactus—decorated the open terrain. A few chunky mountains squatted miles in the distance. They weren't true mountains, more like big boulders than the arrowhead peaks of the high Rockies he'd heard so much about.

As a boy he'd wanted to see those peaks. At times his parents had talked about it. A land of cool clear streams, clean air, and carpets of grass so green it hurt a man's eyes.

After a midday meal of hardtack, Abel turned his horse north on the trail toward Mesilla. By first crossing into Juarez, then looping back into the New Mexico territory he hoped to throw off any pursuit. A posse from El Paso wouldn't dare cross into Mexico, and he doubted any of the railroad's hired thugs would think to look for him back to the north.

While traveling he thought back on the strange turn of events that had driven him to rob the railroad.

How could a few short weeks have changed so much?

The Yankee, Isaac, and another man, one he came to know as O'Massey, had visited his ranch almost two weeks ago. Both were from back east, their faces sun-burnt and peeling from the hot Texas sun. The second man drove their buckboard, bouncing over the rocky trail up to the house. Each wore fancy black suits and derby hats, but the two could not be more different. The spectacled Isaac looked like a bookkeeper or store owner of sorts. The stocky O'Massey had wide, flat knuckles and his nose crooked sharply to the left where it had been broken at least once. Beneath a heavy brow line his eyes were beady, dark, and cruel. Some sort of fighter or boxer Abel had guessed.

Abel had been putting new rails up on the corral when they arrived.

"Abel Lang?" Isaac asked.

"Who's asking?" Abel looked at them over the top rail.

"Mr. Lang, we represent the Greater Pacific Railroad and we want to purchase your land. The ideal route for the line takes it up from the river, around the base of this very hill, and on toward El Paso. I can offer you five thousand gold in recompense."

"Not interested," Abel replied.

Isaac had tilted his head like a bird examining something of inter-est. "Mr. Lang, these days five thousand gold would make you a reasonably wealthy man. Are you sure you won't even consider my offer?"

"Considered it just now. Still not interested."

"If it's more money you're after then I am authorized to pay as much as," Isaac paused while thumbing through a brown leather-bound ledger. He landed on the proper page and pointed. "Nine thousand gold, but not a penny more. We only want a two-hundred-foot easement on either side of the hill's base."

"My father settled this place after the Mexican-American war. He was with General Taylor for the war's duration. Afterward, he and my mother started the ranch here on the only year-round spring for twenty miles. They built the house, brought in cattle, endured through drought and famine, fought off the Apaches and then the bandits. They're both gone now, buried behind the barn where they can look out over the place."

Abel paused then continued. "I ain't sellin."

"I didn't want it to come to this, but Mr. Lang the Governor himself is personally invested in this project. Have you heard of eminent domain? It's a law that the government may seize your land for the benefit of the public. I can be back here with a signed letter to seize your land by the end of the week. Now, won't you just take the nine thousand and save us all the trouble?"

"When you bring your signed letter, you better have a lot of help with you."

"Help, Mr. Lang?" Isaac adjusted his glasses.

"You'll need help," Abel said. "Cause I will kill anyone who tries taking this ranch."

A wide grin spread over the stocky man's face while Isaac tucked away his ledger. Through all of this O'Massey hadn't uttered a single word. When he spoke his voice was hard and cracked like it came up through a bed of broken glass.

"We'll bring plenty of help. Don't worry about that none."

Once Isaac was seated, the big man snapped the reins and turned the buckboard back down the road toward the proposed rail line below.

The next day Sheriff Bowden arrived alone. Abel was just finishing up with the last rail on the corral fence when he arrived.

"Hard to get wood out here," Bowden offered. "Costs a pretty penny to get it."

"It does. Set down a spell," he said.

Sheriff Bowden was an older man, of age with Abel's own father, and a longtime friend to the family. He dismounted and eyed the corral, the barn, the house.

"Abel you've really kept the place up. Improved it even. Your parents would be proud," Bowden said.

"I hope so. Next year I'll start digging an irrigation ditch from the spring. This desert will bloom if I can just give it some water. Then the stock will have some better feed and I'll have room to expand the garden. I talked with Farson about buying one of his young shorthorn bulls."

"Abel, son you need to get shut of this business."

"What?"

Bowden sighed then went on. "The railroad aims to have this land, and the Governor aims to have the railroad. They'll burn the place, hunt you down, and take it. They've a dozen hired thugs in town. O'Massey, the big man who I heard visited you earlier, sends them to 'persuade' landowners to give up their rights."

"They can't do this. People won't stand for it," Abel said.

"They can and they are. Yours isn't the first place that refused to sell. Steve Jackson, east of here, turned down their offer. They killed him and his oldest boy last week. His wife and their youngsters took the money and headed back east. Same thing happened to Mike Bishop."

"Mike Bishop?" Abel couldn't believe it. Mike was a known man, tough, and no nonsense. *If they drove Mike Bishop out.* "And you, Sheriff? You know this isn't right. Where do you stand in all this?"

Bowden's eyes softened for a split second then his face hardened into stone. "El Paso needs the railroad. O'Massey is getting his orders directly from the Governor's men. He said he's going to ride out and run you off. Whatever my personal feelings, it's all going to be legal with this eminent domain nonsense, and there's not a thing I can do."

"It's theft, plain and simple," Abel said.

"Yes," the Sheriff nodded. "Tomorrow they'll ride out here to force you off. Just take the money Abel. Your Ma and Pa wanted you to have the land, but he wouldn't want you to die for it."

"Pa fought for this place. Half the time you fought beside him, first in the war and then to settle this country. How many times did you ask him to scout after wild Indians or some posse chasing down bandits?"

"Too many to count."

"And how many times did he turn you down?"

"Not once," Bowden's voice was low and full of shame.

"And when he was gone who did your scouting?"

"You did," Bowden answered. "Your Pa saved my life more than once and never asked anything in return. I owe him a debt. That's why I'm here trying to help you."

"Help me fight then."

"This isn't like some band of wild Apaches. This isn't something you can win. The best thing you can do is make them a counter-offer and sell out."

"That's your advice? Ask for more money and then give up?"

"It is," Bowden nodded. "And I'm sorry for it."

"I can fight. I'll hold them off," Abel said.

"I know you can. You like to fight, always have. You're a tough man, like your Pa, good with a rifle and deadly with a pistol. Most of them are tenderfeet. You know the area and could kill several of them before they got you. But Abel, there's a lot of them, and more back east. Sooner or later they'll get you. Nobody can buck those kind of odds. Not for long. And they'll get the law involved."

"You'd come after me Sheriff?" Abel couldn't believe it. His father's friend hunting after him.

"I won't have a choice," Bowden said.

Abel grew silent. He could hear the truth in the Sheriff's words. He looked up toward the cabin his father had built.

Strong and sturdy, it wasn't much to look at. The sides were made from thick planks he'd salvaged from a wrecked river barge. It took three weeks to haul all that wood up from the river bottom. When the cabin was done there was enough left over for a wooden floor. Mama was always proud of that floor. Except for what Abel had done himself the last few years, there wasn't a single piece of this place his father hadn't built with his own hands.

Abel looked back to the Sheriff. "I just can't sell it."

Without another word, Bowden mounted up and rode west back to El Paso. Abel watched him go. Bowden was his father's oldest friend. 'A man to be trusted,' his father had always said. Only now he was telling Abel to give up and sell out.

A tumbleweed rolled over the ground between the house and barn.

True to the Sheriff's prediction, a group of armed men arrived at the ranch the following day. Abel watched them from behind a boulder on the crest of a nearby hillside. Four of them wasted no time riding right up to the door, kicking it in, and emptying their rifles inside where he'd left a set of rolled up blankets. Abel felt the anger now. The old battle rages his father had spoken of whenever he'd had too much to drink. The thing that he taught Abel to both fear and respect.

What kind of men would jump someone in bed without giving him a chance?

If this O'Massey and his men wanted to play rough, then he would show them what rough could be.

Abel lined up the Winchester's sights on one of those who had remained outside. He took a breath, squeezed the trigger, and put his first shot through the man's chest. Coyotes like these deserved no warning. Levering another round into the chamber, he picked off a second man running for cover.

Then they were scrambling. The yard below emptied like church after one of Reverend Tomlin's painfully-long services. Only the two dead men lay out in the open. Four gunmen were trapped in the house—those who'd shot into his blankets—and the others had scattered among the rocks and shallow gullies below.

Abel's position was good. With his rifle from here he could command the yard below indefinitely. He knew the area like no other. There wasn't a single hiding place down there he hadn't used one time or another. He knew what those men down there would be considering. When they made a break for him, he knew where they would run, how long they would be exposed in the open.

A rifle barrel showed from the house's window pointed uphill, well away from his location. Sunlight glinted off it. The barrel vanished when Abel put a bullet though the open window.

An hour crept by and nothing stirred down below. He'd worked out where several of the gunmen outside the house hid. One of them peeked out from behind the water trough, but Abel waited for a better shot. No use giving away his position for a likely miss. He chewed on a salty chunk of jerked beef and drank from his canteen. It was cool in the boulder's shade, much cooler than where most of the intruders hid. The hot sun beat down on them mercilessly.

Soon a puff of white smoke emerged from the chimney. Someone must have decided on coffee.

They'll soon regret that, he thought. He pointed his Winchester to cover the door.

An explosion shook the cabin. Yesterday Abel had placed a stick of dynamite in the fireplace beneath the ashes. Dust and dirt billowed out from the windows and door. A man tried to escape dragging a wounded leg, and Abel's shot caught him two steps outside the door. Abel then shifted the rifle and snapped off three quick rounds into the water trough. Three holes appeared in it, draining the water out onto the hidden man.

Well, it is hot out and he must be thirsty, Abel chuckled.

Screams came from the cabin. At least one poor bastard hadn't been killed outright in the blast.

Serves them right. They shouldn't have come after me.

Maybe six down and maybe six more to go. He hadn't made a

good count when they arrived. After the shooting, they would at least have an idea of where he was now. Next some would try to circle him, probably from the left. He held his rifle over the spot where they would emerge.

There wasn't an inch of ground on this place he hadn't ridden across, walked over, or played in since he was just a few years old.

Someone below yelled and all at once several men started to fire. Angry ricochets screamed around Abel like hornets. Men from below the barn and the drenched man from the trough all fired up into the boulders. Two broke from cover and raced off to the left where he'd expected them. Ignoring the scattered shots around him, Abel fired four times and clipped one of them in the shoulder. The wound wasn't serious. He'd live, unfortunately.

Abel studied where they'd gone. Soon the pair would work their way around and up toward his position and then they'd have him trapped in a vise.

Time to go.

He crawled back from the boulder, down into a narrow ravine. His horse waited at the bottom. He was a mile away when the shots started back at the ranch. First, they would find his empty shells, then his trail, and finally where he'd picketed his horse. From there the chase would be on.

For the next three days, Abel led his pursuers through the barren West Texas landscape. He made it his mission to make their lives as uncomfortable as possible. By day he kept well ahead and always out of sight. At night he crept near their camp and fired into it to deny them any rest. One of them headed off to El Paso and returned with a half dozen others. Abel didn't mind. He used their size against them. He avoided the larger water holes, taking a deliberately harder route. During the long chase Abel killed or wounded three more, but after six hard days they pushed him to the border. Bullets smashed down into the Rio Grande while his horse swam across the murky river. That was when he'd picked up the bullet wound. Once across, he fired the last of his rounds and sent his pursuers scrambling for shelter. By now they all knew not to underestimate his aim.

Luckily, the railroad's hired gunmen chose not to follow him into Mexico.

In the end Sheriff Bowden had been right though. Now he could see it. The stubborn streak he'd inherited from his father had given way to his mother's calm insight. He'd miss the old home. Though in truth it hadn't felt much like home since his parents died.

The Greater Pacific was just too big to fight but—after his arrangement with Isaac—Abel had managed to at least get a fair price for his ranch. That was enough to get a new start at least.

Maybe I'll try the Rockies.

ALSO BY CARSON MCCLOUD

The Buckshot War

Devlin's Ride

Devlin's Return

Blood on the Bighorns

Sonoran Gold

Made in United States
Orlando, FL
23 February 2022

15097083R00200